A New Dawn Over Devon

Books by Michael Phillips

Best Friends for Life (with Judy Phillips)
The Garden at the Edge of Beyond
A God to Call Father†
Good Things to Remember
A Rift In Time†
Hidden in Time†
*The Stonewycke Legacy**
*The Stonewycke Trilogy**

CALEDONIA

    Legend of the Celtic Stone   *An Ancient Strife*

THE JOURNALS OF CORRIE BELLE HOLLISTER

    *My Father's World**   *Sea to Shining Sea*
    *Daughter of Grace**   *Into the Long Dark Night*
    On the Trail of the Truth   *Land of the Brave and the Free*
    A Place in the Sun   *A Home for the Heart*

    Grayfox (Zack's story)

THE JOURNALS OF CORRIE AND CHRISTOPHER

    The Braxtons of Miracle Springs   *A New Beginning*

THE RUSSIANS*

    The Crown and the Crucible   *Travail and Triumph*
    A House Divided

THE SECRET OF THE ROSE†

    The Eleventh Hour   *Escape to Freedom*
    A Rose Remembered   *Dawn of Liberty*

THE SECRETS OF HEATHERSLEIGH HALL

    Wild Grows the Heather in Devon *Heathersleigh Homecoming*
    Wayward Winds   *A New Dawn Over Devon*

*with Judith Pella   †Tyndale House

A NEW DAWN OVER DEVON

MICHAEL PHILLIPS

BETHANY HOUSE PUBLISHERS
MINNEAPOLIS, MINNESOTA 55438

Published by Bethany House Publishers
A Ministry of Bethany Fellowship International
11400 Hampshire Avenue South
Bloomington, Minnesota 55438

Printed in the United States of America

ISBN 0-7642-2441-7

Contents

— ✦✦✦ —

Part II: Autumn 1915

Part III: Spring 1916

Part IV: Spring–Fall 1916

Part V: 1917

Part VI: 1918–1919

Part VII: 1920–1923

Introduction
Reconciliation–The Highest Truth

———— ♦♦♦ ————

This series of books you have been reading has many themes. But mostly it is a story of reconciliation.

I did not intentionally set out to write about reconciliation. But perhaps because I believe that reconciliation is God's ultimate purpose in the universe, and that such is the ultimate destiny and climax of every human drama, such a theme simply emerged as the Heathersleigh story unfolded.

All stories and all lives must tell the story of reconciliation if they are to accurately reflect the human condition and the highest truth in the universe. That high truth is simply this, that God will make all things right in the end.

However, during our brief sojourn on the earth, we each are called to live out incomplete portions of that great story. Most human lives contain heartbreak. We live in a fallen world. We are sinners who are rebellious and stubborn and independent of heart. Therefore, it is occasionally difficult not to rant against God for the bitterness of our lot. I must confess myself guilty as well. But we only do so because we lose sight of the fact that we occupy but one tiny role in that universal story whose glorious ending is yet to be told.

That ending is reconciliation, restitution, healing. God is good, and I repeat: He will make all things right in the end.

Foundational and intrinsic in reconciliation—between ourselves and God, and ourselves and others—is forgiveness. There can be no healing without forgiveness. Therefore, any story of reconciliation must of necessity also be a story of forgiveness. God is ever sending his forgiveness in pursuit of us in our waywardness, that he might bring us back into the fold of his eternal family—restored, forgiven, and whole. For such a purpose did he send his Son Jesus Christ to die and make atonement for our sins—to send his love and forgiveness into our midst, to reclaim his creation and bring it home.

Accepting this divine forgiveness, however, as important as it is to salvation, is often only the beginning of healing. As we struggle to incorporate forgiveness into our daily lives, learning to forgive *ourselves* is one of the most difficult aspects of the cross to appropriate in a practical way. We may not face exactly the same struggles that confront Amanda Rutherford. Yet if we are honest with ourselves, I think most of us will admit to great difficulty in bringing forgiveness all the way inside.

But Amanda's life demonstrates that it is never too late to accept God's forgiveness, to forgive oneself, and then to pray for a restoration of the years the locusts have eaten.

God is in the business of working personal, private, invisible miracles of healing and restoration. More than any other of his magnificent works in the universe, this is what God *does*:

He heals hearts.

He fixes human brokenness.

He brings sons and daughters back to their fathers.

He restores.

He makes whole.

He sends his forgiveness after his wayward, hurting, broken, lonely children, like a probe of light, to pierce deep into those private regions of anguish and hopelessness that have been covered over for years. He says, "My child ... I love you, I understand, I not only forgive the world of its sins through my Son, I forgive *you*. Now you can also forgive those who have hurt you, because I forgive them ... and you can forgive yourself. Rise up and be my child—be whole, be clean, be restored, and walk in forgiveness."

It is never too late to have a happy childhood, though the pain may have stolen its memories from you for a time, or your own wrong attitudes may have caused you to lose sight of them along the way. It is never too late, because the probing miracle-working spade of divine forgiveness can go back and retill the soil of memory and bring new life to long buried flowers within the garden of your soul, whose pleasant fragrance can fill your later years with sweetness no matter what may have come before.

It may surprise you when I say that one of the characters I find most intriguing in this entire series is Bishop Arthur Crompton.

He was originally but a minor character whose role in my author's brain never extended beyond that of a brief walk-on appearance. He wasn't supposed to get under my skin. But he did. And I found my heart growing very tender toward him—sin and false motives and hypocrisy and all—as he aged, and as he began looking inward.

Don't you suppose this is how God looks at us—*tenderly*, in the midst of our foolishness, our hypocrisy, our selfish motives, and our sin—*gently speaking* through conscience, through circumstances, through the maturity that the years gradually bring, *quietly waiting* for us to begin asking the right kinds of questions about what our lives have been about. And when we do, he is there as our own loving Father to accept our humble regrets, to listen to the quiet prayers no one else in all the world hears, and do what he can to make sons and daughters of us, even though our years living for self be many, and our years obeying his voice be few.

As I myself grew tender toward Bishop Crompton, it opened a new window of understanding toward God's love for me, and for all men.

Arthur Crompton, therefore, though a minor character, typifies this reconciliatory work of the heavenly Father in the lives of his children— a man gone wrong, a man who gave lip service to the service of God for most of his life, but a man whose heart was finally softened in the end by the incessant wooing of his Father's loving, tender, forgiving, restoring voice.

With regard to the criticism certain to result from Timothy Diggorsfeld's discussion with his church leaders, I would emphasize again, as I did in the introduction to *Wild Grows the Heather in Devon*, that Timothy Diggorsfeld's ideas represent a historical point of view commonly held in the late nineteenth century. I hope you will be able to read this as an accurate slice of perspective into the church of one hundred years ago without wrongly assuming an attempt on this author's part to promote a controversial doctrine. I happen to find it interesting to explore the various issues which concerned the Church of that time. Whether or not one personally embraces Diggorsfeld's views is far less important in my opinion than that we follow his example of not being afraid to ask what our loving Father might do. I hope the same will always be said of me, irrespective of whether I happen to agree with all his conclusions.

If you are interested in my own personal feelings on the matter in more detail, I refer you to the postscript at the end of this book.

Michael Phillips

HEATHERSLEIGH HALL

FIRST FLOOR

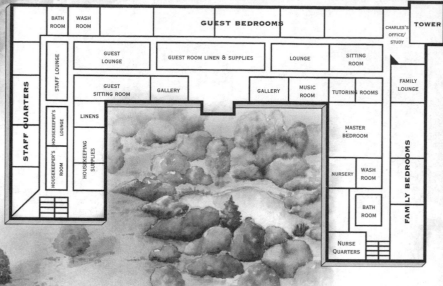

TOWER

CHARLES'S OFFICE/STUDY

BATH ROOM

WASH ROOM

GUEST BEDROOMS

STAFF LOUNGE

GUEST LOUNGE

GUEST ROOM LINEN & SUPPLIES

LOUNGE

SITTING ROOM

FAMILY LOUNGE

STAFF QUARTERS

HOUSEKEEPER'S LOUNGE

GUEST SITTING ROOM

GALLERY

GALLERY

MUSIC ROOM

TUTORING ROOMS

LINENS

HOUSEKEEPER'S ROOM

HOUSEKEEPING SUPPLIES

MASTER BEDROOM

FAMILY BEDROOMS

NURSERY

WASH ROOM

BATH ROOM

NURSE QUARTERS

GROUND FLOOR

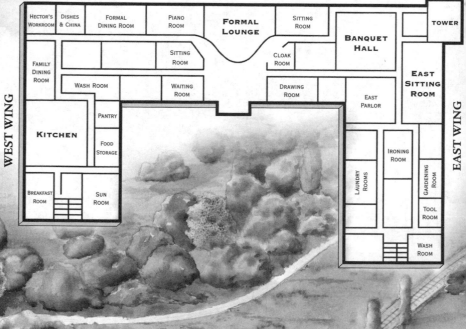

HECTOR'S WORKROOM

DISHES & CHINA

FORMAL DINING ROOM

PIANO ROOM

FORMAL LOUNGE

SITTING ROOM

BANQUET HALL

TOWER

FAMILY DINING ROOM

SITTING ROOM

CLOAK ROOM

EAST SITTING ROOM

WASH ROOM

WAITING ROOM

DRAWING ROOM

WEST WING

PANTRY

EAST PARLOR

EAST WING

KITCHEN

FOOD STORAGE

LAUNDRY ROOMS

IRONING ROOM

GARDENING ROOM

BREAKFAST ROOM

SUN ROOM

TOOL ROOM

WASH ROOM

GARRET

SECRET PASSAGE FROM TOWER · TOWER

SECRET ROOM

SECOND FLOOR

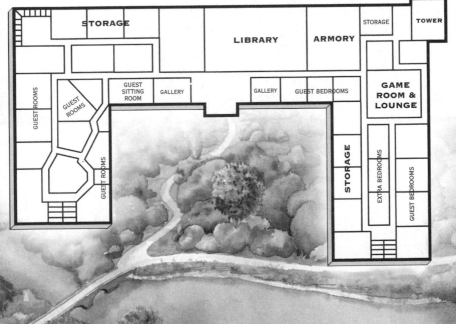

STORAGE

LIBRARY

ARMORY

STORAGE

TOWER

GUEST ROOMS

GUEST ROOMS

GUEST SITTING ROOM

GALLERY

GALLERY

GUEST BEDROOMS

GAME ROOM & LOUNGE

GUEST ROOMS

STORAGE

EXTRA BEDROOMS

GUEST BEDROOMS

Prologue

—◆◆◆—

The Secrets of
Heathersleigh Hall

—◆◆◆—

1629-1915

Clandestine Discovery

❖❖❖

1762

A thick mist blanketed the southern coast of Devon.

It was exactly this kind of night smugglers hoped for—to land, unload their goods, and escape back into the south channel without detection. Being caught meant the gallows. It was worth waiting for the fog.

Two daring lads crouched on a high bluff gazing down toward the rocky water's edge, well bundled and anticipating what adventure the night might bring. Whether they were afraid, neither would admit to the other. Bravado and daring formed the creed of such youth.

Both bore names of distinction in southwest England. But their fathers' reputations provided few thrills. Discovering the identity of the fabled smuggler known as the Devonshire Bandit, and who his accomplices onshore might be, offered a challenge they could not resist. What they would do with the information neither had paused to ask. That there was a secret to be discovered, knowledge of which was accompanied by no little danger, was incentive enough to stir the blood of any teen boy.

The sixteen-year-old was a Rutherford of Heathersleigh. His eighteen-year-old companion, and the chief instigator of the clandestine plot, was a Powell of Holsworthy.

They had arrived two hours before and by now were shivering in the night chill.

"I've had enough," said young Rutherford in exasperation. "We've got the wrong spot. There's nobody within miles of here but the gulls."

He rose and took several steps inland in the direction they had come. As he did he began raising the wick of his lantern.

"Wait—I think I see something!" whispered Powell. "Douse that light."

Rutherford quickly turned the lantern down and knelt again at his companion's side squinting into the fog.

"A ship is coming," said Powell. "I hear creaking, and water splashing against wood. Hand me the glass."

He took it, put the telescope to his eye, and peered through the fog. "Too dark and misty," he said. "I can't make out a thing."

"Let's climb down for a closer look."

Leaving telescope and lanterns out of sight where they were, they rose and carefully scrambled over the rocky incline, being careful to send no stones tumbling ahead of them into the water giving warning of their approach. Halfway down they paused, listening through the night.

"I hear something too," whispered Rutherford. "Was that a voice?"

"Sounded like it."

"Can you see anything?"

"Not yet. We've got to get lower."

"How deep is the water here?"

"Deep. And it's high tide—they'll come all the way to shore. They say the Spanish landed spies in this cove two hundred years ago during Drake's time."

Again they began climbing down. Gruff voices could be heard, muted through the fog, but unmistakable now.

Suddenly the huge ghostly outline of a ship's prow, masts reaching high into the blackness above, came into sight less than two hundred feet in front of them.

Whispered exclamations of shock and momentary terror escaped their lips. They had no idea the ship was so close. It looked as though they could reach out and touch it! Dim figures moved about on deck, with ropes and disembarking planks at the ready, while a half-dozen burly sailors wielded long poles to steady their movement and ease the ship's approach to the shoals.

"What is that they're speaking?" whispered Rutherford at his friend's ear. "I can't make out a word of it."

Powell listened a moment.

"By all the—!" He swore under his breath. "They're Turks. It's not the Bandit at all!"

"*Pirates!*" exclaimed Rutherford, rising to his feet.

"Shut up and stay where you are!" said Powell, laying a restraining hand on his friend's arm and pulling him back down.

"We've got to get out of here!"

"They're too close. They'll be landing below us in less than two minutes. If we try to make for the top now, they'll hear us for sure, then come after us and slit our throats."

"But—"

"Just sit down and keep your mouth closed," said Powell in an urgent whisper. "If we don't make a move, they'll never know we're here."

Moments later the leading edge of the hull thudded against the shoreline. A few shouts followed. The boys heard a scurrying of movement and ropes and planks and jumping and strange shouts in Arabic as the crew secured the vessel. Within minutes a line of dark-skinned thieves began streaming back and forth between ship and shore carrying crates and boxes.

"What are they doing?" whispered Rutherford into his companion's ear.

"Unloading some kind of cargo. I can't tell what. They must be stashing it somewhere down there."

They could make out little through the foggy blackness, only the tramping of feet back and forth across the planks, evil-sounding voices, and the movement of dim shadows. They sat shivering and motionless for an hour.

Gradually it became clear the operation was nearing completion. As suddenly as they had come, they now quickly withdrew the planks and heaved the ropes on board. The pikemen again took their positions and leaned heavily against their poles. Inch by inch the great vessel separated from the rocks.

"Are they leaving?" whispered Rutherford anxiously.

"Looks like it. The tide's probably about to turn."

"I'm heading back to the top!"

"No—wait till they're gone."

Gradually the sight of the ship receded mysteriously and silently into the mist. When they heard no more, Powell rose and motioned for his friend to follow. Carefully they crept back up to the bluff.

"I'm getting out of here!" said Rutherford, pausing to pick up his lantern where he had stashed it behind some large stones.

"What are you talking about?" rejoined Powell. "We're safe now. Let's wait till first light and see what we can find."

"Are you crazy? What if one of them stayed behind to guard the loot?"

"Have it your way, but I'm staying."

Powell lay down and covered himself with his overcoat. Rutherford hesitated a moment. As afraid as he was of the pirates, he was just as uneasy about heading back out across the Devonshire downs alone. He knew someone would come after the stash, and probably soon. He didn't want to meet them. Reluctantly he sat down with a sigh. Fitfully both boys dozed off.

When Rutherford next became aware of himself, the thin grey light of a frigid morning had arrived. He opened his eyes and glanced around. He was alone.

He stood and stretched, glancing down toward the sea. The water was still, quiet, and empty. He could make out but twenty or thirty feet of it before the grey-green of the channel disappeared in a wall of white mist. The only sounds reaching his ears were the gentle splashing of the tide against the rocky shoreline mingled with the cry of gulls soaring about in search of breakfast.

Glancing around further, he saw his friend scrambling back down the bluff. Rutherford rose and began easing his way toward where they had been the night before.

"What are you doing?" he said, hurrying after him.

"Finding out what they unloaded," replied Powell. "There's a cave under that ledge. It's got to be the place."

"What if someone's there?"

"I don't hear anything," replied Powell, though at the words one of his hands went unconsciously to the knife at his belt and unfastened its buckle. "Run back up and get the lantern."

Four minutes later, with Powell in the lead holding the light, the two ducked their heads and ventured tentatively into the blackness of one of hundreds of such caves along the southern coast of England. This particular one—not easily visible from above or from the sea, and with a large dry inner chamber—was singularly well suited for the purpose.

"Look at this!" exclaimed Powell.

Rutherford followed around a protruding wall of stone and now beheld what had prompted the outcry. The dancing light from his friend's hand illuminated a booty of what seemed a fabulous wealth. Already Powell had set down the light and begun to examine the contents of the cave.

"We'll be rich if we can get this out of here!"

"We can't just . . . *steal* it," objected the younger of the two, remembering vividly the frightening images and voices of the previous night.

"Why not? They don't even know we exist."

"Somebody is bound to find out. What if someone sees us carting it away?"

"Who?"

"I don't know—whoever they were delivering it to."

"We'll be careful. I don't know about you, but I'm taking all I can!"

He had already located a heavy chest and began lugging it toward the mouth of the cave.

"What I can't get on my horse's back," he said, "I'll hide up there somewhere. There are plenty of places where it will never be seen."

His friend knew from the gleam in his eye that there was no dissuading him. Almost as if resigning himself to the inevitable, Rutherford glanced about so as not to leave empty-handed himself. In the time it took Powell to make three or four eager trips back and forth to the bluff, he had finally located a somewhat modest-sized metal chest whose weight of some fifty pounds he thought he could manage.

"I've got what I'm taking," he said.

"Is that all!" laughed Powell. "Look around, Broughton—we can set ourselves up for the rest of our lives!"

"This is all I want. If we take too much—"

"Don't be a coward," interrupted Powell, his hands already full again.

"I'm getting out of here," said Rutherford. "I'm nervous being here so long. I'm going back to the horses and starting for home . . . with this chest and nothing else."

He headed for the mouth of the cave.

"Suit yourself," laughed Powell. "But wait for me. I'll be along in a minute. I still say you're loony for not taking all you can."

As he bent down to deposit his latest haul with the rest, Powell's knife, still loose, fell to the ground, along with several other small items he was carrying. But without noticing, he was already off for more. His friend saw them, stooped to pick up the knife, compass, and spyglass—he could take no chances of anything being found; he would give them back to Rufus later—and deposited them in his coat, where he quickly forgot them for the rest of the day.

Twenty minutes later, to young Rutherford's great relief, the two were riding on their heavily laden mounts back the way they had come the previous afternoon. Fortunately, they saw not another soul on their way, and managed to get their goods safely hidden at their respective homes without detection.

◆◆◆

When the news came to Heathersleigh Hall three weeks later, it was with difficulty that sixteen-year-old Broughton Rutherford disguised his disbelief and horror.

"I am afraid I have some dreadful news, son," his father said as he dismounted his horse outside the Hall. "I've just learned that your friend Rufus Powell is dead."

"What!" exclaimed Broughton, turning pale.

"His body was found south of here, on the moor near the coast."

"But . . . how did he die?"

"No one knows. Murdered apparently, and brutally from the reports. There were numerous knife wounds."

Broughton staggered back half a step.

"No one has any idea what could be the motive," William Rutherford went on as he led his mount toward the stables. "When is the last time you and he rode together?"

"Uh . . . I don't know . . . a week or two ago," answered Broughton vaguely.

"Well, it's a mystery . . . everyone's talking about it."

That night, alone in his room and afraid for his life, young Broughton Rutherford crept to his closet and withdrew the chest he had taken from the pirates' cave.

He had to get rid of this. What if they found him too!

Luckily he had removed nothing but two or three small ships' logs, written in English, that were probably stolen anyway and of no interest to anyone. He might keep them out and look through them to see what he could learn. But the rest of it, he would stash good and out of sight, for fear someone might accidentally run across it.

Rufus had obviously been careless. He must have talked and been overheard by the wrong people, or else tried to go back to the cave for more.

The Turks or their accomplices surely knew he had not acted alone. They were probably scouring the countryside even now, watching

Rufus's friends. He would have to guard his every move.

The greedy fool, he thought to himself. Everything would have been fine if Rufus had just been satisfied. Now Broughton would be looking over his shoulder the rest of his life. He could never divulge that he possessed anything unusual of value. Pirates, they said, had long memories.

Not only did he have to hide it, he could never make use of it, never look at it, and never let on that he knew a thing about it. He couldn't let slip so much as a look or a glance to indicate other than that he was just as mystified at Rufus's death as everyone else. He could not even tell his father or his twelve-year-old brother, Robert.

No one must ever know, or eventually those same knives would split his skin too.

Origins

♦ ♦ ♦

1629-1789

*C*onstruction on the stately grey mansion known as Heathersleigh Hall began in 1629.

Its original owners, a certain Jeremiah and Mary Rutherford, were in fact a relatively simple man and woman of deep spiritual convictions. An older cousin of the Scots minister and covenanter Samuel Rutherford, Jeremiah migrated south from Scotland to England as a young man—bringing with him a reminder of his native land, a variety of heather plants which he determined would always bloom wherever he lived.

There his strong religious beliefs led him into association with the Puritans, resulting in his meeting and later marrying his wife, Mary. When the migration of Puritan separatists began to Holland and Massachusetts in the late 1620s—at about the same time Jeremiah's cousin was graduating in divinity from Edinburgh and embarking on the preaching and writing career that would bring him fame—Jeremiah and Mary Rutherford made the decision to not join the exodus of Pilgrims across the sea, but rather to live out their own "separation" from the world in the rural wilds of Devonshire.

To this end they purchased an enormous tract of land, prayed and dedicated it to the glory of God and his purposes, and then set about designing the edifice that would become their home and would house the generations of these English Rutherfords for centuries to come.

When the site for the building was established, even before a stone had been laid, Jeremiah next decided on the location to grow the wiry reminders of his beloved homeland. He proceeded to set his heather plants in the ground just east of where the house would soon rise, asking God, still on his knees as he lovingly patted down the soil, to cause them to flourish, then rose with a smile and turned to his wife.

"Mary," he said, "I think the Lord has just given me the name for our new home. We shall call it Heathersleigh."

◆ ◆ ◆

The initial building of what came to be known as Heathersleigh Hall was personally overseen by Jeremiah Rutherford and lasted eighteen years. He and Mary and their young family, however, were able to take up residence in their new home in 1631 while the rest of the building progressed slowly about them. In time Jeremiah and his three sons completed most of the later work themselves. Mary and her two daughters, meanwhile, cultivated and developed the surrounding landscape, planting lawns and hedges, flower gardens and ornamental trees, and enlarging the original heather garden with many new species.

By the time the structure was at last completed in 1647, Heathersleigh had become one of the stateliest and most beautiful estates in Devon.

Even as mortar on the final stones was drying, the sixty-four-year-old visionary whose dream this had been from the start—head grey with the wisdom of obedience, hands rough with years of hard labor, and heart tender from a lifetime spent seeking his Master's will—gathered his family about him with a smile of weary contentment. He shook each of their hands, after which numerous hugs followed, and tears flowed from the eyes of father and mother as they stood in the great open meadow to the north and gazed upon what they had accomplished.

"You did it, Jeremiah," whispered Mary.

"No, Mother," he replied, "*we* did it . . . with the Lord's help, we all did it together."

He sank to his knees on the sun-warmed earth and was soon joined by wife, sons, daughters, two daughters-in-law, a son-in-law, and seven grandchildren.

"*Gracious heavenly Father,*" he prayed, "*thank you for your faithful provision, and for carrying out your work in the raising of these beautiful stones. Thank you for giving us strength to do what you gave us to do. May your will be done in this place, and your purposes fulfilled. May this home and all who inhabit it live to your glory, their lives a light, a witness, and a testimony to your goodness. May your Spirit never depart from this land and this home that you have provided, and may all who dwell here be given life by that Spirit. May that life deepen and spread and draw many to you. As the years go by we pray that Heathersleigh will be a place where men and women, boys and girls, all whom you lead, will find faith, hope, and love through those of your people who make this their home. Amen.*"

Soft "amens" followed from all the rest. Slowly they rose.

"Well, Mother," said an exuberant Jeremiah, "what have you and the girls prepared as a celebration feast for this family of hungry laborers!"

❖❖❖

Throughout England's tumultuous seventeenth century, Heathersleigh Hall became an oasis of light and spiritual refuge for many. Jeremiah and Mary's eldest son, David, added the east wing to the Hall between 1661 and 1678, and moved the family's quarters to the new wing. Much of the ground floor of the vacated north wing was thus converted from living space and made suitable for more formal use. A sizeable gamekeeper's cottage was added at the northern edge of the estate in a wooded region between the Hall and the village in the 1730s.

But in the mystery of the generations and a divine plan that is difficult to apprehend amid life's heartaches, sons and daughters and those who come after them do not always follow the dictates of their parents' consciences, the convictions of their faith, or even the principles they have been taught. Surely it would have been a grief to this patriarch and matriarch of the Rutherford clan of Devon to see what weeds would later grow in the family garden as the centuries advanced, and what greedy motives of self would come for a time to dominate this place.

Their prayers, however, would not die out altogether, but would return after many years. Indeed God's will would be accomplished again at Heathersleigh as it had been during their own time, and during the years of their sons and grandsons.

The title "Lord of the Manor" was first bestowed on David's son Nathan Rutherford in 1710, and was then passed down from father to son. The peculiarities of the unique appellation dictated that both title and property would always pass to a following generation at the death of the titleholder—son, daughter, even nephew or cousin—but never transfer laterally to a spouse.

Anxious to make his own personal stamp on the Hall, and without wife or family to consume his time, Nathan's great-grandson Broughton Rutherford, shortly after his assumption to the title, began work on the third and final portion of the great house, the west wing. There was little need to add to the already massive structure, for by then the family in residence had dwindled and the number of workers and servants was in decline, and most of the new rooms added would sit vacant throughout the year. But Broughton was fond of an occasional party of lavish proportions, inviting half the gentry and aristocracy of London and southern England, and thus always felt cramped for space.

Meanwhile, his younger brother, Robert, married and had a son, Henry, in 1783.

A freak hunting accident took Robert's life suddenly and prematurely just six years later. His wife, Wallis, never entirely recovered from the shock of his death and, as she had no means of her own, retired to live out the remainder of her days at the Hall in relative seclusion with her young son. Broughton Rutherford, therefore, became the male guardian for his nephew, a wild boy whom the passage of years did little to tame.

As the generations of a legacy ebb and flow according to the character choices made by its members, the family Rutherford now entered a murky era, when secrets, rather than the light prayed for by old Jeremiah Rutherford, came to predominate the spiritual mood within Heathersleigh's walls. Weeds, therefore, began to grow in the soil of the Rutherford family garden, gradually covering over and forcing into dormancy the seeds of light and truth planted by its founders.

The prayers of the old patriarch would be heard again in the fullness of time, though much darkness would have to be endured before the Son of Truth would again rise over the estate of Heathersleigh.

Season of Secrets

1799-1854

*B*roughton Rutherford, now Lord of the Manor of Heathersleigh Hall, climbed the stairs to the garret and looked around. The year was 1799.

Yes, this would be perfect, he thought. He had explored these upper regions of the house as a boy. Now he would put them to good use for his own protection.

The old metal box had haunted him for thirty-seven years.

Rumors abounded throughout the region, and he had been tormented since his youth with a fear that the pirates and their smuggling associates had never given up their search for him. He became obsessed with the idea of having to make an escape from their clutches at a moment's notice, convinced that the day would surely arrive when they would come for him. Thus, he remained ever on the lookout for new and cleverer means that would enable him to hide and elude their grasp. He had to find a place to stash the box and its contents where he would have access to what it contained should he need it, but without his being seen. The Hall's upper regions were perfect.

To this end, as the west wing grew, he devised various cunning doors and intricate passageways to include in its construction, eventually leading into the other two wings as well. If ever he saw unfriendly faces approaching, he would be able to take refuge behind walls and in secret chambers and then get completely out of the Hall and to safety while they were still busy searching his quarters.

Secrecy remained imperative. His nephew Henry was not one he could trust with the knowledge of what he was doing. He had a loose tongue and was a braggart. If he knew the secret, it was only a matter of time before the young fool let something slip. They could all wind up dead just like Rufus Powell. Later, when the boy was older and in a position to inherit, perhaps then Broughton would tell him everything.

In the meantime, he would again employ Webley Kyrkwode from the village for his new garret project. The man was a hard worker, possessed skills with unusual mechanisms, and had always proved reliable. But he would have to keep Henry away from Kyrkwode's daughter, Orelia. He didn't need that kind of a scandal to go along with his other troubles.

———————— ◆ ◆ ◆ ————————

Broughton Rutherford's fears did not materialize. He never saw pirates around Heathersleigh. Nor did he ever confide his secrets to his nephew. When he died suddenly of a heart attack in 1801, the west wing not yet complete, his brother's now eighteen-year-old son became lord of the manor.

Though rumors of amorous affairs circulated for years concerning Henry, he neither married nor produced offspring during all the years of his youth and young adulthood. He became more interested in the Hall itself as he grew into adulthood, gradually resuming construction of and eventually completing the west wing. With Kyrkwode's help, he discovered and added to many of the secret passages contrived by his uncle. But though he had long suspected his uncle the possessor of something of enormous value, the garret's secret forever remained a sealed book to him.

When at thirty-nine years of age he married Eliza Gretton in 1822, he was already becoming frantic to sire a son. When she did not give him one within a year or two, his rage toward her mounted.

Then came the fateful night of February 11, 1829, when suddenly the barren womb of Lord Henry's wife burst into fruitfulness with *two* Rutherford heirs, giving Henry the son he had so long desired.

Alas, poor Eliza did not live the night.

Local midwife Orelia Moylan, who had known Henry all her life and, in spite of her God-fearing heart, despised him, tended both the births and the death, and witnessed the transaction between the lord of the manor and the parish vicar, one Arthur Crompton, who was paid for his silence as she watched from above.

But Orelia's conscience would not let her rest with what she knew. Two weeks later, in the dead of night, she sneaked back into the Hall. She knew its passages and corridors well from much time spent here when her father was under the employ of old Lord Broughton.

She crept into the tower, where she had often played with one of the young maids. She knew where the keys were hidden and also about the secret passage her father had helped build. Using both, and creeping through the blackness with care, she made her way through the narrow hidden corridor to the library on the second floor of the east wing.

It was but the work of a minute or two to locate the large family Bible on the sideboard. She opened it and added the clue she hoped would one day bring the events of recent days to light.

To hide the Bible, her father's craftsmanship again came to her aid. Soon the great book was resting in the secret chamber of the secretary her father had made to match the one in their own home.

She closed the secret panel, slid in the drawer that hid its lock from visibility, then pocketed the key, took it with her as she left the library, and returned through the secret passage to the old stone tower, where she placed it on the ring with the key to the door into the passageway she had just used connecting the two regions of the Hall.

Returning home, she added similar clues to the pages of her own Bible that hopefully one day would lead curious eyes to retrace the very steps she had taken this night. In the margin of Mark 4, next to the words *To you is given to understand the mystery of the kingdom,* she made the notation "There is a mystery, and the key is closer than you think. The key . . . find the key and unlock the mystery." Beneath them, in tiny letters, she added the reference "Genesis 25:31–33."

Only a few more clues remained to be noted. She turned to the familiar passage in the holy text's first book, and beside the thirty-third verse, she carefully noted in the margin "Proverbs 20." This she followed back and forth through her Bible, with no little work, to locate the appropriate selections, until the message was complete.

The references made, she could now rest.

♦ ♦ ♦

The passage of years proved more fortuitous for Vicar Crompton than for either the lord of the manor or Orelia Moylan.

Crompton rose in the Church to the position of bishop, while Henry Rutherford's financial affairs went from bad to worse. Knowing nothing of his uncle Broughton's secret, he was forced to take extreme measures to save himself from bankruptcy.

A certain highly lucrative but questionable scheme kept him from ruin. His invisible partner in the affair, however, was none other than Crompton himself, who promised continued silence regarding both matters in exchange for the donation and sale of the gamekeeper's cottage his uncle had built half a century earlier. Though he was reluctant to part with it, his finances and threat of exposure gave him little choice. His son Ashby's standing, in addition, must be preserved. The transaction was consummated in 1849.

It was when aging Bishop Crompton happened upon old Orelia Moylan in the streets of Milverscombe two years later that the fateful encounter took place that would add still more mysteries to the growing string of rumors surrounding the Heathersleigh estate, and would perplex many local inhabitants for decades to come.

The former midwife was now sixty-five and her own daughter Grace had two children—the eldest a thirteen-year-old daughter by the name of Margaret—and was even then with child in preparation for a third.

The two now elderly former colleagues in Henry Rutherford's deception both recognized one another as they walked along the street near the old stone church where Crompton had once presided as vicar. They had not seen each other since that fateful night at the Hall.

Already Crompton's conscience had begun to whisper to him concerning many things he had done, as well as the manner of man he had been. A gradual decline of his health contributed to this waking. The unexpected encounter deepened the force of those pangs. Yet he could not quite bring himself to answer them. The voice of conscience, when heeded, makes one humble and one's manner tender. That same voice, while yet its demands are resisted, makes one surly. With a stiff nod of acknowledgment, therefore, he tried to continue on past her.

But Orelia, who had been thinking of that night more frequently of late and asking God what she should do with what she knew, stopped and spoke to him.

"I know why you are in Heathersleigh Cottage," she said.

Crompton now paused as well, then turned.

"Yes, and what is that to me?" he said. His unease, in the absence of steps yet taken toward restitution, caused him to vent his anger at himself on the woman, whose sight goaded his conscience all the more.

"Just that there you are with plenty to eat, while me and mine have nothing but gruel to keep us alive," she rejoined. "You received fifty pounds and the house. What have I got to show for my silence?"

"What do you expect me to do about it?"

"I have a married daughter who now has two young ones of her own, and another on the way. It's all any of us can do to put food down our throats. These are evil times, Vicar, especially for one who knows what I know. Surely a man such as yourself is not beyond feeling compassion for the likes of us."

Squirming behind his collar, Crompton managed a few moments later to conclude the awkward interview.

But for weeks the woman's words plagued him. He could not deny them to be true. He had all his life enjoyed plenty. She, whose need was greater, possessed next to nothing.

Yet what could he do?

Perhaps, he said to himself, the question ought to be, what *should* he do?

A Bishop's Restitution

1855-1856

$\mathcal{B}$ishop Arthur Crompton's health continued to decline as his age advanced. And still further did his spirit awaken. He retired from his official position, took up permanent residence in his wooded cottage in Devon, which had from the moment of dubious transfer belonged to him rather than the Church.

About a year later his health took a sudden serious turn. He knew immediately that he was dying.

As eternity beckoned, his conscience—which was in reality his Creator-Father's voice speaking into his innermost regions—became all the more imperative. More importantly, he finally began to heed its whispers.

He saw all too clearly that he had not lived a life worthy of his calling. He could not undo what he had done, but he could at least acknowledge his childness toward his heavenly Father, and live out his final days in His care. And what *did* lie in his power to do by way of Zacchaeus' restitution, that much at least he would undertake to do.

To that end, before his strength failed him altogether, he paid a visit to his former church in the village. Knowing well enough where the records were kept, and knowing that the case was never locked, he added a new entry to that he had made twenty-six years earlier. To have simply altered the entry would have been easier, though it would surely have aroused suspicion. And he must uphold the sanctity of the records, even if he knew their falsehood. He would leave his clue in this manner and hope its truth would be uncovered one day.

To further this end, he also arranged for a visit to the Exeter solicitors' firm of Crumholtz, Sutclyff, Stonehaugh, & Crumholtz. When his business was concluded, two documents were left behind with his signature, where they would remain in the possession of his longtime friend Lethbridge Crumholtz and his firm for as long as circumstances demanded.

The first was a newly executed will, the chief provision of which would, upon his death, transfer the deed to Heathersleigh Cottage that he had purchased from Henry Rutherford—and which document he gave to the firm for safekeeping—to Orelia (Kyrkwode) Moylan. Upon the deed was added the somewhat unusual provision that the property should pass to Orelia Moylan's heirs until or unless it came into the possession of a final heir with no clear descendant, after whom it would pass to the Church of England.

The second document was a letter, written in his own hand the night prior to his journey to Exeter, in which he detailed exactly what had taken place on that winter's night in February of 1829, how he and the midwife had been drawn into Henry Rutherford's lie, as well as what he had done in 1849 to originally purchase the cottage, concluding with his motives now for its final disposition. Truth, he realized, demanded that a full disclosure be made. He was concerned no longer for his own reputation. But lest any repercussions of a damaging nature should accrue to Orelia Moylan or her heirs, his final instructions indicated that this letter of disclosure should not be made public until the same condition was fulfilled as specified on the deed—the decease of her last remaining heir. At that time, and only then, should the principals of Crumholtz, Sutclyff, Stonehaugh, & Crumholtz open it and divulge its contents. The terms of his will by then would have long since already been carried out.

With these burdens at last lifted from his conscience, his final months were the happiest of his life. They were marked by his discovery of the joy of that greatest of all secrets that so few in the human race ever find, the mysterious wonder that he was a child who was cared for in every way by a good and loving Father. That the discovery came late in his life may have been unfortunate, but it was not too late to make a man of him in the end.

When Bishop Arthur Crompton died early in the year 1856, all those for miles around Milverscombe were baffled by the irregularity of an unmarried man who had risen so high in ecclesiastical circles leaving his home to an aging local peasant woman whom not a single individual could recall once seeing him with.

They would not have considered it strange had they heard the words feebly whispered from his dying lips that January night: *"My Father, it has been a life too much wasted loving myself, too little given to listening to you and doing what you told me. I cannot help it, for this life is done. I shall serve you more diligently in the next. Forgive my foolishness. You have been a good Father to me, though I have been a childish son. Perhaps now you will be able to make a true man of me. In the meantime, do your best with this place. Make good come of it, though I obtained it by deceit. Bless the woman and those who follow. Give life to all who enter this door. May they know you sooner than I."*

He paused, closed his eyes in near exhaustion, then added inaudibly—

And now . . . I am ready . . . take me home.

None heard the words, save him to whom they had been spoken.

Arthur Crompton was discovered dead in his bed the following morning, a smile on his lips, according to the lady from the village who came in to cook for him, and who entered that day when he did not answer her knock.

Most vexed of all by the curious turn was Henry Rutherford himself, the aging Lord of the Manor of Heathersleigh Hall, who, now that his fortunes had again reversed, would have done anything to resecure the property and oust the old woman. But he had no legal recourse. The will, brought forth by Lethbridge Crumholtz of Exeter, was legally irrefutable.

There were now only two alive who knew the connection existing between man of the cloth and the woman of swaddling clothes—Orelia Moylan herself, and the lord of the manor whose secret both had sworn to protect. It was a secret she never revealed, as originally planned. She could not but conclude in the end that perhaps, as in the verses she had noted in both Bibles, the blessing had indeed been passed on as God intended.

Bishop and peasant each carried the knowledge of their unknown alliance to their respective graves.

Everyone said the woman's former profession must have made her privy to some fact which resulted in the strange bequest of the former bishop's country home. No living soul ever discovered what that secret was.

Hints and Clues

1865-1911

Generations went by, and those who came and went in Heathersleigh Hall pieced together fragmentary clues pointing toward the many mysteries about the place that the passage of time had obscured.

In 1865 a five-year-old visiting youngster from the dispossessed branch of the family tree by the name of Gifford nearly uncovered the root of strife that would later possess him when, leaving his cousin Charles, with whom he was supposed to be playing, he ventured toward the darkened bedchamber of his aging grandfather.

He had seen the nurse leave a few moments earlier. Now curiosity drove him toward the door. He cast a peep inside. The room was dusky, for heavy curtains were pulled to keep out the sunlight. He inched through without touching the door and entered the room.

Across the floor, on a bed between sheets of white, lay the thin form of old Lord Henry, who seemed to have left the reckoning of earthly years behind altogether. One of his thin arms lay outside the bedcovers, appearing even whiter to the youngster than the sheet, though not quite so white as what hair he still possessed atop a skull over which the skin seemed to have been stretched more tightly than seemed comfortable.

With eyes wide in fascinated awe, the boy crept forward, unable to keep the verses out of his head that Charlie had repeated to him only yesterday:

Look where you go, watch what you do,
  or Lord Henry will snatch and make you a stew.
He'll cut you in pieces, like he did that night
  when his poor Eliza screamed out in such fright.
With his own hand he killed her, or so they say,
  and began to go batty the very next day.
It will happen to you, no one will hear your call,
  if you venture too close to Heathersleigh Hall.

He reached the bedside and gazed down upon the white face. No expression on the countenance indicated that life still existed inside him. All the rumors about his grandfather, along with the words of the spooky poem, went through the boy's brain as he stared at the bed with heart pounding.

Suddenly both the old man's eyelashes fluttered and twitched, as if his eyes were rolling about inside their sockets.

In panic the boy tried to flee. But his feet remained nailed to the floor. The ancient eyes opened, as if the sense of presence beside the bed had awakened him. He spied a form, yet knew it not as his grandson from London. His pupils widened and locked on to those of the boy, which returned their gaze with mute terror.

Suddenly the thin arm shot from the bed. The grip of ancient fingers closed around the youngster's arm with a strength they had not exercised in years.

In abject horror, the boy's heart pounded like a drum.

"Cynthia . . . my dear young Cynthia," he whispered, "—you've come back, just like I prayed you would. We'll set all right now—"

He closed his eyes and relaxed a moment to draw in a breath.

"I . . . I was a fool . . ." he tried to begin again, ". . . they were terrible times . . . I had to protect . . . they tried to take the Hall . . . it was your mother . . . if she had only—"

Suddenly light blazed into the room.

"Giffy!" cried the nurse, bounding through the door. "What are you doing bothering your grandfather?"

"I . . . I only came in for a look," stammered the boy.

"Don't you know he mustn't be disturbed!" she reproached, hurrying toward the bedside. "You stay with Charlie, do you hear!"

She took hold of the thin ancient hand, unwrapped its fingers from the boy's arm, and laid it at his side on the bed.

While the fussy nurse attended to him, chastising herself for her carelessness, the boy crept silently out, the possessor of a secret whose significance he was as unaware of as what the old man's strange words might mean. The shock of seeing the dying man pushed the odd words for some time from his mind.

Henry Rutherford died later that same night, speaking not another word to a living soul.

◆ ◆ ◆

As the years passed, along with wealth accumulated in the business world, the words he had heard as a boy, mingled with the expressed dissatisfaction of his father, Albert, continued to haunt Gifford Rutherford with the fixation of somehow laying claim to the estate where his cousin Charles rose not only to become lord of the manor but also a highly respected member of Parliament and a knight of the realm.

Gifford was indeed of Rutherford blood. But whereas his cousin eventually manifested the spiritual inclinations of old Jeremiah, Gifford's bent was more reminiscent of Broughton and Henry.

Gifford passed on both his character and his greed to his only son, Geoffrey, who came close to stumbling on the key to the secret his father had nearly uncovered as a boy. During a visit of the London Rutherfords to Heathersleigh Hall in 1899, Geoffrey found himself locked in the northeast tower of the Hall as a prank at the hands of his cousin Amanda. Though terrified, the boy accidentally dislodged a loose stone in the wall, finding concealed behind it an ancient key ring. It contained that which would have enabled him to escape the tower through a secret wall-door, by means of a lock hidden behind a small sliding panel of stone, and thus turn the tables on Amanda for good. It also held a tiny key placed on the ring by none other than Orelia Moylan. It was a key which opened more than even Orelia herself knew about, for her father had been shrewd in the matter of the most secretive of all chambers he had been hired to build.

Alas, young Geoffrey was only eight. It did not occur to him that he held in his chubby hand that which, had he known where to locate the secretary to which the key belonged, as well as where to insert it, would have uncovered exactly what his father lusted for.

Therefore he trousered the keys, and neither he nor his father was any nearer the root of things when they left that day than when they came.

And though the elder of the banker Rutherfords continued curious through the years about the missing family Bible, and set stealthy inquiries afoot to steal it out of the Hall, it continued to gather dust, safely out of sight where Orelia had stowed it.

♦ ♦ ♦

Amanda's older brother George had been curious about the great Hall that was his home almost from the day he could walk. He inherited his father's love for exploration, and for asking questions about how things worked and why. And whereas much of Charles's innate curiosity was directed toward mechanisms and people, as a lad George turned his curiosity toward what lay under the floors, behind the walls, and above the ceilings of Heathersleigh Hall.

He had discovered oddities in the garret at nine, and stumbled on yet more fragments of the past in 1904 as a curious sixteen-year-old.

An old wooden chest first drew his attention as he rummaged about in a little-used storeroom on the second floor of the north wing. Opening it, George momentarily had his very hands on that which would have helped explain the riddle of the garret construction that had puzzled him as a boy. But he was not interested in papers and journals. He was more interested in what was to be found beneath the chest. Therefore, he tossed back two ships' logs that had been taken from a cave on the coast 142 years before, and set about dragging the chest away from the wall. Written documents were not as fascinating as the hole in the floor he found beneath the loose boards the chest had been sitting on. Minutes later he was winding down a circular stone stairway into a labyrinth of concealed passages designed by his great-great-grandfather.

He did not stop to ask what could be the motive behind these hidden places. At the moment he was too excited about the hidden invisible world of clandestine twistings and turnings he had found, which led him eventually through the wall on a swiveling bookcase, and unexpectedly into the library, where his astonished parents sat reading. It did not take George many more days to connect the passage with another that led to the tower, through the back side of the concealed doorway that had not been put to use since the night Orelia Moylan had stolen into the house, as well as another passage leading up steep, narrow wooden steps into the garret.

In 1911 George again came close to learning more from that same chest when he brought his younger sister, Catharine, through the hidden passages to the same storeroom. At last the chest's contents had drawn his interest, as he proceeded to explain to Catharine. But his attention was now on the ledgers revealing the construction progress of the Hall. But neither of the two young people noticed the log books. Thus the mystery of young Broughton Rutherford's ill-fated adventure with Rufus Powell and its links with the Heathersleigh attic regions remained undetected in the midst of their other discoveries.

Nor did Catharine realize that the missing family Bible her cousin Geoffrey's father had been so intent to find, which had curiously disappeared from various of Heathersleigh's portraits in the gallery, itself contained clues that would one day alter their family's history. Had she known where to look, she might have discovered parallel clues that same afternoon from the smaller worn Bible in the cottage of bewildering transfer, the names of whose former owners she and Maggie pored over together in the midst of their needlework.

The three Heathersleigh women walked the passage from library to tower upon Amanda's return to England in 1915, and on that day first put to use the key to the disguised tower door they again possessed after Geoffrey returned the ring, sixteen years after he had taken it, at Charles's funeral. The purpose of the large key was at last known. The smaller, however—though its twin had by now been found in the drawer in the cottage—remained on the tower ring, a riddle unsolved.

Many had indeed brushed close to one or another of the secrets of Heathersleigh Hall, yet still much of the past remained cloaked in mystery.

In the end, it would remain for Margaret Crawford McFee to bring that past further into the light.

Maggie's Revelations

1914-1915

*O*relia Moylan's granddaughter Margaret married Irishman Robert McFee in the early 1860s. The two inherited Heathersleigh Cottage at the death of Margaret's mother, Grace Moylan Crawford, and came to be known to the community simply as Bobby and Maggie.

They never had children, and many considered them odd. In earlier times, children in Milverscombe had feared the name McFee and, in the sort of curious mingling and distortion that occurs through the years, came to associate the peculiar couple with the scary rumors about old Lord Henry Rutherford, and would venture too close neither to Heathersleigh Hall *nor* its former gamekeeper's cottage.

Yet none could deny that the two were indispensable to the community. Bobby's knowledge of animals was so vast that few could have managed without him. And his wife made herself useful to the villagers in a thousand ways. She knew much that was not commonly known, about medicine and weather, about herbs and other plants, and about humanity in general. The poor of the region considered her as an angel. The well-to-do didn't know what to think of her, and cared even less.

Those who took the trouble to acquaint themselves deeply with Maggie and Bobby knew them to be a simple man and woman of God. Their close affiliation with Charles and Jocelyn Rutherford, in particular, as the nineteenth century drew to a close, served in time to make the two aging McFees among everyone's favorites, in no small measure due to the spiritual esteem in which they were held.

It was prayer, and her childhood recollections of her grandmother's favorite Scripture, that contributed to Maggie's first subconscious stirrings in the direction of the mystery whose keys she had herself possessed for the better part of her life without knowing it.

A visit to the cottage by nine-year-old Amanda Rutherford prompted a discussion between the girl and the odd couple, as she childishly judged them, containing more significance than any of them realized at the time. Maggie had taken a worn, old black leather Bible from the open desk of the curiously ornate oak secretary made by her great-grandfather, and opened it with reverence to the eleventh verse of the fourth chapter of Mark's Gospel.

"This is my mother's Bible, Amanda," she said, "and my grand-mother's before her. I can remember my grandmother telling me that if a body doesn't begin early in life to see the mysteries of the kingdom, they become harder to see as one gets older. The high things of God take a lifetime to learn. That's why you must point your eyes toward them as early as you can. The Lord will take anybody, anytime, and will do his best with them. But whoever's got the chance ought to get their eyes open early so that the Almighty has time to let his mysteries get down deep into their character.

"This was her favorite passage," Maggie added.

" 'Unto you is given,' " she read, " 'to know the mystery of the king-dom of God, but unto them that are on the outside, all these things are said in parables.' "

Maggie paused, then glanced across the table toward the girl.

"Do you hear, Amanda?" she said. "—*Mystery*. That is what the Lord calls life in the kingdom of God. It takes a special kind of eyes to see into it."

Maggie's words continued to play on her own mind as the years went by even more than they did the girl's for whom they were intended. When Amanda's independent spirit drove her from home at the age of seventeen, Maggie McFee, along with Amanda's family, was driven to renewed depths of prayer for the prodigal they all loved. And as is often the result of such communion with the divine will, as Maggie prayed that Amanda would come to understand the mystery of the kingdom, her prayers opened new channels in her *own* understanding.

That understanding exploded into light soon after the death of her beloved Bobby in 1914, just as the world was being plunged into war. Two weeks after his passing, as she sat slowly rocking and thinking of the dear husband with whom she had shared her life, his final words to Amanda came back to her. *"Open yer eyes, lass,"* Bobby had said. *"Don't wait too long. Ye got t' discover yer heritage. 'Tis different than folks think, differ-ent than ye imagine. 'Tis a legacy ye're given t' discover, though it be hidden from yer eyes at present. A hidden legacy, lass, do ye hear me? Find it. Ye must find it!"*

Bobby's words continued to haunt his wife. Later that same night, Maggie suddenly awoke out of a deep sleep as if an arrow of clarity had stabbed her brain, with Bobby's words reverberating in her memory.

A hidden legacy . . . different than folks think . . . ye must find it.

She rose and sought the Bible that had been passed from her great-grandmother, Mrs. Webley Kyrkwode, to her grandmother Orelia, who had used it cryptically to record knowledge concerning which her tongue had been silenced. Now all at once, with the benefit of her grandmother's scarcely legible marginal note, the double meaning of the passage struck her. Why had she never paid attention to the addition before?

There were the words, faint now with the passing of years, added in the margin in her grandmother's own hand—words as familiar to her as this Bible itself. She had seen the brief note most of her life, thinking it merely a reference to the importance of the verse. She had tried to impress that importance on young Amanda long ago in this very cottage whose origins and history were now on her mind.

She read them again, puzzling over the strange handwritten anno-tation.

There is a mystery, her grandmother had written, *and the key is closer than you think. The key . . . find the key and unlock the mystery.*

Suddenly the words jumped out at her. How could she not have made the connection before now?

A small, old, peculiar key had been kicking around all her life in the drawer of the secretary. No one knew what it was for.

Could its purpose be connected to her grandmother's words!

Below the note had been added a reference to Genesis 25:31–33.

Quickly she flipped back to the halfway point of the sacred volume's first book and scanned down the page. What had her grandmother been trying to convey? Were her marginal notes meant as a message about this key . . . a mystery . . . a birthright?

Again Maggie turned back to the Gospel of Mark—*Find the key and unlock the mystery. . . .*

Suddenly her mind began to race—the key . . . the mystery . . . the sale of the birthright!

Maggie rose, set her Bible aside, and walked to the ancient secretary. With trembling hand she lowered the lid. Above the desk was a small four-inch-wide drawer. Carefully she pulled it out. Her eyes fell on the key inside she had seen resting there all her life.

She removed it and turned it over slowly in her fingers.

What mystery was this key meant to unlock?

She began snooping about the old cabinet, first pulling the small drawer above the desk all the way out. Key still clutched in her left hand, she sent the fingers of her right probing into the opening, investigating with the tips of her fingers.

The back panel was loose!

Jostling it, she managed to slide it half an inch to one side. She stuck a finger into the crack and soon had it sliding along grooves embedded in the wood. In the opening behind it her fingers felt a small metal apparatus. A brass lock was built into the hidden recess of the cabinet! With fingers trembling, she took the key and inserted it, and turned the key. From somewhere inside she heard the faint metallic sound of a lock releasing.

Below the drawer, the back wall of the desk gave way and opened toward her. A hidden panel swiveled smoothly down on embedded pivots, revealing a faceless shelf. On it lay a single folded sheet of heavy paper.

Maggie removed it, brought it out to the light, sat back down in her chair, and unfolded it.

Some time later Maggie still sat, shaking her head in disbelief. To think it had been here all along—the key, the lock, the hidden drawer—in front of her very eyes—and the answer to the mystery that had given rise to so many stories and rumors for over half a century—how the cottage of the Heathersleigh estate had come into the hands of a poor local peasant family with hardly two shillings to rub together.

In her hands, Maggie held the deed to Heathersleigh Cottage—this very cottage, sold, as was written on it, in the year 1849 from Henry Rutherford, Lord of the Manor of Heathersleigh Hall, to one Arthur Crompton.

What could its significance be but that to which her grandmother was referring as the sale of the birthright of the Genesis passage? Further documentation seven years later, in the year 1856, apparently upon Crompton's death, recorded the transfer of the deed to Orelia Crawford, Maggie's own grandmother, to be passed to her descendents after her, or, absent heirs, to the Church of England. The stamp of the solicitors' firm Crumholtz, Sutclyff, Stonehaugh, & Crumholtz attested to the legality of the 1856 transfer.

She had discovered the legal origins to the long-concealed mystery... but still not the *why*.

Gradually sleep returned. Maggie extinguished her light and went back to bed.

The next day, at the earliest possible hour, she was bound for the parish church in the village. The ancient journals and parish records were produced for her examination. It did not take Maggie long to locate what she wanted—the connection between the deed she had discovered and the fateful night of Eliza's death.

Not only was Arthur Crompton at the Hall that night, her grandmother, the only midwife in the region, must have been too. That was the connection between vicar and midwife. Whatever secret had been hatched that night, they had clearly shared it.

But as Maggie left the church to make her way home, a feeling of unease began growing within her. She had nothing against the Church, but it seemed the Cottage ought to belong to those for whom it rightfully had been intended.

She would consult the solicitors' firm whose name was on the deed. She could not undo what had been done years before. But she could at least, if it lay in her power legally to do so, put her home back into the hands of the true heirs of the Heathersleigh birthright.

And she must write down what she had discovered and leave new clues and information explaining it. She also must make a will.

To that end, on the very next day, she boarded the train in Milverscombe, to the amazement of the entire village, and traveled to Exeter to visit the offices of Crumholtz, Sutclyff, Stonehaugh, & Crumholtz, where she concluded her business and left the necessary documents in the hands of Bradbury Crumholtz, senior partner of the firm.

Several months later, after Charles's death and funeral and Amanda's return, and sensing that her own remaining years could be few, Maggie explained to Jocelyn, Amanda, and Catharine what she had learned, telling them how the cottage had come into the hands of her family, and that she had drawn up a will that would give it back to them when she went to join her Bobby.

At last the mystery of Heathersleigh Cottage appeared to have been solved. Temporarily the four women all felt a great sense of relief.

But in time the two younger girls, who had, like their brother, been given curious, thoughtful, and inquisitive mentalities by their father, realized that the family Bible was still missing.

And that the older mystery of the Hall and its garret yet remained.

PART I

Summer 1915

1

A Time to Remember

An attractive young woman, by appearance in her midtwenties, stood at the window of a thick stone wall gazing out upon a serene English countryside.

A calm radiated from her posture and bearing which, had an observer been present, might have seemed almost too peaceful for her years. Full waves of light brown hair flowed down onto her shoulders.

Was she what the world would term beautiful? From the look in her eyes at this moment, it would have been difficult to say. It was a compelling face, not because of the attractiveness of its features, but for what lay beneath the surface . . . an expression hinting at mystery.

Who was she? How had she come to be here?

In partial answer to such inquiries, a closer look would have revealed that the eyes bore an aspect of pain, a good deal of it recent. Their expressiveness explained much of what was to be known about her personal history that had come before, as well as what yet lay ahead in the story being written on the pages of her life.

The colors of the rolling terrain of meadows of the Devonshire downs, broken here and there by clumps of trees, were muted by the subdued oranges and pinks of the late afternoon's sun. It was a landscape she had been intimately familiar with since earliest childhood.

It meant more to her now than she would have thought possible at an earlier season of her life. She once gazed out this same window with far different eyes. But that time was now long past. At last she had begun to apprehend the heritage that was truly hers, and had been all along.

The tower in which she stood rose from the northeast corner of a great country house too old to be called a mansion yet not quite so austere and grey to be comfortable with the term *castle*. For as long as anyone could remember the place had been known as Heathersleigh Hall. It was an estate of ancient date, whose walls contained many secrets—some of which yet lay awaiting discovery.

Her eyes now fell on the small village of Milverscombe two or three miles in the distance. The thatch and slate roofs were all she could make out from this vantage point of the forty or fifty cottages and homes which housed its population. Several larger buildings rose above the level of these roofs, most visibly the old stone church, and a modern train station.

She now looked toward a small wooded area to the west of the village situated about a third of the way toward it from the Hall. Nothing stood out as so remarkable about the collection of birch and pine trees enclosing a small dell between the slopes of two adjoining hillsides. There were a thousand such places in the southwest of England. But this one was special, and not only because it lay just across the boundary of the estate.

She stood for several long moments as her gaze stretched across the fields. Even as unconscious prayers gathered themselves within her heart, the memory of an afternoon not so very different from this came to focus from out of the past in her mind's eye.

In the measure of eternity the years since had not really been so many. Yet the day she now recalled had in truth been another lifetime ago.

Her thoughts were interrupted by footsteps echoing from the passage behind her.

"Amanda . . . Amanda, are you up there?" came her sister's voice up the narrow staircase.

"Yes, Catharine," she answered softly, half turning behind her. "I'm in the tower."

Amanda sent one final wistful gaze of poignant memory out the window, then turned into the small room just as Catharine entered through the large oak door that stood open where Amanda had left it a few minutes earlier.

"Hi . . . what are you doing?" said Catharine with a buoyant smile.

"Just coming to terms with a few memories," said Amanda, returning her smile. "I have a lot to get used to now, things to put right from when I was so mixed up before."

"I know," rejoined Catharine, giving Amanda an affectionate hug, "—do you want to be alone? I didn't mean to interrupt."

"No, it's all right. I'm through."

"Would you like to go for a ride? That's why I was looking for you."

"Where are you going?" asked Amanda as arm in arm they left the tower and began the descent together.

"I was thinking about riding out to see Grandma Maggie."

"Yes, I think I would like that," answered Amanda. "In fact, I was just thinking about her."

"Good, I was hoping you would—I already asked Hector to saddle both horses."

———————— ◆ ◆ ◆ ————————

Another young woman stood at the wood stove of a tiny flat in one of the coastal towns of that far southeastern portion of England known as Cornwall. She was neither old enough nor experienced enough to be as reflective as her Devonshire counterpart. But she stood staring at the sizzling skillet in front of her with eyes that might have been reflective had they anything to think about.

She was but thirteen, and hers had not been an easy life. The struggle merely to survive and make the best of it consumed the days that made up her existence. She did not stop to consider whether she was happy or unhappy, or whether life was a good or an evil thing. Life was simply life. It was hard, but she had never known anything else and did not question it. She was still a child, though hints of changes gradually coming to her body gave evidence that womanhood was not far away.

She stood at the stove watching the small slab of meat that was her father's breakfast brown over the heat. He had not come home last night, and whenever he must work through the long hours when she had to stay alone, he arrived home in the morning hungry. She did not know what he did, only knew that some of it had to do with ships. What else occupied him at such times, she did not need to know. She knew enough not to ask, knew that the people she sometimes saw with him were bad people, knew enough to realize that when he spoke with them in low tones it was about things they would not want the bobby who sometimes walked their street to hear.

Sully Conlin was a rough man, with rough friends. He laughed with them, swore with them, and drank with them, and sometimes fought with them. She thought ill neither of them nor her father because of it. She was not shocked by what she saw and heard. As much as is possible the crude language and coarse behavior passed over her. She did not know otherwise, and took it as one of the laws of existence that men did such things and that girls like her did their best to take care of them.

That Conlin had once been a sailor he had not exactly told his daughter in so many words, but she knew it from the purple tattoo of anchors and ropes on his burly forearm, from the way he spoke, knew it from his dream of taking her away from Cornwall and showing her the world. He never talked about leaving or going somewhere... but always of *sailing* away.

She knew it too from the fond gleam in his eye whenever he spoke of the sea.

"The sea, Betsy," he had said many times, especially after hard days of backbreaking labor on the docks, "the sea is our only friend. It may be hard, but the sea is fair, and treats all men the same. It took your mother, and to the sea we will all return in the end. If ever you are lost, find the sea and follow it."

But whatever he had been, and whatever kind of life he lived, Sully was good to his little girl and treated her gently. He was her father, and she loved him.

Her mother had been dead now many years. All she had to remember her was a small oval photograph that her father kept beside his bed.

Sometimes when he was gone, she would stare at the tiny picture and try to force to the surface from some region deep in her mind an image from her own life, a living memory that moved and spoke, whose voice she might faintly hear in the distance of the past.

But it was no use. She had been aware of the photograph all the days of her life, and there had never been a time when it did not sit at her father's bedside. Whatever actual memory might at one time have been alive in her brain was now too faded and indistinct to be distinguished from the photograph itself.

Reality from the past and the small brown-faded image had by now blurred into a single hazy image, and she did not know whether she had actually known, or had ever even seen, the woman of the photograph. She knew it was her mother, yet her experience with women was so slight that in a practical way she hardly knew what the word *mother* meant.

Her father often stared at the photograph too, especially when he came home and was quiet. She knew that at these times he had been involved with the bad men. Such moments brought a look to his face that made her tremble.

"Ah, Elsbet," he might say, gazing into her face as he cradled her white chin in his great rough palm, "it's an evil world we live in."

What could she do but stare back with wide expression, wondering what he meant. Then he would turn, walk heavily to the bed and ease his huge weary frame onto it with a sigh, pick up the photograph while he sunk into reverie. The wife of Sully Conlin's youthful manhood had been taken from him young. All he now had to remember her by was a tiny fading photograph, and the memory of her eyes that lit the expression of the daughter he had brought into the world with the only woman he had ever loved.

And as he stared at the face now gone, quieting as he gazed upon it, his lips began to move in murmured remembrance.

The watching girl knew he was talking to the woman of the picture, but could make out nothing of what he said. Yet something within her dawning intelligence sensed that at such times the poor man's heart was smiting him with painful memories, and ached with a deeper loneliness than she could possibly understand.

2

The London Rutherfords

◆◆◆

In the London home of Gifford and Martha Rutherford, the mood at the breakfast table was quiet, formal, and somewhat strained, almost as if the three family members quietly partaking of their eggs, bacon, toast, and tea were strangers. Here too, as well as at the estate of their cousins in Devonshire, something was dramatically altered since the sudden death of Gifford's first cousin Charles and his son George in the war. This change was most noticeable in Martha's sad countenance, and to a lesser degree in her grown son Geoffrey, who resided at home and worked with his father in the Bank of London.

"I have an appointment out in Devon tomorrow," commented Gifford, hardly glancing up. "Care to accompany me?" It was obvious he was addressing his son. He would never have invited his wife along on anything of a business nature.

"I don't think so," replied Geoffrey. "I have things to do here." From his tone, however, he was clearly making an excuse.

Gifford opened his mouth and was about to ask, "What's wrong with you lately?" but thought better of it. On reflection, he concluded that he had best carry out his business alone. His son had grown curiously softhearted of late toward their cousins, hardly what he would have expected after having his proposal of marriage so rudely rebuffed by Amanda last year. To be truthful, Gifford was a little concerned about the boy. He was given to disturbing fits of quiet these days, even melancholy. It wasn't like him. Gifford had thought of consulting his physician again to see if something might *really* be wrong with Geoffrey, even though to all appearances he seemed perfectly healthy.

He would come around again, thought Gifford, glancing over the top of the financial section of the *Times* and across the table. He would make sure of it. He would leave nothing to chance. If the boy didn't have the necessary fight to reach the top of the business world on his own, Gifford himself would insure his son's future.

A few minutes later Geoffrey excused himself from the table and went to his room to be alone. Thoughts of Devon, and business of his father, which he could only assume had to do with Heathersleigh, had put him in an irritable mood. In truth the sudden death of Charles and George had shaken him. It was not just that they were dead; he could not escape a nagging sense of guilt that his father's influence had kept *him* out of the war, and that the dubious physical report from his father's doctor had been faked for exactly that purpose. Even after four months he could not get the tragedy out of his mind. He couldn't focus on his work. He couldn't seem to focus on anything. Other things had been playing on his mind as well.

Downstairs husband and wife concluded their strained morning repast without a word passing between them. Gifford rose and left the breakfast room. Martha poured herself another cup of tea and silently sighed.

Forty minutes later Martha Rutherford watched her husband leave the expensively appointed residence on Curzon Street, then turned back from the window into the empty house. Her thoughts, like her son's, had gathered this morning about their Rutherford cousins of Devon.

She missed Amanda. She had so enjoyed their time together, the dresses they had made, all the places they had gone, the parties, the balls. What light and joy and laughter she had brought to the house. It had not been the same since.

Martha's thoughts turned to Amanda's mother. She would like to go visit Jocelyn and the girls. They had always been nice to her. What they must be going through with poor Charles and George gone. But she knew Gifford would never hear of such a visit.

A lonely tear rose in her eye. She knew it was impossible to make the slightest move toward friendship in that direction without her husband's permission, and that was something he was not likely to give.

She was not exactly afraid of him. Gifford would never hurt her, except by his silence, by his rude aloofness, by his cold indifference. As badly as she wanted a life outside the lonely walls of this palatial house, she was too unsure of herself to try to find it. It had been so long since she had had any real friends, she could hardly remember what it felt like. She would try to stay active with her few activities and helping with the war effort. But none of that could take away the terrible aloneness.

Gifford gave her nothing. But he was all she had. And Martha Rutherford feared being left alone more than anything.

3

Heathersleigh Cottage

❖❖❖

Twenty minutes after setting out, the two Rutherford sisters rode into the sunny clearing of Heathersleigh Cottage, where, as did not surprise them, they found their friend and adoptive grandmother Margaret McFee, widowed now just less than a year, on hands and knees in her luxuriant flower garden. Despite Maggie's years now stretching into the late seventies, evidenced by a head of unruly but pure white hair, her garden continued to grow, as inch by inch she tamed more of the surrounding clearing in the middle of the Devon woodland.

Behind her rose the white-thatched home, large to go by the name cottage as it still did, built originally as a gamekeeper's residence, whose mysterious history and curious changes of ownership had aroused such speculation throughout the community these past sixty years.

During the final years of his life, as the callings of eternity had penetrated closer to his heart, the brief occupant, Bishop Arthur Crompton, had first flowered a sunny patch of earth along the cottage's south wall. Neglect had come to it, however, for a short time after his death. But a fondness for flowers had early in her life become one of Maggie's passions, and even while her mother still lived, Maggie began to reclaim some of the original garden. By the time it came into her own hands, the cottage was already surrounded with flower beds of various kinds, extending north, south, east, and west from its four walls through the clearing, toward her Bobby's barn—a smaller replica of the house in design and appearance—and in places encroaching on the forest itself. In midspring, when in full bloom, the only approach to the cottage lay on two narrow, winding, hard-packed dirt paths through the maze of color.

An altogether homier and cheerier setting it would be difficult to imagine, though now the ten-room cottage and sizeable barn seemed vacant and lonely to Maggie without her Bobby's wit and laughter to fill them.

Maggie's faithful cow Flora was also gone. But she was too old to think of trying to care for another. The life-giving cottage in the woods was now home only to Maggie, her flowers, and a few ducks and geese that fended for themselves and made more racket and offered less friendship than either Flora or the flowers. Jocelyn provided all Maggie's earthly needs in abundance, as a true daughter to a spiritual mother, and had done her best to encourage the dear lady to come live at the Hall with them. But Maggie said it was her heart's wish to remain at the cottage until she was unable to take care of herself. If a time came when she could not, then she would consider the kind offer.

Maggie glanced up from her work and smiled broadly as she saw her visitors. With a creak or two, she rose and ambled toward them while Catharine and Amanda dismounted and tethered their horses.

"Hello, Grandma Maggie!" said Catharine, bounding forward and embracing her warmly.

"Catharine . . . Amanda—how good of you to come."

"Good morning, Grandma Maggie," said Amanda. "Whenever I see you, you are in your garden."

"It's summer, my dear—time when growing things are at their best.

And what would I do without dirt to put my hands in to see what I might make grow from it? I was about to have my morning tea—I'll go inside and put the water on."

As Maggie turned, Amanda began to walk pensively about, recalling many past visits to this place when her eyes were unable to perceive what life dwelt here. Unconsciously she meandered toward the barn.

Catharine and Maggie glanced silently at one another as they watched her go, more than half suspecting what was on her mind. Though both had prayed for this day, their hearts were sore for the one they loved. They would spare her the inner anguish of this long-delayed homecoming if they could, but knew they could not, and knew also that Amanda's full healing required a measure of pain.

Amanda wandered into the barn, now cool, dark, and silent. No snort or stamp of cow's hoof, no *swoosh* from Bobby's plane could now be heard except in the memories that gradually came alive in her brain. It all *looked* the same, yet *felt* so very different to the eyes of her adulthood, colored with the sadness of nostalgia and tinged in Amanda's case with the bitterness of regret. Everywhere she walked, everything upon which her eyes fell, from the tower back at the Hall to the empty stalls and rusty tools and cracking leather harnesses of dear old Bobby's barn, brought painful realizations of what she had been, and of those who were now gone whose forgiveness it was too late to seek. With her thoughts of Bobby came again the reminder—so common these days— that she could not go back and recapture a past she had let slip away without knowing how precious it would one day be to her.

A tear came to her eye as she heard Bobby's voice speaking to a nine-year-old girl. *"What are you going to think,"* he said, *"when you're older and God tries to tell you what to do?"*

Now she was older, Amanda thought, and the lessons from God's voice had become painful necessities because she had waited so long to listen.

Amanda walked out of the barn back into the sunlight and slowly made her way toward the cottage. She found the others busy over a bit of lace Catharine had brought to ask Maggie about.

Amanda smiled wistfully to herself. She wondered if it was too late for her to learn such things. Hearing her footsteps coming through the open door, they glanced up and Amanda turned what remained of her smile toward their faces.

"I am so sorry about Bobby, Grandma Maggie," she said. "It is one

of my deepest regrets that I was away and out of the country when—"
Again the tears began to flow. "I am . . . sorry about so many things."

Maggie walked forward and took her in her arms. They stood a moment or two until Amanda had regained her composure.

"Regrets are part of life, dear," said Maggie, stepping back. "We all must live with difficult memories because no one lives a perfect life. The pain helps us grow."

"Sometimes it is almost more than I can bear."

"I know, dear. But it will lessen, and you will be stronger for it. We all must also learn to go forward with thankfulness in our hearts."

"I cannot imagine ever being thankful for what I have done," said Amanda.

"Perhaps not for that," rejoined Maggie, "but you *can* be thankful for how God will use it, and bring good out of it in the end.—But come, the tea is ready. Let us go to the sitting room."

As they walked out of the kitchen and into the largest room of the house, Amanda noticed again the oak secretary built by Maggie's great-grandfather, where, as Maggie had shown them a few months earlier, she had discovered the deed to Heathersleigh Cottage.

"Grandma Maggie," said Amanda as she sat down, "do you remember the day when I came for a visit, and you told me about your grandmother's favorite Bible verse?"

"Indeed I do," replied Maggie, handing each of the girls a cup of tea.

"I had a pretty sour disposition, as I remember," said Amanda. "Of course back then I think I always did—"

"Not always," interjected Catharine. "We had a lot of fun together. I have very happy memories of playing together."

"That is kind of you to say, Catharine," said Amanda, turning a smile toward her sister. "But I often was grumpy, and I'm sure Grandma Maggie remembers even if you do not. But what I was saying is that your speaking of the mystery of the kingdom that day, and the passage from Mark 4, had a double meaning, didn't it? You were trying to help me see the mystery of the kingdom of God. Yet there was also the mystery of your bureau and what was hidden inside it."

"Which even I hadn't an idea about at the time," said Maggie.

"And how this cottage passed out of the family and to the bishop," Catharine added.

"Which I have put right in my will," concluded Maggie. "Do not forget, girls, that when I die, this cottage will again belong to you and your mother."

"Please, Grandma Maggie," said Catharine, "don't you talk of dying. You are as healthy as ever and will be with us at least another thirty years."

"Ah, Catharine, my dear," Maggie chuckled, "when a body gets to my age, one begins to feel that moving on to the next life isn't such a worrisome thing. Speaking for myself, I do not want to live another thirty years! In any event, all I ask is that once in a while the two of you enjoy a cup of tea together here and remember your grandma Maggie and grandpa Bobby, and that they loved you and your brother and your dear father and mother as if you were all our own."

"Oh, Grandma Maggie," said Catharine, "that is so sweet. Of course we will always remember you. We could never think of Heathersleigh Cottage and its beautiful growing things everywhere without thinking of you along with it."

As the girls rode away from the cottage an hour later, Amanda remained quiet. After some time Catharine glanced toward her and saw that her older sister was crying.

"Amanda dear," she said, "what is it?"

"You can't know the grief I feel, Catharine," replied Amanda, "what it is like to realize I have spent a lifetime seeing only through the eyes of self, and how much hurt I have caused. It's so hard, like nothing I have ever known. Even such a simple thing as watching how close you and Grandma Maggie are—I am not envious, I think it's wonderful . . . but it brings a stab to my heart to realize all I threw away. And I feel such guilt that I will never see Grandpa Bobby again. The rest of you were all here when he died, to spend his last days with him. But I was on another continent, not even knowing. What grief it must have caused him to die never seeing me again. Now it's too late. It is something I can never undo."

Catharine remained silent. There was much she wanted to say. Yet she knew that Amanda was right. She herself *couldn't* fully understand. She had never faced what Amanda was feeling. Therefore, she would give her no advice without considering her words carefully.

"I'm so sorry, Amanda," she said, reaching across a tender hand.

"I know, Catharine," replied Amanda, forcing a teary smile. "Thank you. But sometimes I don't know how I will ever be able to forgive myself."

"I'm certain the Lord will show you when the time comes."

Amanda nodded. "You know," she said, drawing in a deep breath, "I think I need to be alone for a while. Maybe I'll just . . . I don't know, ride into the village or out into the country. I need some time to think.—Do you mind?"

"Of course not," replied Catharine. "I'll see you back at the Hall."

◆ ◆ ◆

Elsbet heard footsteps approaching at the end of the street outside. She set down the cooking fork in her hand and hurried from the stove. She opened the door with an eager smile to greet her father.

The sight that met her eyes was not what she expected. He was running along the street faster than she had ever seen him move, with a frantic look on his face, an expression one did not see on a strong man who knew how to take care of himself.

He called out the instant she appeared, "Get away, run Elsbet—run from the house!"

She stood in the doorway confused.

"Get away . . . run," he panted as he lumbered toward her.

In fearful uncertainty she backed inside and stood waiting.

Seconds later he bounded up the three steps and yanked the door closed behind him in exhaustion.

He stumbled into the room, glancing about desperately. All the while the bewildered girl stared up at him silently.

"It's too late to get away now," he gasped. "They will see you—into the garret with you."

He now turned toward her, trying to calm himself. He stooped and gazed earnestly into his daughter's face. His eyes flashed with unmistakable terror.

"Elsbet," he said, still breathing heavily and looking into her face seriously, "I want you to get into the garret . . . quickly!"

With big eyes, at last growing afraid from what she saw in her father's eyes, she nodded.

"Go, now," he said, rushing her to the ladder, "—that's a good lass, up you go. Close the door behind you and don't make a sound . . . not a peep, do you hear, Elsbet—not a peep."

Within seconds she had scrambled into the loft. With a great heave,

Sully shot the ladder into the opening behind her.

"Lower the door," he added, "close it tight. Good girl . . . be still, not a whisper."

She let down the door.

"Papa," she whimpered through the final crack of disappearing light from the room below as she began to cry. "Papa, I love you."

But he did not hear the poignant words. Already he had turned and was making for the street to continue his escape.

It was too late.

Before he reached it, the door burst open with a terrible crash, and instantly the small flat was filled with angry voices. In terror Elsbet lay down on the floor, peering through a narrow slit between two ceiling boards. She recognized two or three of her father's worst companions.

Terrible yelling and fighting and accusations broke out.

"Let's have it, Conlin!" shouted one.

"I had nothing to do—!"

"It's no use lying. We saw you with him!" A violent curse filled the air.

The man suddenly cried out in pain from a blow delivered by Sully's fist cracking his jaw. Two of his companions surged forward. The burly sailor stumbled back, splintering the table on which his daughter had been preparing to set his breakfast, and crashed onto the bed behind it. The two pounced on top of him. One pulled a pistol from his pocket.

The next instant a great explosion sounded. From where she watched, Elsbet leapt out of her skin at the deafening sound. As the echo from the gunshot faded, none of the men below heard the terrified shriek above them that had accompanied it.

"Now you've done it—let's get out of here!" cried the ringleader through his broken jaw. Footsteps bounded across the floor even as the dying echo of gunfire reverberated off the walls.

For several long seconds Elsbet waited.

"Papa," she whimpered at length.

No sound answered.

"Papa," she called out again a little louder. Still he did not answer. A terrible coldness, as of an icy hand, gripped the girl's heart.

She sat up and raised the door of the loft. With great effort she managed to drag the ladder across the boards, lift one end and maneuver the other through the hole. It took all her strength to lower it to the floor without dropping it. When the bottom was securely on the floor, she climbed down. It did not take long for her to see the horrible truth of what the dreadful sound had been.

Shock at the horror of the sight silenced her lips. She crept forward and reached out a tentative hand toward the warm pool of blood that drenched her father's chest.

She had never seen death before this moment. But she knew from the empty stare of his open eyes that her father was no longer the man she had known, and that her life with him was over.

The silence of her tongue lasted but a moment. At the touch of the blood upon her hand, suddenly the streets for blocks rang with the despairing shriek of the little orphan.

The days of innocence for Elsbet Conlin were gone. Though she had never before felt such an emotion toward others of her kind, hatred now rose within her toward the men who had done this evil thing. Through clenched teeth and with a heart of stone, she vowed that she would kill every one of them if ever she had it in her power. She would remember their faces, their voices, and when she was older she would return and find them.

But she could not tarry long. They might be back. And she could not kill them now. Impulsively she pried apart her father's fingers and withdrew what they had clutched in the last moment of his life, cast one last tearful look into his face, then stole carefully out the door. Looking to the right and left, she bolted along the street and away from the house that had become a place of death. Behind her the slice of meat slowly curled into smoky blackness on the stove.

Where she ran she hardly knew; only that she ran until her lungs ached. Still she ran. The streets and the houses of the town grew farther apart. On she ran, not knowing where. Gradually she left the town behind. When she slowly became aware of herself, an hour or two had passed and she was alone, without human habitation in sight, on a lonely moorland overlooking the sea.

She paused to catch her breath, then stared out at the water below.

She had no destination. All she could think were her father's words, "The sea is our friend . . . find the sea . . . follow the sea."

With her father gone, the great expanse of blue he had loved was now the only link to her life with him. Movement gradually again came to her legs, and slowly she continued on. No thoughts or plans entered her mind, only an impulse to keep the sea in sight. If the sea had taken her mother, maybe it would now take her. She must remain near it.

4

A Little Girl Named Chelsea

*A*manda rode into Milverscombe, tied her horse, and absently walked into one of the town's few shops. She had nothing on her mind to do other than distract herself from the unpleasant reminders that the visit to Maggie had stirred up within her. She did not necessarily want to avoid the thoughts—she knew this time of growth was necessary—but did not want to be alone with them.

"Hello, Miss Rutherford," said the shopkeeper warmly as she entered. "Is there something I can help you find?"

"No, but thank you, Mrs. Feldstone," replied Amanda. "I just thought I would look at some of your fabric."

Amanda wandered through the few bolts of cloth the shop had on hand and toward the back of the store. But in her present frame of mind nothing here was of interest. She smiled at the round-faced woman and left, continuing along the street in the direction of the station.

Suddenly she heard footsteps behind her running along the boarded walk. She turned and saw a girl of eleven or twelve whom she did not recognize running toward her. The moment she saw Amanda turn, the girl stopped.

For an uncertain second or two they stared at one another. At last the girl spoke.

"You're Amanda Rutherford," she said excitedly.

"Yes . . . yes, I am," replied Amanda. "How did you know?"

"Oh, I know who *you* are. My mother told me how you went to London to join the suffragettes. It was so exciting. I always wanted to be like you."

The sting of hot tears filled Amanda's eyes and she looked away. She could not hold the gaze even of a little girl for the shame of what she had just heard.

After a moment she turned back, brushed at her eyes, and knelt down.

"What is your name?" she asked.

"Chelsea... Chelsea Winters," said the girl.

"Oh yes," smiled Amanda, "now I remember... I know your mother." She paused, looking earnestly into the girl's face. "Chelsea," she went on seriously. "I am going to tell you something I hope you will remember and think about."

The girl's eyes returned Amanda's stare with wide silence.

"I am not a person you should want to be like, Chelsea," Amanda went on. "When I was your age I did not know how much my parents loved me. I did not pay enough attention to what they told me, and it landed me in a great deal of trouble."

The awestruck expression on the face gazing back at her sobered.

"Do you understand, Chelsea?"

Slowly the girl nodded.

"Be a good girl, Chelsea, not a proud and selfish one like Amanda Rutherford was."

Amanda felt her voice beginning to fail her. She rose and walked away, leaving little Chelsea Winters silently staring after her.

♦ ♦ ♦

Somehow the day passed. When shadows of evening began to lengthen, Elsbet's stout little legs were easily fifteen or twenty miles along the coast away from the town she had never set foot outside of before that day. Even had her father's murderers known they had been observed, they could never hope to find her now.

Night gradually fell. Fear mingled with her hatred for the evil men, and Elsbet knew she must find a place to hide for the night. She began to look for a crevice in the hills along the water.

She crept into a cave and lay down in exhaustion. Weariness was her best friend on this most dreadful first night, for it dulled her brain and made her drowsy. With the sounds of the waves lulling together in her mind with memories of her father, she finally cried herself to sleep.

Within less than fifty feet from the water's edge, the fatherless girl managed to pass a fitful night.

Elsbet Conlin awoke to the same rhythmic sounds of water slopping and sloshing at the rocks that had lulled her to sleep outside the mouth of the cave. As she drank in the sound, her first few moments of wakefulness were peaceful.

Suddenly the terrible nightmare crashed back upon her. She wept the bitter tears of the motherless who was now suddenly fatherless as well. With renewed horror, visions of the previous day returned, adding tenfold to her sense of isolation, and a hundredfold to the hatred digging itself deep into her soul.

Elsbet shivered. In the chilly morning, the coldness of life overwhelmed her. She was damp to the bone with the sticky, clammy, salty dew of the sea.

She rose and left the cave, seeking movement and activity as the sole antidote for her grief. The morning was grey and still, the sun not yet up. At last she had begun to feel pangs of hunger and was very thirsty. She knew her temporary shelter offered no hope of satisfying either.

She soon quenched her thirst in a small stream tumbling down the rocks into the ocean a half mile farther on. With no destination in mind, she continued in the direction she had been walking, moving along the shore itself and occasionally on the bluffs overlooking the sea, her father's cryptic words the sole motivating force pushing her steps along.

The sun rose, the day warmed, and still she walked. By midday, hunger had asserted itself more vigorously. The birds overhead and an occasional rabbit or squirrel brought interest to the day and gave her something alive to talk to and share her struggle with against the elements.

By afternoon the conclusion had grown obvious that she was unlikely to find anything to eat on her present course and that food and water would be more accessible inland. Thus she gradually turned away from the sea into a region of desolate countryside.

Even legs that are small make good time when they keep moving, and by the evening of the second day of her sojourn she had indeed covered a good distance, probably forty or more miles from the place she once called home. Without knowing anything of the borders of the land, she had by now left Cornwall behind and was walking through the county of England called Devonshire.

Despite her hunger, sleep came that night more easily. Dusk had scarcely fallen when her legs fairly collapsed beneath her in the hollow of an open field.

The next day she continued on again, drinking from streams but still finding nothing to eat but some berries that only succeeded in giving her a stomachache. She began to encounter a few cows and sheep, but was afraid of the people she saw in the fields tending them and kept out of sight. What if they were *all* killers?

By nightfall she was famished. For a third night since her departure from the town, darkness closed around her.

She trudged on. The night deepened. At length she saw a building ahead. She knew she was now in a more peopled region and that it might not be safe to sleep in the open. The few drops of rain that had begun to fall added to her resolve. As she approached the building, she heard the familiar sounds of animals. She was not afraid of them!

She continued forward. The door was unlocked. She pushed it open and from inside came the homey smells of horseflesh, grass, and feed.

She crept inside the dry barn and was soon fast asleep on a pile of hay.

5

Hector's Surprise
♦ ♦ ♦

*H*ector Farnham, longtime faithful groom and servant to the Rutherfords of Heathersleigh Hall, awoke, as was his custom, an hour before the rest of the household.

He rose, dressed, went downstairs, and ambled out into the kitchen, where he stoked the coals in the stove and added two fresh chunks of oak to make the fire ready for the housekeeper, Sarah Minsterly, and Lady Jocelyn when they awoke. He put water on for his own tea, then left the house by the kitchen door and made his way toward the barn to give the horses their first installment of breakfast, two fresh piles of fragrant alfalfa hay.

He moved more slowly than in previous years. But even at sixty-one he still put in nearly as long a day as twenty years ago, and was more devoted than ever to his mistress and her two daughters now that the war had taken their men from them.

He opened the barn door and entered. The familiar aromas and a few snorts and stamps of waiting hooves greeted him, the very sounds and smells of heaven to one who loved these majestic beasts as Hector did.

He paused. Something was different this morning. The animals seemed jittery and agitated.

Hector glanced about in the semidarkness. Could one of the horses be down? he wondered. Or had one somehow managed to get out of the barn during the night? Slowly he made his way farther inside, checking each of the stalls. He petted each long nose as he went, mumbling a few words of affection to each, while the breathy snorts of the occupants indicated their impatience to be about the business of breakfast.

A sound disturbed the quiet behind him.

"What's that?" he exclaimed, spinning around with a start. "Who's there!"

Had a weasel or fox managed to get in and mistaken the barn for the chicken shed?

His hand fell upon a nearby pitchfork as he crept toward the corner farthest from him. He didn't want to come upon any uninvited guest unprepared.

Another sound. Louder this time. Whatever the intruder was, it was too large for a fox.

Hector squinted into the darkness. Suddenly a form darted out of the shadows toward the door.

"Not so fast!" shouted Hector, deftly lunging to the right with his fork and blocking the way.

"Whatever you are, this is—"

The broken light from the door behind him fell on the face of the creature he had roused from its hiding place. The sight momentarily silenced his tongue.

"Why . . . why you're a bit of a girl!" he exclaimed.

6

Bath and Breakfast

◆ ◆ ◆

*H*ector walked into the kitchen with the waif in tow. Sarah had just come down to begin her morning duties. She took one look at Hector, then turned and ran back upstairs to fetch the lady of the house.

It took less than a minute of his attempted explanation of the dirty, cold, straggly haired, wild-eyed thirteen-year-old at his side before Jocelyn's mother-heart took over. While Hector still stood with a bewildered expression on his face, Jocelyn and Amanda were already climbing the stairs with the girl. Catharine had disappeared ahead of them to begin preparing water for a bath.

"What is your name, child?" were the last words Hector heard his mistress say as they disappeared around the landing. He turned, still shaking his head at the strange affair, and went out for a second time that morning to attend to his creature friends.

Meanwhile, in the first-floor bathroom, after the bath had been prepared, Jocelyn handed their new guest, whose name she had at last managed to ascertain, a towel, a stack of fresh clean undergarments, and a nice fluffy robe.

"When you are finished with your bath, Elsbet, dear," she said, "come out and I will be waiting for you right here. We will find you a dress and then have breakfast together."

Still too bewildered at the turn of events that had so suddenly come over her, and hardly knowing what to think at finding herself whisked from a cold, smelly barn into the lap of luxury, little Elsbet Conlin merely nodded, expressionless.

Jocelyn began to close the door, wondering whether the child had ever taken a hot bath in such a tub before, then paused. A strange expression had come over the girl's face. She seemed to be trying to say something.

"What is it, child?" Jocelyn asked.

"Why is there red all over your face?" she said. "Is it blood?"

"No, dear," smiled Jocelyn. "This is a mark God gave me to remind me how much he loves me."

"But it looks funny."

"To some people it does. But that is only because they do not know it is God's fingerprint."

Again Elsbet hesitated.

"Would you . . . would you keep this?" she said. Slowly she held out her hand. In it she held a small framed oval photograph with several dark splotches on it. "I don't want it to get wet."

"Of course," said Jocelyn, taking it from her. She glanced down at the photo. "Who is it, dear?"

"My mother," replied Elsbet, then turned away. Slowly Jocelyn closed the door, now with more to think about than before. Catharine and Amanda stood waiting behind her.

"She just handed me this," said Jocelyn, showing her daughters the photograph. All three looked at it for a moment in silence.

"She is a beautiful lady," said Amanda. "I wonder who she is."

"Elsbet said it was her mother," replied Jocelyn.

"But look," added Catharine, "—those dark stains . . . they look like dried blood."

"That is what I thought too," nodded Jocelyn. "I noticed similar stains on her dress and arm."

"Do you think she is in trouble?" said Amanda.

"I don't know," sighed Jocelyn. "If so, we can only hope she will let us help her."

They returned downstairs to the kitchen to prepare breakfast, talking and wondering together where the poor child could have come from, and what she was doing alone so far out in the country.

Forty minutes later, the three Rutherford women sat around the table in the kitchen. Their guest had already gobbled down two eggs and several pieces of toast with jam. She showed no sign of slowing down as Sarah continued to bring more food to the table. As she ate, however, she cast suspicious glances about the room, as if she still hadn't made up her mind yet whether to trust them, but was not about to ask too many questions before her stomach was full. All their attempts to engage her in conversation had been unsuccessful. She reminded them of a frightened animal.

Amanda sat silently watching the girl, unable to get out of her mind the parallel between herself and Sister Gretchen at the Milan train station. How ironic, she thought, that *she* now occupied just the opposite role, and was involved in the attempt to befriend a young girl in need, possibly on the run exactly as she had been.

When she had eaten her fill, Elsbet rose without a word, again clutching the photograph of her mother that Jocelyn had laid beside her place at the table, and made for the door. Then she seemed to remember something. She paused and turned around.

"Where are my clothes?" she asked without expression.

"You may wear that dress, Elsbet," replied Jocelyn.

"I want my own," the girl replied.

"Sarah will wash them for you."

"I do not need them washed. I must go."

"Where . . . *why* must you go?"

"I don't know. I just must. They might find me."

"Who might find you, Elsbet?"

"Nobody. Please—may I have my clothes?"

"You may stay with us, Elsbet. No harm will come to you."

"I want to go," she repeated.

"Where are you going, then, Elsbet?" asked Jocelyn. "Perhaps I can drive you there."

"No—I am going nowhere. I just must go."

"Are you going to your mother, Elsbet?"

"No—my mother is at the sea. I cannot go to her."

"Where, then?" said Jocelyn, more perplexed than ever. "Would you like us to help you find your family?"

"I have no family."

"Your mother is very beautiful—what about her? Does she live near the sea?"

"The sea took her. I cannot go to her until the sea takes me too."

"What about your father?"

"He is—"

Her voice began to choke, and Jocelyn saw her eyes begin to glisten.

"—he is dead," said Elsbet, starting to cry.

Tears filled Jocelyn's eyes. But her eldest daughter, weeping freely by now, was already moving across the floor ahead of her. Amanda approached and placed two loving arms around the poor girl and drew her to her chest. The poor waif melted into the embrace and cried freely.

"Then stay with us for a little while, Elsbet," she said softly. "My mother will take the best care of you in the world."

7

Rollo Black

How Gifford Rutherford obtained the name Rollo Black might have been an interesting inquiry in its own right. His banking associations, though mostly carried out with three-piece suits and silk shirts, occasionally put him in touch with another class of individuals, namely those facing financial and other sorts of difficulties that would not generally be found in Mayfair. From one such contact had the name of the shadowy Mr. Black surfaced. The banker had filed the contact away for future reference, in case he should ever need someone with the kinds of skills this Black reportedly possessed.

That day had now come.

As Gifford made his way along the dark street of Seaton on the south Devon coast, glancing about nervously for sight of any thugs who might be lurking in the shadows of this waterfront district waiting for an easy mark, he found himself wondering if coming here had been such a good idea.

Ahead he saw a hanging sign waving back and forth in the wind.

R. BLACK, DISCREET INVESTIGATIONS.

He continued forward, turned and made his way up the rickety flight of outside stairs, and knocked on the door that presented itself at the landing.

A gruff noise bellowed from inside. Gifford took it as a summons to enter and tried the latch. The door opened.

The man he saw behind a cluttered desk inside wore at least a four-day growth of beard and looked as if he hadn't slept in days. The fellow's red beady eyes squinted imperceptibly at sight of his well-dressed potential client, revealing that, despite his appearance, he was a shrewd judge of character.

"Are you Black?" said Gifford.

The man nodded.

"I was told that you can find out anything about anybody."

"Perhaps not quite," Black rasped in reply. "But what there is to be found, I can uncover. What is it you want to know?"

"I need information regarding some old deeds and property transfers."

"What kind of information?" asked Black.

"That is for me to keep to myself for the present."

"Look—I don't know who you are," Black shot back. "From the sound of your tongue and the cut of your clothes I take you for a Londoner. But that means nothing to me. If you want my services, then you tell me everything. Otherwise, get back to London and take your money with you."

"All right, no need to get testy," rejoined Gifford. "I simply want to authenticate the deeds I mention, as well as look into certain other facts pertaining to the property in question."

"You wouldn't have come to me unless you had more in mind."

"If the deeds are genuine, I want to know what loopholes might exist. That is where the rest of the information comes in. If they are not genuine, or if the loopholes are sufficiently ambiguous, then the information will provide me grounds for asserting my rights of ownership to an ancient family estate."

"I thought as much. You're trying to get your hands on someone else's property, and you want me to help you. Why don't you talk to your solicitor?"

"I have. He's the one who sent me to you. If you find what I am looking for, he will take steps to file the necessary documents. Until then he doesn't want to dirty his hands."

"Who is he?"

Gifford told him. Black nodded.

"We've had dealings together in the past. A conniving bloke. He's willing to bend the law if need be."

"I don't care what he is so long as I get what I want."

Black did not reply immediately, but continued to stare at the banker in front of him, as if making one final assessment of whether he wanted to involve himself in this man's affairs.

"All right, then," he said at length, "show me the color of your money, then tell me about this estate."

8

A Drive to the Coast

◆◆◆

$\mathcal{S}$ummer came to Devon. But the fragrant middle months of 1915 brought little warmth to Heathersleigh, only nostalgically painful reminders of Charles Rutherford's favorite time of the year.

In mid-June the telephone rang, itself a reminder of Charles's fascination with invention and technology and the many modern advances he had brought to the region. Jocelyn answered it to find their friend and spiritual mentor, Timothy Diggorsfeld, on the other end of the line, calling from London.

"Timothy, it's so good to hear from you," she said. "I was commenting to Catharine and Amanda only yesterday that we needed to get you down for a visit."

"Actually, that's why I called," replied Timothy. "I wondered if next week would be convenient with you for a battle-weary London pastor to escape to the country for a respite with his friends."

"Of course, Timothy—you are welcome anytime. When should we expect you?"

"I will take the first train out Monday morning."

"Then we will meet you at the station.—Oh, I am so glad! It has been rather dreary lately. It's hard not to think of Charles all the time."

The phone went silent a moment.

"I miss him, Timothy," Jocelyn added softly.

Timothy could hear the quaver in her voice. "I know, my dear," he said. "So do I. We shall have a cry again together on Monday, and remind one another of the happy times his life brought us."

Both widow and pastor were in tears when they hung up their respective telephones a minute or two afterward.

Timothy arrived in Milverscombe as planned five days later.

As he stepped out of the train, however, he saw four ladies awaiting him, not three, one of them obviously quite young. The moment his foot touched the platform, Catharine bounded forward and smothered him in a huge embrace. The others followed with more reserve.

"Timothy, how wonderful to see you," said Jocelyn, approaching with a smile. Hugs followed as Catharine stepped back.

"And meet the newest member of our family," she went on, "—for now, I should say. Timothy, this is Elsbet Conlin. Elsbet, I would like you to meet our dear friend, Rev. Timothy Diggorsfeld."

"Hello, Elsbet," said Timothy, bending his lanky frame down slightly so that he might look into the girl's face from her own height. "I'm very happy to meet you."

She smiled and shook his offered hand.

"Let me get my bag. Then, Elsbet, you can tell me how you come to be here."

That evening the three Heathersleigh women sat with their two guests in the sitting room enjoying tea and biscuits. After sharing memories and shedding tears remembering Charles and George again together, with smiles on their faces and love in their hearts, Timothy gradually managed to draw Elsbet into conversation. By evening's end he had succeeded in getting more smiles to break out on her face than had any of the others in two weeks. She had just told him about her night in the cave.

"You know what sounds good to me after all this talk of caves," said Jocelyn as the evening advanced and yawns and silences indicated that beds were beckoning, "—a picnic at the sea. Who would like to drive down to the coast tomorrow?"

"A capital idea!" consented Timothy. "I've never actually been to the coast of Devon. I hear there are great stands of chalk like at Dover."

"Then, girls, we shall get busy early and have Sarah help us pack a basket of provisions.—What do you think, Elsbet?" asked Jocelyn. "Would you like to drive to the sea?"

"My father loved the sea," she replied indirectly.

"And you lived near the sea with him, did you not?"

She nodded quietly.

"Perhaps you could show us where you lived," Jocelyn added.

Elsbet glanced down.

Jocelyn had not been successful in learning any details of Elsbet's past life, and was concerned that someone must be looking for the girl.

"We will just go for a drive and enjoy the coast, then," she added with a smile.

♦♦♦

The next morning a little after ten o'clock, the Rutherford Peugeot was filled with the two Rutherford daughters, Elsbet, Timothy Diggorsfeld, and Jocelyn at the wheel, bounding through the Devonshire countryside for the coast some twenty miles to the south.

Jocelyn was able to drive to a flat clearing about a quarter mile from the ocean. They piled out of the car and walked the rest of the way, Amanda carrying blankets and pullovers, Jocelyn and Timothy each holding an end of the basket laden with provisions.

Slowly Elsbet and Catharine inched ahead, as if the smell of the ocean was drawing them like the aroma of hay in the barn to a weary horse. By the time they were halfway, both girls broke into a run together.

A few minutes later, all five stood at the edge of a plateau which sloped down unevenly toward the water. The day was warm, and both sky and sea were a brilliant blue.

"It is positively spectacular!" said Timothy.

Though the bluff overlooking the sea was high, within minutes Catharine found a place where it was possible to climb down and was already scrambling in the direction of the water.

"Look," she cried back above her, "there are caves in the bluff!"

Seconds later Amanda and Elsbet were after her.

"Timothy," said Jocelyn as she began spreading out the blankets on the grass, "thank you for coming. We needed this."

"So did I," he replied. "How are you and the girls doing?"

"We manage. But every day is filled with painful reminders."

"I know, my dear," said Timothy, laying a tender hand on Jocelyn's arm. "You are in my constant thoughts and prayers."

"I know we are supposed to give thanks and even to be joyful, but how is it possible?"

"I don't know if we are supposed to be joyful," replied Timothy. "I haven't been very good at that either. We've each lost our best friend. Who says we should be joyful? But we *can* give thanks. Not that it happened. I cannot *thank* God that Charles and George are gone. But I can

77

thank him that he is good and will make good come of it in the end. But that will never make me joyful. I still wish it had not happened."

Jocelyn nodded. "It is reassuring to hear you say it," she replied. "Elsbet's sudden appearance, I must admit, has been a welcome distraction. Sometimes having someone else to worry about helps take your mind off your own troubles, if only briefly."

"And you know nothing about her?"

"Only that apparently both her mother and father are dead. But whether she has other family ... we haven't been able to learn. It sounds as though her father was murdered."

"Would you like me to make some inquiries?" asked Timothy.

"Oh, I would be appreciative," replied Jocelyn.

"And her family name ... is Conlin?"

"That's right."

"But you have no idea of the father's name?"

"None."

"Well, I will see if I can learn anything."

After about an hour Timothy and Jocelyn heard the girls' voices climbing back toward them. A few minutes later Catharine's head appeared, then Elsbet's, and finally Amanda's. Breathing heavily and perspiring from the climb, they threw themselves on the grass and blankets, where Jocelyn had a sumptuous cold lunch set out before them.

"Mother, it looks delicious!" exclaimed Catharine. "I worked up an appetite down there."

"What did you find?"

"Several caves and—"

"It's not so big as the one where I slept," interrupted Elsbet.

"Any hidden pirate treasure?" asked Timothy.

"Only crabs and smelly sticky grass," answered Elsbet.

They all laughed as the girls dived into lunch. The mood quieted. Catharine was the first to rise back to her feet twenty or thirty minutes later. Slowly the others rose also and found themselves going their own ways. The urge to explore was still strong in Catharine, and before long she had disappeared again. As Elsbet began to walk after her, Jocelyn rose and followed. An undefined fear that she might wander off came over her. She did not want to leave their enigmatic guest alone. She hoped the setting might prompt their new friend to talk.

Amanda's thoughts turned inward. She rose also and walked in the opposite direction from her mother until she had gone some distance along the bluff.

The high view of the sea reminded her of the Dover overlook where Ramsay had taken her. Soon she was engulfed in sad and painful reflections of the prodigal sojourn that had taken her to Vienna a year ago as the war had broken out, then to Switzerland and finally back to Devon. Would the memories ever stop haunting her?

After walking some thirty or forty minutes along the bluff, and gradually encountering more rocky terrain, she turned back. In the distance she saw Timothy walking the way she had come two hundred yards away. She did not shy away from the encounter as she might have a year or two earlier, but continued forward, and gradually approached him. She smiled warmly as they met. Timothy paused, then turned and continued at her side.

9
Layers of Self-Insight

♦ ♦ ♦

They walked for a minute or two in silence.

"I am always struck with how peaceful life seems to become once you get out of the city," sighed Timothy at length. "I should definitely do it more often. This setting is so beautiful. There is something about the sounds and smells and sight of the sea that cannot help but get into your spirit."

Amanda nodded. After another several steps, Timothy spoke again.

"You've been thinking about your father, haven't you?"

"How did you know?" replied Amanda softly.

"For one who understands something of what you are going through, it is not difficult to see." Timothy paused, then added, "My ears and heart are open if you would like to share your thoughts with one who also loved him."

Amanda nodded reflectively.

"It will take me a long time," she said as they went, "to fit everything together. There is so much to get used to, so many changes. More thoughts have been tumbling through my brain than I know what to do with. I've been such a slow learner."

She paused briefly, struggling to find the right words.

"Please don't think me stupid, Timothy," she said. "I know it is a simple thing, but I think I am finally realizing how important it is what kind of person you make of yourself."

"I would never think you stupid, Amanda," said Timothy.

"But I have been. Maybe you are too kind to say it, but I can."

"We all have lessons to learn in life—myself no less than you," said Timothy. "Truth comes to us in layers of deepening insight. We each have to reach the point, through the circumstances of our lives and through the consequences of our choices, where we are able to peel off successively more of those layers."

"That is a good description," said Amanda. "But it feels like I'm peeling off my skin. It hurts to see what I have been."

"Some truth is painful," Timothy agreed. "And what may appear a simple realization for one individual may represent half a lifetime's struggle for another."

"But why should truth be painful?"

"Because the uncovered layers bite deep into the heart and soul of each of us uniquely. And if there is sin to deal with in the process, the revelations hurt."

Amanda did not reply. That fact she knew only too well.

"You are now learning truths," Timothy went on, "that some men and women never discover. Do not think your growth insignificant because it comes now and did not come sooner in your life."

"But it would have been so much better had I begun the process long ago."

"In some ways perhaps. But there are other ways in which you may not have been ready for it until now. Who can say why? The story of your life is like no one else's, as is mine, your father's, your mother's, Catharine's, George's, even little Betsy's, whose story we don't even know."

"I suppose you're right."

"Don't forget, even your father did not turn his face toward the Lord until his late thirties. We all must respond to God in the circumstances in which we find ourselves."

"I see what you mean," Amanda nodded.

"And, too, I believe that everything occurs by God's timing. Therefore, the development of your faith is in his hands. Your responsibility is to fall in with it now that it has come, exactly as your father and mother did when that moment of response came for them."

"Thank you, Timothy," said Amanda. "You have always been so kind to me, more kind than I deserve. I will always regret how I used to treat you. I don't know how you can stand me."

"Amanda, please, don't even think it," rejoined Timothy. "But tell me what you were reflecting on a moment ago when I met you."

"About what I used to be like," replied Amanda with a sad smile. She paused briefly. Timothy waited.

"When I was younger I always thought I wanted to make a difference," Amanda went on, "to do great things, to change the world. That's why I left home. But I was so naive and self-centered. I looked at Father and Mother after they became Christians and thought they were accomplishing nothing of value. Yet now I see how much influence they actually had in so many lives in the community."

"Not just in Devon," added Timothy, "but in London as well."

"The outpouring of affection that I have seen toward my father since I came home, and toward Mother too, has been remarkable," Amanda continued. "There's no one who doesn't have a story to tell about something one of them did."

"I'm certain it would be the same if you could question the men your father served with in Parliament."

"I never saw all that before. I don't know how I could have been so blind all those years. It has made me realize that God's way is different than I always assumed, upside down from how I used to look at things. I wanted to change the world by a massive stroke, like my joining the suffragette movement. What I find myself thinking now is that perhaps God would have people change it one little piece at a time, even if in ways that are invisible to others."

"A keen insight, Amanda. That was something your father certainly believed."

Amanda nodded. "He understood far more than I gave him credit for," she said, "such as that the kind of person you are becoming is more important than what you do. That is the part of the world we are most supposed to change one little bit at a time, isn't it?—*ourselves.*"

They walked along for some moments in silence.

"Our father taught us to think, and to think in big ways," Amanda went on. "It was probably his greatest gift to George, Catharine, and me as we were growing up. So many snatches of conversation now come back to me, times when he would probe and question us."

"I can envision it even as you describe it."

"He always tried to stretch our minds and how we looked at things. Yet I used that gift to turn away from him. Not very logical, is it?"

"Young people aren't usually terribly logical in their responses."

"He gave me freedom to think and dream in ways many fathers don't. He encouraged us to imagine possibilities, to look at every side of a question, even to disagree with him, in order to sharpen our brains and our thinking skills. My father was following God's example, wasn't he, Mr. Diggorsfeld—excuse me, Timothy—in the way God gave man free will. My father gave *me* free thought, so to speak, by training my mind when I was young. It breaks my heart to realize what I did with such a gift."

She turned away, eyes flooding with tears.

"I thought one of your resentments," Timothy probed, "used to be that he urged you toward Christian ideas. I thought you were angry at being forced to adopt his value system."

Amanda thought a moment.

"Yes, I suppose I did resent that," she said at length. "My mixed-up reactions still confuse me. At the time I thought he and Mother were trying to control every aspect of my life. I felt constrained by it."

"Yet now you are talking about the freedom and latitude he gave you?"

"Freedom is the last word I would have used to describe it back then," rejoined Amanda with a sad smile. "Yet now everything looks different. They really did give us freedom, didn't they? But not the kind of freedom my immaturity wanted. I'm certain both George and Catharine would say it was a very liberating environment in which to grow up, while I found it constraining. The difference was because of *me*, wasn't it? Not Mother and Father. I thought I was escaping their restraints by leaving home, when actually all I was doing was living out the consequences of my wrong use of that freedom."

"Might it be," suggested Timothy, "that your father gave you intellectual and imaginative freedom by encouraging you to think in large and diverse ways, while in the area of attitudes, behavior, and how you treated others, he expected you to obey certain standards?"

"That may be it exactly," nodded Amanda, "the distinction between attitudes and behavior on the one hand, and the intellect on the other.

My parents didn't give us the same latitude ethically and behaviorally that they did creatively and intellectually. You're right, they expected a standard of respect and gracious behavior."

"Does that seem so unfair to you now?"

"Not at all," replied Amanda. "Why I resented those restraints on my independence is hard to understand. As I look back, it seems that they were insisting on nothing more than common sense and normal kindness. All parents try to teach their children proper attitudes and behavior, don't they? The problem with me was that I was so completely self-centered, so filled with selfish attitudes, that I didn't want anyone telling me what to do."

10

Visitor to the Parsonage

───── ♦♦♦ ─────

As the Rutherford women and their two friends walked and explored at the coast, back at Milverscombe a visitor had arrived in the village and now walked toward the church. Though he had done his best to make himself look respectable, at first glance he did not appear to be a man whose dealings with houses of God had been particularly frequent. He made his way past a few tombstones without so much as a shiver or the moment's compunction that would have been of great benefit with respect to his own eternal destiny, and soon arrived at the front door of the adjoining parsonage.

Vicar Coleridge answered the sound of the door knocker himself.

"Would you be the reverend, sir?" said the man standing in front of him, forcing a smile through thin teeth not of the whitest.

"Yes, I am Stuart Coleridge," replied the vicar. "And you?"

"If you please, sir," answered the man in a scratchy voice, "I would prefer keeping my name out of it for the time being. Let me just say that I am on an errand of mercy for a friend."

Vicar Coleridge had spent enough time amongst the humble folk of Milverscombe parish to recognize a wolf in sheep's clothing when he encountered one. The slight squint of this man's eye put him immediately on guard.

"And how might I be of service to . . . uh, your friend?" asked the vicar.

"If I might just have a look at your parish record books, Gov—er, Reverend, that is. Won't take but a minute or two and then I won't bother you again."

"I see," nodded Coleridge. "I suppose there can be no harm in that. Come with me, then—they are in the church."

From the churchyard ten minutes later, Vicar Coleridge watched the man go. The moment he was out of sight on his way toward the station, the vicar hurried back inside the parsonage, grabbed his coat, walking stick, and hat, left the house again in the opposite direction, and made his way straight to Heathersleigh Hall.

"Hello, Sarah," he said when Sarah Minsterly answered the door. "May I please speak with Lady Jocelyn?"

"I am sorry, sir," Sarah replied, "they are at the coast."

"Oh . . . I see."

"Rev. Diggorsfeld came down for a visit, and they all went for a drive together."

"Ah, I see. Well, Sarah, I have important business to discuss with Lady Jocelyn. And I would like to see Rev. Diggorsfeld while he is in Devon. Would you please either have them come see me in the village, or send word to me when would be a convenient time I might call?"

"I will tell them as soon as they arrive home, sir."

"Thank you, Sarah. Good day."

"Good day, sir."

11

Invisible Scratches of Character

*A*manda and Timothy continued along the coastal bluff, and she smiled nostalgically.

"When I came home briefly last year before leaving for the Continent," she said as they went, "a strange thing happened. As I opened the door of the Hall, I was surprised at how easily it swung open. I suddenly realized the reason it didn't squeak was because my father kept the hinges oiled. Then I remembered his always trying to make things the best he could. I never saw that I too was one of those things he was trying to make better. It wasn't just *things*, though . . . he wanted *people* to be better too—himself most of all. He wasn't trying to control or dominate me. He was trying to help me become a better person—a young lady of virtue and character."

Timothy nodded.

"Now it strikes me," Amanda went on, "that in a way his whole life was spent encouraging everything to be the best it possibly could—as I said, especially his own character. He loved the idea of people and ideas and things of all kinds reaching their potential. The heather garden, the front door, a machine he might be tinkering with, and his own family— he wanted things to be the best they could."

"Listening to you," smiled Timothy, "is like listening to Charles himself. You have gained such insight into him. I never actually put words to it before, but what you say is exactly true. He wanted all of life, as you say, to reach its potential, because he believed such to be the reason God placed us on this earth, to grow into beings that reflect his nature."

"Why do you think he felt so strongly about that?" asked Amanda.

"He was one of those who believed that there is a Master of men, a *perfect* Master who demands of them that they also shall be right and true men and women. It is not a popular view in these days of compromise and lukewarm faith where people imagine that because God accepts them as they are, he does not mind that they never grow to be better. Your father's was a view that people cannot readily understand, nor one that many Christians like."

"I used to resent it," added Amanda. "Now it seems an honorable position for a man to hold."

Amanda smiled. "I thought of those silent hinges again just the other day," she went on. "I realized that there are other reminders of my father like that, things, as you've said, that I can continue to learn about him if only I have eyes to see—"

She stopped. It was obvious a thought had just come into her mind. Timothy waited. A smile slowly spread over her face. "I just remembered something I saw my father do that I never understood before. At last it makes perfect sense."

"Tell me about it," said Timothy.

"I must have been twelve or thirteen. I had already developed a nasty attitude by that time and was constantly grumpy. I don't know how they stood to have me around. I came upon my father in his workshop sanding a piece of wood for a set of shelves he was making for the library. I was such a sourpuss, I don't know why I was even in his workshop. But I disinterestedly asked him what he was doing, and he proceeded to lecture me, as I saw it then. He would use any incident to teach us and stretch our outlook. Every tiniest detail was filled with worlds of meaning for him, and he was constantly opening his mind to us about what he was thinking. Nothing was meaningless. His motto might have been: We ought to learn from everything. But back then I only saw it as him lecturing me and I hated it.

"He said, 'I'm trying to sand a scratch out of this board.'

"I looked at it and could hardly see the scratch he was talking about. I said, 'It looks fine to me.' He stopped and pointed to the tiny spot he was working on. And it really was little and by most standards insignificant. So I said, 'But no one will ever notice. I can hardly see it.'

"Then he said, 'God will know, even if no one else does.'

"I remember thinking how ridiculous his words sounded. It seemed to me at the time that everything was God this and God that with him. I grew to resent God just as much as my father because he was always talking about Him.

"Then he went on with his little spiritual lecture. Now that I think about it, I wonder if he realized that his words would come back and take root in me one day, so he just continued to teach me day after day, year after year, even though he knew I was paying no attention."

"No doubt he prayed that such would be the case," said Timothy.

"I wonder how much of my present change in outlook is due to his prayers for me through the years," said Amanda sadly. "I owe him so much."

She glanced away and blinked back a rush of tears. Again Timothy waited.

"In any event," Amanda went on after a moment, "as I said, he continued to talk to me. It's amazing that I was so uninterested, yet his every word comes back to me now as if it happened yesterday."

"What did he say?" asked Timothy.

" 'Amanda,' he said, 'if something is worth doing, it is worth doing well. If God gives me a shelf to build, then that shelf deserves my best. Excellence isn't something to strive for so that people will notice, but so that our lives will reflect God's character. And as I have been sanding, I've thought how like this board I am myself—pretty good, a decently well-constructed board to all appearances . . . but with little scratches and blemishes and sins all through me that no one sees but God. Am I going to say that those little sins of attitude, those little imperfections of character, those little immaturities and selfish, un-Christlike ways of looking at things, don't matter because people passing me on the street don't see them? Of course not. You see, Amanda, I cannot be satisfied with scratches on my own character any more than I can the scratch on this board. There's no fooling God. So as I have been sanding away on this board, I've been thinking of how I need to place my own self under God's trusting hand, while he works away to remove the scratches and help me overcome *my* sins and make me the best man he can.' "

Amanda paused, and again smiled.

"That was my father, wasn't it, Timothy?" she said. "He was always trying to help people work on their scratches so that they would reflect God's nature."

Timothy did not reply. Amanda glanced to her side and saw that he was quietly weeping.

"It is so moving to hear you speak of him," Timothy said softly, his voice shaky. "Yes—what you say is true, that was your father. Listening to you—it is as if he is here with us. Such feelings welled up inside me as you were talking, I could hardly contain them. He is truly living on in you."

"I'm not sure what to even think about what you say," replied Amanda. "Now that he is gone, I miss him so much. I saw him as critical and presumptuous back then. It seemed he was always unsatisfied, but actually he just wanted things to be as good as they could. He was forever talking about the meaning of this or the implications of that, or what we ought to do about something else. I especially hated that he wanted *me* better. But all the while he was subjecting his own board to the most careful sanding of all, wasn't he?"

"If you could have been with us during many of our talks," replied Timothy, eyes glistening, "you would know how very true that is. I have seen him literally weep for some trivial lapse in himself, as he saw it, in love or patience or kindness toward someone who did not even realize what Charles had done. I have seen him cry out to God for forgiveness for a sin no greater than allowing a brief flirtation with some worldly ambition to take hold in him. Things that most men would consider utterly insignificant would drive him to his knees begging God to strip from him every trace of worldly values. He had no interest in mediocrity. Christlikeness was his constant prayer."

They continued to walk along in silence for two or three minutes, during which both were lost in poignant reminiscences of the man who had drawn their lives together.

12

What *Might* God Do vs. What *Won't* He Do

◆◆◆

*A*manda looked up to see her mother and Betsy approaching hand in hand.

In that moment her heart swelled with love for the woman who had given her life. In the flash of an instant she saw deep into her mother's soul and perceived in a new way the reservoirs of love that dwelt there, saw that she was now pouring out that love to a little stranger girl who was opening herself to it more than she herself ever had at the same age.

A stab now went through Amanda's heart. She had been given the best mother in the world, and yet had left home and rejected the very affection her mother had lavished on her. Little Betsy, without a mother at all, was able to receive in just two short weeks what she could have been drinking of every day of so many wasted years—a true mother's heart.

They approached. Amanda's eyes flooded with tears. She walked to Jocelyn and embraced her. They held one another for several long seconds.

"I am so sorry, Mother," she whispered. "You were so good to me. I am sorry I did not have eyes to see it. I love you."

Catharine reappeared from somewhere almost the same moment, and gradually they all returned to the blankets and lunch and began gathering together their things. Soon they were walking back to the car.

With Jocelyn driving and returning the way they had come half an hour later, Timothy was the first to break a long, contented silence. "Being with you all is such a tonic to my spirit," he said. "I feel so much better."

"Better . . . better than what?" said Catharine. "Have you been ill?"

"No, dear, just fatigue from my job."

"When you telephoned last week," Jocelyn now said, "you sounded so unlike yourself. What did you mean when you called yourself battle weary?"

"I cannot slip anything past you, can I?" laughed Timothy. "I've just been a little discouraged lately. Occupational hazard at times, I suppose."

"From what, Timothy?" asked Catharine.

Timothy glanced back to where she sat with Amanda and Betsy in the rear seat and smiled. "A long story, Catharine. Suffice it to say that some in my congregation do not find my views to their liking. A few of them have raised objections to the denomination."

"Not—" began Jocelyn.

"Not your sister or brother-in-law," added Timothy quickly. "Hugh and Edlyn have been attending with some regularity and have been entirely delightful. No, the objections come from other quarters. That the complaints have been endured, say the reports, for some years without a single individual once coming to talk to me about them is as painful to me as that the letters to denominational headquarters occurred behind my back. Without my having so much as an inkling anything was amiss, suddenly I find myself in the sort of church imbroglio I never thought I would face."

"Timothy, I *am* sorry," said Jocelyn. "Why didn't you tell us?"

"I didn't want to add to your troubles by complaining about my own."

"You have helped us all so many times, prayed with us and wept with us in our trials, you must know how willing we would be to share yours with you."

Amanda heard the words and they stung her afresh. She said nothing, quietly knowing she herself was the origin of many of those trials of which her mother spoke.

"You are always so considerate of our needs," Jocelyn went on. "I have never seen you take a thought for yourself. Won't you give us the chance to listen to you for a change?"

"You'll have to forgive me," replied Timothy to her request. "To be honest, at first I thought it was much ado about nothing. I was certain it would blow over quickly. But as it has escalated, to be truthful, I find myself embarrassed. I never dreamed I would be at the center of such a controversy. I suppose I am more comfortable sharing the burdens of other people's problems than letting them share mine. Perhaps that is one of the things the Lord is trying to teach me."

"What could anyone possibly object to?" now asked Amanda, trying to put her thoughts of herself out of her mind and enter into the conversation. "Do they object to you, your ideas, what? I cannot imagine . . ."

"You would be surprised, Amanda dear," replied Timothy. "Believe it or not, when a man's theology is suspect in people's minds, they will willingly believe almost anything of him. It seems they *want* to think the worst of him because of it. Though it pains me to say it, there have been rumors circulating that I have been secretly involved in politics, even that I have—" His voice broke and he stared ahead at the road.

"Timothy, what is it?" said Jocelyn. "You can tell us."

With difficulty he struggled to continue.

"Of course, I know that. I just didn't want you to have to know."

"Know what, Timothy?'

"My frequent trips out of London," he said softly, "my visits to my dear Devonshire friends—I am sorry, my dear," he added, glancing toward Jocelyn, "I had no intention of ever bringing this up . . . but there have been rumors that the reason for my trips is an affair . . . and some people are only too willing to believe it."

"Good heavens!" exclaimed Jocelyn.

"That's nonsense!" added Catharine.

"Timothy, I am so sorry," Jocelyn went on. "Who could possibly believe such a thing about you? You are one of the most upright men I have ever met. Don't they know you, know your heart?"

"Apparently not," he sighed.

"I just can't believe it," huffed Catharine angrily.

"When people of a certain sort get it into their heads that a man is unorthodox by their narrow definition of doctrinal purity," Timothy said, pausing to exhale sadly, "they begin to see boogiemen in everything he says. They are all too eager to assume that his suspect theology has led to ethical wreckage as well. They delight in believing such things, for it proves that the theology they so dislike must be intrinsically evil."

"But what theology?" persisted Catharine.

"Besides the purported moral case against me," replied Timothy, "the charge to my denominational leaders is that I am a *liberal*, as if that were tantamount to being the devil himself. Not that I consider anything so evil in liberality. Yet I am so far from being what they call a liberal as I can imagine."

"I still do not understand their complaint," said Amanda. "Or are they like I was, completely irrational in their response to things?"

Timothy laughed lightly.

"I will make no comment about you, my dear," he replied, "except to say that it delights me that you are responding to the Lord now, and that fact erases all past irrationalities from my thoughts. But to answer your question in a nutshell about the people in question, I suppose I am not rigid and narrow enough to suit them. I like to think of what great possibilities might exist in the divine plan of God. Many are uncomfortable with such an approach to theology. They prefer to think of all the things God *won't* do, rather than to imagine what wonderfully large things he *might* do. They want the lines of their doctrine drawn tightly around both themselves and God. All the while, of course, they say the God they worship is infinite and almighty, when those are the very last terms any logical man or woman would ascribe to the crimped being whom they say must never move outside their narrow boxes. They insist that God conform to their small definitions, but see no incumbency upon themselves to enlarge their own spiritual mentalities to consider what *almighty* truly means. They *say* 'almighty,' but contradict themselves immediately by adding that God cannot—"

Suddenly he stopped and gave an embarrassed chuckle.

"Forgive me," he added. "I don't mean to rant. In the midst of the pain this dispute causes me, the foolish things these so-called guardians of doctrinal purity say of God also anger me."

"I still can't imagine why they would object to a large view of what God might do," said Catharine.

"I'm not sure I can help you, Catharine," replied Timothy. "I don't understand it either. They do not want an imaginative God, a creative God, a large God, or an infinitely redeeming God."

"What kind of God *do* they want?" asked Catharine.

"In a word," replied Timothy, "—a *comfortable* God. A God they can control, a God who will make no demands either on their intellects or their hearts . . . especially on their obedience."

"That is ridiculous," rejoined Catharine. "It is that aspect of God's nature that draws me."

"Exactly as it was for your father," added Jocelyn. "If you had not portrayed God in such a large and wonderful way, Timothy," she added, "we might not know him now. Charles would never have been drawn by a tight and narrow kind of Christianity. He became a Christian in the first place because it offered answers consistent with his reason and his intellect, which were expansive to say the least."

"That is exactly the point I have been trying to make to my denominational inquisitors," sighed Timothy with frustration, "that a large God, the God of the Scriptures, the God who was the Father of Jesus Christ, is precisely what the world is hungry for. This narrow mentality flatters itself that only its particular brand of fundamentalism can be truly evangelistic, when in fact I think the world would respond far more enthusiastically to a—excuse my use of the word—a more liberal and less confining and restrictive gospel. By that I only mean the gospel of Jesus Christ himself that accepts all men where they are, then says to them, 'You have a good Father in heaven who loves you. Seek him and obey him, and you will know life indeed.' "

"What do they say to such things?" asked Amanda.

"They would rather send people to hell than enlarge their concept of God. I will give you an example of the kind of mentality I find myself up against. Several months ago, during a Sunday evening sermon, I chanced to make a remark about animals and the afterlife. It was an innocent conjecture on my part that greatly upset two of the individuals involved and brought matters to a head."

"What did you say?" asked Jocelyn.

"Actually, I wasn't talking about animals going to heaven at all," answered Timothy. "I had never thought much about it before. My text was, 'Love is eternal.' I was talking about the love we feel for one another in this life and that it will continue into the next. As I was speaking, the thought suddenly occurred to me, and I voiced it, that if we also love, say, a special horse or a pet dog or cat, is that love *also* eternal? If so, might the animals also have some manner of soul, different from man's, of course, but still capable of living beyond death? Then I added, 'I don't know whether there will be animals in heaven. But isn't it a wonderful possibility to contemplate? Just how large might eternity be, and how vast God's miraculously reconciling work!' I remember the words exactly because I have said them over and over to myself many times since, trying to think what could possibly be so scandalous in them. And now, because of a chance mention of animals possibly going to heaven, I find my ministry in jeopardy."

"That is preposterous!" exclaimed Catharine, breaking into laughter. "What could possibly be upsetting in that?"

"I honestly do not know," replied Timothy, shaking his head. "I confess myself utterly bewildered by the narrowness that is threatened by a too-large God. Speaking for myself, I choose to believe that the God I worship and serve and strive to obey truly *is* infinite and almighty, and that no possibility is too great for him. That does not mean that he *will* do everything, only that he *can* do anything and everything it is his will to do."

"Amen!" added Jocelyn.

13

The Most Difficult Forgiveness

───── ◆◆◆ ─────

*L*istening to Timothy share his woes reminded Amanda again that hurtful talk about others always has widening consequences, and of the pain she had herself inflicted upon someone much closer to them all than Timothy's parishioners.

"Did the letter I wrote and the things I said about him affect my father like the pain this is causing you?" she asked at length.

Timothy glanced back toward Amanda and smiled. It was a sad smile, yet one which sent the ministry of compassion ahead of his words for what he was compelled to say.

"Yes," he replied. "I would not be honest with you, Amanda, if I said they did not hurt him deeply. What you did broke his heart. But for love of *you*, not concern for himself. He didn't worry so much about his own reputation, or his own hurt, but mostly—for I think he foresaw this day—the pain *you* would feel one day from knowing what you had done. Of course, he always anticipated being there to share your sorrow with you, and to help ease your suffering with the tender father-arms of his own forgiveness."

Amanda began to weep. Catharine put her arm around her sister.

"Oh, it is so dreadful that I can never ask his forgiveness!" she said.

"One chooses to extend forgiveness whether he is asked for it or not," rejoined Timothy.

The words seemed momentarily to register only confusion on Amanda's face.

"I don't see what you mean," she said, pulling out her handkerchief and wiping her nose and eyes.

"When Jesus was on the cross," Timothy continued, "he forgave those who crucified him. Yet those very scribes and Pharisees and priests and Roman soldiers never asked him for forgiveness. They did not repent of their wrong, but he forgave them regardless."

Timothy paused and glanced back at Amanda, trying to convey with his eyes the love he felt for her at this moment.

"What I am saying," he went on, "is that forgiveness need not wait for such a repentance. It acts immediately. I need to forgive those in my church spreading these tales about me whether the tales are true or not. I need to forgive the loose tongues that have allowed these lies to circulate. I need to forgive those whose thoughtlessness even hurts you dear ones and clouds the memory of your dear Charles. What they have done makes me angry. But I know the only path before me is not to defend myself, not even to try to combat the charges, but to forgive . . . whether they ask my forgiveness or not."

"What does all this have to do with my father?" asked Amanda.

"It has everything to do with him. We must forgive those who injure us whether or not they ever acknowledge their wrongs. There is no other way to move on in life. Your father forgave you, Amanda. He forgave you the minute these things happened. He forgave you for the letter you wrote before the ink on it was dry. He forgave every unkind thing you ever said to him the moment they fell upon his ears. The words hurt him, because it pained him to see you living in rebellion to the life and truth within you. But that pain did not prevent his forgiveness. Forgiveness flowed out to you from his heart long before you wanted forgiving. Forgiveness is what love does. God's complete forgiveness of *all* sin is what the cross is all about."

Amanda was quiet. The car bounced along more slowly now in thoughtful silence.

"There is something even more important," said Catharine, breaking the silence.

Amanda looked at her sister with glistening eyes.

"You have asked God's forgiveness," Catharine went on. "I have heard you. You have asked Mother's forgiveness, and Timothy's, all of ours. And Timothy is right, Amanda—Father forgave you long ago. You know that. We all know it. He forgave you. Mother forgives you. God forgives you."

She paused and gazed intently into Amanda's eyes.

"Everyone forgives you," she added seriously. "Now you have to forgive yourself."

At the words, Amanda burst into a wail.

"I can never forgive myself!" she cried.

"Your dear sister is right, Amanda," said Timothy, speaking again. "The only way to move on and do what God put you on this earth to do is to forgive yourself. It is the one final door that will complete the healing God is carrying out within you."

"But how . . . how can I possibly forgive myself!"

"That doesn't mean you won't always feel pain at the memory," said Timothy. "That may continue all your life. The consequences of your actions, even past words, will not disappear. That is why forgiveness of oneself is the most difficult forgiveness in the world. Difficult but necessary if God's work is to be complete in our hearts. He forgives, always forgives, and forgives completely . . . but we must *take* that forgiveness from his offered hand and receive its full measure. The cross is our constant reminder of God's forgiveness. Because of the cross, that forgiveness is offered to *all* men, but each must reach out and receive that work of Christ's death into his and her own heart. Forgiveness allows us to shed our tears, then stand up and move forward."

Again the car fell silent and continued so for several long minutes.

14

For God So Loved the World

*B*etsy listened intrigued but could hardly make sense of it all. She had never heard such talk in her life. She had heard the words "Jesus Christ," of course, but only on the lips of an occasional friend of her father's as an exclamation or curse. As she heard them now, they scarcely conveyed an inkling to her brain of an actual man who had actually lived, whom these people spoke of with loving respect.

And as she heard the word *forgiveness*, neither was any idea conveyed to her that remotely suggested any concept within the orbit of her existence. Nor did the word cause any connection to rise within her of the Jesus Christ to whom they had referred. A subconscious association with the word, however, caused her to think briefly of the men who had killed her father, sending a new wave of hatred through her.

Even as Timothy had been speaking, turning occasionally toward Jocelyn where she sat, and Catharine and Amanda in the rear seat, he sensed a perking up of the inner ears of the girl beside them.

"Do you know who Jesus Christ is, Elsbet?" he asked at length, turning around toward her.

"No," she answered simply.

"He was a man who lived a long time ago," Timothy went on. "He is the most unusual man who ever walked on the earth, because though he was a man who lived and died like the rest of us, he was also the Son of God. Do you know what that means?"

She shook her head.

"It is another way of saying that he was actually God himself. And because he was God, when he died he did not stay dead but actually rose up again and walked right out of his grave. That probably seems hard to imagine, but he did. And he kept on living, and he still lives right now. But his life today is very different than the life of other people. It is an *invisible* life because he lives in a very special place. Do you know where that is, Elsbet?"

"No, Mr. Diggorsfeld," answered Betsy.

"It is inside our hearts. The spirit of Jesus Christ himself lives inside my heart right now, even though neither you nor I can see him. Does that seem hard to believe?"

"Yes. How can a man live inside someone else?"

"I agree with you, it is very difficult to believe," said Timothy. "But that does not mean it is not true. He can live there because he no longer has a body, only a spirit. And that spirit takes up no space. It can live inside a person, or fill up the whole earth. That's how Jesus and God, who is his Father, are. And do you know a wonderful thing—Jesus will come to live inside the heart of *anyone* who invites him to. He wants to come live inside your heart too, Elsbet. He is only waiting for you to ask him."

"Why do you want someone else living inside you, Mr. Diggorsfeld?"

"Because Jesus is God himself," answered Timothy. "Think what a marvelous thing it is for God to be with us all the time. He loves us so much he wants to be a close and special Father to us. I cannot tell you how glad I am that God lives in my heart. He is helping me all the time to become a better man. He is not only God, he is also my special friend. I can talk to him and ask him what he wants me to do. Then I try to do what he tells me. That is how I become a better man. But there is something even more marvelous than that. Would you like me to tell you what?"

"Yes."

"Do you remember I told you that Jesus Christ lived and died like other men?"

Betsy nodded.

"Well, his death was not quite like any other man's. You see, because he was God he didn't *have* to die. He could have just kept living forever without dying. But he chose to die so that we wouldn't have to."

"My father died," said Betsy.

"Yes, Elsbet, I know he did," said Timothy tenderly. "I am very sorry. Did you love your father?"

"Oh yes. He was such a good man."

"But he died, didn't he? All men and women die eventually, don't they? Do you know why?"

"Because they get old, or because someone kills them."

The words momentarily shocked Timothy, but he did his best not to show it. "Yes, that's right," he said. "But that isn't the real reason people die. They only get old, and bad people kill other people, for another reason. Do you know what sins are, Elsbet?"

"No."

"Sins are the things we do that displease God. Everybody sins. Even good people like Lady Rutherford and your father, and even you and me, Elsbet—we all sin. We don't live the way God wants us to. That's why we die. It is sin that causes death. But because Jesus was God, and because he didn't sin, he didn't have to die at all. But he *chose* to die."

"Why?"

"That is the most important question in all the world, Elsbet," said Timothy. "He chose to die because of how greatly both his Father and Jesus loved us. Jesus loved us all—everyone in the whole world!—so much, that he gathered all the sins of all the people who have ever lived—my sins and yours and your papa's and everyone's—he gathered them into his heart, and he took them into the grave with him when he died. But then when he rose back to life again, he left all those sins there in the grave. They didn't come back to life with him. They stayed dead. So you see, our sins were put to death and got buried away forever so that they would never be able to bother us again. Then Jesus came out of the grave and said, 'You are all free from your sins. Now you do not have to die.' "

"But my father died," persisted Elsbet.

"Yes, his *body* died," replied Timothy. "Just like the body of Jesus Christ died and was buried. But do you remember that I said the *spirit* of Jesus still lives. That is the invisible life that was inside him that didn't die at all. Your father had a spirit like that too, Elsbet. That was the *inside* part of your father, not just his hands and his hair and his skin and his legs. That was the part of him that you loved. And that part of your father, his spirit, is still alive."

"My father . . . he is still alive," said Betsy, her eyes growing wider. Her interest had been slowly mounting as Timothy spoke. Now she began to sit forward in the seat.

"Yes he is, Elsbet," Timothy went on. "But you cannot see him, just like we cannot see Jesus, even though his spirit lives in our hearts. You see, Jesus died for your father's sins too, and your mother's, just like for yours and mine and for the whole world's."

"When will I see him again?"

"I don't know, Elsbet," replied Timothy. "We don't know very much about the kind of life that is on the other side of what we call death."

"Will I see my mother too?"

"I believe you will, Elsbet. But I cannot tell you when or where. All we know is that because of Jesus' death, people don't have to die—their spirits can keep living. We don't know what that new life is like, though. That is why we must be content with making sure we will see Jesus one day ourselves by inviting him to live inside our own hearts and doing what he tells us to do."

Timothy stopped. He could see that Elsbet had had enough to absorb for one day. Slowly she sat back in the seat, her expression full of many new things to ponder.

He turned back toward the front in quiet prayer, thankful for the opportunity to occupy his heart with someone other than himself. The silence in the car this time lasted until Jocelyn pulled into the drive of Heathersleigh Hall.

Timothy Diggorsfeld had been a pastor long enough to see that had he pressed, he could have easily extracted a certain recited prayer from young Elsbet's lips, of the type with which many of his clerical colleagues were highly enamored. But he recognized that such prayers, though easily enough induced by the evangelistically impatient, were difficult to deeply root in the soil of experience. If salvation were to come to any man or woman, he would rather see that salvation blossom slowly of their own volition and thrive in reality, rather than be force-germinated in an artificial spiritual hothouse, only to wither when subjected to the winds and rains of real life.

Nor would he take advantage of a moment of heightened emotion to bolster his own spiritual ego. He knew, with the ground thus tilled, that the seeds planted in Elsbet's mind and heart would receive careful watering and nurturing by the motherly compassion of Jocelyn Rutherford. Unless he was badly mistaken, by week's end Jocelyn would be opening one of the several Bibles at the Hall every night before bed, Elsbet at her side, teaching her that which she loved, not that which she had been taught, reading to the waif who had been sent to them as surely as had the Lord himself knocked on the door, telling her of Jesus and his deeds and his words, his thoughts and his life.

Timothy had seen sufficient from the vantage point of his London pulpit through the years to care no longer, as he had in his younger days, for the urgency of its opening or the shape of the door by which the Lord entered into the house of a man's or woman's heart and took possession of it. Nor did he take any pride in that most false of ecclesiastical measuring sticks, his own personal tally of "souls" won.

He had learned well from his literary mentor, he whom he called simply the Scotsman, whose words concerning the matter Timothy had never forgotten. Like the fictional Janet Grant, Timothy had no inclination to trouble his own head, or Elsbet's heart, with what men called the plan of salvation.

It was enough for him to know that she would one day follow his Master.

◆◆◆

That evening, after they arrived home and were told of the vicar's call to the Hall, Jocelyn and Timothy drove into the village. Vicar Coleridge invited them warmly into the parsonage, and as soon as they were seated with tea, he told Jocelyn of the strange visitor he had had earlier in the day.

"I have no idea whether it concerned you or Charles or Heathersleigh in any way," said Coleridge. "But an inner sense told me that you should know about it. I did not like the man's look."

"Thank you, Stuart," replied Jocelyn. "But I don't know what is to be done. I'm sure it had nothing to do with us."

"How did the interview conclude?" asked Timothy.

"I showed him what he asked for," replied the vicar. "He perused the books for a few minutes, then left with no expression on his face that indicated anything one way or another."

"What do you think it means, Stuart?" asked Jocelyn.

"I don't know, Lady Jocelyn. But I will keep you informed if I learn anything further.—Tell me, Timothy," he went on in a different vein, turning toward Timothy, "how long are you down for?"

"Only a couple of days."

"I would be honored if you would take my pulpit on Sunday."

"The honor would be mine," returned Timothy. "But I am afraid I must return to occupy my own," he added almost sadly. "I would, however, appreciate an hour of your time tomorrow. I have been sharing some of my pastoral difficulties with Jocelyn and the girls, and I am hungry also for the insight of a brother clergyman. Perhaps we could pray together as well."

"Nothing could delight me more, Timothy," rejoined Vicar Coleridge. "My morning is yours."

15

Surprise Visitor

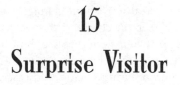

An expensive roadster pulled to the front of Heathersleigh Hall one day in early July. The officially clad young man at the wheel got out and walked with confident bearing to the front door and sounded the knocker.

Sarah Minsterly appeared a few moments later.

"Good morning, ma'am," said the visitor. "I am here to see Lady Rutherford and Miss Catharine and Miss Amanda."

"I am afraid they are not at home," replied the housekeeper.

"When do you expect them? I have come quite some distance."

"I really could not say, sir. They went to the cottage for the afternoon."

"The cottage?"

"Heathersleigh Cottage, just across the meadow and through the wood north of the house."

"Perhaps I shall go see them there."

"There is no road, sir—only a wagon road, that is."

"Then I shall walk, if you would be good enough to point the way out for me."

Forty minutes later, Maggie, Jocelyn, and the girls were on their hands and knees in the soft, moist earth of her tulip bed carefully digging up the spring bulbs for drying in the barn. Several geese were making a racket, distracting them at the moment from hearing the footsteps coming through the wood.

Maggie herself was the first to observe the approach of a tall white-uniformed stranger who had just emerged from the wood and was now striding toward the cottage. She rose, wiping the dirt from her hands on her apron, assuming his business to be with her. The most belligerent goose, an elderly though vigorous male who considered himself proprietor and bodyguard of the place, had spotted him seconds before Maggie. He now scurried toward the newcomer in a screeching wrath of flapping flurry.

"Get back, you fool creature!" shouted Maggie, hurrying after him.

But nothing would stop the charge of the protective watch-bird now.

"He'll take a chunk of your flesh if you let him close to you, sir!" she cried. "If you value your leg, give him a swift kick with your foot!"

The newcomer did not require being told twice. He had grown up around just such pesky animals and knew their danger well enough. A well-aimed blow from his boot sent the unsuspecting fat white ball skidding backward. Its honking increased to a shrill frenzy, though it called off the attack and now waddled furiously in the opposite direction in fierce dudgeon, shrieking and honking to his comrades to join in the battle. Betsy had just emerged from the cottage, leaving the door open, and toward it the irate goose now bore, neck outstretched to at least double its normal length.

"Stop him!" cried Maggie. "He'll be the end of my quilt that's all laid out!"

She turned and made for the house as fast as her legs would carry her. Catherine, however, closer by half, jumped up and bolted after the white marauder.

"I'll get him!" cried the masculine voice whose owner had sent the bird on its present course. But Catharine's eyes were on the danger. Once on her feet and up to speed, she neither slowed nor glanced toward the sound.

Suddenly a white form dashed in front of her, intercepting the goose and moving to block the doorway. At full speed, Catharine crashed into him and sent both of them tumbling over one another into a bed of pansies bordering the walkway.

The stranger was first to regain his feet. He offered Catharine his hand.

"Thank you . . . Lieutenant Langham!" Catharine now suddenly exclaimed as for the first time she set eyes on his face. "I didn't recognize you at first. All I saw was a blur run in front of me."

"I am sorry for my clumsiness," the lieutenant laughed, pulling Catharine to her feet.

"But what are you doing here!" smiled Catharine exuberantly as her mother and Amanda came forward and greeted their visitor.

"I drove out for a visit," he replied, shaking each of the other's hands. "Hello, Lady Rutherford, Hello, Miss Rutherford.—Hello," he added to Maggie, extending his hand as she now walked up puffing. "You can be none other than the Mrs. McFee of whom I have heard so many loving reports. I am Terrill Langham. I hope I did not injure your goose."

"I hope perhaps you *did*, Mr. Langham!" rejoined Maggie. "Nothing could please me more than to roast him for my supper. I don't know why I put up with the cantankerous thing."

Lieutenant Langham laughed with delight.

"To what do we owe this unexpected appearance, Lieutenant?" said Jocelyn.

"I thought it was time I drove down to Devonshire for a visit."

"I'm afraid your uniform is a sight," said Catharine.

"Not to worry," replied Langham, brushing himself off. "A little honest dirt is occasionally good for naval trousers and jackets."

"Come inside," said Maggie, "and we shall have tea."

"I want to see this quilt I had a hand in saving from the destruction of the goose," said the lieutenant as he followed his hostess through the open door.

"I've been laying out squares for weeks, sir," said Maggie as they entered the kitchen. "If that creature had got inside, they would have been sent flying in every direction. I am greatly in your debt."

A pleasant, lively talk around Maggie's table followed. An hour and a half later, the three Rutherford women walked leisurely with their visitor through the wood toward the meadow that led from Heathersleigh Cottage back to the Hall. They had made arrangements for Betsy to remain with Maggie and spend the night.

As they walked, Lieutenant Langham reflected how wonderful it was to see these three attractive and aristocratic women—a stately mother and her two grown daughters—in simple dresses, heavy shoes, and muslin aprons splotched with dirt from their work in the tulip bed. The country bred a different outlook on life than was possible in London, he thought to himself. In his naval uniform—notwithstanding its own soiled spots from the goose incident—he was the most overdressed of them all!

Langham glanced from one to the other as they went, noting the sisterly resemblance between Amanda and Catharine, as well as the obvious affection and respect the two young women had for one another.

The older was obviously more careworn, carrying a slight melancholy in her expression that hinted at experiences no young lady of her years should have had to endure. The younger was tall and robust and still possessed the exuberance and innocence of youth. He also detected a hint of mischief in her eyes, whose acquaintance he had already had occasion to witness a time or two on previous visits. She was attractive, even what he would call pretty, as well as nimble on her feet. But at the same time was nearly as big as he. She had the look of one who could take on the world, and probably would not be afraid to try. Neither of the two girls was so much younger than he at twenty-seven.

His glance now passed to Lady Rutherford. He was unable to keep his eyes from dwelling momentarily on the red mark that so defined her face. Yet she seemed serene and perfectly at ease with the blemish, and bore the aspect of a lady in whom the years had deepened a mature serenity with respect to who she was.

Why were some women, he wondered, chosen to bear tragedy, while others, it seemed, went through life unscathed by heartbreak? This was quite a family, he thought, that Commander Charles Rutherford and his son had left behind.

"Let's go by the stream!" said Catharine, bounding ahead.

"But that way is longer," said Jocelyn.

"And more lovely. I haven't gone that path in ages." Already Catharine was running ahead. "Come, Lieutenant Langham, I'll show you!"

By the time the rest of them reached the clearing in the pine wood, Catharine had already bounded across the vigorous little brook.

"Now I remember why I don't come this way," laughed Jocelyn. "The stream is too wide. Catharine, my legs are not as long as yours!"

"It's easy, Mother—look!" replied Catharine. She leapt back and forth twice more with the ease of a deer.

Jocelyn laughed. "You were always my young athlete, Catharine! But it's not so easy at my age."

"I don't want to get my feet wet either," objected Amanda.

"I will help you across, Miss Rutherford," said Lieutenant Langham.

Taking a run of several steps, he jumped over to join Catharine, then turned back at the water's edge and stretched his hand across to Amanda.

"Take my hand, Miss Rutherford, then just give a little jump. You will be over in no time."

Amanda did so. Five seconds later she was safely on the bank beside Catharine.

"Now, Lady Rutherford..." said Langham, turning and reaching across again.

"I don't know if I—"

"You can do it," encouraged the lieutenant.

"But I can't quite reach your hand."

The lieutenant inched closer to the flowing water, placed one of his feet at the water's edge and bent his knees, then stretched his hand as far as he could and strained to take Jocelyn's hand.

She was just able to clutch his fingers.

"There we go," Langham said, though his own position was slightly precarious as he leaned off-balance toward her. "I've got you. Now give a jump and I'll pull you over."

Jocelyn hesitated but a moment, then gave a leap. Langham yanked as gently as he could while his foot dug into the soft earth of the stream bank. But he had miscalculated the pull of Jocelyn's weight. As she flew onto the opposite bank, his one foot slipped.

"Look out!" shouted Catharine.

It was too late. His other foot sloshed into the water as he struggled desperately to keep his balance.

"Lieutenant!" cried Jocelyn.

Catharine jumped into the stream to grab his flailing hand. On the bank, Amanda reached for the other, and together they steadied him and kept him from tumbling on his face into the foot-deep water. With some effort they pulled him back to the bank, his white naval trousers soaked above his boots to the knees. Catharine's dress was in a similar condition, though she was loving every minute of it.

"I will never live this down," he said, "having to be rescued from a little stream barely four feet wide. We naval officers are supposed to be more skilled on water than that!"

Still laughing, they recovered themselves and gradually continued on their way, their footsteps squishing as they walked.

"I am so sorry, Lieutenant," said Jocelyn. "This is all my fault."

"No, it was mine," said Catharine, "for insisting we come this way. I apologize to you all," she added. But even as the words were out of her mouth, she was giggling again.

"Not to worry," laughed the lieutenant. "No harm done, except to my pride. It was an adventure I am sure I shall long remember ... and never live down among my naval colleagues—if I tell them, that is!"

"You can put the blame entirely on me," laughed Catharine.

"But tell me about little Betsy," Langham went on, changing the subject as they sloshed away from the stream. "Who is she?"

"Actually, we know very little about her," replied Jocelyn, and then went on to explain briefly.

Even before she had finished explaining Betsy's strange appearance at Hector's side at their kitchen door, Catharine was again romping ahead.

Lieutenant Langham and Jocelyn continued to talk while Amanda listened quietly.

"Both Mr. Churchill and I have been concerned about you all," the lieutenant was saying. "One of the reasons for my visit was to see how you were getting on."

"I will not say it is not difficult without my husband," replied Jocelyn. "But we know that God is good, and that helps us manage."

"His memory is highly respected in the navy."

"Thank you, Lieutenant."

"And Mr. Churchill sends his personal regards."

"Thank you. Please express my appreciation to him."

"I will be certain to do so."

They walked awhile in silence.

"One thing I have been curious about, Lady Rutherford," said Lieutenant Langham as they now made their way out of the woods and into the more open country that would lead them toward the Hall, "—has Miss Rutherford—Miss . . . Amanda, that is—told you everything about what happened at the lighthouse, and how brave she was?"

"No . . . no, she hasn't," replied Jocelyn. "—What is all this, Amanda?" she added, turning to Amanda.

"It all happened so suddenly," she said, "and then with Father's death and the funeral . . . we just never seemed to get around to talking about it."

Langham glanced toward Amanda. "May I tell them?" he asked.

Amanda smiled and nodded. Overhearing the lieutenant's question, Catharine now joined them again.

"It was a story of high intrigue and no little bravery on the part of your daughter, Lady Rutherford," Langham said. "It all began one day when a London minister came to the door of the Lord of the Admiralty, asking to speak with Mr. Churchill, with a certain very attractive young lady at his side."

As she listened Amanda smiled, then laughed occasionally to hear the lieutenant brag of her exploits. Gradually she quieted, and Jocelyn noticed a change come over her mood. Catharine, meanwhile, hung on the lieutenant's every word, supplying the narrative with just the right number of questions and exclamations.

By the time the tale was completed, they had nearly arrived back at the Hall.

"Would you join us for tea, Lieutenant?" asked Jocelyn. "Sarah made fresh bread this morning. In fact, as it is too late to return to London today, we would be delighted to have you stay the night. We have not had enough occasion to make use of our guest rooms lately."

The invitation took the lieutenant by surprise, though he was clearly pleased.

"I made arrangements at the inn in Exeter," he said slowly, revolving the thing in his mind. "But . . . yes, I think I would like that very much. I accept your kind offer."

16

Name Out of the Past

Two hours later Amanda left the house following evening tea, still in a thoughtful mood.

The reminder of what had happened at the lighthouse sent her thoughts plunging back to Ramsay and the years of her prodigal sojourn in London and on the Continent.

As if he had read her mind, Lieutenant Langham followed her outside a few minutes later. Amanda heard him coming and slowed her step. He quickly caught her, fell into step beside her and offered his arm. She took it as they continued on in the same direction, unintentionally moving toward the heather garden.

"I hope I did not embarrass you earlier," said Langham, "when I was telling your mother and sister what happened."

"Only that you greatly exaggerated my role in it," said Amanda, glancing toward him with a smile.

"Not so much," rejoined the lieutenant. "Such organizations that surround themselves with the gloss of piety and respectability, and which use a certain amount of mind control, can never be brought down without the help of someone from the inside exposing the deception for what it is. Had you not come to us with what you knew, we would never have been able to shut down the spy ring connected to the lighthouse."

"Did it really help?"

"Absolutely. It has already made a difference."

"I am glad to hear it."

"Mr. Churchill believes the tide of the war is turning. And that fact is certainly aided by the assurance that our shores are safe from German and Austrian spies. Although I am sorry to say that he is falling under a great deal of criticism for his conduct of the Dardanelles campaign. I fear he may not last much longer as First Lord of the Admiralty."

It fell silent. They entered the narrow, winding paths.

"This is a wonderful little garden—and so many varieties of heather," said Langham, glancing about him. "Is this how Heathersleigh got its name?"

"I don't think so," replied Amanda. "Perhaps it did originally, but no one knows exactly where the name came from. My father and mother planted most of these shrubs."

"A great deal of work."

"They were always out here when I was young—planting, weeding, pruning, making new paths."

"They must have loved this garden very much. Their care and hard work is obvious. It is a lovely setting."

They continued to walk. In a first-floor window behind them, Catharine watched as they disappeared from view. She was pleased that Amanda had someone besides her and her mother who understood what she had been through.

Slowly a smile spread over her face. *You two look very nice together*, Catharine said to herself. *Maybe . . .*

She allowed her youthful romantic musings to drift off vaguely without completing the thought, though the smile remained on her lips.

"I am glad for this opportunity to speak with you alone, Miss Rutherford," Lieutenant Langham was saying as they walked. "I was hesitant to bring up the subject until we were free to talk, but I did have another reason for coming than merely conveying Mr. Churchill's concern for your mother."

"What is it, Lieutenant?" asked Amanda.

"Our intelligence sources have located Ramsay Halifax," Langham replied.

Amanda immediately tensed.

"Where?" she said in a shaky voice.

"On the Continent . . . southern France, then Austria."

"Will he . . . ?"

"We do not think you are in any danger," the lieutenant went on. "But we felt you ought to be informed. Colonel Forsythe has been instrumental in shutting down their operations on British soil."

"At least that is a relief."

"There are, however," he added, "indications of continued activity by the Fountain of Light on the mainland. There has been no attempt to contact you?"

"None," replied Amanda. "Do you think they will?"

"There is no way to know. We only want to make sure no danger comes to you or your family."

"Thank you, Lieutenant. I cannot tell you how much your concern means. But I hope I never see any of them again."

"Be assured we will continue to monitor the situation. I am in close touch with Jack Whyte of the intelligence service. We will not let them come near you."

"I appreciate your confidence," said Amanda, "though knowing them as I do, I realize all too well that they have not forgotten me. I cannot help occasionally being nervous. They are not likely to forget my defection anytime soon."

17
Difficult Thoughts About the Future

◆ ◆ ◆

*T*wo mornings after Lieutenant Langham's departure, Jocelyn awoke to strange sounds above her in the house. Her first thought was a reminder of George. As her brain made its rapid journey from sleep to wakefulness, she found herself wondering if his ghost had returned to carry out the explorations of the house he had been unable to complete before.

Gradually she came to herself, then rose, put on her dressing gown, and went to investigate. Almost directly above her own bedroom she found Betsy rummaging about on the third floor.

"Betsy dear, what are you doing?" she asked.

"Just exploring," replied the girl enthusiastically. "The house is so huge. I never knew houses were so big in all the world. Catharine said it would be all right."

"Yes, that's fine," nodded Jocelyn, smiling to herself in humorous though poignant disappointment that it had not been George whom she had discovered. "You may go into any room that is unlocked. Only leave things as they are."

"Yes, ma'am."

On her way downstairs, Jocelyn glanced through the window and saw Amanda outside walking. She paused and now saw Catharine come bounding out of the house as well. The morning was windy, and in the distance clouds appeared to be approaching at the front of a storm. After a moment, Jocelyn continued down to the ground floor and outside to join them.

Amanda had awoken early. After an hour with her Bible, retracing many now familiar scriptures for insights she might have missed, she had gone out into the frenetic morning. Lieutenant Langham's visit had stirred many thoughts—both happy and sad, both new and old—and she had been restless ever since his leaving. She left the house, enjoying the blustery summer tumult.

She had scarcely been out of the house five minutes when she heard footsteps running up behind her. She turned to meet them.

"Catharine!" she exclaimed. "Good morning—you're up early!"

"So are you. Thinking of Terrill?"

"*Terrill!*" laughed Amanda. "You are on a first-name basis so soon?"

"Only to myself. I so love it when he calls me *Miss* Catharine," she giggled.

"You're as bad as a silly schoolgirl! Why do you say that?"

"I don't know. It just sounds funny, so old-fashioned and formal. What does he call you?"

"Miss Rutherford, I suppose, now that I think about it."

They walked on a few steps.

"I saw you and him alone in the heather garden the other evening," said Catharine in a teasing tone. "With your hand through his arm, you looked very..."

She allowed her voice to trail off significantly. Her intended meaning was not lost on Amanda.

"What are you suggesting, Catharine?" said Amanda, glancing toward her sister.

"Only that he is very handsome, and that despite whatever he said to Mother about Mr. Churchill and the war and all that, he obviously came out here to see you."

"To... *see* me?"

"You know what I mean, Amanda. You must know that he likes you."

"You're not actually thinking—" she began, then paused briefly and looked at Catharine in disbelief. "—Catharine, I'm *married*," she said. "Much as I would like to forget that fact, I cannot."

"Perhaps you won't be forever," persisted Catharine with a coy smile. "And he *is* handsome."

"There is nothing between Lieutenant Langham and me," insisted Amanda good-naturedly but firmly. "I cannot imagine you would even think it."

Just then Jocelyn walked up behind them.

"I agree with you, Catharine," she said. "The lieutenant is indeed a handsome young man. In a way, he reminds me of your father when he was young—dashing, friendly, courteous, full of hopes and plans. No wonder I fell in love with him—*Charles*, I mean," she added laughing. "If anyone's going to fall in love with Lieutenant Langham, I'm afraid it will have to be one of you!"

Amanda said nothing. Catharine realized she had disturbed her sister's tranquility. She now turned back for the house so that the other two could be alone.

"Well, I'm going back inside," she said and ran off.

Jocelyn and Amanda continued on some minutes in silence until they were well away from the Hall.

"That's just the trouble, Mother," said Amanda at length in a more serious tone.

"What's the trouble, dear?" asked Jocelyn.

"Catharine was teasing me about Lieutenant Langham. She thought he was paying *me* some kind of romantic social call. I know she meant nothing by it, but it made me uncomfortable."

"You don't think he was?"

"Of course not," rejoined Amanda. "When we went out walking, remember, after tea, it was only so that he could tell me about Ramsay. I am certain he knows I'm married. I can't exactly remember if he heard when Ramsay told everyone—I think he was outside somewhere. But why else would he come all this way to inform me about him?"

"I don't know, dear. He does seem very fond of you."

"But I am *married*, Mother." Amanda paused briefly. "Sometimes I just don't know what I am going to do!" she burst out after a moment.

Again it was silent for several pensive seconds.

"Have you considered a divorce?" asked Jocelyn.

"Of course I have thought about it," replied Amanda. "How could I not? The thought of what to do is with me constantly. But—"

"What is it, dear?" asked Jocelyn.

"I don't know if divorce is right. And I *couldn't* face having to locate Ramsay to sign papers. I don't ever want to see him or have anything to do with him again."

"Why don't you talk to Vicar Coleridge?"

"I hardly know him, Mother."

"He is a very nice man. Sometimes it helps to get an outside opinion on such things."

"But I don't want someone's opinion. I want to know what is *right*. There are right opinions and wrong ones."

"Your father was extremely fond of the vicar," said Jocelyn. "He would not have respected him unless he thought him a wise man."

Jocelyn paused and glanced about. The dark clouds had moved nearly overhead and the wind had intensified.

"If we stay out here much longer," she said, "we may get soaked. And look at me—I'm still in my dressing gown! I have the feeling this is going to be quite a storm."

Gradually they turned and began making their way back toward the Hall by way of the heather garden.

18

Crumholtz, Sutclyff, Stonehaugh, & Crumholtz

The storm about to engulf southwest England was born on winds slanting down from Scandinavia. Its northeast rains therefore hit Exeter a few minutes before arriving at the westernmost portions of Devon. And they hit suddenly and with fury.

The expensively dressed man hurrying along the walkway of Exeter's High Street glanced up, silently cursing whatever gods were responsible for such things, and pulled his overcoat more tightly around his neck. He had been caught unsuspecting without an umbrella on his way from his hotel, and his shoulders and feet were nearly drenched. Unfortunately, the hotel was farther behind him than his destination was ahead, and he had no choice but to continue. He quickened his pace to an awkward run.

A long minute later he sloshed his way under a faded green awning, paused briefly to compose himself and catch his breath, then entered the door ahead of him.

"Good morning," he said to the secretary who greeted him. "I have an appointment with Mr. Crumholtz."

"Yes . . . Mr. Rutherford, is it?" she replied. "Mr. Crumholtz is expecting you. I will tell him you are here."

She rose and disappeared into an inner office while Gifford Rutherford moved about uneasily on his cold feet, hoping the activity would keep him from freezing to death.

She reemerged a few minutes later. "This way please, Mr. Rutherford," she said as she led him into the lawyer's office, introduced him to her employer, then left the two men alone.

"I have been conducting some investigations for a period of several years," began Gifford when he was seated.

"Investigations . . . of what nature?" inquired Bradbury Crumholtz.

"Dealing with an ancient family property about which there are some ambiguities of title," replied Gifford. "It is, I believe, an estate with which you are familiar, as your firm has executed several wills and deeds for certain of its principals."

"What do you know about my firm's transactions?"

"As I said, I have been conducting an investigation of my own—a *thorough* investigation," added Gifford, and the emphasis was not lost on Mr. Crumholtz. "That is why I am here—because I know you have had dealings in the affair. My own solicitor felt that your services would be invaluable, and that the necessary documents would carry more force coming from your office. It may be that you possess, or are in a position to obtain, the necessary information to right the wrongs done to my family once and for all."

Crumholtz listened without betraying his annoyance at the fellow's manner. From the cut of his suit, even wet, and his speech, he knew his visitor came from London and was wealthy—no doubt influential too. But already he didn't like him.

"The estate is that known as Heathersleigh," continued Gifford. "As I am sure you know, it lies northwest of here just outside the village of Milverscombe."

Crumholtz nodded. "And?" he intoned slowly. "What is it exactly you want me to do?"

"It is simple, really," replied Gifford. "I want you to initiate legal proceedings against Jocelyn Rutherford, the current resident of Heathersleigh Hall. She is, though this fact is of no consequence in the case, the widow of the late Charles Rutherford, who was my cousin."

"What kind of proceedings?" asked Crumholtz.

"Putting forth my legal claim to the Heathersleigh estate," replied Gifford, now shoving several sheets he had removed from inside his coat across the desk in front of the solicitor.

Crumholtz eyed the papers carefully, letting no twitch or expression betray his suspicions. A gnawing caution in the pit of his stomach told him to tread lightly with this man.

The office grew quiet. Crumholtz picked up the papers and pretended to review them. In truth, his mind was racing as he quickly tried to marshal what he knew about the estate in his brain, connecting various pieces from out of his memory. Suddenly he recalled the old McFee woman. She was connected to Heathersleigh as well.

"I will look into it, Mr. Rutherford," he said after a moment, "though it may take a little time. These things always do. Though I am not at the current time a specific agent representing the present owner, there may be conflict-of-interest issues to be resolved. Where may I contact you?"

Gifford reached forward and handed him his card.

"I will make it worth your while," said Gifford.

Crumholtz nodded. "And I may . . . keep these papers?" he said.

"Of course," said Gifford, rising. "They are duplicates."

Gifford departed and the solicitor remained seated another minute or two, continuing to turn the matter over in his mind.

Then he rose, walked to his safe, opened it, and thoughtfully removed the documents, including the sealed envelopes, that had been entrusted to the firm for safekeeping. He sat down at his desk again, spreading both new papers and old out in front of him.

What can it all mean? he puzzled to himself. *And who is this new London Rutherford?*

19

The Garret

———— ◆◆◆ ————

*M*eanwhile Betsy had left the room where Jocelyn found her and had wandered some distance along the corridor of the east wing, then turned into the north. Passing the library, whose treasures had not yet drawn her, she reached the end of the wide hallway, turned right into a narrower corridor, then left again until she came to its end at the northwest corner of the building.

As she paused Betsy saw to her right a small door barely two feet in width. Rarely used, for it had no apparent purpose except to provide access to a garret, which to all appearances was itself useless, the door was altogether unlike any of the other large doors she had seen in the Hall. The instant it caught her eye, the narrow entry to places unknown invited exploration.

Testing the latch, she found it unlocked. She opened the door and crept through it and immediately found herself facing a steep, narrow wooden staircase. The cool, musty aroma of disuse met her face, drifting on an imperceptible breeze from unseen regions above coming down through the door. Intrigue swept through her. She placed a tentative foot on the first step, then took another. The stairs creaked to the weight of her feet, and slowly she continued. The very smell of the narrow passage, as she rose into darkness, spoke of antiquity and mystery.

An inquisitive girl by nature, she had grown even more so since arriving at Heathersleigh. Not only had she never imagined houses so big, she had never dreamed of clothes so clean, food so delicious, beds so soft, or people so kind. Whenever she thought of the past, hatred continued to rise in her for her father's murderers. But being among such loving women as had temporarily adopted her was gradually drawing the latent instincts of approaching womanhood from her soul. And with them came a gradual softening of the rough edges that her upbringing could not help to have left upon her.

But she was not thinking of such things as the thin illumination from the corridor below receded behind her through the door she had left open. A gust of air swirled momentarily about her head, then died back down, evidence that the approaching storm outside was playing havoc with roof and tower of Heathersleigh Hall. Outside and above her, the wind racing through the ceiling tiles whistled and moaned eerily through the upper portions of the structure. Betsy shivered briefly, though it was not cold, and continued on.

At length she arrived at the end of the staircase. She paused and glanced about where she stood at the corner of the garret where the north and west wings of the house connected.

Betsy found herself in a narrow room that from its cobwebby appearance had likely had no visitors in years. A thin light came from an air vent high on the wall of the far end, though it was scarcely enough to see by.

She felt about, found a light switch, and flipped it. The space around her filled with light. How could she have known that she owed the bulb above her to the very young man whose feet had been the last before hers to venture here? In truth it was not a room in which she stood at all, but merely a wide-open corridor of sorts running along the length of the north wing garret. Wall-like partitions approximately six feet in height had been erected from the floor to the open beams of the roof rafters, blocking from sight the lower portion of the roof as it sloped down to meet the floor. But the large central space was apparently not used for anything. The floorboards were uneven and overspread with the accumulated dust of years, and cobwebs covered every inch above her where the huge beams of the sloping rafters met in the center at the apex of the roof.

She glanced about uneasily for a few moments, for, with the wind still moaning and blowing above her, the place could not help but make her shiver from sensations other than cold. Slowly she walked across the floor and came to another door leading beyond. She opened it. Another light switch illuminated the passage in front of her. She now found herself in a narrow corridor that led at an angle away from the door, the open beams of the roof above her head such that she occasionally had to brush away the cobwebs to prevent them from matting her hair. The passage turned and twisted to the right and left at such odd angles as she followed that she quickly lost her sense of direction. She walked and walked until eventually she was above the library, though she did not know it. Whether there were closets or rooms, or anything at all, for that matter, behind the walls enclosing her as she continued on, it was impossible to tell. From all appearances the circuitous hallway served no purpose and led nowhere.

Then suddenly, as if to confirm that fact, Betsy rounded a turn to the left and the passage ended abruptly. She found herself facing a solid wall. No door or latch or indication of any way through it was visible. She stood puzzled for a moment or two, then rapped against the boards that had so abruptly ended her exploration. A dull, hollow echo came back from the sound of her fist. Whatever was behind this wall, she thought, it was not the solid stone from which the major structural portions of the Hall were constructed.

As her knocking investigation quieted, suddenly she was startled by a loud clattering noise almost directly above her. She jumped momentarily, then glanced up and around. Seeing nothing, she realized it must be the wind outside making mischief with a loose roof tile. Again she probed the walls about her, pounding once more upon them, but still without discovery.

At length she had no choice but to turn around and leave the garret the way she had come.

On her way back down into the inhabited portions of the house, as she reentered the second-floor corridor and walked along it past the library, she met Catharine coming up the main staircase.

"Hello, Betsy," said Catharine with a smile. "Having a good time exploring?"

"I was until the hall up in the garret ended."

"You were up there?" rejoined Catharine in some surprise. "You were brave, Betsy! I used to be scared to death to go up there with my brother. I was always afraid we would stumble on some old bones. How did you get there?"

"Through that little doorway back there," answered Betsy, pointing behind her.

"Oh, that explains it. And you came to the end of a narrow, twisting hall?"

Betsy nodded.

"Then you have *much* more exploring to do!" said Catharine excitedly. "You were on the wrong side, that's all."

"Wrong side of what?" said Betsy, now excited again herself. "More exploring to do where?"

"You were on the wrong side of the wall," replied Catharine. "There is a secret room behind it."

"A secret room!" exclaimed Betsy, suddenly coming to life.

"Yes, I'll show you," said Catharine.

"How do you get to it!" Betsy asked as she hurried to keep up. Already Catharine was walking toward the library.

"Come with me!"

Catharine led through the large library doors, turned on the light, and then strode quickly through the bookshelves to the rear of the room.

"But this is the library," said Betsy. "The garret is above us."

"Just be patient, Betsy. You won't believe what I am about to show you. My brother, George, discovered all this when he wasn't much older than you. He loved to explore too."

20
Difficult Options

♦♦♦

*J*ocelyn and Amanda sat down on one of benches in the heather garden, ready to make a dash for it if the sky suddenly emptied.

Amanda seemed for the first time to notice the intricate woodwork of the bench's design.

"I don't remember this bench, Mother," she said. "Has it always been here?"

"Your father built it after you left home," replied Jocelyn. "He built most of the benches in the heather garden."

"I don't know why I never noticed them before."

"He tried to make them all different, and in distinctive woods."

Amanda pondered her mother's words.

"Why?" she asked. "That seems like a lot of extra work."

"You know your father's passion to understand things."

Amanda nodded.

"Whenever variety presented itself, he wanted to grasp every side of it. You know how he was with ideas—always trying to look at issues and situations from different angles. And when it came to objects that fascinated him or that he found useful, he could never be satisfied with just one," chuckled Jocelyn. "You know his watch collection, all his various tools—"

"And his Bible collection," interjected Amanda.

"Exactly. He had to have *every* available translation. When we became interested in heather, he had to try to find *every* kind of heather. When he discovered the Scotsman's writings, he searched high and low until he had *every* book the man had written. Had Charles lived, I don't doubt that eventually we might have had five or six different cars. When he started building benches, he had to make them all unique and use a different kind of wood. That's just how he was. He loved variety. And he always had to investigate everything that crossed his path to the ultimate."

119

"He was a very creative man, wasn't he?" smiled Amanda.

" 'Creatively restless' one of his friends once said about him." Jocelyn now smiled too at the memory. "Charles always laughed at the phrase," she said, "but it fit him perfectly. He always had some new idea or project to try."

"What kind of wood is this?" asked Amanda.

"It's called redwood," Jocelyn answered. "Your father had it shipped from a small, obscure seaport in northern California. It was quite costly, but he found it such a joy to work with."

Gradually Amanda's thoughts returned to her personal dilemma.

"I don't know, Mother," said Amanda after a brief silence, "I understand what you say about Vicar Coleridge. But I really want *your* counsel more than anyone's."

"I have never faced what you are going through."

"Neither has Vicar Coleridge."

"I suppose you are right," replied Jocelyn. "There is also Timothy to think of. He would be glad to talk to you. But you know I will do whatever I can."

"Then tell me what *you* think I ought to do," said Amanda. "If someone you didn't know was in my position, and you were the only person she had to turn to, what would you tell her? What if it were Betsy? She has no one else—what would you tell *her* to do? Even if you haven't been in my situation, what do you *think* is right?"

"Well, dear," answered Jocelyn thoughtfully, "I suppose the first thing would be to look at what options you see before you. What comes to my mind immediately is the most straightforward—stay married but not see Ramsay again."

"That would be the simplest and easiest possibility," Amanda nodded, "just to do nothing. I have thought of that, of course. But I do not think I could bear knowing that for the rest of my life my legal name was Mrs. Ramsay Halifax." Amanda shook her head and sighed at the very sound of the words. "And I suppose, as we are talking about my options, there is always the possibility of actually going back to Ramsay," she added, "but I could never do that."

"Then let me turn the question back on you," said Jocelyn, "and ask what you asked me a moment ago—what do *you* want to do? What does *your* heart tell you?"

"I don't know," groaned Amanda, "—I want to do what is *right*. I just don't know what that is."

"And remarriage?" said Jocelyn.

"Isn't that getting the cart a little ahead of the horse, Mother?"

"I don't see how you can resolve the present without looking ahead to the future, dear. The present and the future are always linked. I think you must look at the entire prospect of what is facing you—present as well as future."

"I see what you are saying," nodded Amanda. "To answer you, then, I don't see how I could ever remarry, Mother."

"Why not?"

"Even if I divorce Ramsay, I must still bear the consequences of what I did. On that point I do agree with Sister Anika."

21

The Secret Room

In the Hall, thirteen-year-old Elsbet Conlin glanced about her with wide eyes of wonder as she followed Catharine through the back of the moveable bookcase in the library, along a tight corridor, and around two turns.

"We are between the walls of the library and main corridor," said Catharine as they went. To Betsy's ears Catharine's voice sounded so different in here. It seemed they had stepped back in time a hundred years—as in truth they had. "From inside any of those rooms," Catharine went on, "it is impossible to know all this is here."

"How can there be space for this walkway?" asked Betsy.

"The walls were constructed with a void or empty space behind them. My brother explained it all to me, and drew me pictures and diagrams, but it took me a long time to make sense of it. That's where we are walking, in the empty spaces behind the walls. Many of them are connected, and you can go almost anywhere in the house through these hidden passageways. But there are only four ways to get into the maze— at least that's all George ever found. You can go all the way down to the basement and outside, or to the tower."

"What about the secret room?" asked Betsy.

"That's what I will show you now," replied Catharine. "It is just as George discovered it. You can't get there any other way but this. It's just like a hidden cave right in the middle of the house. It's so well hidden that no one knew about it for years, until George discovered it."

Catharine led on, not following the descent and later ascent to the storage room by which George had first discovered the labyrinth under the old chest of records and journals, but instead leading Betsy around various turns paralleling the walls of the rooms, arriving finally at a stairway going straight up above them like a corkscrew. She took it. Betsy followed up into darkness. At the top, Catharine paused, then pushed up on the ceiling above her. A two-foot square panel of wood fastened to invisible hinges swung up and out of sight. The next thing Betsy knew she saw Catharine disappearing into the hole. She scrambled up after her.

"Here we are!" said Catharine "And, thanks to George, there is even a light."

She flipped a switch and the room filled with the light of a dim bulb hanging overhead.

Betsy found herself on the floor of a room some eight feet square, with the same open beams of the roof above her as before. The wind was still blowing fiercely outside, and they heard it all the louder the moment they climbed into the secret room from below.

"What's that noise?" said Catharine, glancing about.

"I think it's a roof tile," said Betsy. The clattering and scraping was now right above them. "I heard it before, in the garret hallway."

"You were on the other side of this wall," said Catharine, pointing to her left. "And this one," she added, indicating the other, "was built to block the passage to the tower. These boards you see are exactly like the ones on the other side. George said this room was built later by blocking off the passage right in the middle. So you can't get all the way through the garret of the north wing now because both corridors end at these two walls."

"But why?" asked Betsy.

"George didn't know. We had a great-grandfather that George said was more than a little eccentric, and his uncle was lord of the manor before him and was the same way. George said it probably had something to do with one of them."

"But why would they have built it like this?" persisted Betsy.

"George thought they made it for a hiding place."

"From what?"

"I don't know. Neither did George."

22

How Far Should Accountability Go?

*W*ouldn't your grief, and the divorce itself," Jocelyn had just asked Amanda as Betsy and Catharine sat talking in the secret room, "be bearing the consequences?"

"In a way, perhaps," answered Amanda. "But I could not simply go on afterward as if nothing had happened."

"What do you mean?" asked Jocelyn.

"I cannot ignore the Scriptures just for my own convenience merely to escape my accountability."

"But you have said that you were not yourself, that you were not thinking clearly."

"Ramsay may have been a cad, and maybe to a degree I was brainwashed, though I certainly did not think so at the time. But I am still accountable. No one *made* me marry Ramsay."

"I still do not understand why you feel so strongly that you can never marry again."

"Because of what I just read in Matthew 5:32 this morning. It is a passage Sister Anika told me about."

"What does it say?"

"That to remarry would be adultery," answered Amanda.

"Adultery!" repeated Jocelyn, shocked at Amanda's blunt statement.

"There is no other way to look at it. 'Whoever marries a divorced woman commits adultery.' There it is, Mother, in Jesus' own words. I would be a divorced woman—"

At the words, Amanda turned away and began to cry. Jocelyn took her in her arms, and they sat quietly for a moment.

"The sound of it is too horrible to think about," said Amanda after a while, wiping her eyes. "But if a man would be committing adultery to marry me—after a divorce, I mean—then I would just as surely be committing adultery myself."

"Those are strong words, Amanda. Surely God would not condemn you so harshly for making a mistake."

"It is not that God will condemn me, it is about my doing what is right. And I was reading several other passages, too, before I came out this morning," Amanda went on. "Another passage Sister Anika told me about is in Mark 10. It is even clearer than the verse in Matthew."

"And?"

"It says that if a woman divorces her husband and marries another man, she is an adulteress."

Again the word jolted Jocelyn's sensitive ears. She was familiar enough with the passage, but to think of Jesus' hard words in relation to her own daughter had taken her by surprise.

"I wish it wasn't there," continued Amanda. "I hate what those words make me feel like, so dirty and unclean. But even if Ramsay committed adultery and I am free to divorce, the verse still says that I cannot remarry without being an adulteress."

"Dear, please—that is such a terrible word. I just don't think—"

"But the words are clear, Mother, in black and white," insisted Amanda.

"But surely you don't want to remain unmarried."

"Of course I don't want to live the rest of my life alone. But can I ignore that passage, and say the words don't *really* apply to me and my situation, just for the sake of my own happiness? What kind of obedience to the Scriptures is that? You and Father taught us that the Bible was to be obeyed. I didn't do very well back then. I resented it every time either of you would say it. But I am trying to take the Bible seriously now."

"You are convinced that's what it means?"

"I don't know, Mother!" said Amanda in frustration. "I just don't see where Jesus or Paul say that certain men and women *may* remarry because they later found out things about their husbands and wives they didn't know before. Maybe I am missing something. I haven't studied the Bible very diligently, that's for sure. But it seems to say that remarriage after divorce is adultery and that's it. Oh, it is so confusing!"

A lengthy silence intervened. Finally Amanda spoke again.

"I have spent my whole life resisting authority," she said, "caring nothing for what was right or for what God wanted, only what I wanted.

I didn't learn how to submit to you and Father when I was supposed to. So I must begin to live that way now. How else can I know God fully if I never learn what he wants me to learn? I don't want to add to my troubles now by ignoring what the Bible says just so that I won't be lonely for the rest of my life."

"In the matter of your future," remarked Jocelyn, "much will depend on how you feel God leading you inside. I have never thought of these things."

"If loneliness is the price I must pay for getting myself into a marriage I shouldn't have," Amanda went on, "then perhaps I have to be willing to pay it. I can no longer make light of morality issues. I know what I did hurt you and Father deeply. It cut against all you stood for as Christians and as a husband and wife. If I am going to turn my life around, I have to start sometime. And I think that time has to be now. I have to start making decisions in a new way than I ever did before, saying not what do I want to do, but what is the *right* thing to do."

Again Amanda sighed.

"I wish Daddy were here," she said. "I would just ask him what to do. But since he is not, I must turn to you."

"I know, dear. But honestly, I don't know what to tell you. Even with your father gone, I would never remarry. He is the only husband I ever want to have. It is different for you. You are much younger and—"

"Uh-oh . . . here comes the rain!" cried Amanda suddenly.

The next instant mother and daughter were on their feet and bolting for the house.

PART II

Autumn 1915

23

Something Is at Hand

◆◆◆

The storm that drenched Heathersleigh Hall and all of England had also blown through Switzerland, and was now past. On the morning after the showers, the sun shone brilliantly over the mountain landscape, creating a dewy blanket of diamonds everywhere. Every flower and blade of grass surrounding the Chalet of Hope near Wengen, Switzerland, sparkled with a thousand subtle colors of a jeweled rainbow.

Hope Guinarde came down into the large room of the chalet, whose great fireplace sat quiet during these months of late summer, and realized she was the first of the household to stir. Even Sister Agatha, usually awake before everyone, had not yet made an appearance. She added fresh wood to the cook stove, put on water to boil, and went out into the crisp but sunny morning.

She walked down the sloping pathway toward the pond, surrounded at this time of year with lush grasses and abundant flowers of great variety and every color. This was such a beautiful and peaceful place, she thought. Could any spot on earth more visibly lift the human spirit toward its Creator than the high alpine meadows of Switzerland?

You are so good to me, Lord, she whispered. *I do not deserve it, yet you constantly lavish me with blessing. I am so grateful.*

Slowly she made her way about the pond, her thoughts gradually drifting across the miles to their guest of the previous year who had so gotten under their collective skin. She had read Amanda's first letter again just last night before retiring. Every time she thought of it she was struck anew with the remarkable work God was able to do at this place, even, sometimes, in spite of her own lack of faith. She felt that she was often too blunt, so weak and immature at times. Yet God continued to change lives, not because of her, not because of any of *them,* but because this was *his* place, his work.

A sense had begun growing upon her that a work in some *new* life was about to begin. The sense of preparation, of needing to get a new

room ready was building again in her heart—a feeling so familiar because it had come on so many occasions, yet also surprisingly new every
time, as the quiet voice of the Spirit's leading always is.

And with that leading, Amanda too had been occupying her
thoughts.

After some time of prayerful reflection, Sister Hope turned and
began walking up the hill back to the chalet. She saw Sister Gretchen
standing on the porch waiting for her. Behind the house, Sister Marjolaine's tiny form was visible walking toward the chicken shed, basket in
hand, to gather the morning's eggs for their breakfast.

"Good morning, Gretchen," she said, smiling as she walked toward
the house.

"Good morning, Hope—it is spectacular, isn't it!"

"As long as I live, I will never tire of this place."

"Sister Agatha has coffee brewing . . . and I can see that *something* is
on your mind."

Sister Hope laughed. "Haven't you been sensing it too," she said,
"the undefined stirring . . . the expectation?"

"Perhaps," replied Sister Gretchen. "But I think this time it comes
more from watching it come upon you."

"You've seen it?"

"Of course."

Again Sister Hope laughed. "I hadn't realized I was so transparent."

"Maybe not to all the others . . . but you are to me. Tell me—what
are you thinking?"

"Nothing specific, only that perhaps this time it will not be someone
coming to us, but rather someone we must go find."

"Like Amanda in Milan."

"Exactly. And speaking of Amanda, she has been on my mind a great
deal as well, as if she is involved in whatever is approaching for us."

"Perhaps she is coming back."

"Her most recent letter indicated nothing. Yet I feel . . . I don't know,
as if I need to see her again."

"How wonderful that would be," said Sister Gretchen, "now that . . ."

"I know what you mean," added Sister Hope, finishing her friend's
uncompleted thought, "—now that she is *right* with herself."

The two women were silent a moment or two, both their thoughts
revolving around Amanda.

"Since we received her first letter after she was home," Sister

Gretchen said after a minute, "I have often wondered if she might return, and might even become one of us."

Sister Hope nodded.

"I have thought often of that first conversation you and I had about her soon after her arrival," Sister Gretchen went on, "and the sense we both had, even then, that her life was destined for service and ministry in the Lord's work."

Sister Hope smiled at the thought. "It was difficult to see back then. But I still believe it to be true."

"As do I," agreed Sister Gretchen. "He has *something* for her."

As they were talking the door opened behind them, and two beautiful but very distinctive young women walked out to join them.

"Good morning, Kasmira . . . Hello, Sister Anika," said Sister Hope.

"Good morning, sisters," replied Kasmira with a bright smile. "A lovely day," she added in a thick accent.

24

To London

Two weeks after their conversation, Amanda sought Jocelyn in the sun-room.

"Mother," she said, "I have been thinking about what you said when we were talking before. I think it was good advice when you recommended that I speak with either Vicar Coleridge or Timothy. I would like to do that. I realize that the first step in learning to make decisions differently is probably to follow wise counsel from those who love me, not reject it as I did yours and Father's years ago. So . . . you gave me that advice, and I am going to take it."

"What are you going to do?" asked Jocelyn.

"As much as I do not want to go to the city again, I think I should talk to Timothy."

"He would be glad to come here."

"I know he would. But something tells me this is a step I need to take, and go to London this time for the right reason—to learn how to obey. Will you go with me?"

"I'm not sure I should," replied Jocelyn. "We have Betsy to think of."

"Yes, of course—what was I thinking?"

"Why don't you ask Catharine?"

"That's a great idea. I think I will!"

◆ ◆ ◆

On a cold and drizzly morning a week later, the two sisters sat on the train bound for London. Amanda was quiet and pensive. The bare trees evidencing the approach of winter were the perfect landscape for her thoughts. Would a new spring ever bloom again in *her* life? Catharine had noticed her mood ever since their departure from Milverscombe. She glanced over several times, then finally spoke up cheerily, trying to draw her sister out.

"You have changed so much, Amanda," said Catharine brightly. "You have grown so wonderfully in the Lord since you came home. What a story you have to tell about what God has done for you. I know he will use it to help others."

Amanda looked toward her and smiled, but said nothing.

"In a way, though it sounds funny to say it," Catharine went on, "I am almost envious."

Now Amanda's expression as she listened turned questioning.

"I admire how you have been able to befriend Betsy," Catharine went on. "I cannot help but think it must be because you have suffered too. I haven't had that experience. I haven't got that kind of story to tell."

"How fortunate you are that you don't," rejoined Amanda sadly. "I'm sure it must please the Lord that you grew in obedience and godliness all your life. You have something I will never have."

"What is that?" asked Catharine.

"Purity," answered Amanda sadly. "I often think these days of that short phrase describing Jesus' childhood, that he grew in wisdom and in stature and in favor with God and man. How sad it makes me now to realize I did not use the opportunity God gave me to do the same when I was young."

Her words took Catharine by surprise and she did not reply. They rode along some moments in silence.

"I learned at the chalet," Amanda continued at length, "that every-one has a story God can use somehow. The sisters were so different, yet each of their lives and all those differences helped me in some unique way. So I suppose what you say is true. But in another way, it is a terrible price to pay in one's own life just to be able to have an experience to share with others. Once you give your purity away, it's not something you can ever get back."

Now it was Catharine's turn to lapse into an uncharacteristic mo-ment of melancholy. Suddenly their roles from only a moment ago were reversed.

"What is it, Catharine?" asked Amanda.

"I'm not sure I do have a story to tell," replied Catharine. "It seems that all the sisters you've told us about had stories involving some kind of hardship or suffering. I've not suffered in the same way you have, except losing Father and George recently, of course, and I cried and cried afterward. But I mean with the burden of guilt you feel. I know it's painful for you, what you've been through. But you have something truly valuable to give to others."

"But you are living the best story of all," replied Amanda.

"What story?" asked Catharine.

"A life lived *without* rebellion. I wish I could say that. You are a shin-ing example of a life lived pleasing to God."

Catharine nodded, trying to take in the new thought that her ordi-nary and normal life might actually be a testimony of God's goodness more than she had realized.

"Yes, maybe God will use my waywardness," Amanda went on, "but how much more can he use a life that has honored him without turning its back on his voice. I am so lucky to have you for my sister."

Another silence followed. Both young women had a great deal to think about.

"Will you pray for me, Catharine?" Amanda asked at length.

"I always do," smiled Catharine. "I have been for years."

"You have?"

"Of course. George and I used to pray for you together after you left—sometimes in the secret room."

The words were too poignantly painful for Amanda. Quietly she began to cry. Catharine reached out a tender arm of comfort. The two sisters drew close to one another, holding each other for several long minutes, then quietly began to pray.

"*Lord,*" said Catharine, "*I do thank you for Amanda, and for what you are teaching her even through the pain of what she must endure. I ask you to use her life for you, and to help others. Use Amanda's life, Lord, to turn other young people toward their mothers and fathers, and toward you. Continue to mature her and deepen obedience and wisdom within her. And help us both to move on with thankful hearts, even though we cannot help the grief of losing Papa and George. And we pray for Mother, too, and thank you so much for her.*"

Amanda gave Catharine a squeeze of affection, sniffed through her tears a time or two, then began herself to pray.

"*Help me learn to be a good daughter, heavenly Father,*" she said. "*Thank you so much for giving me a sister like Catharine, and for such a loving mother as we have. I am sorry again for not paying attention to so many things soon enough. But help me learn now. Show me what to do about Ramsay. And if you do want to use my experiences in some way, like Catharine says, show me what you want me to do. I would rather just forget what I used to be like. But if you have another plan for me, I am willing to do whatever you want, especially if I can help prevent other parents from having to experience what I put Mother and Father through.*"

She stopped, and gradually they sat back in their seats. Amanda began quietly crying again. Catharine took her hand and held it in hers as they rode along for the next hour in relative silence.

They arrived in London and immediately took a taxi to New Hope Chapel. Timothy was expecting them.

"Hello, Catharine, Amanda," he greeted them, "—come in!"

He led them inside the parsonage. "Let us have some tea and a talk," he said. "I've asked Mrs. Alvington to prepare us a light tea. I thought you might want something after your train trip."

After they had visited briefly, Catharine turned as if to leave.

"Where are you going?" asked Amanda in surprise.

"Into the city," replied Catharine. "I asked the taxi driver to wait."

"Why, aren't you staying?"

"I thought it would be best."

"But why?"

"You need to talk to Timothy alone. You will be able to share more freely without me."

"But you can't go into the city yourself."

"Of course I can," laughed Catharine. "I'm a big girl now too, Amanda. I'll be fine."

"But what will you do?"

"Mother gave me a message to take to Mr. Churchill. Afterward, I thought I would go to Hyde Park, or maybe the museum."

"All right, but—"

"Don't worry. I'll be fine, I promise . . . I'll see you at the hotel later."

25

A Garden of Dormant Seeds

$\mathcal{Y}$ou look well, Amanda," said Timothy once he and Amanda were seated. "How are you feeling . . . inside, I mean?"

"I don't know . . . reasonably well, I suppose," replied Amanda. "The memories are sometimes difficult to bear. Yet I am learning from them."

"I am glad to hear it."

"Just as you said a while back, so many things about my father are returning to me. Everywhere I turn, it seems, I see him standing there in my mind, laughing, working on a project, telling us about something."

"But it is painful?" asked Timothy.

"Occasionally," replied Amanda. "But I am coming rather to enjoy some of these occasions more often than not. It's something that is . . . well, bittersweet."

"I think I understand."

"Not long ago Mother and I were in the heather garden, and suddenly I noticed the bench we were sitting on, as if I had never seen it before. I made a comment to her about it, and we found ourselves talking about Father and his creativity. So I have come almost to welcome the memories, even though, as I say, they are sometimes difficult to bear."

"You will continue to have moments such as you have been telling me about, Amanda," said Timothy with a smile. "I do not doubt that you will find many memories coming back to you in just this way now that your heart is open to your father. If my example is any indication, it may continue for the rest of your life. It is a form of spiritual gardening in which I have been engaged myself for some years, ever since I discovered its necessity."

"A form of ... *gardening?*" asked Amanda with a puzzled expression as she turned toward him. "What do you mean?"

Timothy chuckled lightly. "An admittedly odd way of viewing the matter," he said, "but one that helps me visualize the process more practically. Shall I explain what I mean?"

"Please do."

"It began shortly after I took up residence at New Hope Chapel," Timothy began. "I should say, my understanding of what I call spiritual gardening began then. Actually, the internal process had been at work within me some time previously. You probably did not notice when you visited before, but outside this sitting room, through those two narrow French doors there, is a small garden."

Amanda glanced in the direction Timothy indicated.

"It sits at the back of the church, as you can see, surrounded by a wing of the building itself, two high stone walls, and my living quarters. It is only some twelve by fifteen feet. But I have always fancied gardens; therefore, when I moved here to New Hope, one of the first projects I sought to undertake was to bring some order to it and plant it full of bulbs and flowers and thus brighten the view from my window."

"It's beautiful now," said Amanda. "Was nothing growing when you began?"

"Oh, it was full of growth," replied Timothy. "Weeds and grass, briars that were trying to take over, wild ivy, and several gangly shrubs of no value I could see. It was a positive jungle of overgrowth, some of it up to three and four feet high. My predecessor, and for all I know his predecessor before him, had done nothing with the space except let nature take its course—which is the worst thing for the development either of a human being or a flower garden. I could hardly open the French doors for the wildness encroaching against them."

"What did you do?"

"I determined to reclaim the place and try to cultivate it into a little square of loveliness."

"It is obvious that you succeeded."

"It is nice now, I must admit."

"But a lot of work from the sound of it."

"Indeed," nodded Timothy. "Once I managed to get the doors open and through to the outside, I began cutting and chopping and whacking, at first merely to prune back the wild greenery so that I could get at the earth itself. That alone took me several weeks of spare time. Then I burned the grass and weeds and shrubbery prunings, until at last I had the place cleared of growth. Even that was a great improvement, though all I had at that point was bare ground, the stubbly grass ends, and a small pile of ashes. But at last, I thought, I could begin to till and prepare the ground in preparation for filling it with bulbs and seeds.

"I should explain that I took up residence at New Hope at the first of the year, and this all took place in the months of January and February, as weather permitted. My aim was to have the garden planted by early March. I was anticipating the spring months with eagerness, and throughout the last two weeks of February, I dug and tilled with every spare minute, digging down some eighteen inches below the surface, removing roots, upturning and knocking at the hard earth and cultivating it into what I hoped in time would become soft, crumbly, moist loam.

"As a lad I had always marveled to observe the farmers near my home, how the hard-packed crust of the autumn harvest could be ploughed and reploughed and transformed into the softest, most luxuriant soil by the following spring, so light and airy as it awaited planting with the season's new seeds that I could plunge my hand into it past my young wrist. Somehow I knew, even at that young age, that the soil itself was the key to growth, and that without proper preparation, growth would be stunted and would not bear its appointed harvest.

"As I began my project to transform my little jungle into a garden, therefore, my hope was to turn the hard, neglected earth into that soil I'd seen as a child, soft, crumbly dirt that would fall through my fingers and into which I could reach my hand six or eight inches, in which I could plant seeds and bulbs that would thrive."

"It reminds me of Mother and Father in the heather," said Amanda.

"My back paid a dreadful price," laughed Timothy. "I developed painful blisters on every one of my ten fingers from the shovel work. I enjoyed it, of course. Nothing is as invigorating as a job whose hope is a reward you intend to enjoy yourself, as your father knew. His hands were rough too. It always took me aback when I shook hands with him, thinking of him as a member of Parliament, to feel the hand of what could have been a common laborer. In any event, after two weeks' time, having turned and knocked and spaded the entire garden three times, as I said, in places to a depth of over a foot, I thought that I was at last ready to begin planting.

"Alas," Timothy went on, "at exactly that moment, my mother fell seriously ill. I immediately dropped, not only the work on the garden, but my pastoral duties as well, quickly arranging for a supply minister to take my place, and hurried north to be with her."

"Did she. . . ?" began Amanda.

"No, she recovered and lived several more years. But the illness was serious, and I was away for two months. When I returned, with spring well advanced—for by then it was May—imagine my surprise to see my little garden once again alive with growth."

"All the grass and weeds had come back?"

"They were there all right," replied Timothy. "But the unexpected surprise was that flowers had sprouted everywhere as well."

"*Flowers*—but I didn't think you had planted any yet."

"I hadn't."

"What could account for it, then?" asked Amanda.

"That was the wonderful mystery. My spade work, bringing light and air to the depths beneath the surface, had caused long dormant seeds and bulbs to explode suddenly out of the soil with new life."

"But . . . I don't understand how that could be."

"It is a little-recognized fact that many of the seeds which lie buried in the ground, too deep and in earth too hard to allow for germination, strange to say, yet retain the power of growth. Some perhaps fall in their pods or shells, and before they are sufficiently decayed to allow the sun and moisture and air to reach them, they get covered up in the soil too deep for those influences to reach. It is said that fish trapped alive and imbedded in ice for a long time will come to life again. I do not know if that is true. But it is well known that if you dig deep in any old garden, ancient—perhaps forgotten—flowers will appear. They have been neglected or uprooted, but all the time their life is hid below."

"It is a marvelous thought. I wonder if there are such lost or forgotten plants at Heathersleigh."

"I think it very likely."

They sat a few moments in silence.

"As I reflected on my experience in the little garden outside my kitchen," Timothy went on at length, "I began to perceive a larger truth to which it pointed—that there are dormant invisible seeds in the soils of the lives of men and women too, buried deep and perhaps covered over by layers of earth hardened by self-centeredness and neglect. And like the seeds of my garden, these too are seeds that can sprout to life if we spade up these soils and bring sunshine and warmth to them. And who can tell but that it may perhaps also require the rain of our own tears to water them and give them life.

"And I especially thought how the Great Husbandman plants many of these seeds designed for our maturing and our growth and our understanding of life, indeed for so many eternal purposes, into the soils of our fathers and mothers. Some parental soils are rich; some are hard and appear as though nothing could grow in them. But God has planted seeds in *all* human soils. To enable them to sprout and then grow the truths God wants us to learn about him, we must upturn that ground and bring air and rain and the warmth of sunlight to bear on those seeds."

"What about orphans?" asked Amanda, thinking of Sister Hope and Sister Clariss, and now Betsy. "And people with cruel fathers and mothers?"

"Even orphans have parents," replied Timothy, "though they may not know them. Often orphans have wonderful ideas of who their parents might have been. There are seeds of truth God wants them to discover too. They will not be the same truths that you are learning. Betsy certainly has fond memories of her father, even though he may have been a rough sort of man. Every flower garden God plants in the soils of our lives is completely unique. He has planted different seeds for orphans to discover, and still different seeds yet for discovery by children of cruel parents. But the process is one *every* man and every woman in all the world shares."

Timothy paused and thought a moment.

"It is natural, even in cases where parents live full lives, that their sons and daughters do not apprehend everything they are supposed to from those lives. It takes maturity to do so, and often parents are gone before that maturity comes.

"In any event, that is what I call spiritual gardening—upturning those soils to discover what invisible seeds God has for us to discover. They then become flowers of truth we can transplant into the gardens of our own natures. How marvelous of God to enrich our lives in this way."

Amanda nodded, trying to take in the largeness of the concept. "That is a beautiful picture," she said quietly. "What you say reminds me of the last thing I ever heard from dear Bobby's lips."

"I would be interested to hear it."

"He said that the legacies we are meant to discover are often hidden legacies."

"How right the dear man was," said Timothy. "You have already discovered the seeds of your father's hidden legacy sprouting within you. The oiled hinge sprouted the truth that God is always doing the very best he can for his creatures. The scratched board in need of sanding showed you something else, then the bench you just told me about—all these were seeds that were, until those moments of revelation, invisible to you, but which had been planted long before by God in your father, the memory of whose character-soil *you* needed to upturn to bring them to life. Some of these are painful ploughs, tearing deep into the family soil, that seeds of lost virtues and forgotten truths may once more be brought within reach of sun and air and dew."

"And you would call my father's death such a plough in my life?"

"So it seems to me. God works good from all things. And through the pain of his death, the plough has driven deep into your heart. Yet through that breaking are the truth-flowers of his character and his teaching coming to life within you. You didn't come home only sorry for what you had done. You've come home, sorry . . . yes—but also wanting to grow."

Amanda began to cry. Timothy reached out a reassuring hand and laid it on her shoulder.

"I feel so horrible," sobbed Amanda softly. "Now I *want* to know him. I am hungry to know everything about him, about what he thought and did. Yet I was with him all those years, and I wasted them. I could have had so much!"

Another long silence followed. It was broken by the entry of Timothy's housekeeper from the kitchen.

"I have some tea things, Mr. Diggorsfeld," she said.

"Ah, thank you, Mrs. Alvington," said Timothy, rising. "Here, let me take that tray."

She handed him a tray containing two plates and silverware, biscuits, sliced bread with meats and cheeses, napkins, and butter. He set it on a low table between his own chair and the couch where Amanda sat.

"I'll just be back in a minute with the pot of tea," said the housekeeper and left the room.

Amanda's tears subsided. She dabbed her eyes and rose at Timothy's invitation to have something to eat.

26
Light Goes Out of the Fountain

In Vienna, Mrs. Hildegard Halifax sat silently in her favorite easy chair in the sitting room, her large black eyes staring straight ahead.

The huge house on Ebendorfer Strasse, once so full of life and bustling with activity, was empty and quiet like a great many-roomed mausoleum. Its many windows had become like intrusive eyes probing inward with their accusing stares. The Fountain of Light it had once been called. But if there had ever truly been light existing within these brick and windowed walls, there was none now. Whatever it might have more accurately been called, it was now rapidly being extinguished by a power its inhabitants had vastly underestimated—the power of right and truth.

Mrs. Halifax had been reading the morning newspaper, but it now lay still on her lap. Beside her sat a small writing table with her stationery, cards, envelopes, and favorite pens. But she had no more interest in writing at the moment than she did in reading.

She was not a woman given to morose reflection. But some stray thought had inexplicably triggered her thoughts in the direction of events of the previous year. The reminder sent her brain into a renewal of smoldering fury. She had never thought of Amanda as actually her own daughter-in-law. The marriage, if such it could be called, had been hastily arranged merely to insure that the girl remain with them when old Mrs. Thorndike returned to England. The temporary visit to Vienna, which Amanda had originally assumed would last no more than a week or two, would not have allowed them time to turn her fully to their dark cause. A marriage offered the perfect solution. But there had been no permanent affection for her. She had merely been useful to them. She was merely an object to help them achieve their ends. And at first it seemed they had succeeded.

But then she had outwitted them and escaped. How, Mrs. Halifax still couldn't imagine. As a result they were now out of favor with the higher powers of the Alliance. Her house, once a thriving hubbub of intelligence activity, even empty was now scarcely large enough to keep her and Hartwell Barclay out of one another's way, each blaming the other, and both blaming her son Ramsay, for the breakdown that led to Amanda's escape and their subsequent fall from grace. Their petty natures, obscured by people and activity and self-importance, now came to the surface and grated on each other every moment.

Barclay came and went. She hadn't seen Ramsay in weeks. The war was going badly. And Mrs. Halifax had the uncomfortable feeling that she was going to be caught beneath the house of cards when it finally fell.

She did not like being alone.

She was a woman ill at ease, but unfortunately not from the healthy pangs of conscience. Whether or not her conscience was still alive at all would have been a difficult question to get to the bottom of. Instead, she was ill at ease from the indignation that consumed her—anger toward Amanda, toward Ramsay for not being able to control her, toward Barclay for his quiet demeanor and calm superciliousness that never took blame for anything. She was angry with everyone. She would not have been capable of recognizing it as such, but in her own way, Hildegard Halifax was even angry with herself.

She had always been cold and calculating. She cared about the cause, of course, but mostly for the benefits and wealth that came to her as a result. But things were not turning out as she had planned when she took the first steps down this road.

When she and her young son had been sent to England years ago, she knew what was expected of her. And there was no denying that she enjoyed the danger and intrigue. She was proud of having snagged Lord Halifax. He never had so much as a clue he was being seduced until it was too late for him to back out. She had not been a young woman even then, but she had used her wiles to maximum effect. He had been putty in her hands. Seduction came easily for her, one who was consumed with herself. And she had to admit that the luxury she had enjoyed in England was more pleasant than living within the war zone here on the Continent.

Ramsay's mother smiled. In a way it was too bad the old man had died. She might have turned him to the cause eventually too.

Yes, everything according to plan . . . until Amanda—the little vixen! The dark scowl returned to her face. How could such a stupid little thing have turned the tables on them! It was almost as if some invisible power had protected her and kept her out of sight across Europe. All Ramsay's attempts to locate her had been useless until she was safely in England, and it was too late.

Their network was undone, and everyone was blaming them!

A great imprecation suddenly burst from the woman's lips. The same moment her hand came crashing down on her writing table, breaking the eerie silence throughout the house and sending pens and stationery flying in all directions.

27

Timothy's Counsel

Timothy allowed Amanda to compose herself as they prepared their plates and waited for the tea. When they were seated with steaming cups in their hands, he spoke again.

"But this is not why you came to London," he began. "On the telephone you indicated that you wanted to ask for my counsel about your marriage."

Amanda nodded.

"Mother and I have discussed it at length," she said, "but I just don't know what to do."

She went on to share with him the gist of her own thoughts and the conversation she had had with her mother about her options, as well as telling him briefly about Sister Anika and Sister Agatha and their differing views.

Timothy listened carefully. When Amanda was finished he sat for a few moments quietly thinking.

"How long were you actually married before you left?" he asked at length.

"About two weeks," answered Amanda.

"And your, uh . . . Mr. Halifax—I am so sorry to bring this up, but . . .

he was involved with another woman at the time?"

Amanda nodded with embarrassment

"And from what I understand, he later threatened you?"

"He said he would shoot me if I didn't come with him, if that's what you mean."

Timothy nodded slowly as he took in the information.

"Well, Amanda," he said at length, "it seems clear to me that both legally and scripturally, a divorce would certainly be in order. No judge in England would deny such an application. And as a minister, I would say, too, that scripturally the same is true. Your husband committed adultery and that *is* the one clear biblical ground for divorce."

Timothy paused for a moment.

"Tell me about the marriage itself," he asked. "Were you coerced?"

"How do you mean?" replied Amanda. "No one *made* me do it. I was foolish, but I knew what I was doing."

"But according to your mother, there was apparently a certain amount of mind control involved, was there not?"

"I was not myself—that much is for certain. Yes, they twisted my thoughts around. But I went along, foolish though it was."

"Would you say you were pressured, then?"

"Perhaps," nodded Amanda. "Yes . . . pressure was definitely applied when suddenly they suggested Ramsay and I marry so quickly. But I cannot in good conscience say that I was coerced. I was terribly bewildered. Mrs. Thorndike was returning to England. I had no money. I thought I had nowhere to go back here in England. I see now how stupid it was to think that, but that's how confused I was at the time. I couldn't go back to the Pankhursts' home. I didn't want to go to Cousin Gifford's and Martha's. I felt almost as though I had no choice but to stay. And Mr. Barclay convinced me that I would be seen as a spy if I returned."

Again Timothy was silent. When he spoke again, his words were not what Amanda had expected to hear.

"Amanda," he said, "have you considered the possibility of an annulment?"

Amanda stared back across the table.

"An . . . annulment?" she repeated.

"That's right—filing papers to have the marriage declared invalid . . . as if it had never existed."

"No . . . I hadn't thought of such a thing. Is that a possibility?"

"I will have to look into it," replied Timothy. "But I think a strong case could be made in favor of it, especially given your family background and what is now known about Mr. Halifax and his mother's spy connections. I think it is a strong possibility that their chief motive may have been to lure you into their camp for the purpose of their spy ring and the war. That alone might be sufficient grounds. The fact that you escaped and left him immediately after learning of the other woman, and that you and he were only married for two weeks prior to that time—yes, I think you have a very strong case for annulment."

"It would certainly be a relief not having to go through life as a divorced woman. But I want to make sure it is also the right thing to do."

"We shall all pray about it further," said Timothy. "You talk to your mother. In the meantime I will consult with a solicitor who is in my congregation. We will need to think through the implications. It may even be that the marriage would not be recognized in England at all. But I will look into all that for you."

"I am so grateful," said Amanda.

"And if and when the time comes, I will help you with the papers and legalities."

"Perhaps Uncle Hugh would help."

"I will talk to him as well."

"Thank you, Timothy. I owe you so much . . . we all do. I only wish I had known sooner what a good friend you were."

Another long silence followed. When Timothy spoke again, it was in an entirely new vein, and was even more unexpected than his suggestion of a few minutes earlier.

"Amanda," he said, "I would like to talk to you about something else—your future after all this is settled."

"My future?" repeated Amanda, puzzled.

Timothy nodded. "It is no accident," he said, "that in God's economy you are now seeing things much differently than you once did. I believe God has a purpose in it."

"What kind of purpose?"

"A purpose for you."

"What do you mean?"

"I believe God intends to use your experience in the lives of others."

Amanda smiled. "Catharine said almost the same thing on the way here."

"Then perhaps this is more than simply a whim of mine. It may well be that other young women who do not understand how to rightly relate to the authorities in their lives, especially their parents, will benefit by what you have to tell them. Betsy, for example. I think her coming may be involved in what I am saying."

"But how could I help them? I'm the worst kind of example."

"Perhaps that is the very thing God will use."

"But how?"

"By sharing your experience and the wisdom you have gained from it. Virtue is so desperately needed today among young people. God may want to use your experience, even your mistakes—*especially* your mistakes—to help others see the need for virtue."

Amanda considered his words thoughtfully.

"I suppose that would be some consolation," she said, "if good could come out of it somehow."

"That's always the way God works—bringing good out of circumstances that seem worthless to us. Never forget, it is dung, refuse, and waste that makes living things grow most vigorously."

Amanda smiled at the analogy.

"I appreciate what you have said, Timothy," she said. "I have been so unvirtuous in my attitudes all my life. So what you say sounds strange and foreign. But I can promise you that I will pray and think about it further."

"That is all I could hope for."

"On the train Catharine and I prayed together. One of the things I prayed was that God would show me what to do with regard to my future. After what you have said, I will continue to pray in the same way."

The two fell silent a moment.

"—But we have been talking for nearly an hour about me and my problems," said Amanda. "I am curious how things are with *you*—your church and your parishioners, I mean."

Timothy tried to smile, but without success.

"I am afraid things are not much better on that front," he said, "though I very much appreciate your asking."

"People are still complaining?"

Timothy nodded. "Yes, and I fear their complaints are striking root at denominational headquarters in Birmingham. I have preached nothing within a hundred miles of controversy since the trouble broke, but

I am met with the same cold, silent stares from half the congregation every Sunday."

"What is to be done?"

"I honestly do not know, my dear ... I honestly don't know."

28

Hang On to the Lifeline— God Is Good

♦ ♦ ♦

*L*ater that afternoon Timothy accompanied Amanda by taxi to her hotel, where they met Catharine and enjoyed dinner together. The following morning the two sisters rode again to New Hope for breakfast with the minister before their eleven-o'clock train back to Devon.

The moment Timothy had seen them off at the station, he returned home and telephoned Jocelyn.

"Hello, Jocelyn, my dear," he said when she came on the line. "I just left your two lovely daughters at the train—they are on their way back to you."

"Was it a good visit?" asked Jocelyn.

"Wonderful. Amanda and I had an excellent talk. I hope I gave her some helpful things to think about. I'm sure she will fill you in. She is maturing greatly in the Lord, Jocelyn. You have a great deal to be proud of."

The telephone was silent for several moments.

"Jocelyn...?"

"Yes, I am still here, Timothy," said Jocelyn. "I just—"

Her voice faltered.

"What is it, my dear?"

"Yes, I see that Amanda is doing well, but sometimes I ... I just become—"

She began to cry.

"I'm sorry ... I can't help it. Sometimes ... I become so angry for what happened, for what she went through ... for what we all went through."

"Angry ... angry at who, Jocelyn? Angry at God?"

"I don't know, Timothy," Jocelyn replied, "—at everyone. Angry at the Pankhursts, angry at my brother-in-law Hugh, especially angry at the Halifaxes and that Hartwell Barclay—angry at them all for being so willing to take advantage of Amanda's resentments. Any of them could have turned Amanda's heart toward home at any time. But none of them did. They used her. And sometimes I'm even angry with Amanda herself for being so foolish and stubborn all those years. Not Amanda as she is now, but I confess I still get angry with the old Amanda, for putting us through this—for putting herself through it when it was all so unnecessary. We were a good family, Timothy, a fun family—*why* couldn't she see it!"

Jocelyn broke down, crying in earnest.

"Now it's all gone," she went on. "I even get angry at myself and Charles too. Oh, if only we hadn't been so hard on Amanda! If only we had let her live a more normal life here at home. I don't know, Timothy ... maybe anger toward God is mixed up in it all too. It just hurts so much to have lost Charles and George, and to see Amanda have to suffer now."

"I know ... I hope I understand some of your pain," replied Timothy tenderly. "In the midst of my own grief for Charles I battle with similar emotions. Yet all that has happened to you has helped make you who you are today, and to deepen your trust in our Father."

"But I don't care about myself!" sobbed Jocelyn. "Timothy, if God is sovereign, then why did George and Charles have to die, and why does Amanda have to suffer, so that I can be who I am today? It's not fair that *they* should have had to suffer so that I could be strong! I don't want to be strong—I only wanted a godly family, and now it's gone!"

"They did not suffer *so* that you could be strong," said Timothy. "Suffering is one of the intrinsic components God has allowed as part of human existence. People do not understand why he has done so, and even use the fact to say they do not believe in God at all. Yet God's purposes are eternal not temporary. If he is able to use the suffering of this life toward eternal good, then foolish is the man or woman who looks at this very tool in his hand—a tool he will use for our ultimate benefit, even, it may be, our ultimate perfection in the next life—and say they do not believe in the Father-sculptor who wields it."

"But it is so hard to understand when you're in the middle of it!"

"We do not have to enjoy suffering. How can we? But we must look to the Father and see it as his divine instrument, not the working of a cruel and impersonal fate. Suffering came to your family—why, I do not know. Only God does. But through suffering, God will always make us strong if we will let him, as you have let him through yours."

"But I'm so tired of it, Timothy! I'm tired of having to be strong, tired of having to trust God. It is so hard! Sometimes I can't help but think we would all have been better off if Charles and I had never tried so hard to follow the Bible, never become Christians at all. Oh, you know I don't mean that, but it is so confusing!"

"I have no answers, Jocelyn," said Timothy softly. "In this world there is suffering, and why it is dispensed where and when it is will remain one of the great mysteries of life and the human equation. I only know that God will make all right in the end, and having done so, all his creation will look back and say, 'Everything was *always* right, only we did not know how to see it.' I believe your dear husband believed that. And I know down in your heart you believe it too. Therefore, the best way to revere Charles's memory is to hang on to his lifeline, that God is good, and always will be good, and that all will work for good."

Gradually the passion of Jocelyn's tears subsided.

"I would trade anything that I am," Jocelyn said at length, "I would trade all my own growth to have them back."

"Charles and George joined the navy knowing they might be giving their lives for their country," said Timothy. "They didn't die *so* you could be strong, but you will grow strong if you can trust the Father in the midst of your grief."

"And I just cannot help thinking there might have been something more we could have done to hasten Amanda's homecoming."

"You mustn't blame yourself. You could not have known what was going to happen. Homecoming always depends on the prodigal. The father in the Lord's parable prayed and waited patiently, but could not urge his son home until the son *himself* said, 'I will arise and go.' Amanda could have come home anytime she wanted. She could have ended her sojourn in the far country years sooner. But she didn't. I believe she always knew in her heart of hearts, during the darkest nights when she was alone with her thoughts, that you were here waiting to love her. But she waited. And the cost of that waiting is something you all have to bear."

Timothy paused.

"But she *is* home now," he added. "For that we are all grateful. Some prodigals never do return in this life. But yours has. It is a return that will always be tinged with grief, but is nonetheless a return of her heart to its home."

"I know... I know. Forgive me, Timothy," sighed Jocelyn. "Sometimes, even now, the sadness overwhelms me. But I realize we went above and beyond trying to do what we *thought* was right, even though it all seemed to turn out so wrong."

"Not all. You mustn't forget George and Catharine. And you did more than what you thought was right—you *did* right."

"But you must see that it is very confusing."

"Of course."

"When Amanda was gone, I wanted so badly to try to find her and go see her. I wanted to write her letters and send her packages and gifts and birthday reminders. I wanted to do so much. But I knew I had to respect her wishes to let her alone, give her freedom to live by her decision, give her the very freedom she never thought we were capable of giving her. She will never know how hard that was, just to let her go, and let her wallow in her waywardness and do nothing when everything in my mother's heart cried out to love her!"

Again Jocelyn began to cry, this time softly.

"I feel so worthless and unspiritual, Timothy," she said. "You talk about the strength this has brought me. I certainly feel none of it. I just feel helpless! How can I help Amanda through this grief she feels for her father and her brother, when I feel it too? How can I help her through the dilemma she is in about her marriage?"

"Jocelyn, you need to just be who you are, and hang on to that lifeline that God is good. Amanda needs that more than anything—to remember that God is good."

"But none of this seems good!" Jocelyn said, crying again. "How can it be from God?"

"The tragedy is not *sent* by God," replied Timothy, "but it is *used* by him. God is our holy Father. Though this world is fallen, it is still his, and suffering and tragedy, prodigality and pain, all result because his independent, rebellious children insist on taking their lives into their own hands. But he *will* make all right in the end. We know that, and we must hang on to it."

Another pause came over the telephone line for several long seconds.

"Every human pain, every disappointment, every tear," Timothy added after a moment, "is specially designed for use by the Father's hand to sculpt our characters into their eternal shape. We can trust him, Jocelyn dear... we can *trust* him to do that work within us. And if we will but yield the tool into his hand, he will mold our beings into the likeness of his own dear Son."

29

Thoughtful Return

*L*ike her mother after the telephone conversation with Timothy, Amanda too was thoughtful that afternoon on the train as she and Catharine rode back to Devon. Little was said as they sat side by side gazing out at the passing countryside. In contrast to Amanda's pensive mood, Catharine was even more bubbly than usual, with an occasional smile breaking out on her face, though from what cause she didn't say. At the same time she seemed to sense her sister's need to keep to herself.

As the train continued along, Amanda's thoughts drifted back to all that she and Timothy had discussed on the previous afternoon, especially allowing seeds from the garden of her father's nature to sprout and blossom in the soil of her own life. Then her thoughts came to dwell on his final comments about her future.

Thinking about what lay ahead was new for Amanda. For years, especially during the months since leaving Vienna, merely getting through the present had been challenge enough. All of a sudden Timothy had put the notion in her brain that life could be good again. It was almost too overwhelming a thought to take—that even now, after all this, her life might actually amount to something.

She had had such dreams and plans when she was young. How shortsighted they all seemed now! She had changed the world, all right... for the worse. She had hurt so many people, herself most of all. But if what Timothy said was true and God did have a purpose for her life even after such failure, was it really possible that she might have the chance to give back a little, to help where she had hurt, to make restitution for what she had done and been?

She knew she could never make it up to her father. That realization would pain her for the rest of her days. So restitution would have to come in other ways. She could try to make it up as best she might to her mother and Catharine. And perhaps, as Timothy said, she could help other girls and young women, that healing might grow in their families out of the soil of her own mistakes.

She smiled as she remembered Timothy's analogy. That's what she had made of her life all right—manure! Yet perhaps she could put that manure of failure to work to help cause good things to grow in other people's lives.

The thought sent a surge of hopefulness through her heart. She realized she had not felt *hope* for longer than she could remember. She had been so discouraged for so long, thinking that life could never again contain happiness. She had almost given up altogether, resigning herself to living out her existence in a dreary continuum of enduring one grey day after another. She had forgotten what hope and optimism, enthusiasm and joy, even felt like.

Amanda smiled to herself. It was a smile that contained both sadness for the past and new hope for the future. Perhaps, she thought, the way God's people were meant to change the world was by being men and women of goodness and character, being true sons and daughters of God, rather than by changing things about the world itself. She had had it all backward when she was young.

Her father understood that principle, she thought. The realization led him to step aside from the world's politics in order to carry out a work in a much different realm—a realm she did not have eyes to see at the time. The very characteristics that used to bother her about him were nothing more than the natural result of his trying to live—really live!—by the principles of the Sermon on the Mount. He was trying to be a man of spiritual character. He had come to recognize the requirement she had for so long been unable to see—the need to change, not the world, but oneself.

I am sorry again, Lord, Amanda breathed to herself. *And I am sorry for not seeing your work in my father for what it was. But, Lord, I want to submit myself now to your transforming hand. I always thought I wanted to become someone of importance in the world. Now I ask you to truly make a lady of me—your daughter. I want to make a difference in the world, Lord—but for you and your kingdom. I ask you to carry out your work in me. And if there is anything you can use to help other girls, as Timothy said, then please do so. I was not a good girl. I was too selfish for good qualities to grow within me. But I ask you now, Lord, to take what is left of my life and make a virtuous woman of me. And if the story of my prodigalness can help anyone else, then I will be glad. I am willing for you to do what you want with me.*

She closed her eyes and sat back as the train continued to bounce along, at peace with her thoughts. Gradually she dozed off. When she came to herself an hour later, the train was slowing down and they were nearly home.

Almost as if in answer to her conversation with Timothy and her own prayer, as they left the Milverscombe train station, Amanda saw Chelsea Winters on the sidewalk. She smiled and stopped.

"Hello, Chelsea," said Amanda. "How have you been? I haven't seen you for a long time."

"Hello, Miss Rutherford," replied Chelsea. "I saw you come out of the station, but I didn't know if you would remember me."

"Of course I remember you, Chelsea," rejoined Amanda. She glanced around, but the girl was apparently alone.

"Where is your mother, Chelsea?"

"I came to town by myself."

"Have you thought about what I told you before?"

"Yes, Miss Rutherford."

"I hope you are not thinking any more about going away to London to be a suffragette like a foolish girl named Amanda Rutherford."

"I don't know... sometimes I think I would like to do something exciting like that."

"It is not exciting at all," rejoined Amanda, "but a way to get yourself into a great deal of trouble."

Amanda paused momentarily as a thought struck her.

"Why don't you come to the Hall with Catharine and me," said Amanda. "Would you like to do that?"

"Yes, Miss Rutherford!"

"When is your mother expecting you home?"

"Not for two hours."

"Good—we will have tea and biscuits and then take you home after a little while. Have you met Betsy?"

"Who's Betsy?" asked Chelsea as she began walking between Amanda and Catharine to where Hector sat waiting for them with a horse and two-seater buggy.

"A girl about your age who is staying with us."

"Why is she staying with you?"

"Because her daddy was killed, and God sent her to us."

"Did God really send her?" asked Chelsea.

"I think so."

"Why would God send her to you, Miss Rutherford?"

"I don't know, Chelsea. Perhaps so that she could learn some things she needed to know."

"What kinds of things?"

"I don't know yet. Sometimes we are not able to see all that God is doing. Maybe one of the reasons is so that you and she could become friends."

30

The Greater Victory

◆ ◆ ◆

*L*ater that same night, Amanda lay in bed recalling the events of the afternoon.

She could hardly believe what had come out of her mouth when she was talking to Chelsea and Betsy. The comments, when they came, were so unexpected that she hardly had time to stop and ask herself how she could have had such words to say in the first place.

◆ ◆ ◆

Was your father really killed?" Amanda overheard Chelsea ask Betsy when the two girls were alone for a few minutes after the others had gone into the next room.

Amanda and Jocelyn were in the corridor just outside the open door. They had not been able to get Betsy to utter so much as a word about what had happened, so when they heard Chelsea's question, they could not help pausing to stand out of sight and listen.

A barely whispered "yes" prompted Chelsea's next question. "How do you know? Were you there?" she persisted.

"Uh-huh," Betsy said almost inaudibly.

"Were you scared?" they heard Chelsea ask.

"Oh yes," Betsy spoke up. "I thought they would kill me too."

"What happened? Did they have a gun?"

"Yes, and they came in after my father, yelling at him, and I was hiding in the loft where he had just put me a minute before. Then they argued, and they shot him."

Jocelyn's eyes were already filling with tears as she and Amanda listened from the hallway. It was obvious from the quiver in Betsy's voice that she was about to cry. What the poor child must have been through!

But all at once a hardness came into the girl's voice that prevented the tears.

"I hate them," she said. "When I grow up, I will go back to Looe. I will find them and kill them myself. I hate them, I hate them!"

At this outburst, Chelsea fell silent.

Jocelyn and Amanda looked at each other in shock. They had never heard Betsy say such a thing. Mother and daughter hesitated only a moment before Amanda left her mother's side and walked into the room.

Chelsea stood motionless—momentarily cowed into silence—an expression of fear on her face at Betsy's vehement declaration.

"There is something even better than killing your enemies that you can do to repay them, Betsy," Amanda said calmly as she approached.

"What!" retorted Betsy, glancing around, her voice still angry, her dark hazel eyes afire.

Amanda waited a moment before answering, hoping Betsy would calm down. She put her hand on her shoulder and slowly sat down beside her. Chelsea came and stood on the other side.

"You can forgive them," said Amanda at length.

"I will never forgive the men who killed my father!" shouted Betsy.

"Then you will one day become just as bad as they are."

"No I won't!"

"Hate is hate, Betsy," said Amanda, speaking slowly and

calmly. "It was hate that made them shoot your father. If you hate them in return, you have become just like them. The only way to win, and have victory over both those men and the memory of what they did, is to forgive them."

Betsy seemed hardly able to take in the idea. Perhaps it was the thought of gaining victory over her father's murderers that temporarily silenced her.

"You see, Betsy," Amanda went on, "sometimes hate *is* justified. This can be a terrible world, and sometimes bad things happen. It was an evil thing those men did. They are bad men. No one would blame you for hating them. No one would say you were wrong to hate them. It is natural to be angry with those who have done us wrong, or have done wrong to someone we love. But God wants us to lay down our anger and our hatred so that he can grow something better in its place in our hearts."

"What?" asked Betsy, her voice calming.

"Love," answered Amanda. "God wants to help us *love* those who have done us wrong."

"How could I possibly love them?" said Betsy, more in disbelief than anger.

"God loves them."

"I could never love the men who killed my father."

"I think perhaps you will one day, Betsy. And you will be happier for it."

"I don't want to love them. I want to hate them."

"God will help you want to love them," replied Amanda. "Then he will help you forgive them so that you can love them. It is not something you can do all by yourself. None of us are able to love very well. Do you know, Betsy, I did not even love my father as I should. So in that way, I am even worse than you, for I am sure you loved your father very much, didn't you?"

Betsy nodded. "My father was a good man," she said, "and sometimes I cannot stand it." She began to cry.

"I'm sure he was," replied Amanda, drawing the girl to her tenderly. "I wish I could have known him. But, Betsy, my father is dead now too. That is something you and I share. And though you hate those men who killed your father, I actually hated my own father for a time, even though he was a good man. Hatred was inside me, Betsy, and it nearly ruined my life. I also hated

God. All that hatred that was in me I am now finally learning to get rid of. It is hard because, as my dear sister told me not long ago, the person I need to forgive most of all is myself. I feel terribly guilty and unworthy of God's love, for I was a very unkind and selfish girl. But I know that forgiveness will heal my guilt, though it hasn't done so completely yet, just as it will heal your hatred. I hope you will get rid of your hatred too. Jesus will help you, if you will let him."

Amanda could hear her mother quietly weeping in the hallway as she softly hurried away to her room.

◆ ◆ ◆

Amanda lay in her bed, eyes open, staring into the quiet blackness of the night as the memory of the day's incident receded.

Something had changed for her. She couldn't quite put her finger on it, but a sense of peace had slowly begun to steal upon her—a peace she hadn't felt in a very long time—a peace, now that she thought of it, she had perhaps *never* felt before. And with it came the growing conviction, still vague and undefined, that Timothy was right, that she indeed had something to offer girls such as Betsy and Chelsea.

"Thank you, Lord," Amanda breathed quietly. *"I think I am beginning to know—really know—that you love me . . . thank you."*

31

Be a Good Girl

◆ ◆ ◆

*A*lone in her own bed, Elsbet Conlin also lay awake.

The reliving of her father's murder followed by Amanda's words had triggered a memory she had till then all but forgotten. If this was the season at Heathersleigh for remembering a father's words, the Spirit-prompted activity was not limited to the daughter of Sir Charles Rutherford.

Betsy had been overwhelmed these last few weeks with the knowledge that her father was dead. But now for a few moments her father was alive again in her thoughts. Just when this incident she was remembering had taken place she wasn't sure. She was probably nine or ten.

──────── ◆ ◆ ◆ ────────

Betsy," said Sully Conlin, sitting his daughter down on a wooden chair and gazing intently into her eyes. "If anything ever happens to me, I want you to be a good girl."

Betsy stared back, not exactly alarmed to hear him talk so, but sobered by his tone and expression. He looked weary and suddenly older than she had ever seen him. How could she possibly understand the world he lived in, and his occasional worries if something went wrong?

"My own mama always told me to be a good boy," Conlin said in a strangely nostalgic tone. Then he smiled sadly. "I haven't been as good as I should have been," he went on. "Because when a man goes to sea he sometimes gets mixed up with bad men."

He leaned close and cupped her soft white chin and cheeks in his rough, scarred hand and looked deep into her eyes. "But, Betsy, don't get mixed up with bad people," he said. "Listen to your papa when he tells you to find *good* people after I'm gone— good people that will help you be good too. Will you promise that?"

"Yes, Papa," nodded Betsy, "I promise."

"If you are a good girl," he said, leaning back, "you will grow up to be a lady like your mother. You want to be like your mother, don't you, Betsy?"

Betsy nodded vigorously.

"Then you be a good girl, Betsy. And you find people to help you be good. If you do, you'll make me proud of you. That's all I want, Betsy, is for you to be a good girl like your mother."

──────── ◆ ◆ ◆ ────────

Even though Betsy had forgotten her father's words for a time, they now penetrated deep.

"Be a good girl... grow up to be a lady... make me proud of you... find people to help you be good...."

She was only a month from her fourteenth birthday and was becoming a woman more rapidly than she realized. With good food, regular meals, and work and exercise, her body was filling out and changing even more quickly since her arrival at Heathersleigh. But the changes coming to her were not all physical. Now she was beginning to think... think about important things... think about what kind of person she wanted to be, and what she wanted the girl called Elsbet Conlin to become.

In every life there is a time for remembering, a season when thoughts turn inward, a time when decisions are made to point one's footsteps in lifelong directions. That moment might come at fifty or at ten. For Amanda, circumstances had forced it upon her at twenty-five. Her father and mother had not begun to reflect and turn inward until their late thirties. But for Betsy Conlin, though she was much younger, such a season was now at hand.

As both Amanda and Betsy privately recalled the conversation they had shared earlier that day, neither knew how deeply Amanda's words had penetrated into her mother's heart.

The widow of Charles Rutherford also lay in bed thinking and praying that night.

It was heartbreakingly bittersweet to think of, but with tears in her eyes, Jocelyn realized that the vision of her husband—the dear man who had loved her into self-assurance, into personhood, almost into faith itself (for how could she have ever experienced God's love had he not loved her first?)—was still alive. Even in his death, like God's Son whom he served, Charles continued to give life. In his own way, his spirit continued on in this house, this refuge of life as he had made it for her, and was still giving life to others.

She thought about Heathersleigh and what it had always been to her. Charles had helped make it the personal retreat and oasis where she could grow and become the person God wanted her to be.

As she lay thinking, Jocelyn remembered the card she had given Charles just after his fifty-third birthday, with the picture of the great sprawling tree in full leaf. The moment she had seen it, she had been reminded of her husband. Charles had always been, she told him, a towering oak, a permanent trunk of strength in a crowded and busy world. He was a secure stronghold that would never change, and she was not the only one who had found rest under the protective shade of his branches.

But now he was gone. And people were looking to her to be what Charles had been. Sometimes it overwhelmed her.

And yet . . . if his spirit and vision did live on, perhaps that place of rest, that oasis, that refuge, could continue on too in the lives of others. Even now, in the daughter whose homecoming he had not lived to see, Charles's life was bearing fruit.

Then she thought of the acorns of an oak, which must die in order to be ground into meal, then washed with ashes to remove the bitterness. And with the thought came Jesus' words, "Unless a grain of wheat fall into the ground and die it remains alone, but if it die it brings forth much fruit."

Jocelyn remembered what Timothy had said on the evening of their return from the memorial service several months ago, when he had challenged them to look toward the future as an opportunity rather than a tragedy.

"*In many ways,*" came Timothy's voice into her memory, "*women are the stronger of the two halves of humanity when something greater than physical strength is required. I am excited to see what might lie ahead. I think God has some great thing in store. Whatever it is will grow out of the ashes of your pain, and will flower as the result of the compassion perfected by your suffering.*"

And with the words came again the reminder of the Chalet of Hope, where Amanda had at last been turned toward home.

What do you have to do here, Lord? Jocelyn prayed. *You have provided such abundance. And though Charles is gone, the peace and strength he gave somehow lives on at Heathersleigh. How do you want to use it in the lives of others?*

Her prayers fell silent and her thoughts returned to the man who had been her oak tree. Would such a time come when Heathersleigh was again giving life as Charles had allowed it to give her—a place of peace, a place to learn who you were, a place to learn to accept God's love?

Recalling the conversation between Amanda and the two girls earlier that day, Jocelyn thought, perhaps that time had already begun.

PART III

Spring 1916

32

A Letter

*T*he letter from Sister Hope that arrived at Heathersleigh Hall just after the first of the new year was greeted with great excitement. The moment Amanda saw the postmark, she sat down and hastily tore open the envelope.

Dear Amanda, she read,
   All the sisters send their warm greetings. We still talk of you often and wish the distance between us were not so great so we could see you. Many have come and gone to and from the chalet through the years, but few have made the impact in our hearts that you did. I am not certain I can explain it other than to say that you are greatly loved, and we all remember you—in spite of all that happened—very fondly.

As Amanda read the words, tears filled her eyes.

   This is one of the reasons I am writing. I feel God saying that perhaps I do need to see you again. For some years I have been putting off a visit to England. It is something I know I need to do for several reasons. There are two or three people I must see, and some unresolved mission business concerning my late husband that should have been attended to years ago. And, too, perhaps it is time for me to put a few of the memories of my own past to rest in a deeper way than I have been able to do from afar. But most of all, Amanda, I feel I am to see you.
   You know how we rely on the Lord's leading concerning those who come to the chalet. For some time I have felt him telling me that you are involved in what—or whom—he has next for us. I do not know why, nor do I know how you are involved. But somehow I feel a deep urgency simply to see you again face-to-face.
   What would you and your mother think of having a guest from Switzerland visit you for a brief stay?
   I plan to be in England in April.
   Again . . . to you, your mother, and your sister, our deepest sympathies

*and prayers continue to be with you for the loss of your loved ones. God will
give you strength—trust him!*

With great love, your sister in Christ,
Hope Guinarde

"Mother . . . Mother, look!" cried Amanda, running and handing the
letter to Jocelyn. "Sister Hope wants to come for a visit! I'm going to
write her back immediately!"

33

A Fall

$\mathcal{A}$ spring celebration was planned for Maggie's seventy-eighth birthday. All the inhabitants of Heathersleigh rose with Hector and the animals in order to begin preparations for the feast that would be held that
afternoon at the Hall in Maggie's honor.

Midway through the morning, Betsy came into the kitchen with a
handful of roses she had just picked.

"They are beautiful, Betsy dear!" said Jocelyn.

"May I take them over to Grandma Maggie?" asked Betsy.

"You mean . . . now? I don't suppose there would be any harm.—In
fact, that is a good idea!" added Jocelyn. "Wish her a wonderful birthday, and tell her we shall be over a little after noon to bring her to the
Hall."

Betsy was out the door like a flash and running across the meadow,
black hair, yellow dress, and multicolored clump of roses in her hand
all flying in the breeze.

Jocelyn laughed as she watched the girl's short, stocky legs flying
across the grass. "If half those roses survive by the time she reaches the
cottage," she said, "it will be a miracle!"

"She really loves Grandma Maggie, doesn't she?" said Catharine at
the table behind her as she put the finishing touches on the frosting of
a large layer cake.

"And it warms my heart to see it," nodded Jocelyn. "What must it have been like to grow up without a mother, or grandmother, or even an aunt—the poor girl!"

Jocelyn was passing the window again some twenty minutes later when she saw Betsy walking slowly back across the meadow, the same bouquet of flowers still clutched in her hand.

"What is it, Betsy?" she said as Betsy entered the house. "Why didn't you give Maggie the flowers?"

"I couldn't find her," answered Betsy.

"What do you mean?" asked Jocelyn, puzzled.

"I knocked and knocked, but she never came to the door."

"Did you look around? She might have been in the garden," said Jocelyn.

"I walked all around the cottage, then to the barn," said Betsy. "I called out too, but she didn't answer."

Jocelyn's eyebrows knit together.

"Catharine, Amanda," she called up the stairs behind her. "I am going over to Maggie's."

"But I thought we weren't going until—" began Catharine from the landing.

"Maggie didn't answer Betsy's knock," interrupted Jocelyn. "I have an uneasy feeling. I want to check on her."

Both her daughters were already downstairs and on the way outside with her. Without waiting for Hector's help, they hitched one of the buggies and climbed in. Jocelyn slapped the reins with her wrist and yelled to the horse, and did not let up with her shouts until he was in full gallop across the meadow.

They flew into the clearing three or four minutes later. Jocelyn leapt out before the carriage was fully stopped and sprinted toward the cottage. The door was unlocked as always. Jocelyn hurried in, her two daughters on her heels.

"Maggie . . . Maggie, are you home!" called Jocelyn as she ran through the rooms. She found her elderly friend lying on the pantry floor.

"Maggie—what happened!" cried Jocelyn, kneeling down beside her.

"I am all right, Jocelyn dear," moaned Maggie softly. "I just couldn't make Betsy hear my voice. But I am not in too much pain."

"Where does it hurt?"

"It's my hip. I was being clumsy and tried to reach too high. . . ."

"Did you fall?"

Maggie nodded. "I'm afraid I slipped," she said softly.

"Your face is pale.—Catharine, run for Dr. Cecil."

In seconds Catharine was out the door.

"What can I do for you, Grandma Maggie?" asked Amanda. "Would you like tea . . . or water?"

"That sounds delightful, dear. Some water . . . then when I can sit up to drink it, I would enjoy a cup of tea."

"How long have you been here?" asked Jocelyn, trying to get herself under Maggie and gently lift her to a sitting position without causing more pain.

"Perhaps two or three hours. But you are here now—I will be fine."

Amanda arrived with a glass of water and helped her swallow two or three sips.

"Thank you, dear . . . I am feeling better already," sighed Maggie wearily. "—Not much of a birthday," she added. "I am sorry to be such a bother, and that I've ruined your party for today."

"Maggie—think nothing of it," said Jocelyn. "We will just bring our party here and spend the day with you instead."

"What about all the people who were coming?"

"Let us take care of everything," insisted Jocelyn. "You just rest.— Here, put your arm around my shoulder . . . come, Amanda . . . we will try to get you into your bed, if it doesn't hurt too much."

Slowly and carefully Jocelyn and Amanda got Maggie to her feet, then made their way to her bed, mostly carrying her to keep weight off the hip which Jocelyn feared might be broken. Neither of them missed the wince of pain that came to Maggie's face when they lifted her.

"I don't care how you object," said Jocelyn as at length they eased her down. "We are finally going to have a telephone line installed here to the cottage. That will be your birthday present."

"It would have done me no good today, dear—I was unable to move."

"Nevertheless, you *must* be able to get in touch with us."

Maggie nodded. She did not like to give in either to the advancement of technology or the advancement of age. But she could no longer deny that both were rapidly gaining on her.

"You are right," smiled Maggie. "I am sorry for being such a stubborn old woman."

"You are a *dear* old woman!" rejoined Jocelyn. "And I love you too much not to take the best care of you I can."

34

I Want to Be Good Like Daddy Said

A week later Amanda came upon Betsy sitting alone and quiet on the first-floor stair landing.

Amanda approached. "You look like you're thinking about something," she said.

Betsy glanced up toward her.

"I have two ears that are available for listening if you would like them," Amanda added, sitting down beside her.

"I was thinking about something my daddy once said to me," said Betsy.

"What did he tell you?"

"That he wanted me to grow up to be a good girl."

"That is good advice," smiled Amanda. "And do you want to be?"

"Yes . . . I want to be good like Daddy said my mother was."

It was quiet a moment or two.

"I was also remembering," Betsy added, "what you said about things growing in my heart."

Amanda took in Betsy's words with surprise, though she did not show it. She had not suspected that the serious things they discussed had penetrated into the girl's consciousness. At Betsy's age, it was difficult to tell what she was thinking, and to distinguish between the child-girl oblivious to life's meaning, and the slowly dawning woman awakening within her that was beginning to be drawn by deeper currents.

As Amanda sat quietly at Betsy's side, a silent prayer rose within her. *Lord,* she prayed, *whatever Betsy needs at this moment, give me the right words.*

At last she turned toward Betsy. "Do you know something, Betsy?" said Amanda. "Your daddy was a wise man to tell you to be good. But do you know that you can't be good all by yourself? You need someone's help."

"Whose?"

"Do you remember Mr. Diggorsfeld from London?"

Betsy nodded. "Can *he* help me be good?"

Amanda smiled. "Well, Mr. Diggorsfeld has helped me," she said, "and he has helped our whole family. But the greatest help he has given us is to tell us about someone *else*. Do you remember when he told you about the man called Jesus?"

"Yes. I remember him saying that he lived in people's hearts, though I still cannot understand it. I don't think my daddy knew about Jesus."

"Neither did my daddy until Mr. Diggorsfeld told him. But he does now. And maybe your father knows about Jesus now too. What Mr. Diggorsfeld said," Amanda went on, "is that when Jesus lives in our hearts, he helps us to become better children, and better men and women. So, Betsy, *Jesus* is the one who helps us become good."

"My daddy told me to find people who would help me be good."

"That was wise of him to say. Jesus is that person, though your father didn't know it before he died. He is the *only* one who can."

"How does he do it?"

"You have to ask for his help," replied Amanda.

"But didn't Mr. Diggorsfeld say we couldn't see him?"

"Yes, but he can still help us . . . inside."

A puzzled look came over Betsy's face.

"There is a garden in your heart, Betsy. And if you ask him to come live there, Jesus will be the gardener and will make good things grow in it and help take out the ugly, nasty weeds."

Amanda paused and looked at Betsy. When she spoke again, her voice was tender.

"Do you know that there are weeds growing in the garden of your heart?" she said. "The weeds are called sin. We all need Jesus' help to get rid of those weeds so that good flowers will grow. You're not as good as you want to be, are you, Betsy?"

Betsy shook her head.

"Neither am I," said Amanda. "I am not good at all. But I want to be too, just like you do. You have told me that there is hatred growing in your garden."

"My heart doesn't feel like there are good flowers growing in it," said Betsy sadly.

"You're right. Hatred is a dreadfully ugly weed," rejoined Amanda. "And it will ruin your whole garden if you do not get rid of it. It is not very pretty, just like selfishness and meanness. All those weeds were

growing in my garden too. I was not a nice person at all, Betsy. I was
mean and cranky and disrespectful."

"You!"

"Yes—I wasn't very nice at all."

"Are those weeds gone now?" asked Betsy. "They must be, because
you are one of the nicest people I have ever known."

"Thank you, Betsy," smiled Amanda. She put her arm around the
girl and drew her close. Betsy let her head rest on Amanda's shoulder.
"They are not completely gone. But Jesus helps me every day to pull a
few more weeds out of my garden to make room for the flowers he is
growing inside me."

"Does he pull the weeds out for you?"

"No, we have to pull out our own weeds."

"I don't know how to."

"He helps us."

"How?"

Amanda thought a moment.

"I was a very selfish girl for most of my life," she went on. "I thought
about no one but myself for so many years that the weed of selfishness
became a very big weed with very deep roots. The selfishness weed grew
so big within me that there was hardly room for anything else to grow.
It is not the kind of weed that can be pulled out all at once. And Jesus
wants *me* to pull it out because that is part of what he wants me to
learn, how to put others first instead of myself. But even though he
doesn't pull that weed out for me, every time I reach down to try, he
places his hand on top of mine and gives me the strength to pull up the
sin-weed a little more. So Jesus and I are working hard together to get
selfishness out of me. And I hope that one day soon, if I *keep* trying and
keep letting him help me, that the weed of selfishness will be gone from
the garden of my heart. The roots may never come out altogether, and
may keep sprouting tiny selfishness weeds all my life. But with the main
weed gone, I will be able to pull those out myself whenever they start to
grow. That's how it is with all my sin-weeds. Jesus can't just make them
go away. I have to stoop down and grab hold of them first, then he helps
me."

"Why can he help pull them and we can't?" asked Betsy.

"Because Jesus is God's Son, and because he died for us," replied
Amanda. "That gives him a very special kind of power over sin that we
do not have. The Bible says that he has conquered sin and can save us.

Because of that, he can conquer it within us too. And the way he conquers sin within us is to help *us* conquer it ourselves by helping us pull out our own sin-weeds. That is why he is called our Savior. He has saved us from sin and can help get rid of the sin in our lives. He can also help you forgive the men who killed your father."

"It all sounds confusing," said Betsy.

Amanda smiled. "At first, perhaps," she said. "But once you get to know Jesus, then it is wonderful. Let me try to explain it another way—you see, because Jesus died for us, he forgives all our sin—*your* hatred and *my* anger toward my father. Do you remember when Mr. Diggorsfeld said that Jesus took our sin to the grave with him?"

Betsy nodded.

"But the weeds of that sin are still growing in our hearts. So though God has forgiven us, we must still pull out the weeds. And when we invite him into our hearts, he helps us. He forgives you for your hatred, and he will help you get rid of it by helping you forgive those men. And with the hate-weed gone, even when it starts to be gone, he will begin to grow nice-smelling flowers inside you instead—flowers like kindness and goodness and happiness."

Betsy thought a moment or two. Amanda said nothing. For a long minute they sat quietly together.

"I would like him to live in my heart," said Betsy at length. "I want to get rid of the weeds so I can be a lady—a good lady like you, Amanda."

At the words, Amanda's heart stung her, and tears quickly rose to her eyes. She drew in a deep breath and blinked them back.

"You would like to invite Jesus into your heart like Mr. Diggorsfeld said?" she said.

Betsy nodded.

Amanda rose, wiping at her eyes. "Betsy," she said, "let's you and I go up to the secret room in the garret and pray there together."

Betsy stood. Amanda offered her hand and led her to the library. Hand in hand they walked through the bookcases into the secret corridor. Moments later they were making their way through the now familiar hidden corridor toward the topmost portions of Heathersleigh Hall.

35

Secret Garden-Room of the Heart

$\mathscr{A}$manda and Betsy arrived at the secret room. Amanda closed the floor-door behind them; then they sat down on the bare wood together. The room was dark and Amanda left it that way. No words had passed between them as they came, and now they were quiet a few more moments as the serious mood between them deepened. At length Amanda spoke.

"This room," she said, "is just like your heart, Betsy. It is in the middle of the house where no one can see it. Someone looking from the outside would never know it is here. And for years no one *did* know it was here, until my brother discovered it."

She paused briefly.

"That's the way our hearts are," Amanda went on. "Most people don't even know they contain a secret place just like this room—a secret place where Jesus wants to live. We all have a secret room inside us, but most people don't even know it. That's too bad, isn't it?"

"Yes," replied Betsy. "What if they never find it?"

"It is very sad, but some people never do. They never know about the room in their heart. They go through life and never explore the secret places of their house. Grandma Maggie once told me that it was like a mystery—the most important mystery in the world—and that every person must solve that mystery and discover that secret for himself, in the same way that George discovered the mystery of this secret room."

Amanda paused briefly.

"But you know about your secret room now, don't you, Betsy?" she went on. "So you don't have to be one of those people who never solve the mystery. You *can* discover your secret room."

Betsy took in her words thoughtfully.

"And when we invite Jesus to come live in the secret room of our hearts," Amanda went on, "he will be there always with us, a special friend living in our house, a friend we can see and visit and talk to anytime we want—our very own special friend. Isn't that a wonderful thought?"

"Oh yes," replied Betsy, eyes aglow. The moment she realized she *wanted* to be good, and *wanted* Jesus' help, the doors of her soul began to open. It is within the hearts of those whose desire it is to grow and change toward goodness that the daystar of understanding will always arise, as it was now rising in the heart of Elsbet Conlin.

"It is as if there was a secret treasure right here in this room—"

As Amanda said the words Betsy could not help glancing around, even in the darkness, with sudden curiosity.

"—But Jesus living in our hearts is even better than a secret treasure," said Amanda. "Because sometimes treasure makes people greedy. But Jesus helps us be good, and makes *nice* things grow. That's the difference between this room and the secret place of our hearts where Jesus lives. This is just an empty room with nothing in it. But imagine if this room had a skylight instead of a roof, a skylight to let in sun and rain. And imagine if this floor wasn't made of wood but was good, rich dirt, and that this secret room was able to grow beautiful flowers in it. That's the way our hearts are. There is a *garden* inside it. So when we invite Jesus to come live there, he changes the dark secret room into a garden and gets very busy tending it, making nice character-flowers grow."

"I want him living in my heart," said Betsy. "I want Jesus to be in my secret room."

"Then all you have to do is ask him. The door to the room is unlocked. He will come in as soon as you open the door."

"How do I open the door?"

"Just talk to him, invite him to make his home in your heart. As soon as you do, he comes in."

"Will I . . . hear him or feel him?"

"No . . . you will just know he has come in."

"Then . . . *how* should I ask him?" said Betsy. "Where is he?"

"He is everywhere. He is here with us right now."

"He is!"

"Yes, and he is listening and just waiting for you to ask."

When the moment is right, no prodding is necessary. And Betsy needed none.

"*Jesus, wherever you are,*" she began at once, eyes wide and expectant, "*please come into the secret room of my heart, like Amanda says. I want you to*

*live inside me, and to be my friend and make me good like my daddy said. I
want nice flowers to grow inside me. I am sorry for hating those bad men. . . ."*

As Amanda listened, she remembered the day her father led her and
George through a prayer to accept the Lord as their Savior many years
ago. She had done so, and meant it, as much as she was capable of at
the time with so many conflicting thoughts in her young brain about
the sudden spiritual changes that had come to their family. And
through the years since, as she had grown and drifted away, she had
known all along that she was still a Christian, even if a rebellious one.

And now she found herself praying similar words to Betsy's to reaf-
firm her own new commitment to the faith that had earlier been her
father's.

Lord, prayed Amanda silently, *I too am sorry for the weeds I have allowed
to grow in my heart's garden. It is sin and I know it. Please forgive me. Thank
you for not giving up on me during all those years I tried to give up on you. I
know you are in my heart because you never left. But I want now to rededicate
myself to you—not partially, but completely. So I give myself anew to you, every
part of my life. Take me over completely. Thank you for dying for me, and for
the new life of your resurrection. I feel almost as if I had been dead myself and
have been raised with you. If anyone deserved to die, it was me, not my father or
you. Yet you kept loving me all through my rebellious years. Even though my
father is now with you, I feel more alive than ever before. All I can do is thank
you and devote myself to you completely.*

Amanda had hardly been listening, but now Betsy's voice again came
into her hearing.

*". . . and I will try to be good, if you will help me pull bad weeds out of my
heart."*

Betsy stopped and turned toward Amanda.

"What do I do now?" she asked. "I don't feel any different."

"Jesus is in your heart now," replied Amanda. "So start talking to
him as your friend, and keep asking him to help you pull the weeds of
sin and grow sweet-smelling flowers. Go to the secret room whenever
you can, just as we come here whenever we want. With Jesus in our
hearts we can go there too, to visit him and talk to him, ask for his help
with the sin-weeds that are troubling us, and especially to ask him what
he wants us to do."

"How does he tell you?" asked Betsy.

"By putting the feeling of what is right and what is wrong inside
you," replied Amanda, "and then urging you to do what is right. He also

says things in the Bible that we are to do. Mother and Catharine and I can help you learn some of those things. Like forgiving our enemies. That is something we may not *feel* like doing, or sometimes may not even *want* to do. But with Jesus in our hearts, we have to do it, because he tells us to. He is not only our friend, he is also our Master. So we must do as he says."

"It sounds fun," said Betsy. "Is he really alive and right with us all the time?"

"He is. But some of the things he tells us to do can be very hard. It is not easy to forgive your enemies. But when we do those difficult things, he will make us much happier for it."

Amanda reached over and found the switch to turn on the light. The two of them squinted at first as their eyes became accustomed to the brightness.

"Do you know what you just did, Betsy?" said Amanda. "You turned on the light in your secret room by inviting Jesus to come in. Now it will never be dark in there again."

36
Another Key
♦ ♦ ♦

*M*aggie was still mostly bedridden after two weeks and could only get about with help. One of the Heathersleigh women stayed with her at the cottage every night and throughout most days.

Dr. Cecil Armbruster had declared the hip suffering from a hairline fracture, not an outright break.

"You should be able to walk on it within a month," he said to Maggie and Jocelyn on the day of his diagnosis. "But, young lady," he added, poking a stern finger toward Maggie while flashing a quick grin in Jocelyn's direction, "I know you! Your doctor is giving you strict orders to stay out of your garden until I pronounce you fit."

"But the weeds—" Maggie began to protest.

"Will still be there waiting for you a month from now," interrupted the doctor.

"They will take over."

"And we will help you," interjected Jocelyn. "Betsy will love to get her hands into your dirt. That is all she is talking about these days, pulling weeds. She will have a splendid time, and the rest of us will all help her."

──────── ◆◆◆ ────────

"Amanda dear," said Maggie one afternoon when Amanda was spending the latter half of the day at the cottage, "would you bring me my Bible? I think your mother put it on the secretary—you know, there in the sitting room—when she was here this morning."

Amanda rose from her chair, walked into the sitting room, and picked up Maggie's Bible. As she made her way back to the bedroom, Bible in hand, she paused and glanced back and took another long look at the open secretary from which she had just lifted it.

Suddenly it struck her how similar it was to the one in the library at the Hall she had noticed just a few days ago when she and Betsy were on their way to the secret room. Was she remembering correctly, that the cubbyholes and drawers in back of the lid-desk were on the *right* of the secretary back at the Hall? If so, the two cabinets would be nearly exact mirror replicas of each other. And why not? Maggie's great-great-grandfather had built them both. For here, as Amanda looked at the open desk, the drawers were on the *left*, and the ornate panel hiding the compartment Maggie had shown them was on the right.

What *other* similarities might there be that were not discernible at first glance?

Amanda continued to stare at Maggie's cabinet, the wheels of her brain slowly turning in a new direction. She recalled months ago sitting here with Catharine and her mother as Maggie explained about finding the secret panel and shelf where the deed to Heathersleigh Cottage had lain so long hidden.

Slowly she made her way back to the secretary, pulled out the drawer, just as Maggie had shown them. There sat the key, just as Maggie had described finding it.

Her curiosity heightened and her thoughts accelerating, Amanda reached into the drawer, picked up the little key, and held it a moment, turning it over in her fingers.

175

Suddenly an explosion went off in her brain.

She knew this key!

Or one just like it. She had known it for years! Geoffrey knew it too. And it still sat on the same key ring where it had baffled them all this time!

She stood back and beheld the secretary again.

What if—

By now Amanda's brain was spinning rapidly.

If the same craftsman had built the two cabinets, why shouldn't both pieces of furniture be alike . . . *down to every detail!*

"Grandma Maggie—here is your Bible," she cried, hurrying into the bedroom. "I have to run home!"

"What is it, Amanda dear?" asked Maggie in alarm.

"Maybe nothing—I'll tell you about it as soon as I get back."

Already Amanda was out the door and flying through the woods toward Heathersleigh Hall.

37

Discovery

$\mathcal{P}$anting for breath, Amanda burst into the east sitting room, where she entered by the side door. Jocelyn glanced up. A sudden fear seized her heart.

"What is it, Amanda!" said Jocelyn, beginning to rise. "Is Maggie—"

"No, she's fine, Mother," said Amanda, dashing through the room.

"But what—"

"I'm going to the tower! Where's Catharine?"

Two minutes later, still breathing hard, Amanda stood in the familiar tower, the footsteps of her mother and sister echoing from the stone stairway behind her. When Catharine ran through the door a few seconds later, Amanda was stooped over, fumbling with frantic fingers at the loose stone in front of the tiny recessed chamber where Geoffrey had long ago discovered the key ring.

"Amanda, what—"

"The keys, Catharine! I think I know—"

The stone fell to the floor. Amanda grabbed the key ring off the iron hook in the recess with its two keys. By the time her mother reached the tower a few seconds later, Amanda was disappearing through the wall of the opposite side into the hidden maze of corridors.

"Catharine, do you know—" began Jocelyn.

"I know nothing, Mother," replied Catharine. "I just saw her grab the two keys, open the hidden door with the one, then run through it."

Again mother and sister hurried after Amanda.

"Amanda . . . where are you going?" yelled Catharine into the maze after her.

" . . . the library!" were the only words Catharine heard echoing back through the blackness.

When Catharine and Jocelyn reached the library two minutes later, they found Amanda standing in front of the ancient cabinet that had been there longer than any of them could remember.

"What is it, Amanda?" asked Jocelyn, hurrying up beside her.

"All these years we have known that Maggie's great-grandfather built both this secretary and the one at the cottage," she answered. "Yet even after Maggie showed us the hidden panel in hers a few months ago, I never made the connection."

"What connection?" asked Jocelyn.

Amanda showed them the key ring she had taken from the tower.

"This," she said, "—the small mystery key! We knew the larger of the two opened the door George discovered in the wall of the tower. But this tiny one—"

"Looks exactly like the key Maggie found in the drawer of her secretary!" exclaimed Catharine.

All three now approached the cabinet built by Webley Kyrkwode for Broughton Rutherford.

Amanda pulled down the lid, revealing an open secretary-desk just like Maggie's—with, as she thought, the drawers, cubbyholes, and rear panel exactly reversed. Slowly Amanda pulled out the drawer above the ornate rear panel. She took it all the way out, as she had seen Maggie do, set it aside, then reached inside the drawer space with her hand, probing with her fingers.

Jocelyn and Catharine saw her eyes widen and knew she had found something.

"Hand me the key, Catharine," she said.

Catharine did so. Amanda again reached into the space and, with some effort, inserted the key into the locking mechanism she had discovered. Just like with Maggie's cabinet, the vertical panel gave way and swiveled toward her on its invisible pivot. Upon the shelf that was revealed sat, not a deed this time, but a large and ornately bound book.

"The family Bible!" exclaimed all three women nearly at once.

Amanda took it in her two hands, brought it forward, and set it on the desk.

"It has been here all this time right in front of us," she said, "and we never knew it."

Jocelyn leaned forward and opened the cover board, then began thumbing through it slowly and reverently.

"Oh, how I wish Charles and George could be here for this," she said.

"Maybe they are," Catharine added.

38

Preparations

$\mathcal{T}$he scene at the Chalet of Hope was nearly as full of expectancy and excitement as if a guest were coming rather than that Sister Hope was leaving.

Hope herself was both nervous and excited, bustling about, packing, trying to remember everything, and struggling most of all not to cry.

London was the last place she would have chosen to go. It represented so many shattered dreams in her life—dreams of a happy childhood, dreams of the mission work, dreams of a long marriage, dreams of a family. All these lay on an altar somewhere in England.

Part of her feared that God might require her to once again lay another dream on yet another altar. But what could it be? And who was she to question it if God should demand a sacrifice of her? Wasn't he always good and generous?

Listen to me, she thought to herself. *I believe that God is good. Why should I fear any gift from him?*

Behind her, Gretchen entered the room with some fresh laundry.

"Gretchen, have you seen my blue dress?" asked Hope, trying to banish the anxious thoughts from her mind.

"I have it right here. Are you almost ready?"

"I think so ... but I cannot help being nervous!"

"You will have a good time. The Lord will be with you, and we will be with you in prayer and spirit. You know that the Lord is calling you back to England. He has something there for you."

"I know, and I am excited too ... but a little afraid."

"Of the war?"

"I don't think it is that so much."

"Afraid of what, then?" said Gretchen, setting down her armload on the bed.

"Every time I left London," replied Hope, "it was with the hope that I would never return. I left once for Birmingham, then again for New Zealand, then yet again for Switzerland. All these happy years here I never thought I would go back. I never *wanted* to go back. Now here I am preparing to go to London again. As I said, I cannot help being a little afraid."

Hope smiled. "But at least this time I know that it is just for a visit," she added, "and that I will return. That makes the parting bearable. I will soon be home again with my wonderful family of sisters."

Hope turned and gave her friend a long hug, trying to hide the lingering pang that had come to her heart with the last words she had spoken. She only hoped they were true, and that she *did* come back soon.

Meanwhile, in Sister Galiana's room, preparations of a more secretive nature were under way. Galiana was making a card for each of them to sign and was busy at the moment creating a beautiful likeness of the chalet with their beloved mountains in the background.

"How do you do it?" said Sister Anika. "That is beautiful enough to frame!"

Below, Sister Marjolaine was at that moment sneaking into the house with a brown paper parcel in her hand. She hurried on tiptoe up the stairs and glanced about for sign of Sister Hope. Hearing her and Sister Gretchen down the hall, she crept into Galiana's room and closed the door behind her. Several busy heads turned toward her.

"I've borrowed the most delightful book from Herr Buchmann," she said excitedly in her characteristic high-pitched voice. "It is filled with wonderful short stories that take place in the Alps. That way Sister Hope will be able to read for a bit as the mood strikes her rather than read an entire book."

"I wish Herr Buchmann would write *his* story," said Sister Agatha. "What a book that would make."

"Perhaps one of us will have to write it for him," suggested Sister Marjolaine as she began to unwrap the book so that she could wrap it again in colored paper. She also planned to add some Alpine flowers she had pressed between its pages. "I don't think he has any idea how much people would enjoy it. Why don't you write it, Sister Agatha?"

"I could never write a book!" she exclaimed.

"Just let him tell you the story and then write it down in his own words."

"Right now I am too busy with my package for Sister Hope to think about such things," she answered. "See, I filled a little lace bag with small hard candies. I know that a train ride can get very long and one's mouth gets dry. I want her to have something sweet to keep in her mouth."

"It is lovely. She will enjoy it very much."

"This was such a wonderful idea of yours, Sister Agatha," said Sister Luane. "She is going to be so surprised when she opens her bag and finds gifts from each one of us."

"What are you putting in, Luane?"

An embarrassed look came over her face.

"I've written a little story," she said shyly, "about our chalet . . . and about us."

"How wonderful! May we read it?"

"Not now—I would be too embarrassed. I want to give it to Sister Hope to remember us all when she is away."

"Perhaps *you* are the one to write Herr Buchmann's story," said Sister Marjolaine.

Sister Clariss walked into the room and placed a small packet of handkerchiefs tied with a yellow ribbon on Sister Galiana's bed, and the enthusiastic discussion continued.

Throughout the day the surprise parcel continued to grow, with homemade sweet biscuits, dried fruit and raisins, and more handmade notes and cards.

Later in the afternoon Sister Galiana found Sister Gretchen alone in the kitchen.

"What will you be hiding in Sister Hope's satchel?" she asked.

"I have written out several Scripture passages on little pieces of colored paper," Gretchen answered. "I am rolling each one up and tying them with ribbon. I plan to fill up a little paper box with them, and on the top I will write, 'Open and unroll one of these little treasures whenever you are feeling tired or lonely.' "

"That is a wonderful idea," said Galiana. "I think we will have Sister Hope's bag so full of unexpected treats and gifts that it will take her all the way to England to find them all."

Kasmira had been watching the preparations for several days without saying anything. Gradually Sister Hope noticed that the young Muslim believer had become more withdrawn and anxious, and less like her new peaceful self.

"What is it, Kasmira?" she asked finally as they passed in the upstairs hallway later that same day.

Kasmira dropped her eyes.

"Will you go outdoors with me?" she said softly.

"Of course," nodded Hope.

They walked downstairs and out the door together, and made their way silently around to the front of the chalet near where the crèche was set up at Christmas. It was Kasmira's favorite place, and she often came here to reflect and pray.

"I live with war all my life," Kasmira began at length in her thick accent. Her words were still soft. "Each moment around me was danger and fear. But here I have peace and safety. . . ."

Her voice began to quiver as she glanced up into Sister Hope's eyes.

"I have fear for you . . . if—"

Kasmira began to cry.

Hope took her in her arms and pulled her close.

"I will be in our Lord's hands all the way," she said tenderly. "God is my good Father, and we have nothing to fear. I will be back with you before you know it."

39

Visitor From Switzerland

As the time grew short and the miles shrank, Hope Guinarde's heart beat more and more rapidly within her. It had been a long and tiring train ride, not to mention a somewhat bumpy channel ferry crossing. She had been gone from the chalet almost a week, and, after a day in London before leaving for Devon, she was now nearly at the end of her journey.

By the time the train began to slow and the conductor announced Milverscombe, she could hardly contain her anticipation.

She had only known Amanda a few brief months. The girl was young enough to be her daughter, and at the time of their acquaintance in Switzerland, they had hardly hit it off as the closest of friends. And their parting had been strained to say the least. Yet Hope felt she was returning to visit a lifelong friend.

She stepped off the train full of so many emotions, not knowing what she would find, yet knowing the Lord had something unknown and wonderful waiting for her. She hardly had a chance to glance around before she heard her name called out above the hissing steam of the engine.

"Sister Hope!" cried the familiar voice.

If Hope had had any lingering doubts about how Amanda would receive her after their tense meeting a year and a half earlier, they were gone in an instant.

She looked toward the sound to see Amanda running toward her with arms outstretched. Vaguely she saw two or three other figures behind her. But she had no chance to think of them further, for the next moment Amanda had her in her arms. She returned the hug, tears flowing freely.

"Oh, Amanda," said Hope, "it is so good to see you."

She leaned back and looked deeply into Amanda's eyes. "You look well!" she said.

"As do you," whispered Amanda. "Thank you . . . thank you for everything!"

"For what?" said Hope.

"For loving me enough to send me home."

Hope smiled and nodded. Her heart was too full for words. Notwithstanding the letters they had received at the chalet, she had hardly been able to dare dream that her exhortations of the previous winter would be used to so turn Amanda's life toward home. But one look in Amanda's face showed just how great the transformation had been. The hard, resistant independence had been replaced by a radiant childlikeness, and Hope could see that Amanda was finally at peace with herself.

Behind them, Amanda's small entourage now approached.

"I am so glad you are here!" Amanda said as they withdrew from the embrace, dabbing at their eyes. "Now I want you to meet my family."

Amanda turned, slipped her arm through Hope's, and brought her a few steps forward.

"Mother, meet Hope Guinarde . . . Sister Hope, this is my mother, Jocelyn Rutherford."

Sister Hope extended her hand. "Lady Rutherford—" she began.

But more words never came from her mouth. The next instant Hope found herself swallowed in Jocelyn's embrace. The grateful mother could no longer hold back her emotions and sobbed without reservation.

For several long moments the two women held each other in the silent embrace of mutual love and respect.

At length Jocelyn spoke, whispering into Hope's ear words of gratitude that she had longed to express to this dear woman.

"Thank you so much," she said. "You will never know how grateful I am."

Hope nodded. She could not reply. Her own throat and eyes made speech temporarily impossible.

"And my sister, Catharine . . ." said Amanda, continuing with the introductions. Hope nodded with a smile to Catharine over Jocelyn's shoulder.

"And I would like you to meet a visitor in our home, Elsbet Conlin—Betsy, this is Sister Hope."

Hope and Jocelyn parted.

"Hello, Betsy," said Hope, looking down and smiling as she took the girl's outstretched hand.

At the touch of her fingers and the gaze of her eyes, Hope's heart leapt with love and feelings undefined. She did not yet know that the girl before her was motherless and fatherless. She knew nothing about her. But immediately the look of her eyes plunged straight into Hope's heart, and something told her it was for this child standing in front of her that the Lord had sent her to England.

Betsy returned her gaze, smiling and unflinching, until Amanda spoke again.

"Do you have more bags?" she said, interrupting Hope's thoughts.

Hope turned. "Oh . . . yes, just one," she answered.

"Then shall we get it and be off to the Hall? We have a nice tea all waiting for you!"

40
Preservation of the Doctrine

A small, select committee of ecclesiastics sat in a plain room around an oval wood table. Whether there was a Bible in the room could not be said for certain. A glance around the table revealed none. Had one been present, it would doubtless have remained as closed as the minds here gathered in the name of preserving what were thought to be its sacred creeds.

There had been talk. Various reports had been filed. The complaints had reached this executive body. Discreet investigations, interviews, and personal observations had been carried out. And now these august defenders of the faith must render a decision based on their collective years and their love for the traditions of their elders.

"As I understand it," the chairman began, "the chief charge facing us is unorthodoxy." The speaker was a man whose seventy-three years had provided more abundantly for the expansion of his waistline than his mind. And though he was personally unfamiliar with the case, the briefing of his loyal lieutenants was all he would need to pass judgment. Of all things he could not tolerate, unorthodoxy sat at the top of the list. Doctrinal correctness was far more important in his eyes than ethics, or even morality itself. He would far more quickly cut off fellowship for doctrinal slippage, as he saw it, than for anything to do with a man's or woman's obedience or disobedience to the commands of Christ. Orthodoxy was his God, and he served the idol with all the passion of one from the church at Sardis.

"He is a difficult man to pin down," said the woman to his right, a certain Mrs. Packer, tall, robust of frame, and with ample black-grey hair neatly bundled atop her head. Her demeanor, even her professional dress, made it clear she had learned well from the example of the Pankhursts, though she disdained them, and was the equal of any man in both ambition and determination. She enjoyed the role of authority and had her eye on the chairmanship when Roul stepped aside, as he was reportedly planning to do at year's end. She had first been contacted by one of the church's deacons on behalf of the disturbed membership. Never caring much for Diggorsfeld, she had immediately taken over the investigation with relish. "He avoids saying anything which contradicts Scripture outright," she went on. "But his bias is undeniably liberal. It is clear he does not give proper emphasis to the tenets and doctrines of the denomination."

"Such as?" inquired Chairman Roul.

"Animals in heaven and that church attendance is not mandatory are two of the most obvious," she replied. "In addition, he refuses to urge his people to tithe, and there are hints of scandal involving a married woman."

"I see . . . these *are* serious charges," rejoined Roul in solemn tones. "The latter could be especially useful, if it becomes necessary to rouse the people against him, to illustrate how heretical teaching leads to moral decline. A rumor dropped into the right ears is always effective. Do we have sufficient evidence otherwise to move against him?"

The members of the committee glanced around the table at one another. No one spoke, for none of them did possess such evidence.

"We have been watching him for months now," said the treasurer of the committee, Mrs. Paulus, "ever since the first reports reached us."

"And what have you found?"

"The same points of objection that Mrs. Packer reported."

"But as I look at the chapel's statistics," now put in the only member of the committee who was not convinced, Vice-Chairman Taylor, "it appears that attendance is actually on the rise." He was younger than either Packer or Paulus, and had not completely relinquished his mind to the will of the committee. His capacity to think for himself, however, was diminishing by degrees the more frequently he squelched his objections and went along. As a young seminarian he had been full of spiritual ideals and enthusiasm. But there is no underestimating the power of organizational church orthodoxy to engender a spirit of fear within its membership, the first casualty of which is always the capacity to inquire of God outside the rigid boundaries of that orthodoxy. And sadly, Taylor's former zeal for truth was invisibly being supplanted by the attempt to protect his position within the hierarchy of which he had made himself a part.

Chairman Roul glanced to his right.

"That, uh . . . may be true," replied Mrs. Packer. "There have been reports of increased attendance for some time. It is one of the factors in the case that has puzzled us."

"I thought the dissenters were leaving him."

"Some, it is true, have stopped attending until the matter is resolved."

"But others say his popularity with the people is enormous."

"When I was there the chapel was packed," put in Taylor. "And enthusiastic. I don't know that I have ever seen one of our clergymen so well liked by the people."

"Except, of course, for those raising the complaints."

"Yes . . . of course—I suppose that is true."

41

Good Will Be Called Evil

❖❖❖

*E*ven as the executive committee, unknown to him, pondered his fate, Timothy Diggorsfeld rose to answer the door of his parsonage. There stood a young man he judged to be in his late twenties whom he had never seen before.

"Someone gave me this little leaflet," he said, showing Timothy a small folded paper in his hand. "It had this address on it. Can you tell me . . . is this true, what is written here?"

"Why don't you come in and have some tea with me," said Timothy, "and show me exactly what your question is."

He had to blink back his tears for a second or two, seized by a momentary stab of fond remembrance in his heart, and thinking that standing before him was an angel sent by his good friend Charles Rutherford as a reminder that he was thinking of him.

"—My name is Timothy Diggorsfeld," the pastor added, extending his hand.

Fifteen minutes later he and his visitor were seated in Timothy's parlor. The young man still clutched the tract which had been handed him by one of the members of New Hope Chapel several days before.

"Ever since I read these words," he was saying, "I have not been able to get them out of my mind. *Jesus seeks to introduce us to a life lived with the Father—an ongoing, moment-by-moment experience between loving Father and contented child. He does not protect us from God, he takes us to him. It is toward intimacy with the Father that the Son would guide us. For such he was born, for such he died. This is what a relationship with Christ is all about.*"

He glanced up at Timothy as if the words were the most astonishing thing he had ever heard. "As I read them, an inner explosion went off in my brain," he added.

As Timothy listened he could not help smiling to himself. He knew the words well, for he had written them himself, though his name appeared nowhere on the tract.

"You see, for years I have struggled with what people call the atonement," the young man went on.

"You are . . . or are not, a Christian?" said Timothy.

"I don't know," replied his visitor. "I have never prayed a conversion prayer, if that is what you mean, though I have been a sporadic attendee of various churches. Perhaps I should explain that I am one who tries to make sense of things. Logic is important to me, though I have heard it scoffed at by some preachers. What do you think? Is logic of God or of the devil?"

"Who made it?"

"I'm afraid I don't understand you."

"Who made our minds?"

"God, of course."

"Then logic must be one of his gifts to us."

"But what if it is of the fallen nature?"

"A legitimate concern, for many aspects of our humanity are. Can you tell me—why does such a question occur to you?"

"I don't know. I suppose because so much of the preaching I have heard emphasizes that there is nothing good within us, that everything about man has been tainted by sin. I heard a sermon just last month entitled 'The Total Depravity of Man.'"

Timothy smiled. He was well familiar with that upside-down theology whose deepest foundations were rooted in the sinfulness of man rather than the character of God.

"I would agree," he said, "that everything in us has been tainted by sin. We *are* sinners; there is no doubt about that. By no goodness of our own will we enter the kingdom of heaven, but only through the shed blood of the Savior and the loving forgiveness of his Father. However, I take exception with the *total* depravity view. Sinful . . . yes. In need of a Savior . . . yes. *Totally* depraved . . . no."

"Why do you say that?"

"Because we are still made in God's image, and everything God made was good. Even the Fall cannot change that *in-his-image-ness*. And to return to your question about logic—I consider it too wonderful a thing for the devil to have invented. Of course it is tainted, as you say, by our sin nature. But I stand by what I said, that imperfect as it is, it remains one of God's precious gifts to mankind."

"Do you think logic can aid spirituality?"

"Not only can it, it is *supposed* to. I believe that faith, though by definition it concerns the unseen, *must* be bolstered as much as possible by sound reasoning, and that obedience must likewise be nourished by a wide-awake and thoughtful mentality."

"Why do so few Christians emphasize that?"

"Because 1 Corinthians 1:19–20 and 3:19 are two of the most mis-read passages in the New Testament," replied Timothy, "which foolish people use to justify the shoddy view that we are not supposed to make sense of God's truth. Both Jesus and Paul were crafty and intelligent men, who brought the full weight of their intellects to the aid of their faith."

"I cannot tell you how glad I am to hear you say it," laughed the young man lightly. "I have never been able to accept ideas by rote simply because someone tells me I should. And so much of what I have been told about salvation, I am sorry to say, makes very little sense to me."

"Common sense is one of the much overlooked virtues in theological circles," rejoined Timothy. "I am pleased to see that it is one you value. Would you care to give me an example of something about the common explanations of salvation that grates against your common sense?"

"Such as," replied his guest, "Jesus dying to satisfy the justice of an angry God."

"Why do you think that makes little sense?"

"God punishing sin, even though *he* is the one who created mankind capable of that sin? It is logically backwards. It is as if I punished my dog for being unable to speak English."

"In other words, punishing your dog for being something he cannot help being?"

"Exactly. We cannot help being sinners. Yet they say God created us imperfect and then will condemn us to hell for *not* being perfect unless we go through a process of repentance which our very sinfulness makes it impossible for us to thoroughly understand or embrace. This strikes me as monstrous cruelty. Yet theologians insist such to be evidence of his holiness and righteousness, and all the while maintain that God is love. The illogic of it is enormous."

"You make a strong point," nodded Timothy.

"Well if that is their God," said their visitor, "I want no part of him. That is certainly like no love I am familiar with."

He sighed and glanced away. Timothy waited.

"And yet," he went on in a moment, "I am drawn to Jesus. For in him I see love, tenderness, compassion, reasonableness, intelligence, logic, manliness, humor, truth, and even, if I can say it, down-to-earth common sense. I have read the Gospels numerous times. And part of me desires to give myself to him and be his disciple."

"But something has prevented you?" asked Timothy.

"Yes—the idea that he was a sacrifice to appease an angry God. I simply cannot in good conscience accept such a thing. As much as I respond to Jesus himself, I cannot accept him if that is what it means. So to answer your question, I don't suppose I am a Christian."

"But from the sound of it, you want to be."

"Yes, I think I do. Because I am certain in my heart that Jesus' death and resurrection must mean more than the theologians say."

"You are right, they mean much more," smiled Timothy.

"What do you think they mean?"

"That your image of God the Father is wrong."

"If only I could believe that."

"Do you believe Jesus?"

"I . . . I think I do."

"What did he say of his Father?"

The young man hesitated, then cast Timothy a look of question.

"He said that he was just like the Father," Timothy went on, "—in other words, full of love, compassion, tenderness, gentleness . . . and forgiveness—all the same qualities you say you see in Jesus himself."

"What about his holiness in the face of our sin?"

"Who else but a holy and righteous Father could love and forgive us perfectly and completely?" replied Timothy.

42

Souls at Risk

◆◆◆

I also see that revenues have nearly doubled," said Chairman Roul as he perused the documents he had been provided.

Mrs. Paulus glanced down at her own figures and nodded.

"And yet you say he is not stressing the tithe," went on Roul. "I fail to understand such a dichotomy. People do not contribute to the collection plate unless they are reminded to feel duty bound. The tithe must be preached or we are out of business."

"I also hear there are many conversions," now put in Mr. Riper, who had not yet spoken.

"How can that be?" said Mrs. Packer, growing a little annoyed with her two colleagues who seemed intent on giving Diggorsfeld the benefit of the doubt. "We all know that liberals do not emphasize evangelism."

"He has one of the most evangelistic outreach programs in the city," added Taylor. "It is said to be quite effective."

"A mere rumor," she retorted. "The idea that such a man is capable of winning souls is doubtful to say the least. The question I would raise concerning these so-called conversions is whether they are *true* conversions?"

"If, as you say, his liberalism is well known," now consented Riper, "then you raise a critical question. The wrong words, even uttered in prayer, will not insure salvation."

"I say he is a dangerous influence," rejoined Mrs. Packer.

"But the people listen to him eagerly," added Vice-Chairman Taylor. "I saw some taking notes."

"What in the world for?" asked Mrs. Packer.

"I don't know. But I have never seen such a response to a man's sermons."

"I think we must come back again to the matter of the conversions," said the chairman. "This could make it difficult to prove his liberalism."

"There are conversions and there are conversions," replied Mrs. Packer. "As I hear it, he insists on pointing people toward the Father for salvation rather than our Lord and Savior Jesus Christ."

A few heads began to nod, as if they had him now. Even Vice-Chairman Taylor had to admit that if this were indeed true, he would have no choice but to side with the others and make the vote unanimous.

"If these so-called conversions are not based on the blood of the cross," Mrs. Packer went on, "then however good he may make people feel about the Father's love, those poor unfortunate souls may still be bound for hell. It would be better, our Lord said, for a stone to be put around his neck and he be thrown into the sea."

"Yes, you are right," nodded Chairman Roul. "We must act, and act decisively. Not only is the man dangerous to the doctrine, souls could actually be at risk."

More heads nodded.

"We must put a stop to the spreading of false teaching."

43
The Passion to Forgive

Timothy Diggorsfeld's unexpected visitor tried to take in the minister's last words.

They had fallen like a divine chisel against encrusted traditional explanations of the atonement he had been struggling with for many years. "Because of his holiness—which is a *good* holiness, not a self-righteous holiness," Timothy continued, "God wants to forgive, not punish. *Forgiveness* is the Father's passion toward sin, not retribution. Of course, forgiveness always comes with a price. Yet it is what he is continually striving to achieve.—But tell me about this explosion that went off in your brain."

The young man smiled. "Many explosions seem to be going off," he answered. "I suppose even before I came here today I was gradually seeing glimmers of what you have just been saying. When I read the tract, the phrase 'He does not protect us from God' jumped off the page at me. Suddenly I realized that perhaps God might not be a vindictive, condemning judge, intent on exacting punishment of the innocent to satisfy his divine justice."

"What do you think he might be instead?"

The young man hesitated and glanced down, as if the idea were too wonderful to take in.

"I am still trying to get my mind around it," he said after a moment, "and what you just said adds a new piece to the puzzle. But what I am wondering is whether God might not be the avenging judge theology has made of him, but might rather be a loving Father to whom Jesus wants to take us in order that he may forgive our sins. In other words, a Father whose arms are open to receive us and to whom Jesus takes us, rather than a Father from whom he must protect us . . . a Father—I can hardly say it, but this is what I am thinking—with a smile of welcome on his face rather than a scowl of rebuke."

"An uncommon view," commented Timothy with hint of a smile. "In other words, just like the Father of Jesus Christ."

"Yes," said the young man excitedly. "But . . . could it be true!"

"I think it very likely."

"Do you see what a difference it would make! It would mean that Jesus did not come to rescue us from God's *wrath*, but to introduce us to his Father's *love*. All of a sudden everything in the Gospels makes more sense. Even his death makes sense now. The injustice that fell upon him was *man's*, not God's. Jesus yielded to that injustice because of love. Thus he makes atonement for my sin, not only as a symbol of the Old Testament sacrifice, but to show me how much I am loved by both him and his Father, and to take me to his Father to cleanse me of the very sin that did not stain him."

"I see you have been thinking this through very thoroughly," smiled Timothy. "You almost begin to sound like a theologian yourself."

The young man returned his smile sheepishly.

"I have tried to get to the bottom of what it may mean," he said. "And yes, to be honest, I have studied and thought about the atonement a great deal, even prayed to God for insight about it. I *want* to make sense of it."

"I applaud you for that effort," said Timothy. "If only more Christians were as earnest about their system of beliefs as you are."

"Upon the basis of what I have been thinking since reading this tract, if it is true, I *can* accept Jesus as my Savior and Lord, something I was never prepared to do before."

He paused, then added quietly, "No . . . I *want* to accept him as my Savior and Lord."

He looked earnestly at Timothy.

"So I have to ask you," he said, and his voice was as one dying of thirst in the desert approaching Timothy as his final hope of finding water, "—do you consider this new revelation—at least it is new to me— that Jesus desires to take us *to* the Father rather than save us *from* his wrath . . . do you consider it possible? If not I must surely give up my quest, for I have exhausted every other explanation of Jesus' life and death."

"I not only consider it possible," replied Timothy, "I consider it *true*. Triumphantly true! With all my heart I believe that our salvation as Christians exists in love rather than in the satisfaction of divine justice. Do not get me wrong. There *is* divine justice, and we will all face it. But it is a justice of love, not a justice of retribution. God is a good, fair, and just Judge, not a vindictive, condemning, angry Judge. He is a Judge we will *want* to face, for he will make everything right, including our sin, and will make truth prevail throughout the universe."

"Do you believe in the cross?"

"Of course," replied Timothy. "Without the cross there is no salvation. The death and resurrection of Christ are the greatest demonstrations of love the world has ever known. And by that love, atonement is made for our sins. Atonement originates in the loving forgiveness of a holy, righteous, and forgiving Father, not in the satisfaction of a vengeance, which foolish theologians call 'holy,' yet is anything but. Such demean the holiness of God by expending their energies inventing theological theories rather than doing the truth. They have set themselves to speculate concerning the mysteries of God's forgiveness rather than yield to the Fatherhood out of whose heart that forgiveness flows. They read their Bibles in a condition of heart in which it is impossible for them to unearth its truths. They presume to explain the Christ to whom years of obedience could alone have made them able to comprehend. Forgive me," he said. "I sometimes become quite exasperated with my colleagues."

He smiled and took a deep breath.

"Let me try to put it like this," he went on. "God's wrath is all against sin, not against mankind. He is bound by his holiness, not to *punish the sinner* but to *destroy sin*. And destroy it altogether. Toward this end the death of Christ on the cross is the victorious weapon against which sin, hell, and the devil himself cannot stand. The victory of the cross will be complete."

"You cannot imagine how happy it makes me to hear you talk so," said Timothy's visitor, beaming. "You have set my heart to rest on many things. Would you then tell me what to do to become a Christian, to accept Jesus as my Savior?"

"Nothing would delight me more," said Timothy. "The Bible says to believe by faith in Jesus Christ, and confess that belief. You have already evidenced your belief and confessed it to me today. So you are possibly already a believer. Jesus himself talks about repentance along with belief. And baptism is also an important New Testament symbol that you have become his disciple. All these elements—belief, faith, repentance, confession, and baptism—are involved."

"Yes, I would like to be baptized too."

"Good, we can talk about that later. You must keep in mind that there is not necessarily a formula to be followed," Timothy went on. "God knows each individual heart. The most important thing is responding to him personally. But each of these elements can and usually does accompany that heart response to God to one degree or another."

"I do not want to leave anything out. Once I make up my mind on something, I give myself to it all the way."

"Then why do we not pray together and you can tell the Lord what is in your heart, and that you want to follow him and obey him."

The young man bowed his head and closed his eyes. From the way he spoke and his familiarity with New Testament concepts, Timothy could see that he was no stranger to church life, just as he said, even though having stumbled over the common prescription for salvation.

"*Dear Jesus,*" the young man began, "*I am sorry for being so slow about acknowledging my belief in you. But I just couldn't understand before. I think I do now. I repent of my sins. I thank you for dying on the cross and shedding your blood that my sins could be forgiven. Thank you for showing me the way to deny myself by your willingness to endure suffering and death. I ask you to come into my life and I accept you as my Savior and Lord. I believe in you and trust you by faith for my salvation. I pray that you will help me grow as a Christian. From this day on I want to live for you, obey you, and be your disciple.*"

He opened his eyes and glanced up. Timothy's face was aglow.

"Is there anything else?" he asked.

"I think you should also address the Father," said Timothy. "Remember, Jesus is your Savior because, as you said yourself, he wants to open your heart to intimacy with the Father."

The young man closed his eyes again.

"*Dear heavenly Father,*" he prayed, "*thank you that you are not a tyrant like they say, but that you love the world . . . and that you loved me enough to send your only Son to tell me about you and show me the way to have an intimate relationship with you. I want to be your child and to walk with you as my Father. Thank you for forgiving my sins through the death of your Son. Help me to get to know both you and Jesus better. Help me to begin seeing you as a tender, loving Father. Reveal your character to me and show me what you want me to do.*"

Again he opened his eyes. They were glistening as he smiled at Timothy.

"Thank you," he said. "I cannot tell you what this means to me.—So . . . what should I do now? How do I begin living as Jesus' disciple?"

"It is very simple, really," replied Timothy. "You have been doing a good deal of it already."

A puzzled expression came over the young man's face.

"Keep reading your New Testament," Timothy went on, "—in particular the Gospels. Find what Jesus told his followers to do . . . then do it. I would be happy to have you join in a Bible study or two that we have in the church in which we attempt to help one another toward that end. There is nothing more to the Christian life than that—simply doing what Jesus said. Jesus himself said it this way: *Follow me.*"

44

The Dreaded Word

◆◆◆

*M*eanwhile, the discussion around the oval table continued.

"What of this fellow Wildecott-Browne?" asked Chairman Roul.

"A solicitor . . . relatively new to the church," answered Mrs. Paulus.

"Whose side is he on—is he reasonable?"

"He is highly respected—a former Anglican."

"What is he doing at New Hope Chapel?"

A few heads shook. No one seemed to know.

"Can we interview him . . . discreetly? He is apparently a powerful man in some London legal circles. He could be of great help in making the case against Diggorsfeld."

"He was one of the first the deacons went to because they knew he was close to Diggorsfeld."

"They have already tried to sway him?"

Mrs. Paulus nodded.

"And?"

"The attempt was unsuccessful," said Mr. Riper. "He is one of Diggorsfeld's staunchest supporters."

"Then he will do us no good," rejoined Roul.

"There is also the charge—" Mrs. Packer began, then paused. "I cannot bring myself to say the word," she added.

"You mean . . ." said Mrs. Paulus.

Packer nodded.

"Come, come, we are behind closed doors," huffed the chairman. "There is nothing to fear from saying it. It is written right here. Are you referring to the charge of universalism?"

A momentary heavy silence descended upon the room, as if the speaking of the dreaded word was tantamount to embracing the heresy itself.

The others nodded.

"Is it actually true . . . *is* he a universalist?" asked Vice-Chairman Taylor. If it were true, this would certainly put an end to Taylor's own ambivalence. The board could not let a known believer in the universal victory of the cross continue to speak openly.

"I cannot answer for the man," replied Mr. Riper. "But when I attended one of his Sunday evening services—I was disguised so he would not recognize me—I heard him raise the question—and I wrote it down to be certain we did not charge him falsely—'What marvelous things might it be in God's heart to do?'"

The others took in the words seriously.

"That certainly *could* be grounds for heresy," Roul said at length, "if only we were certain what he was referring to."

"What *else* could he be referring to?" objected Mrs. Packer. "It is obvious, the man is a heretic."

"I agree," nodded Mrs. Paulus.

"I say we formalize the charge and have it drawn up," said Mrs. Packer.

"And what would be the charge . . . exactly?" asked Roul.

"Unorthodoxy, heresy, and working division in the flock."

The chairman nodded. "Yes . . . yes, that should be adequate grounds for dismissal."

45

The Mother and the Motherless

᷐wo evenings later, two women sat down together, each with a cup in hand. Jocelyn had brought tea and a small plate of biscuits to the sitting room next to her bedroom after the three girls had retired and invited Hope to join her.

"Young Betsy is an energetic and delightful girl," smiled Hope as they began sipping at the edges of their cups. "The moment I saw her, something quickened in my spirit."

"She has found her way into all our hearts," smiled Jocelyn. "And already she is so different, so much more outgoing and expressive than when she came," said Jocelyn. "The change is remarkable. She was so withdrawn and silent, no doubt in shock from what had happened. And yet—"

Jocelyn hesitated.

"What I was going to say," she went on after a moment, "is that as much as we have tried to make her feel at home, there still seems to be something missing in Betsy's life. I realize, of course, that in her circumstances it may always be that way. Yet somehow it appears that she may never quite be at home here."

Hope took in the words thoughtfully.

"I cannot help thinking that the Lord has something else for her," Jocelyn went on, "though I have no idea what that might be."

"You still know nothing of the circumstances of Betsy's father's death?" said Hope.

Jocelyn shook her head. "A minister friend of ours in London is trying to learn what he can, but thus far without success."

"It must have been terrible for her."

"I am sure it was. Yet, as I said, she is so much better than when she came. A great deal of the change is due to Amanda. She has been able to draw her out in a way that I haven't myself, though Betsy seems to love Catharine too."

"It appears that she adores them both."

"Yes, she really does," smiled Jocelyn.

"It is not hard to see why," said Sister Hope. "Both your daughters are lovely young women."

"The one in no small measure because of you and your sisters at the chalet," rejoined Jocelyn. "Amanda has told us so much about her time with you—all the way down to Sister Marjolaine's story about the tiny man fighting the dragon—that I feel I know every one."

The reminder brought a smile to Hope's lips. "Perhaps you and Amanda and Catharine can visit us one day," she suggested.

"I can hardly imagine such a long journey," laughed Jocelyn. "But you have come here, and Amanda has traveled over half of Europe, and I myself was raised in India, so I suppose it can be done. From all Amanda has told us, your chalet sounds lovely."

"Our little village is the most spectacular place on earth," smiled Hope. "Although I must admit it is lovely here in Devon as well. I have felt such a great peace since being with you. It began the moment I stepped off the train. In its own way, Heathersleigh Hall reminds me of the Chalet of Hope. God's Spirit is here in a similar way. I feel somehow that I have left the world's cares behind and have found a refuge here. It is exactly how the chalet has always ministered to me."

Jocelyn smiled. "That is exactly what Heathersleigh has been for me, thanks largely to my dear husband. As you can imagine," she went on, gesturing to the red scar covering nearly half her face, "the world was often a cruel place for me. My hardest struggle as a Christian was to believe that God really loved me as I was, even that he had created me as I was. Charles helped me learn to accept God's love. In doing that, he always made sure Heathersleigh was a place where I could be free from the staring eyes and expectations of others and could just be myself. And eventually his love, then God's, got through to me."

"He must have been a very loving man."

"He was indeed. But poor Amanda . . . he was gone before she woke up to realize it."

"But she has realized it now; that is the important thing," rejoined Hope. "Earthly timetables, even the intrusion of death itself, matter far less in God's grand scheme than they do to us."

"I try to keep reminding myself of that, though it is not easy. I miss him too, yet I do not have to carry a tenth the grief she does."

"She will be reunited with him one day very soon," Hope added, "and all will be well between them. As well as had their hearts never been parted at all."

"In some ways it already is," said Jocelyn. "Amanda's heart is so tender and grateful toward Charles's memory."

"So I have gathered from her letters," said Hope. "Does she share them with you?"

"Yes, she does. She wants me to know everything she is thinking."

"That must bring great joy to your heart in the midst of your loss."

Jocelyn nodded.

"But sometimes I do miss Charles and George so much. Yet I feel I must endure some of it alone for fear of adding to the guilt that is so near the surface in Amanda."

"I have found it remarkable to see the change in your daughter in such a short time. It is so clear from her letters. When she was with us, she was expressing the last dying gasps of anger toward your dear husband. I saw it in her eyes, how she would react to things that were said. All along I knew fatherhood to be at the root of her struggle with herself. And yet now her thoughts seem full of your Charles's memory. Everywhere she turns, she has said, she discovers pleasant memories, reminders of things he taught her which at last she is able to receive. I am sure the time will come when she will heal to the point where you will be able fully to express your own grief."

"I marvel as I watch it," nodded Jocelyn. "I don't know whether the parallel is apt, but I am frequently reminded of the Lord's words to his disciples, that it was for their good that he leave them, and that after his death the Spirit would bring many things to their remembrance."

It fell silent for some time. Both women were mature enough in years and life's experiences to enjoy the quietude, and to allow the stillness, in its own way, to knit their hearts even more closely together.

"In so many ways," said Jocelyn at length, "we have you to thank for the changes that have come to Amanda. You will never know what an answer to prayer you have been in our lives. All those years when she was gone, Charles and I prayed that God would send people to her who would be good for her and would love her with God's love. While so many coddled Amanda and justified her prodigality, even used it for their own ends, you were willing to make her face it. You cannot know how grateful I am to have my daughter back, and that the Lord sent her to you."

Hope's eyes filled as she listened.

"It almost seemed too much to hope for, but we prayed especially that she would be led to someone at the right time who would turn her back toward home," Jocelyn went on. "I have so longed for this moment, to be able to thank you personally. As remarkable as it seems that she could wind up high in a little village in the Swiss Alps, it would seem that he led her to you and the other sisters in answer to our prayer. Now that you are here, and because we prayed for you, in a sense, for so long, I feel like I have known you for years."

Hope smiled. "I often imagine the prayers of God's people intertwined in a great invisible tapestry," she said, "in which God weaves many threads together in ways we cannot see, and often will never see. But the prayers of the saints, all taken together, I believe, will result in the magnificent triumph of salvation and reconciliation, healing and growth, restitution and forgiveness, and most of all homecoming, when at last we have heavenly eyes to see it."

"That is a lovely picture!"

"Amanda was as much an answer to our prayers as we were to yours," Hope added. "That is the wonderful thing about our God. He so energetically takes care of us all, and leads us, by his Spirit, all to pray toward the same will that is in his heart to accomplish."

"He certainly used you in answer to ours. I am more thankful than I will ever be able to tell you."

When at last they stood, a long embrace followed.

When they separated, both women were weeping. Jocelyn Rutherford and Hope Guinarde knew they had each discovered in the other a lifelong friend.

46

Betsy and Sister Hope

—— ◆◆◆ ——

Watching from an upstairs window, Jocelyn Rutherford smiled as she saw Betsy outside below on the edge of the lawn. The girl had such a way with animals. She was now slowly inching her way toward a rabbit standing at the edge of the woods. Jocelyn had overheard her on several occasions, talking quietly to birds and sheep and rabbits, even little snails, in a soft voice different than she used for anyone else. She was no doubt speaking in her quiet animal-talk voice now, thought Jocelyn as she watched Betsy creep gently closer with hand outstretched.

Out of the corner of her eye, Jocelyn saw Sister Hope walking out from the house.

Hope paused ten or fifteen feet from the door when she realized what Betsy was trying to do.

The two stood still for several moments. Then Betsy seemed to become aware of the presence behind her. She turned and glanced back toward where Hope stood watching. As she did the rabbit scampered into the woods.

"I'm sorry I frightened your rabbit," said Sister Hope, now walking toward her again.

"That's all right," said Betsy. "He will come back."

"How do you know?" asked Hope as she approached.

"Because I have been making friends with him, and he lets me come a little closer every day. I tell him he has nothing to be afraid of."

"Do you talk to all the animals?"

"Yes."

"Do you think the little rabbit understands you?" asked Hope.

"I don't know," replied Betsy. "But I think he likes the sound of my voice."

"I'm sure he does. I've noticed that you like animals."

"They are my friends."

Hope took Betsy's hand, and they began walking toward the heather garden together.

"We have many animals where I live," said Sister Hope.

"Where is that?" asked Betsy.

"I live in the mountains of Switzerland called the Alps. Do you know where that is?"

Betsy shook her head. "What kinds of animals do you have?" she asked.

"We have chickens and goats, and two donkeys and three cows—"

"Oh, I would like to see the donkeys!" interrupted Betsy.

Hope laughed. "I am sure you would love them. But donkeys can sometimes be naughty."

"I would be so nice to them they would not want to be naughty."

Again Hope laughed. She was quickly falling in love with this girl!

"Perhaps you could come visit and help us take care of them."

"Oh, may I, may I ... please!" exclaimed Betsy. "I would take good care of them!"

"One of the women who lives with me, a lady named Galiana, loves animals just like you do. She makes sure that they are all well cared for. She feeds them every day and gives them nice fresh straw to sleep on. But sometimes she needs help, and whenever she must go away, then the animals need a friend because they miss her."

"I would be their friend."

"I am sure you would be," smiled Hope.

"I like cows too, but they don't seem to notice when I talk to them. When may I come?"

Hope laughed. "We shall see," she said. "It is a very, very long way."

They entered the garden. Hope led her to one of the benches and they sat down.

"What is that in your hand, Betsy?" she asked.

"A picture of my mother," replied the girl. "Would you like to see her?"

"Yes, I would."

Betsy handed her the small stained photograph.

"She is very pretty," said Hope. "You look like her, Betsy."

"Do you really think so?"

"I do."

"My father said she was a good lady, but I cannot remember her. Are you anyone's mother?"

"No, Betsy," smiled Hope. "I have no children."

"I wish you were my mother."

The words took Hope by surprise.

"What about Lady Rutherford?" she asked.

"I love Lady Jocelyn. But she already has two girls."

"She loves you very much."

"I want a mother who doesn't have a daughter and wants me for one."

A stab went into Hope's heart at the words. She glanced away, a sudden lump rising in her throat.

"For as long as I am with you," she said, reaching her arm around Betsy and drawing her close, "I will be as much a mother to you as I can be, Betsy dear."

They sat in contented silence. Gradually Hope began softly to sing a hymn. As she did she felt Betsy relax against her and snuggle imperceptibly closer. She continued to sing.

Christ our Redeemer died on the cross,
Died for the sinner, paid all his due.
Sprinkle your soul with the blood of the Lamb,
And I will pass over you.
When I see the blood, when I see the blood,
I will pass, I will pass over you.

Chiefest of sinners, Jesus will save,
All He has promised that He will do.
Wash in the fountain opened for sin,
And I will pass over you.
When I see the blood, when I see the blood,
I will pass, I will pass over you.

Judgment is coming, all will be there,
Each one receiving justly his due.
Hide in the saving sin-cleansing blood
And I will pass over you.
When I see the blood, when I see the blood,
I will pass, I will pass over you.

O great compassion! O boundless love!
O loving kindness, faithful and true!
Find peace and shelter under the blood,
And I will pass over you.
When I see the blood, when I see the blood,
I will pass, I will pass over you.

When she stopped, Betsy was breathing deeply and Hope realized she was sound asleep.

Tears filled Hope's eyes, and she continued to sit unmoving, the motherless girl sleeping happily in her embrace.

47

Inquisition

◆◆◆

The two women and one man walking along Bloomsbury were not smiling.

They were on business too sacred and important for smiles. It had been five days since their fateful meeting together. Sometimes the Lord's work was unpleasant, but they, his appointed guardians of truth, must take on the unpleasant task of separating the wheat from the chaff in order that the flock under their care not be misled.

They walked to the door of the parsonage of New Hope Chapel and sounded the knocker.

Timothy answered. His smile and greeting were returned by cold stares and nods. He recognized them all, and knew from their faces that they were not bearing happy tidings.

"Please, come in," he said warmly.

The three followed him inside, the man of the triumvirate puffing from the exertion of the walk.

He sat down stiffly. One of the women also joined him. The other preferred to stand.

"Would you care for some tea, Mrs. Packer?" asked Timothy.

"That will not be necessary."

"And you, Mrs. Paulus . . . Mr. Roul?"

The treasurer and chairman both shook their heads. It was uncomfortable enough having the man be nice to them. They wanted to get their business over and done with as soon as possible.

The initial discussion was brief and formal. They presented the charges, which were brief and comprised chiefly of the four points upon which they felt they could make an ouster stick. Although their objections to his theology were many, the four points raised were that the minister had expressed a hope that animals would share in the life to come, that his teachings on the Sabbath and tithing were suspect, that he had given it as a scriptural possibility that some provision may exist for the heathen after death, and finally that in general his ideas were tainted with liberal theology.

Following were listed many minor points that some in the congregation, notably two prominent deacons and their wives, were reported to have raised.

When Timothy finished reading the text that had been put before him, he looked around at his visitors and could not help breaking into a smile, which was followed by a laugh of incredulity.

"You cannot actually be serious?" he said.

"I am afraid we see no humor in the matter, Mr. Diggorsfeld," replied Mrs. Packer, who had refused the chair he had offered, drawing herself up in an offended manner, which, with her hair in a great bun on top of her head, made her appear almost six and a half feet in height. "These are highly serious matters of great import. We must protect the flock and preserve doctrinal truth." It was clear from her expression that she was not about to flinch in the face of adversity, and that Timothy's character and simple honesty would not move her an inch.

"But these statements are so exaggerated as to be not representative of truth at all," said Timothy.

"You do not consider yourself a liberal?"

"Not only do I not *consider* myself one, I am *not* a liberal."

"What are you, then?"

"I hope I am a disciple of Jesus Christ. Beyond that, I do not care for labels."

"Are you an evangelical?"

"As I said, I do not care for the label. But I will consent to it for your sake—yes, I am an evangelical."

"Do you consider yourself conservative on the major doctrines of the historic church?"

"I do."

"And yet you hold to such views as outlined here?" said Chairman Roul, speaking for the first time.

"As I indicated, most of what is written here is so exaggerated and unfounded as to be preposterous. So I don't know how to answer your question. We could take them point by point, but I am not certain that would accomplish a great deal. I will not defend myself. If it is enlightenment you want into my beliefs, as much as I can provide that without defense, I will try to oblige you. Let me respond, therefore, by saying that I do not try to be conservative or liberal. I try to find and live by the truth of the Bible. If others choose to interpret that quest for truth according to certain labels of their devising, that is not something I can prevent. But labels generally do not well serve the search for truth."

"But you *are* an evangelical?"

"Being an evangelical does not mean I do not think. That is the one thing I always try to get my people to do—following, as I see it, the example of our Lord who did exactly the same with his disciples. I realize that many in ecclesiastical leadership are threatened by free and fresh thought. But where there is no *thinking,* I do not see how true faith can exist at all."

"I must take exception to what you say," said Roul.

Timothy nodded respectfully. "At what point, Mr. Roul, if I may inquire?"

"That people should be encouraged to think," he replied. "Any minister who believes that is doomed to fail in the pastorate. It is for theologians to outline the doctrines of truth and then present those doctrines to the people in a simplified manner that they can understand."

"Where in Scripture, if I might ask, did you come up with such an idea?"

"People are not capable of accurately dividing the word of truth," answered Roul, avoiding Timothy's question.

"Then you have less faith in the human mind of God's creation than I do. God *wants* thinking men and women searching for truth in his Word, not swallowing the traditions of the elders without asking which are right and which are wrong."

The chairman paused briefly as he wrote down Timothy's statement, then looked up again.

"What, then, is your role as their pastor?" he went on. "It does not appear that you do much for the people if you intend to leave them floundering without direction."

"Is that what I said?" replied Timothy. "I prefer to see my role as pointing them to faith, and encouraging them in the living of that faith."

"How do you accomplish that?"

"In many ways. One of those ways is to teach and encourage them to ask questions, as I said, to think, and to go both to the Bible and their heavenly Father for answers."

The three looked around at one another with knowing glances.

More notations were added to the growing inventory of incriminating quotes.

"But not to teach them the doctrines of the church?"

"It is my duty," responded Timothy, "to teach the truths of the New Testament and the teachings of our Lord Jesus Christ."

A brief pause followed. Mrs. Packer now decided to drive straight into the crux of the matter with no more beating around the bush.

"What about the charge that you deny the importance of Jesus Christ and the cross for salvation?" she asked.

"It is untrue."

"There are those who say that you look to the Father for salvation."

"I do, exactly as did Jesus Christ himself."

"So you consider the Father more important than Christ for salvation?"

"I consider that our salvation lies in the love of the Father. It was to take us to that love that Jesus came to earth, that he died, and that he rose again, in order that we might know salvation in the Father's love and forgiveness and be one with him."

"Upon what do you base such an unorthodox view?"

"Upon the words of our Lord himself."

"Do you consider Jesus Christ the source of salvation?"

"He is the door to our salvation."

"But I insist that you tell me—what do you consider the *source* of salvation?"

"The love of God."

A long silence followed, during which the chairman and Mrs. Packer made a few additional notes.

48

I Believe

*L*et me ask you another question very directly," now said Chairman Roul again. If the women were afraid to speak the word, he was not. He wanted to get to the bottom of this single question most of all. "Are you or are you not a universalist?"

Timothy took in the question and inwardly sighed. He would prefer to follow the Lord's example and say nothing. He realized his words would be less than useless against such a mentality, and that silence in the face of an accusing spirit was normally the best course of action. Yet on this occasion he felt the need to clarify his position as best he could. Maybe *one* of them would hear him.

"No," he said finally. "I am not a universalist."

"What, then, is your view on the afterlife? Do you believe in hell?"

"Of course," replied Timothy. "It is a clear scriptural truth, one intended, as is everything of God's, for the ultimate benefit of creation. How could I not believe in it? The Bible is the source of truth, and upon it I base everything I believe."

"Oh, so you *do* believe in the Bible," commented Mrs. Packer with obvious sarcasm. "I hadn't been able to tell."

"Certainly I believe in the Bible."

"You believe it is the literal and inspired Word of God?"

"Definitely," replied Timothy, looking at them more perplexed than ever. "My entire life and ministry is based upon its principles and precepts."

"Then ... where do these charges against you originate?" she went on.

"I presume from people who love the Bible's truth less than I do."

She squirmed and was silent.

"So you believe in the literal inspiration of the Bible?" now repeated Mrs. Paulus, still unable to bring herself to accept his affirmation.

"Absolutely."

"But, as I understand it, you are in sympathy with the universalist view?" said Roul, coming back to the sticking point.

"I am intrigued by it," replied Timothy. "But I recognize that the Bible is not clear on the matter, just as it is not clear on many matters. I believe God desires us to inquire into but not be dogmatic on such issues. Therefore, I have formed no definite opinion."

"How can you possibly say the Bible is not clear on the matter?"

"I assumed that you were familiar with the contradictory verses."

"Now you are saying that the Bible contradicts itself!" exclaimed Mrs. Packer.

"Anyone who has studied the Bible knows as much."

"I thought you believed it was the inspired word of God," said Mrs. Paulus.

"I do. But for reasons known only to God, it contains contradictions, or perhaps what should more accurately be called *apparent* contradictions. That is why we must approach it with a thinking and open mentality."

"Give me an example of such a contradiction," said chairman Roul, poising his pen to take down Timothy's words, thinking that this should provide all the evidence they needed.

"Well, since you brought it up, your question about universalism offers a perfect example," replied Timothy. "We have Matthew 25:46, Philippians 2:10, and John 12:32 all staring each other in the face—the first seeming to indicate eternal damnation, the latter two apparently indicating universal salvation through Christ. These three passages force me—as one who believes that *all* Scripture is inspired, not just those portions which bolster my own views—to keep an open mind with regard to the afterlife. I have no alternative but to say, 'I do not know the answer to this scriptural conundrum.' "

The three shifted uneasily. It was not the answer they had expected.

"The Word of God is unequivocal," said Mrs. Packer, quickly gathering herself to resume defense of the faith. " 'And these shall go away into eternal punishment, but the righteous into eternal life.' "

"I agree with you, Mrs. Packer," nodded Timothy, then added a smile as he went on, "those words do seem unequivocal. Just as unequivocal as Jesus' words when he said, 'If I be lifted up from the earth, I will draw *all* men unto me.' It is indeed a mystery, is it not, what is in God's heart to do?"

She did not see what there was to smile about.

"I take it, then, that you believe all men will be saved?" said Roul.

"Not necessarily," replied Timothy. "I don't know. My point is simply that Jesus said he would draw *all* men to himself. Since I take the Bible as truth, I do not know how to reconcile the *everlasting punishment* of Matthew 25:46 with the *all men* of John 12:32 and the *every* knee and *every* tongue of Philippians 2:10. Therefore, being one who believes that we must take the whole Bible as it comes to us, not pick and choose to support our opinions and traditions, I keep an open mind. I say that the Bible has not revealed full truth to us on this matter, just as it has not revealed full truth to us on many matters. In short, I am not a universalist, but neither am I *not* a universalist. I am a disciple of Jesus Christ and a son of his Father. I seek to obey them both, and I leave *full* revelation of truth, and the eternal souls of mankind, believers and unbelievers alike, in his hands."

"Why do you insist on propagating this particular doctrine?" said Mrs. Packer, her face flushed in anger at what she had just heard.

"I don't," replied Timothy. "What I have just said to you behind closed doors, I have never said from the pulpit. I especially do not propagate it because, as I said, I honestly do not know what is in God's heart to do. These are high matters that can be confusing to some who have been so steeped in the tradition of the elders that they have ceased to be capable of thinking without fear of committing some doctrinal indiscretion. I do not care to try to set anyone right about this or that point where that tradition satisfies them, especially if they long for nothing more in the way of meat and drink for their souls. And in particular I have no interest in propagating a view I am uncertain of myself. I simply want people to think, and to approach their Bibles honestly, not fearfully and with closed minds. So I do not talk of these things openly."

"There are those in your congregation who say that you force this view upon others."

"They are in error. They make more of my words than I intend. There are also many people of my acquaintance, and in the church as well, who have no idea I even think about such things. Speculation about the afterlife is no more important to me than any other aspect of faith. Far *less* important than obedience, for example, and many other more important truths upon which I base my ministry."

"And what would those important truths be?"

"That we seek to discover the character and nature of God, and that we obey him."

"And you consider that more important than doctrinal purity?"

"In that doctrinal purity is impossible in this life, I consider knowing who God is and obeying him absolutely more important. We are commanded to love God and live by obedient faith. Nowhere that I know of are we commanded to seek doctrinal purity above those two highest commands."

Timothy paused a moment, then continued.

"My intent as a minister of the gospel is to point people to their heavenly Father. For those many whose image of him has been marred by a centuries-old tradition not based in the Gospels, I attempt to introduce them to their *real* heavenly Father—that is the Father whom Jesus called *Abba*—and tell them that he is good, loving, and trustworthy, exactly as Jesus said he was. Upon that foundation, I try to help Christians think, to encourage them to prayerfully search the Scriptures. On matters of doctrine I try to encourage them to draw their own conclusions as they feel the Spirit of Christ leading them. Raised in the tradition of conservative evangelicalism, I have been a seeker along the same road as most of my people. Even now I do not hesitate to say that my own perspectives remain growing and incomplete."

"Then we want to know your position on these things now," said Mrs. Packer.

"What things?"

"I should think it would be obvious," she answered in a huff, "—the afterlife, heaven and hell, eternal judgment and damnation."

Timothy thought a moment.

"All right, then. I shall try to answer you as best I can. What I am comfortable saying with absolute certainty on the matter is this—"

He paused and glanced at all three. Their pens were ready to take down what he said, and when he opened his mouth he spoke slowly so there could be no mistaking his words.

"—I believe that the love, goodness, forgiveness, and trustworthiness of the Father of Jesus Christ are infinite," Timothy went on. "Therefore, I trust Him completely. Though he slay me, yet will I trust him, and so may all creation likewise trust him. He is a *good* Father, so all he does must be good and can only be good. His essential nature is *love*, so everything that proceeds out of his divine will must reflect that love. It is in his heart to *forgive* infinitely. Jesus told us so. Therefore . . . we may trust him, and trusting him, may trust him for *all* things, for *all* men, for *all* possibilities. What is in the heart of God the Father to do will be full of *love*, full of *goodness*, and full of *forgiveness*. And in those foundational truths of his essential nature and character I rest. In those foundational truths of his essential nature and character are all my questions swallowed up. I am at peace . . . for I trust Him."

"Is that all?" said Mrs. Paulus.

"Beyond that, I care not to go," answered Timothy. "You asked for a statement of my current view, and there you have it."

"That sounds like a liberal speaking, Mr. Diggorsfeld," said Mr. Roul.

"That is your label, not mine."

The chairman squirmed slightly in his chair.

"To speak bluntly," Timothy continued, "in my view the key reason why those on both sides of this issue struggle so hard to systematize their personal theologies, and err in the process, is that they don't trust God enough. That is why this issue has proved so divisive in the church this past half-century in our country. So many feel they must put together a system of belief constructed out of their own incomplete intellects."

"You consider our intellects incomplete and our doctrines in error?"

"Certainly. All of ours are," Timothy went on. "I would far rather trust God for biblical uncertainties than to convince myself that I am sure of his will on every thorny issue as many seem to consider it their duty to do. Being wrong does not frighten me nearly so much as being unable to trust God to do what is right and good, though my fallible human intellect will of a certainty be unable to discern how he will accomplish that in every instance. That is why I do not take sides in this dispute, but say only, 'God knows.' "

A long silence followed.

At length Mrs. Packer, her face still red, nodded to her two colleagues. They rose.

"I think we have heard enough," she said. "Good day, Mr. Diggorsfeld."

Chairman Roul offered a tentative hand in Timothy's direction.

"Just to set your mind at ease," he said, "we had agreed before we came that your salary would continue for a month. You will also have continued use of the parsonage during that time. We will, however, arrange for a supply minister for this Sunday and for all subsequent services until a permanent replacement has been found."

Timothy shook his hand, still not believing what he was hearing, then looked at the two women. Mrs. Packer was unmoved.

"You have preached your last sermon at New Hope Chapel," she said firmly. "Good day, Mr. Diggorsfeld."

She turned and led the others out of the room and to the door, which she opened herself and hurried through before Timothy had a chance to reach it.

49

Refuge

When Timothy Diggorsfeld arrived at Heathersleigh Hall four days later, one look at his face the moment Jocelyn saw him standing at the open door told her something dreadful must have happened. He had not been able to summon the strength to telephone her, but had simply arranged his affairs, notified a few of his parishioners, packed two small bags, and then taken the train to Devon at his earliest opportunity.

"Timothy!" exclaimed Jocelyn. "You look devastated—what is it? Are you ill?"

At sight of his friend, Timothy broke into tears. Jocelyn went to him with open embrace. They stood in one another's arms for several long moments.

"Actually, Jocelyn dear," said Timothy as he stepped back with a thin smile, "I think it was seeing you that finally made me break down more than what happened. But now that I am here, I am already feeling better."

Behind them Catharine and Amanda approached from the kitchen with concerned looks on their faces.

"But what *is* it, Timothy?" repeated Jocelyn as they stepped inside and she closed the door. "*What* happened?"

"I have lost my church," Timothy replied simply.

"Timothy . . . what . . . how!"

"The difficulties I told you about before had escalated more than I was aware. I am being replaced. I was notified four days ago."

"I cannot believe it. Oh, Timothy, I am so sorry!"

"It is not such a bad thing, perhaps. Once the pain ceases, I shall probably be happier for it. But it is not easy when a man's work and lifeblood are rejected by those very ones he has tried to serve. Although no doubt the Lord would have something to say to me about my present attitude with regard to such things."

"It makes me angry!" said Catharine. "How dare they do this to the best minister in London?"

Timothy laughed. "Catharine, you will be a good tonic for me!" he said, still laughing.

"I mean it!" she said. "I have a good mind to make you give me the people's names and then go to the city myself and tell them a thing or two!"

"Well, we shall see, my dear! I must admit," he went on, more seriously again, "that I am concerned for a few in the congregation. Some had begun to make great progress toward seeking the heart of their Father in new ways. I think especially of your sister and brother-in-law, Jocelyn."

"I am certain they will continue in the ways you have taught them."

"Some will. But the engulfing tide of the evangelical elder-traditions will surge in to re-swallow others, and that is unfortunate. However, I must remind myself that God is far more concerned about their—"

He stopped as the unfamiliar figure of a woman descending the staircase caught his eye.

"Oh, I'm sorry . . . I didn't know you had—" he began again.

Glancing back, Jocelyn saw Sister Hope approaching to join them.

"Oh, this is too wonderful," exclaimed Jocelyn, the fact just dawning on her, "having the two of you here together!—Timothy, this is our special guest from Switzerland."

"You remember, Timothy," now put in Amanda excitedly, "—the chalet where I stayed. This is Sister Hope."

"Hope," added Jocelyn, "meet our dear friend, Rev. Timothy Diggorsfeld."

"Hello, Rev. Diggorsfeld," said Hope, walking toward him with a smile and outstretched hand, "I am Hope Guinarde."

"I have indeed heard about you!" said Timothy, receiving her warmly. "But the *Reverend* won't do at all. And I can already tell that neither is this an occasion for the *Mister*. Please call me Timothy. And let me say that it is an honor to make your acquaintance."

"Likewise," smiled Hope.

"This is so exciting," said Jocelyn. "I am sorry, Timothy, about what has happened. But I cannot help being happy you are here!"

"What did happen?" asked Hope. "I missed out on the beginning of the conversation."

"Nothing serious," replied Timothy as they all now made their way into the sitting room. "I have just been ousted from my pastorate is all."

"On what grounds?" she asked.

"Let me just say that I apparently have a disconcerting way of putting things," replied Timothy. "I encourage free thought. I enjoy exploring theological gray areas. And I believe that the Father of Jesus is a good and loving Father. That probably about sums it up, other than to add that the more tradition bound among my denomination tend to find some of my perspectives unnerving."

Hope laughed with delight. "People have the same problem with me!"

"Then you and I will have to have a long talk," rejoined Timothy. "I am anxious to hear about it."

"As I am to learn of your disconcerting perspectives! There is nothing I enjoy more than a disconcerting doctrine."

Timothy roared with glee. He liked this woman already.

Catharine, however, could not get over her profound annoyance at the reason for Timothy's visit.

"I don't see how you can laugh, Timothy," she said. "Don't you care what people think, that they say wrong things about you? It would make me so angry."

Timothy sighed and quieted.

"It hurts if I dwell on it," he answered after a moment, "that I could have given them so many years and yet at the first opportunity these few are ready to believe distortions and untruths about me. But the ones who care to know the truth will come to me and ask for my perspective and will try to sort it out for themselves. As for those who don't care to find out the truth, I don't suppose there is much I can do, and I will have to grow to a point where I no longer care."

"You are not there yet?" asked Hope.

Timothy smiled. "Sad to say, no," he replied. "It hurts, though I am embarrassed to admit it. I wish I were full enough of love that I did not notice when others do me wrong. But then I am not quite done with this life, and the flesh does still pester me more than I would like."

50

Do Your Will, Lord

*L*ater that same evening, all the inhabitants of Heathersleigh Hall, including Sarah Ministerly, Hector Farnham, Elsbet Conlin, Timothy Diggorsfeld, Hope Guinarde, and Jocelyn Rutherford and her two daughters, Amanda and Catharine, gathered informally in the sitting room.

Sarah and Jocelyn were busy serving everyone tea and light snacks. Hope was showing Betsy how to turn a flat sheet of paper, by many twists, folds and unfolds and refolds, and other mysterious crinklings and shapings, into a little paper donkey.

Timothy and Catharine were enjoying yet another laugh over Catharine's plan to march to Birmingham and take the denominational headquarters by storm.

Amanda had asked Hector which had been her father's favorite horses and why, and for the last half an hour had been listening to an animated breeding history of Heathersleigh's stables.

If only Maggie could be with them, thought Jocelyn, then all would be nearly complete.

Timothy intended to stay a few days, then return to London to begin preparations for packing up his belongings and few earthly possessions. Beyond that his plans were uncertain.

He and Hope had hit it off immediately and could not already be two more kindred spirits in the Lord had they known one another for twenty years. That afternoon they had ridden out together to see the recuperating Maggie, had enjoyed a stroll in the heather garden, and had been talking continuously almost from the moment of Timothy's unexpected arrival.

"I hope you will consider my offer, Timothy," Jocelyn said, approaching with a tray of biscuits. "You may have a room to yourself rent free for as long as you like. It could not suit me better if you stayed for the rest of your life! You may use Charles's office for study, for writing, to use as your own."

"Timothy, why don't you write a book!" exclaimed Catharine.

"That's a wonderful idea," replied Sister Hope.

"The Scotsman started writing because he was removed from his church too," added Catharine.

"Yes, I am familiar with the story," said Timothy, "—Arundel, it was."

"Didn't you meet him once?" asked Jocelyn.

"Yes, after discovering his books I made the pilgrimage to Italy to see if I might catch a glimpse of him. I'd forgotten to tell you and Charles about it."

"You actually met him . . . in person?" said Hope.

Timothy nodded. "He received me graciously," he said. "There was a gentleness to his spirit that somehow reminded me of one of the great apostles of old—humility, strength, spiritual fire, even holiness. However, he was very elderly at the time. Our encounter was brief. I wanted to ask about his experience in the pastorate but could not bring myself to do so. I had always wondered what it must have been like for him, so when I returned to England, I visited his former church in Arundel. When several years later I read in the *Times* that he had died, I wept."

"A remarkable story," said Hope. "Perhaps it shall be for you to follow his example."

"It would seem I am following it now in matters of my church more than I would have ever dreamed of doing."

"And perhaps now the time has come for you likewise to leave the pulpit to preach to a wider audience through your pen."

Timothy smiled. "You are all very kind," he said. "I appreciate your encouragement, Jocelyn, and your generous offer. But does the Lord want my new home to be in Devon? That is the question. My heart would leave London in an instant. But I must go where *he* wants me. I must do what he wants. If he wants me in the city, I must be willing. I intend to talk to Stuart tomorrow and seek his counsel and prayer on the matter as well."

"When will you return to London?" asked Hope as Jocelyn set the tray down and took a seat.

"In two or three days," replied Timothy.

"I must return to the city as well," said Hope. "I have a number of things I must attend to there."

"Why not join me?" exclaimed Timothy. "We shall ride in on the train together."

"Splendid," said Hope. "I cannot think of anything I would enjoy more."

"I wish I had a guestroom to offer you, but the parsonage is small, and," Timothy added with a sigh, "as you know, I can hardly any longer even consider it my own. One of my first decisions will be what to do about lodgings after this month is out."

"Timothy," pleaded Catharine, "please come to Devon and live at Heathersleigh and write books! Heathersleigh would become famous if we had a renowned author living here."

He laughed again.

"We shall see, Catharine!"

Gradually the mood quieted. Slowly all the individual conversations ceased, and their collective spirit, as of one accord, was drawn to prayer.

Jocelyn was the first to break the silence.

"*Dear Lord, our Father,*" she prayed, "*how much we have to thank you for, especially one another. None of us have whole families left, yet we are family for each other. You are so good to us. We have all felt the pain of loss. I lost my husband and my son. Hope lost her husband. Betsy and Amanda and Catharine all lost their fathers. Timothy has now lost his church. Yet we have you. You are our good and loving Father, and we praise you even in the midst of our earthly losses and our earthly suffering, because you are good, and you love us, and you always keep us in the palm of your hand.*"

As Jocelyn's prayers ceased, everyone in the room reflected on the words she had just spoken. Except for Hope, who had the sisters at the chalet, and Sarah who had a sister in the city, and Jocelyn's sister Edlyn, this was all the family the rest of them had in the world.

"*We find ourselves facing uncertainty in our lives,*" now prayed Timothy. "*We find sudden change all around us—my dear Jocelyn and Amanda and Catharine with the loss of their Charles and George, Betsy now without her father, and myself now suddenly without my church. We seek your guidance, Lord. Show us your will.*"

"*And about my marriage, Lord,*" added Amanda. "*Show me what you want me to do . . . and give me strength to obey you.*"

"*And how you want us to use Heathersleigh,*" added Jocelyn. "*We desire that our lives and this place you have provided be what you want it to be. We do not know what your purpose for the future is for Heathersleigh or for us, but we want it to be your will that is done, not our own.*"

"We pray too for Grandma Maggie," prayed Catharine. *"Restore her to health and vitality, Lord, and we thank you so much for all her life has meant to us."*

"Lord," prayed Hope after another brief silence, *"as anxious as I was about leaving my dear chalet, I should have known I could trust you. For you were sending me to a new place of life, with new friends, new brothers and sisters. I feel as at home here as if I were back in Switzerland. I pray for my dear sisters at home. Be at work in all their lives, and keep them close to one another."*

Her lips stilled as she silently prayed for guidance concerning the other matter which was on her mind. But she could say nothing openly about it yet.

"Do your will with us, Lord," she added. *"Only your will."*

"Sustain and uplift us in our weakness, Father," Timothy now prayed. *"We confess our weakness to understand and to trust you in our pain, in our uncertainty. We do not always know what you want us to do, except we do know what you want to do in us—that is for us to trust you. Thank you for bringing me to these friends to sustain me in the rich fellowship of the Spirit during this time of trial for me. Thank you for their love and encouragement."*

"And we thank you for Timothy, Lord," added Jocelyn.

"Thank you for the new blessing of allowing me to know my sister and your daughter Hope," Timothy went on. *"Thank you for her contribution to the life at Heathersleigh. We feel life here, Lord . . . your life. We all continue to feel the pain when we think of dear Charles and George. But we know they are with you, and we know you are enriching our lives in new ways, even through this loss."*

Timothy paused, and when he began again his voice was soft and full of emotion. He was near tears as he prayed.

"And with this new loss that has come to me, I ask for your guidance as well as your sustaining strength. Sometimes I feel so weak, so unable to trust you. I have been walking with you so long, and yet have come such a short way. But you know my heart, and that my desire is to walk with you in trust and obedience. Help me, Lord, and guide my steps at this hour when my future is uncertain."

His voice faltered. Hope now prayed again.

"Help us remember in whatever crisis we face," she said, *"that when we feel we are hanging on to a rope for dear life in the middle of a dark, bottomless well, even when the rope is unraveling, that in the center of it is a strong steel cable called* God is good, *and that as long as we hang on, you will eventually pull us up to you."*

"*Amen, Lord,*" said Timothy again. "*And I pray for the dear people at New Hope Chapel, that you will keep them growing toward truth, and growing toward you. I pray especially for my brother Roul and my sisters Packer and Paulus. Be real to them, Lord, in new ways . . . fresh, alive. Prick their brains and hearts to inquire more deeply into your nature and your purposes both for mankind and for themselves. Draw them all close to your heart.*"

"*Guide us through life's uncertainties, hardships, sufferings,*" added Jocelyn. "*Let us never lose sight of your goodness, though circumstances unravel around us.*"

Again it fell silent. For many long minutes they sat in prayerful contemplation. Gradually one by one they rose and made their way to their rooms.

51

Departure

◆◆◆

The next afternoon, Hope again saw Betsy alone outside and followed her out across the lawn. Betsy heard the door close behind her, turned, saw Hope, then came bounding toward her. They met in embrace, then Betsy took Hope's hand and began pulling her across the lawn.

"Come, Sister Hope," she said excitedly.

"Where are you taking me?"

"I have something to show you!"

She led to the edge of the wood and took a few steps into the trees, still tugging on Sister Hope's hand, gradually slowing as she went.

Finally she stopped, took her hand out of Hope's, and gently parted the shrubbery of a bush about four feet high.

"Look what I found, Sister Hope," she said, pointing into the undergrowth.

Hope's eyes followed her finger.

"It's a bird's nest!" said Betsy.

"Oh yes . . . I see . . . so very tiny."

"And look—a little blue egg broken in half."

"It's a hummingbird's nest, Betsy! The egg must have just hatched and the baby flown off with its mother."

"Do you think it will come back?" said Betsy, a little disappointed.

"Probably not until next year," replied Hope. "But if the nest is still here, perhaps the mother hummingbird will use it again."

They turned and made their way hand in hand back out of the wood. It was quiet for a minute; then Hope spoke as they went.

"I have to leave and go to London," she said.

"May I go with you, Sister Hope?" asked Betsy.

"I'm afraid I must go alone," replied Hope.

"Please . . . please let me go with you."

Hope looked away. How she loved this girl!

"I have a great deal to do, Betsy."

"But you are coming back?"

Hope had not planned to return to Devon. Before she had time to consider it further, however, the words were out of her mouth.

"I will come back before returning to Switzerland," she said. "I promise you will see me again. From now on, we will always be the best of friends."

◆ ◆ ◆

The following morning they all rode into Milverscombe together, taking the car and one buggy, to see Timothy and Hope off for London.

As the train pulled into the station and slowed to a steamy, noisy stop, Hector and Timothy began loading the bags.

Betsy began to cry. Hope took her a little way aside, then stretched her arms around her.

"We will be friends forever, remember, Betsy?" she whispered in her ear.

"But I am afraid you will never come back."

"I *will* come back, Betsy. You may trust me."

They returned to the others. More good-byes followed, not nearly as tearful as otherwise might have been the case, since Hope had shared her promise to Betsy with the others. This was only a temporary parting, not a final farewell one.

As the train pulled out five minutes later, both Timothy and Hope sat beside one another quietly absorbed in their own thoughts. Both had expected to leave Heathersleigh alone, but they had been given the unexpected blessing of sharing the departure with a new friend. Yet both felt the breaking of bonds deeply with those they were leaving behind on the platform, especially Hope for the girl whose eyes were red as she stared after the departing train. For the first thirty or forty minutes it remained silent between them. It was the first time their dialog had not been free flowing and energetic since their meeting.

"A remarkable family," commented Timothy at length.

"Indeed," nodded Hope. "I can hardly imagine that a week ago I did not know them—except for Amanda, that is. Now it seems I have known Jocelyn all my life."

Gradually they again began to talk, and soon were laughing and conversing freely. Eventually the discussion came round again to Timothy's church difficulties.

"Hope, will you answer me a simple question?" said Timothy.

"I don't know—I can try."

"Why are some Christians afraid to think? Why are they threatened by ideas outside the comfortable boundaries of what they have been taught?"

"That sounds like two questions," laughed Hope.

"All right, then, two questions. And I will add a third—Why is orthodoxy, by the standards of their peers, a higher thing to seek than the will of God? What *is* it with the tightly constricted mindset of the average evangelical? I do *not* understand it."

"Is it because people are afraid to think for themselves?" suggested Hope.

"But why?"

"Is it that orthodoxy inbreeds fear in order to perpetuate itself? It is something I have often wondered."

"Have you noticed how the moment any question is raised, tradition-loving, fear-bound Christians run to their pastor or favorite theologian to ask what they are 'supposed' to believe. I face it all the time."

"What do you say?"

"I tell them to go to the Gospels and seek God's truth. But most are not capable of such a thing. When they go to the Gospels, they are only capable of seeing their own narrow orthodoxies reflected back to them, and then they wrongly assume those orthodoxies to originate in the Lord's words rather than in the biases of their own brains."

"I agree that fear is a deeply rooted component of the ordinary religious mind," said Hope. "Growth is not viewed as the expansion of spiritual awareness, but the accumulated learning of the correct doctrines in more and more detail."

"Precisely," rejoined Timothy. "And what a trial this has been for me as a pastor. The more doctrines one knows by rote, with accompanying proof-texts, the more evangelicals flatter themselves that they are growing. In fact it is just the opposite. This doctrine preoccupation leads not to growth at all, but to spiritual stagnation and the numbing of the spiritual senses."

"How did you ever wind up in the pastorate in the first place?" asked Hope. "You seem far too free a thinker to be happy in the pulpit."

"Because I love the Church, I love God's people, and I love the Bible," replied Timothy. "I thought that by teaching the Bible and nurturing God's people, perhaps in my own small way I could help change the Church."

"And now?"

"I begin to despair, I must admit. I have given my whole life to these ends, and it is difficult to see much fruit."

"I am sure there is abundant fruit in many individual lives."

Timothy sighed. "I am sure you are right. But being prone to melancholy, sometimes it is difficult for me to keep my head up in the face of daily discouragements."

"There are the Rutherfords of Devon," said Hope, "to come back around to where we started this conversation. Their faith began, as I hear the story, from a tract thrown into the gutter by Jocelyn's husband . . . a tract which led him to you."

Timothy smiled.

"Yes . . . you are right," he said. "Even if there was nothing my ministry had to show for itself than the story of that family, I would have to say God be praised."

They arrived in the great metropolis two hours later.

Timothy took Hope to her hotel. When time came for them to part in the lobby, they paused, looked at one another for a moment and smiled. Neither could find adequate words.

Timothy opened his arms and Hope went straight into them, returning his embrace affectionately.

"Thank you, Timothy," she said. "These have been such wonderful days shared with you."

"I thank God for them too," he said. "You have helped breathe fresh new winds into this tired soul."

They stepped back and smiled again.

"I will call on you tomorrow here at the hotel," said Timothy.

When Hope lay down in her hotel bed that evening, she was thinking about many things, not the least of which was her future, and what she was going to do about a little girl named Elsbet.

PART IV

•••

Spring-Fall 1916

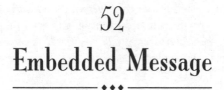

52

Embedded Message

♦♦♦

*T*he hour was late.

Usually her times of prayer and thought came early. But on this night Amanda had been unable to sleep. She rose, not with a sense of anything momentous at hand, but from simple sleeplessness. By the time she had put on a dressing gown and tiptoed through the dark and silent house and upstairs to the library, however, a feeling began to grow upon her that sleep had been kept from her for a reason.

Indeed something momentous *was* at hand. A long-hidden secret was about to be revealed. It had been four days since Timothy and Sister Hope departed. With Heathersleigh again quiet and life resuming its routine, Amanda's thoughts had returned to their former pathways.

She now sat, an hour later, alone in the library, the great family Bible they had only discovered recently open on a table in front of her, a thin desk lamp illuminating a sheet of paper beside the Bible containing various notes, phrases, and scriptural references jotted down in Amanda's hand. It was sometime after one in the morning. All was deathly still. If mice inhabited the walls and hidden passages of Heathersleigh Hall, they were not about. This night had been reserved for silence and revelation.

Amanda glanced at her paper. The unplanned investigation had begun as she perused the family record in the opening pages of the large Bible in front of her and saw the odd reference in the margin next to the names Ashby Rutherford and Cynthia Rutherford, the twins born to Henry Rutherford's wife, Eliza, on February 11, 1829—a tiny handwritten notation, *Genesis 25:24–5; 29:16; 25:26.*

Why had someone entered these references at the edge of the page of birth records?

She recalled Maggie's Bible with similar notations. Maggie had explained them in connection with the discovery of the key and secret panel of her secretary.

What were the passages referred to in Maggie's Bible? It had something to do with the birthright.

Amanda now turned to the three verses indicated and read them in order, first the twenty-fourth and twenty-fifth verses of chapter 25: *And when her days to be delivered were fulfilled, behold, there were twins in her womb. And the first came out red, all over like an hairy garment; and they called his name Esau.*

Then the sixteenth verse of chapter 29: *And Laban had two daughters: the name of the elder was Leah, and the name of the younger was Rachel.*

And finally the twenty-sixth verse, again in chapter 25: *And after that came his brother out, and his hand took hold on Esau's heel: and his name was called Jacob: and Isaac was threescore years old when she bare them.*

Amanda sat back slowly and thought a moment.

What could be the connection between Leah and Rachel, and Jacob and Esau? What did these three strange passages have to do with each other?

Her eyes perused the lines again. As they did, she seemed to notice something strange.

Amanda bent down close to the page and squinted in the pale light. Were her eyes deceiving her, or did she see a faint line, barely visible, apparently made by a lead pencil, underlining a few of the words of the three texts? Whatever the lines were, they were surely not accidental. Someone had made them . . . but why?

Now she read only the underlined portions.

At first they seemed to make no sense. She read them again, this time jotting down the underlined words as she went.

Suddenly her eyes jolted open and she sat back in her chair stunned. Had she just seen what she thought she had seen!

She read over the verses again.

Could it possibly be! Who made these markings!

She looked at her page and read them over a third time, then remembered Maggie's Bible.

She would have to go out to Maggie's tomorrow and look at it again. The notations and clues in the two Bibles must be connected. And perhaps a visit to the church would be in order as well.

She mustn't let her imagination run away with her, Amanda told herself. She would say nothing until she investigated further.

But the cryptic message hidden in the lines of text could not be coincidental. And she had a feeling she knew what it meant!

With great difficulty, but knowing there was nothing further she could do at present, she rose, turned out the light, and returned to her room to try once again to get to sleep.

53

Deciphering the Clues

——— ♦ ♦ ♦ ———

*W*hen Stuart Coleridge opened the door of the parsonage the following morning, he was as surprised to see Amanda standing before him as he was at her request.

"Good morning, Vicar Coleridge," she said. "I wondered if I could look at the parish records."

Again, he thought to himself, reminded of the strange man who had called on him the previous summer. "Of course, Amanda," he replied. "Which ones?"

"Births," she answered.

Wondering what this could all be about, but saying nothing for the present, the vicar led Amanda from the parsonage to the church, where he removed the two large books bound in faded red leather from the case where they were kept and set them on a table before her. Amanda flipped through the first two or three pages of the oldest volume until she came to the early years of the nineteenth century, then began following the entries more closely until she arrived at the year she sought.

There were the births noted on February 11, 1829, exactly as in the family Bible at home: *Ashby Rutherford*, the eldest, followed on the next line by his twin sister, *Cynthia Rutherford*.

To the right, in the margin, was also noted a Scripture reference similar to that in the Bible back at the Hall—*Genesis 25:26, 31; Psalm 27:12*—with the tiny initials *A.C.* and a date beside them, *16–7–55*.

What was it with all these marginal references? thought Amanda, first in Maggie's Bible, then in the family Bible, and now in the parish records!

Had they all been made by the same hand? And yet . . . as she studied this particular note in more detail, it seemed distinctive from that in the

Hall Bible, the hand a little shakier and more upright. But both, though slightly different, began with Genesis 25.

"Do you have a Bible I could borrow for a moment, Vicar Coleridge?" asked Amanda.

"Certainly," he replied. "I will only be a moment."

He turned and left. While he was gone, Amanda took the time to write down the references of the three verses on a fresh sheet of paper. The vicar returned a minute later with a Bible in hand. Amanda looked up the three passages and read them in order, beginning with the twenty-sixth verse exactly as she had read it last night in the library: *And after that came his brother out, and his hand took hold on Esau's heel; and his name was called Jacob: and Isaac was threescore years when she bare them.*

Then the thirty-first: *And Jacob said, Sell me this day thy birthright.*

And finally Psalm 27:12: *Deliver me not over unto the will of mine enemies: for false witnesses are risen up against me, and such as breathe out cruelty.*

Again, she thought, what was the connection between this odd collection of verses?

Her mind full of many questions, Amanda thanked Vicar Coleridge, and began the same walk from the village to Maggie's cottage that she had made long ago at age nine. Today, however, she was on a mission and she had no idea where it would lead.

As she went she reflected on what she had discovered thus far. If the wild notion that the clue in the family Bible had sparked was true, it would certainly seem to be confirmed by the reference in the parish birth record. And it would be confirmed by Maggie's suspicions that Bishop Crompton had indeed been paid off as a false witness.

Amanda quickened her step, the sense growing upon her that Orelia Moylan's old Bible might hold the remaining clues that would unravel the final threads of this mystery.

Hastily she entered the cottage, gave Maggie a hug and kiss, then asked, "Grandma Maggie, may I borrow your Bible?"

"Certainly, dear. What for?"

"I'll tell you later," replied Amanda, picking up the Bible from the open secretary, where it always lay. She kissed Maggie again and was gone as quickly as she had come, leaving Maggie watching after her, wondering what it could all be about.

Amanda hurried back to the library at the Hall, where the family Bible still sat open from the previous night. She placed the two Bibles side by side, then also laid on the table the two sheets of her notes, including the parish record entries she had just written down forty minutes ago.

She turned again to the significant passage in Mark 4 Maggie had shown them months ago where she had found the words about the mystery and the key, and with the tiny reference to Genesis 25:31–33.

Genesis 25 again!

Every clue pointed to the Jacob and Esau passage!

Amanda turned in both Bibles to the now significant passage in Genesis 25 about Esau's sale of his birthright to Jacob, which was noted in all three marginal additions. She glanced back and forth between them. Maggie had assumed the Jacob and Esau reference had only to do with the sale of the cottage to Bishop Crompton. But now Amanda was sure there was more.

She continued to stare at the pages, now focusing her attention, not on the faint underlinings in the family Bible, but on the page in Maggie's small Bible. In the center column, among the various references and cross-references of the study portion, had been added in hand a small additional reference beside the thirty-third verse: *Proverbs 20:21*.

What could Proverbs 20:21 have to do with Jacob and Esau?

Was this a clue meant to be followed?

Quickly Amanda flipped through the pages to the book of Proverbs, then read the indicated twenty-first verse: *An inheritance may be gotten hastily at the beginning; but the end thereof shall not be blessed.*

The verse was underlined, this time boldly and unmistakably in pen.

What could it mean?

Again, in the center column among the printed references, she saw another handwritten notation, this time leading her to *2 Chronicles 10:16*. Hurriedly she turned back toward the front of the book, found 2 Chronicles, and read: *And when all Israel saw that the king would not hearken unto them, the people answered the king, saying, What portion have we in David? And we have none inheritance in the son of Jesse: every man to your tents, O Israel: and now, David, see to thine own house. So all Israel went to their tents.*

This time only the words "we have none inheritance in the son" were underlined.

And again she noted a verse among the center references beside 2 Chronicles 10:16. This time she found herself led to 2 Kings 9:12: *And they said, It is false; tell us now,* Amanda read as soon as she located the verse. *And he said, Thus and thus spake he to me, saying, Thus saith the Lord, I have anointed thee king over Israel.*

Only the words "It is false" were underlined.

By now Amanda's brain was racing feverishly. She realized she had stumbled onto a circuitous scriptural trail laid down generations before, she suspected by Maggie's own grandmother Orelia Moylan, the midwife who had delivered the Rutherford twins. Maggie had probably noticed these underlinings at some time in her years of Bible reading, but had no doubt never followed them in order as Amanda was herself doing now, beginning with the first reference beside Genesis 25:33. And when the underlined portions were read in sequence, they told an incredible tale. Was it possible, thought Amanda, that she had at last unearthed the long-hidden secret about what had actually happened that night back in 1829?

Yet once more she noted a verse among the center references beside 2 Kings 9:12. This time it led her to Numbers 27:8: *And thou shalt speak unto the children of Israel, saying, If a man die, and have no son, then* ye shall cause his inheritance to pass unto his daughter.

And from it to Ezekiel 16:46: *And* thine elder sister *is Samaria, she and her daughters that dwell at thy left hand: and thy younger sister, that dwelleth at thy right hand, is Sodom and her daughters.*

And there the scriptural trail seemed to end. For beside Ezekiel 16:46 no additional reference in the center column was noted.

Amanda sat back, eyes wide, shaking her head as she glanced again over the page of notes she had taken, and the underlined words she had written down while progressing through the verse-to-verse trail.

54

Culmination

❖❖❖

Amanda was more certain than ever that she knew what had happened that night in February of 1829.

It explained everything, all the way down to Bishop Crompton's curious acquisition of Heathersleigh Cottage and his even more curious disposition of it at the time of his death. It might explain why the family Bible had been hidden, and why the London branch of the Rutherfords had always been so anxious to find it.

If only George were here, Amanda thought. He would love all this! And be able to make sense of it in a minute. But he wasn't. So she had to try to figure it out herself.

Her discoveries might explain many of the hidden mysteries about this place that was their home. But they could not tell her what was to be done as a result.

Realizing what these revelations might mean, should she divulge what she had found? If she did, what would be the consequences to them all?

Amanda sat dumbfounded, staring at the Bibles and her papers, for probably thirty or forty minutes.

Gradually her spinning brain began to calm and her spirit quieted. What had begun to dawn on her was too huge. She could hardly take it in.

Half an hour later, still in a near daze, she rose. There was only one place she could pray through these stunning developments, and seek the guidance she knew was required for the decision that must be made. She knew it would not be her decision alone. But she had to know her own heart before she shared it with anyone else. Too much was at stake to speak lightly.

In a deepening mood of prayer, she left the library, descended the stairs, and walked out of the Hall.

Jocelyn came into the library shortly after Amanda's departure. She saw the two Bibles on the table, still open, along with Amanda's pen and several pages of notes spread about.

What had Amanda been working on? she wondered. And why was Maggie's Bible here too?

With curiosity Jocelyn made her way slowly around the library, pausing at the north window. She saw Amanda outside walking slowly across the meadow. Was she on her way to Maggie's? But as she went, Amanda now bore more northward, her step purposeful, toward the wooded area west of the cottage.

Jocelyn watched her for a few moments more, then turned to leave the library, pausing once again at the table where Amanda had been engaged in what looked like such intensive study. She glanced over the papers one more time, having no idea that the thoughts tumbling through her daughter's mind at that moment so deeply concerned her own future.

Amanda reached her father's prayer wood, as she still called it.

So many emotions always filled her every time she came here.

But today was like no other visit she had ever made. She had been given glimpses of the eternal reality of this place on previous occasions. But now for the first time the deepest purpose of Charles Rutherford's prayer sanctuary was sweeping into the maturing spiritual consciousness of his daughter—that purpose to which God ultimately leads all those of his sons and daughters who seek him: the abandonment of their own ambitions, their own very selves, into his higher Will.

For all the years of her life, until these recent months of heartache-stimulated reversal and growth, the daughter of Charles Rutherford had tried to run from this highest of all life's necessities, this ultimate of all life's opportunities, this most precious of all life's choices—the great *privilege* which, if not taken as the privilege it is, will ultimately one day become the great *requirement*, of laying down one's own will, in a glorious moment exemplifying the crowning triumph of human freedom, to say, " 'Not mine, God my Father, but your will be done.' "

Amanda was now approaching that flowering pinnacle of human personhood, which her father's and Timothy's friend the Scotsman called the blossom of humanity: the moment of holy abandonment of herself into Another.

At last were the prayers of the father fulfilled in the daughter.

Amanda knelt down in the soft, moist grass, bowed her head to the ground, and began to pray, not knowing that she was doing exactly what her father had done during so many seasons of his own relinquishment of will.

"Lord, do your will," burst from within her. *"Show me what it is . . . tell me what you want me to do."*

She paused briefly, and then as the tears began to flow, added, *"Make me willing, Lord . . . even to give up Heathersleigh, if that is your will."*

When Amanda rose to walk home half an hour later, her course was clear. She was confident she knew the Father's will, and knew what her own father would have done in the same circumstances. Ultimately it would be her mother's decision. But it would affect both herself and Catharine, as well as their mother, for the rest of their lives. So her own mind had to be clear.

As she went at last she understood that painful laying down of her father's she had so resented years before when he had told them of his decision to leave politics.

Amanda smiled sadly as she went. *He* had known what it meant to relinquish, not only his life, but the ambitions of that life, into God's hands. She had never understood before now. At last she understood his heart.

And now an equally momentous relinquishment faced them all. Her own personal battle with it had just been won, through many tears and much anguish of heart, and was now behind her.

As she was walking across the meadow back toward the Hall, still trying to dry her red eyes, she saw Betsy coming toward her.

"Betsy, have you seen my mother and sister?" asked Amanda.

"No," answered Betsy. "When is Sister Hope coming back?"

"I don't know, Betsy—in a few days, I believe."

"I wish she would hurry." Betsy walked toward the barn.

Amanda continued on. She found Catharine in the kitchen and Jocelyn in the sun-room.

"We have to go to Maggie's," she said. "Mother, would you have Hector hitch a buggy? I have to go get some things from the library."

Before they could ask what it was all about, she was climbing the stairs. Jocelyn knew from the look on her face and the tone of her voice that whatever was on Amanda's mind, it was serious.

She set about making preparations at once.

Upstairs in the library, Amanda began to gather the two Bibles and her notes, then paused and thought a moment.

She turned and walked to the well-familiar shelf that had been her father's favorite, reached up, and took down a thick volume of one of the Scotsman's stories. How she chanced to think of it she hardly knew, but all at once she remembered her father reading the passage to them years ago.

It took her three or four minutes to find it. Then, with the familiar voice of her father in her mind's ear, she sat down and again read the now poignantly significant words:

> To trust in spite of the look of being forgotten; to keep crying out into the vastness whence comes no voice, and where seems no hearing; to struggle after light, where there is no glimmer to guide; to wait patiently, willing to die of hunger, fearing only lest faith

should fail—such is the victory that overcomes the world, such is faith indeed.

After such victory Cosmo had to strive and pray hard. It was difficult for him.

But there was still one earthly clod clinging to Cosmo's heart. There was no essential evil in it, yet it held him back from the freedom of the man who, having parted with everything, possesses all things. The place, the things, the immediate world in which he was born and had grown up had a hold of his heart. The love was born in him and had a power in him. And though it had come down into him from generation after generation of ancestors, Cosmo was not one of those weaklings who find in themselves certain tendencies toward wrong which perhaps originated in the generations before them, who say to themselves, "I cannot help it, so why should I fight it?" and at once create a new evil, and make it their own by obeying the inborn impulse. Such inheritors of a lovely estate, with a dragon in a den which they have to kill that the brood may perish, make friends with the dragon, and so think to save themselves the trouble.

I do not think that Cosmo loved his home too much. I only think he did not love it enough in God. To love a thing divinely is to be ready to yield it without a pang when God wills it. But to Cosmo the thought of parting with the house of his fathers and the land that yet remained was torture. Instead of sleeping the perfect sleep of faith, he would lie open-eyed through half the night, hatching scheme after scheme to retain the house. He had yet to learn to leave the care of it to him who made it, for his castle of stone was God's also. As he lay in the night in the heart of the old place, and heard the wind roaring about its stone roofs, the thought of losing it would sting him almost to madness.

Suddenly one night he became aware that he could not pray. It was a stormy night. The snow-burdened wind was raving and Cosmo lay still, with a stone in his heart, for he was now awake to the fact that he could not say, "Thy will be done." He strained to lift up his heart to God, but could not. Something had arisen between him and his God and beat back his prayer. A thick fog was about him. In his heart not one prayer would come to life.

It was too terrible! Here was a schism at the root of his being. The love of things was closer to him than the love of God. Between him and God rose the rude bulk of a castle of stone. He crept out of bed, lay on his face on the floor, and prayed in an agony. The wind roared and howled, but the desolation of his heart made it seem as nothing.

"God!" he cried, "I thought I knew you, and sought your will. And now I am ashamed before you. I cannot even pray. But hear my deepest will in me. Hear the prayer I cannot offer. Be my perfect Father to fulfill the imperfection of your child. You know me a thousand times better than I know myself—hear me and save me. Make me strong to yield to you. And therefore, even while my heart hangs back, I force my mouth to say the words—*Take from me what you will, only make me clean and pure.* To you I yield the house and all that is in it. It is yours, not mine. Give it to whom you will. I would have nothing but what you choose shall be mine. I have you, and all things are mine."

Thus he prayed, with a reluctant heart, forcing its will by the might of a deeper will that *would* be for God and freedom, in spite of the cleaving of his soul to the dust.

For a time his thoughts ceased in exhaustion.

When thought returned, all at once he found himself at peace. The contest was over, and in a few minutes he was fast asleep.

It was not that after the passing of this crisis on this particular night there was no more stormy weather. Often it blew a gale—often a blast would come creeping in—almost always in the skirts of the hope that God would never require such a sacrifice of him. But he never again found he could not pray. Recalling the strife and great peace, he would always at such times make haste to his Master, compelling the slave in his heart to be free and cry, "Do your will, not mine." Then would the enemy withdraw, and again he breathed the air of the eternal.

When a man comes to the point that he will no longer receive anything except from the hands of him who has the right to withhold, and in whose giving alone lies the value of possession, then is he approaching the inheritance of the saints in light, those whose strength is made perfect in weakness.

With fresh tears in her eyes, Amanda rose, replaced the book, gathered the two Bibles, and went downstairs to join mother and sister.

55

Letter Home

*H*ope Guinarde sat at the writing desk in her room of the Rose Garden Hotel.

She didn't know how much longer she would be in England. Perhaps she would get home before this letter reached the chalet. But her heart was so full that she had to find expression for her thoughts.

Dear Sisters, she wrote, my beloved Gretchen, Luane, Anika, Galiana, Agatha, Marjolaine, Clariss, Regina, and dear Kasmira (I am so pleased to be able to list you as one of our family!):

So much has happened since I came to England I hardly know where to begin. To think I was anxious, even afraid, hardly seems possible, for now I am full of more contented thoughts and feelings than I will ever be able to convey. Your gifts helped so much. Every one was so lovely, personal, and thoughtful, and whenever I grew anxious or lonely they gave me a delightful distraction. I laughed and cried halfway across France.

I was fearful when I actually got to London. The feelings of my youth tried to overwhelm me. But I faced them one at a time—and now am feeling much better, because the old fears have been put away for good.

I have been to the mission board. There were many memories but no regrets. It only made me happier for all the Lord has done in these latter years of my life. London is all so very different now knowing I have a family to return to. I looked up Mrs. Weldon who first befriended me. She is quite elderly and a widow now, but she remembered me, and we shared a fond visit and a laugh or two about my first dreadful days at the mission.

After arriving in London I went to Heathersleigh, Amanda's home. It is a lovely country estate. We had no idea who Amanda was. Her father was an M.P. some years ago. Amanda is so changed I almost did not recognize her as the same young woman who was with us, as indeed she is not. She was in a dark cocoon when she came to us, but now she is a beautiful moth. She reminds me of the stunning and colorful moths we saw in the jungles of New Zealand. But a moth, not a butterfly, for a slight sense of night, a hint of sadness, seems always to cling to her beauty. I recognize the look of grief from when I lost my husband and baby.

As she wrote, a fresh wave of sadness briefly overwhelmed her at the reminder, and hot tears filled her eyes.

"Goodness, Lord," said Hope when the tears were spent, "where did that come from?"

And then there is Betsy! Hope wrote as she continued with her letter.

She is a darling girl of about fourteen whose father was recently killed and who found her way to Heathersleigh, Amanda's home. The moment I laid eyes on her I felt she to be the reason the Lord sent me to England. I think he may have her in mind as the chalet's next guest. I have said nothing to her or Amanda's mother yet. But I am so excited when I think of it, for she is such a dear. I told her about you, Galiana. She loves animals.

Hope set down her pen, her mind full of Betsy.

She rose from the writing table and left the room. She needed to walk . . . and think . . . and pray about this opportunity she had to give a girl the kind of life she had always dreamed of.

She found herself an hour later on the familiar street outside the orphanage where she had spent so many of her own early years, a multitude of thoughts and emotions swirling undefined through her.

Is this where Betsy could ultimately end up, she wondered, or someplace just like it? She could not stay at Heathersleigh forever. Eventually Jocelyn would have no choice but to inform the authorities, and then she would become a ward of the state. What would become of her then?

Memories flooded Hope's heart and brain. How good God had been to her. How he had watched over her all her life. He had brought her out of this dark, cold, granite tomb to the most beautiful place in all the world and given her the lovely chalet built by her husband's father.

She almost laughed aloud to think of the contrast between her past and her present life.

He had protected her all these years, giving her the name *Hope*, knowing that he would fulfill her name and her childhood dream of having a place to belong.

And now she was in a position of being able to do that for another. No . . . not she—he. *He* could do that same thing for Betsy, who, like her, had no mother, no father, no place to call home.

She wished she could take all the girls here back with her. But she knew such a thing was impossible.

She gazed up at the tall, cold stone walls, hardly able to imagine Betsy having to move to such an institution.

As her thoughts and prayers continued to gather themselves around the memory of Betsy's face in her mind's eye, she thought of her own daughter, the precious little one who had not even lived twenty-four hours.

"*Lord,*" Hope began to pray, "*is Betsy meant to be something more than simply a visitor, a guest, a sister at the Chalet? Is she—*"

She could not complete the prayer.

Again her eyes filled with tears as she turned and began walking away from the orphanage. But the power of its memories could no longer touch her, and her heart swelled with joy at what God might intend.

56

Amanda's Unwelcome Proposal

◆◆◆

In the cottage Amanda sat at Maggie's kitchen table with her mother and sister and Maggie, the recently discovered family Bible, Maggie's Bible, and her sheets of handwritten notes, open and spread out before her as she explained her visit to the church and the clues she had found. She had just completed reading the various passages noted in the three sources.

"So if you put it all together," Amanda was saying, "and read only the faintly underlined portions, in order, from the family Bible, it reads..." She paused and glanced at one of the papers. "'... there were twins in her womb. And the first came out... daughter:... the elder was... And after that came... brother out...'"

She set the paper aside and pulled Maggie's Bible toward her, with the sheet on which she had written its clues.

"And then, if you read the words underlined in your Bible, Grandma Maggie," Amanda went on, "in the sequence that I looked them up, the same message is repeated in more detail: 'An inheritance may be gotten hastily at the beginning; but the end thereof shall not be blessed... we have none inheritance in the son . . . It is false . . . If a man die . . . ye shall give his inheritance unto his daughter . . . thine elder sister.' "

Amanda stopped and glanced around the table at the other three.

"Do you see it?" she said. "I think the message is as clear as can be. Cynthia was really the first born of Henry Rutherford's twins, and Daddy's father, Ashby, was born *second*."

The words sank in around the table, though seemed to strike no one with as much force as Amanda had expected. None of the others yet appreciated where the revelation was leading.

"Exactly as I thought," said Maggie, nodding her head after a moment. "I knew the vicar had been paid off for something. That must have been it, and he helped cover it up."

"But why?" asked Jocelyn. "Why reverse the birth order?"

"Because old Henry didn't want a daughter to inherit," said Maggie, her blood beginning to run hot.

"They falsified the order so that Henry's *son* could inherit," added Amanda. "You almost had it solved, Grandma Maggie, just not this one final piece."

"It was no secret how old Henry came to hate his wife," Maggie went on. "He wanted a son; everyone knew it. I thought there was something suspicious about the old villain. So he inverted them in the parish register, just like Jacob and Esau, switched the birthrights even as his wife was dying, and got the vicar to be part of his lie with him, leaving his *true* heir, Cynthia, out of her inheritance. It was a scoundrel thing to do."

"But who left all these clues?" said Jocelyn again.

"Maggie's grandmother, who attended to the birth and would have known what happened better than anyone," answered Amanda. "Afterwards she must have wanted to leave some clue that would point to the truth. That's when I think she made these notations in the family Bible."

"But how did she get to the Bible in the Hall?" asked Catharine.

"I think I can answer that," said Maggie. "She had been there often with her father, who was the carpenter for the lord of the manor. With her lifelong connections to the place, she could easily have got in, written down that reference in the birth record and underlined those words that you found, Amanda, then hidden the Bible in the secretary she knew about because it was just like her father's."

"What about the parish record?" asked Catharine.

"The handwriting looked different to me," said Amanda.

"That clue must have been left by Crompton—the initials A.C.," said Maggie. "What did you say was the date?"

"July 16, 1855."

"Just a year before his death, when this cottage was transferred to my grandmother."

"It is puzzling," said Jocelyn. "Why would he make that notation so many years later?"

"And what I haven't been able to understand," added Amanda, "—if he was going to alter the parish record, why he didn't simply change the original entry?"

"And why didn't my grandmother just tell someone what had happened," added Maggie, "such as my mother, or even me?"

"We may never get to the bottom of some of the mysteries about Heathersleigh," said Amanda.

As she spoke Jocelyn glanced over and saw that Maggie had grown pale and was clutching the table.

"What is it, Maggie?" she said in alarm.

"Nothing, dear," replied Maggie, her breathing shallow. "I think the excitement over old Henry wore me out, that's all. I am still not myself. I get tired too easily. Sometimes I think I am—"

"Nonsense," interrupted Jocelyn. "You just need a little rest. Let me help you over to the divan and you lie down. You will be able to hear everything we say."

"Thank you, dear."

Amanda rose from the table. "Would you like some water, Grandma Maggie?" she asked.

"Yes, dear . . . thank you."

"I wish Charles were here," sighed Jocelyn a minute or two later, once she had Maggie comfortably resting on the couch. "I wonder if he knew anything about all this. Even with all you have discovered, Amanda, we still have no actual proof all this is what happened."

"But don't you think it is likely . . . more than just *likely*—undeniable?"

"It does seem so," replied her mother. "I admit it is difficult to put any other construction on those underlined passages, even though such deductions as you've made would probably not stand up legally or in court."

A long silence followed.

"This is all very interesting," said Catharine at length. "But what difference does any of it make? Cynthia and Ashby have been dead for years. Who cares who was born first? What do legalities and courts have to do with it, for heaven's sake?"

Amanda and Jocelyn looked at one another. Jocelyn had at last begun to apprehend a portion of why Amanda was so serious and why she had been crying earlier. She thought she knew what Amanda's thoughts were pointing toward, though she did not yet see all that had come to Amanda in the prayer wood.

"I think Mother was referring to what might be the consequence if news of what we have discovered fell into other hands," replied Amanda to Catharine's question.

"Whose hands?—I don't know what you're talking about," said Catharine. "Who would care about any of this anyway?"

"Don't you understand, Catharine?" said Amanda. "The inheritance, even perhaps the title itself—though I'm not sure it would have passed to *Cynthia* rather than Ashby—but in any event the bulk of the inheritance followed the *wrong* family line."

"What do you mean, the wrong family line?" asked Catharine with a puzzled expression on her face. "What are you saying?"

"That had the inheritance come down through the years from Henry as it *should* have," Amanda continued, "—that is through his eldest daughter, Cynthia—Heathersleigh Hall would now belong to Cousin Gifford, *Cynthia's* son. In other words, Father would never have been lord of the manor at all."

"What!" exclaimed Catharine.

"That is what makes all this so important," replied Amanda, her voice now growing soft.

The silence which fell around the table this time was long and reflective. It almost seemed dishonoring to the memory of their beloved Charles to imply that he had been an unwitting usurper to a title and estate that should never have belonged to him. The moment the words left Amanda's mouth, they fell like chilly icicles into the hearts of all these women who had loved him so deeply.

"I don't like it," said Catharine at length. "You make it sound as if Daddy did something wrong."

"That's not how Amanda meant it, dear," said Jocelyn. "Your father could not have known."

"Well, I don't even like the sound of it," rejoined Catharine. "I don't want to think about it. Besides, none of it matters now anyway. It's too late. It's all over and done with."

"It might not be *completely* over yet, Catharine," said Amanda.

Catharine glanced toward her with a look of question. She did not like the tone in Amanda's voice.

"What do you mean?" she returned a little sharply. "Daddy's dead. And like Mother said, there is no proof."

"Perhaps the only proof we ought to need is what we know is the truth, not whether it could be legally disputed or not."

"But *why?*" insisted Catharine.

"Catharine," Amanda began, then glanced over at her mother, "don't you see what we have to do?"

"No, I don't see it at all," rejoined Catharine testily.

"If Heathersleigh is not rightfully ours, and never should have been, then we have no other alternative."

"Alternative than what? You're not implying—" began Catharine, at last giving in to her mounting disbelief.

"I feel we should give up Heathersleigh," said Amanda. Her voice was soft but firm. "It should rightfully belong to Cousin Gifford's side of the family."

"Amanda, you can't be serious!" exclaimed Catharine.

Amanda did not reply.

"Even if it is true," Catharine continued, "what good will possibly be accomplished by revealing what you have discovered? You can't be suggesting actually turning Heathersleigh over to Gifford! I don't believe what I am hearing!"

More silence followed.

"Mother," said Catharine after a moment, "tell Amanda this is absurd, that what she is thinking won't help anything."

"I don't know if it is a question of helping anything, Catharine," replied Jocelyn. "What Amanda is saying is that we should perhaps consider it because it may be the *right* thing to do."

"But it is ridiculous! Isn't possession supposed to be nine-tenths of the law or something?"

"I think I agree with Amanda."

With an imploring look, Catharine now glanced over at Maggie.

"Your sister is speaking from the Lord's heart, dear," said Maggie. "I think you should listen."

"Mother . . . please!" Catharine said, turning back toward Jocelyn.

"Though many years have gone, that does not undo a wrong," said Jocelyn, "restitution and truth still have to be sought no matter how long it has been."

"Actually," Amanda now said again, "one thing you said is true, Catharine—I don't suggest turning it over to Gifford."

"I am relieved to hear that!"

"I think the right thing to do might be to place Heathersleigh in *Geoffrey's* hands rather than his father's."

"Oh no—it goes from bad to worse!" cried Catharine. "Geoffrey! How does that help matters?"

"I am not sure I understand you now, Amanda," said Jocelyn.

"It is nothing I can put my finger on exactly, Mother," replied Amanda. "But not only must we do what is right, we also must be good stewards of what has been placed in our hands, even if originally by deceit. I don't think giving Heathersleigh to Gifford would be wise stewardship over the estate, which is the Lord's more than it is any of the rest of ours. I have the feeling he would misuse it, maybe even sell it."

"What makes you think Geoffrey would be any better?" asked Catharine.

"I don't know, just a feeling I have. I think Geoffrey is changing. If we follow through with this and undertake to transfer the estate to him, I have the feeling he would take it very seriously."

"I cannot believe what I am hearing! Don't tell me his proposing to you went to your head. You're not thinking of . . . *marrying* him, are you!"

"Catharine, that was years ago. This has nothing to do with that. No, I'm not thinking of marrying him. I'm not thinking of marrying anyone."

Catharine said nothing.

"But that has nothing to do with the fact that there is no denying that Geoffrey is the true heir to Heathersleigh in the next generation, not you or me."

"I don't believe this," exclaimed Catharine, suddenly jumping up from her chair. "Who do you think you are? You are always wrecking everything. You made Mum and Daddy sad all the time. And now you come back and try to turn our lives all upside down!"

She stopped and stood in horror at what she had said.

"Oh, Amanda . . . Mother—I am so sorry!"

She turned and ran from the cottage.

Maggie and Jocelyn were quietly weeping, not for the possible loss of their beloved home, but for what Amanda had become, and for her willingness to relinquish what would have eventually become hers.

57

Argument

The expensive dinner laid out across the white linen tablecloth in a secluded corner of an exclusive Paris restaurant had been sitting untouched ever since the appearance of the piece of paper Ramsay Halifax still held in one hand.

"Look, Adriane, I have no choice," Ramsay was saying, glancing toward the message he had received that afternoon. "These people are serious."

"I'm tired of it," replied his irritated mistress, Adriane Grünsfeld, alias actress Sadie Greenfield. "You're always leaving, and I never know when or where I'll see you again . . . or *if* I will see you at all."

"There is a war on. Certain sacrifices have to be made."

"Not by me. I'm not interested in this war."

"I'm being well paid, darling. Surely it is worth it so that we can have a good life after the war. And it won't be much longer. I'll carry out this one last assignment and then tell them I'm through."

She laughed, making no attempt to hide her sarcasm.

"And your mother and that man Barclay—I cannot stand the sight of him when he gives me the evil eye. Are you going to tell *them* you're through?"

"I can handle them."

"Like you've handled them till now?" she rejoined, laughing again with disdain.

"What is that supposed to mean?"

"That you always do their bidding. You're twice the man Barclay is, but you always cower around him like he's got some power over you. I hate him."

"I'm doing all right for myself," snapped Ramsay, all the more annoyed with her comment in that he knew there was a certain degree of truth in it.

"All I know is that if you don't get that mess with the English girl resolved so that you can marry me, *I'm* through."

"Soon, I promise . . . just let me take care of this one last assignment, then you and I will settle down together."

"Settle down . . . where! That hardly sounds like you, Ramsay. All of Europe is at war. I have the feeling you like it. Where is someone like you ever going to settle down?—Vienna, here in Paris, the States, perhaps . . . or back in England with—"

She paused abruptly. The comment hadn't been planned. But now that it had nearly escaped her mouth, after a second's hesitation she let it come.

"—with your wife."

"Leave her out of it!" snapped Ramsay testily.

"How can I?" she snapped back. "What am I supposed to think?"

"She means nothing to me."

"Do you really expect me to believe that? You married her."

"I had to. She's probably dead by now anyway."

"And maybe not. Before we go any further, I want her taken care of. I refuse to marry a married man."

"You haven't objected to being with me before now."

"That's different," said Adriane in a huff.

"Relax, darling," said Ramsay, trying to calm her down. "I'll look into it."

Adriane glanced around and made a halfhearted attempt to stab a piece of cold veal with her fork. She was beginning to wonder what she'd gotten herself into.

58

Two Visitors

The three Rutherford women walked slowly and thoughtfully back toward Heathersleigh Hall. As she thought about it, Catharine found the discussion at Maggie's no more agreeable now than when she had first realized where her sister's thoughts were leading. It was the closest she had come to actually being angry with Amanda since she had returned home. She had let out some steam and was sorry, but it still wasn't resolved. She walked a little way apart from the others, silently nursing her stunned disbelief.

As they went they saw a tall figure walking across the meadow toward them.

"I do believe that looks like—" began Jocelyn.

"Terrill—I mean ... it's Lieutenant Langham!" exclaimed Catharine, breaking into a half run. In an instant the cloud over her countenance disappeared.

As she hurried toward their visitor, she saw Betsy now running out from the Hall to join the party.

"Hello, Lieutenant," said Catharine, slowing the same instant Betsy scampered by.

"Hello, Miss Rutherford," he replied, glancing to his right as a blur dashed past them. "Who was that!" he laughed.

"Where did you all go?" cried Betsy, reaching Amanda and Jocelyn. "I've been looking everywhere for you."

"We had to go see Grandma Maggie, dear," laughed Jocelyn. "Hello, Lieutenant Langham," she added, glancing behind Betsy where Catharine and the lieutenant now approached.

"Lady Rutherford ... Miss Amanda," said Langham, nodding first to Jocelyn, then Amanda. "It seems my timing is always a bit off. You are out every time I call. At least on this occasion there are no streams to leap over and geese to tackle!"

They all laughed, glad for the lighthearted memory to replace, even if temporarily, the heaviness of the matters concerning their future which had been occupying them before the lieutenant's unexpected appearance.

"We are glad you are here, Lieutenant," said Jocelyn. "I would say your timing could not be better. It is nearly teatime."

"Thank you, Lady Rutherford," he went on, "but we do not have a great deal of time."

"We?"

"Lieutenant Forbes is with me. He hopes to speak with you for a moment too. But we are on naval business."

"Then we shall hurry right in and get tea on the table," insisted Jocelyn. "—Betsy, how would you like to go visit Grandma Maggie for a little while? I was planning to return to the cottage, but if you would like to, it would be a big help to me, and I know she would like to see you."

"Yes, I'll make her tea," replied Betsy. "She always asks me to read to her out of the Bible."

"Splendid, dear. Be sure to run get me if she needs me. And if she becomes drowsy, let her sleep."

"I will!" replied Betsy and ran off eagerly. Then she paused and turned. "Do you know when Sister Hope will be back?" she asked.

"No, Betsy dear. But I am sure it will not be many more days."

They turned and continued toward the house as Betsy scampered off toward the wood.

Twenty minutes later the three women and two naval officers were gathered in the east sitting room, whose window looked out across the lawn toward the heather garden, enjoying tea and light conversation. It had become obvious to Jocelyn that Lieutenant Forbes was still somewhat shaken by the death of her husband, as well as her son's having saved his life. Though his head injuries appeared to have healed, it was clear that, for his part, the visit had been intended to help put his mind at ease regarding the family of the man who had saved his life and lost his own.

"I am so glad to see that you are all doing well," he had just said.

"Yes, Lieutenant," agreed Jocelyn. "We miss Charles and George, and always will. But we know where they are, and therefore we are at peace."

Forbes took the words in with a thoughtful nod. "It has been difficult for me to put the incident behind me," he said, "but being here with you helps a great deal."

As they continued to chat together, Lieutenant Langham now turned toward Amanda.

"When I saw your sister in London, Miss Rutherford," he said, "she mentioned that you were in the city consulting with Rev. Diggorsfeld about your marriage—"

"You saw Catharine . . . when?" replied Amanda, glancing back and forth between the two.

"When the two of you were in London. Miss Rutherford and I had a visit in Hyde Park."

"I see," nodded Amanda, throwing Catharine a mischievous smile. "I hadn't realized that."

"I wondered," Langham went on, "whether you have had any further contact with Mr. Halifax."

"No . . . none," replied Amanda. "I had hoped you might have some news."

"Unfortunately . . . no, I'm afraid," replied Langham. "We have learned nothing either. So your . . . uh, marital status is unchanged?"

Amanda nodded.

Langham pulled his watch from his pocket and glanced down.

"We do need to be on our way," he said. "We are due in Plymouth in two hours."

"You're not being reassigned?" asked Jocelyn.

"No," Langham replied. "Only a temporary duty which I hope will be brief."

"What is it?" asked Catharine.

"I am sorry, Miss Rutherford," he answered, "but I cannot say."

"Oh, a secret mission!" she said with a smile.

"Something like that. Let me just say that we are on a special assignment."

"It sounds dangerous."

"Let's hope it won't come to that. We are just trying to keep track of someone for the army."

"But you are in the Royal Navy."

"The army and navy have found it necessary to join forces in this case. It may be nothing, but with a war on, we have to be certain."

"You're following someone?"

"I think I have said enough," he said with a light laugh. "Perhaps too much!"

Langham rose as if to leave.

"Before we go," he said, glancing toward Jocelyn, "I wonder if I might have a word with you, Lady Rutherford . . . in private."

The two girls glanced at one another.

"Of course, Lieutenant," replied Jocelyn as she stood. "Come upstairs with me to the family sitting room.—Girls, I am sure you will be able to keep Lieutenant Forbes occupied."

Catharine cast Amanda a look which said that she did not find the older Forbes nearly so interesting as the younger Langham.

"I will say my good-byes to you both now," said Langham, turning toward each of the young women. Miss Rutherford . . ." he said to Catharine, "—Miss Amanda," he added, now nodding toward Amanda.

"Good-bye, Lady Rutherford," said Forbes, rising and shaking Jocelyn's hand. "It was wonderful to see you again. Thank you for your hospitality."

Lieutenant Forbes took his leave and went to wait in the car.

"Amanda," said Catharine when they were alone, "I apologize again for what I said back there. I am *so* sorry."

"Think nothing of it," replied Amanda. "I'm sure what you said was true enough."

"But I don't want you to think I used to think that all the time. There were occasions when I would be confused or frustrated with things you would say and do. I admit it. But they were very rare; you've got to believe me. I have very fond memories of our childhood together."

Amanda smiled, and the two sisters embraced.

About twenty minutes later they heard Lieutenant Langham's booted footsteps coming down the stairs. They waited until the car engine started outside, then bolted from the sitting room and up the stairs in search of their mother. They met Jocelyn as she reached the first-floor landing.

"Mother, what was that all about!" exclaimed Catharine.

"Never mind," said Jocelyn with a smile. "Just a private talk between me and the lieutenant."

"Mother!"

"I'm sorry, but you will get nothing out of me. He made me promise."

"Mother . . . please!"

"Let me turn the question back on you. What was all *that* about,

Catharine—you and he meeting in London?"

"She won't tell me a thing, Mother," Amanda added. "I've been pestering her about it ever since Lieutenant Forbes left. I wondered why she was so bubbly on the train ride back to Devon!"

"And now you know," said Jocelyn. "So, Catharine . . . it comes out that you had arranged to visit Lieutenant Langham all along."

"I didn't," laughed Catharine. "It was a mere coincidence."

"It still sounds suspicious to me," rejoined her mother. "I don't know whether we can believe you or not."

59
Hope's Return

*B*etsy had been watching the windows constantly for two days. Jocelyn had begun to worry that the girl was sinking back into the uncommunicative melancholy of her first days at Heathersleigh. She was slowly withdrawing and growing increasingly restive.

But the moment Betsy saw the carriage coming up the drive, she flew down the stairs and ran out to meet it, grinning from ear to ear. Sister Hope scarcely managed to set foot to the gravel before she was fairly overrun.

"Betsy dear!" she exclaimed laughing, trying to keep her balance amid a charging hug that nearly knocked her over.

"I couldn't wait for you to get back," said Betsy. "I have so many things to show you! I found another hummingbird nest."

"I want to hear all about it," laughed Hope. "First let me get my bags inside. And I have something exciting to tell you about too."

"You do! What?"

"Help me with my bag, and then we shall take a walk together. You can show me the nest, and I will tell you my surprise."

Already Betsy had grabbed one of the bags and was eagerly lugging it toward the house and on up to Hope's room. Hope followed her, pausing to greet Jocelyn, Amanda, and Catharine at the door. Affectionate kisses and hugs followed.

"Betsy has been in an absolute state waiting for you," said Amanda, "—hasn't she, Mother?"

Jocelyn laughed as she nodded. "I have never seen her like this," she said. "Something about you went straight to her heart."

Hope took in the words with quiet thankfulness to the Lord for giving her instant confirmation to what was in her mind to do.

"Jocelyn," she said, "might I be able to have a word with you, just for a moment before Betsy gets back downstairs?"

"Certainly," nodded Jocelyn.

Hope set her bag down, and they walked a little way from the door out away from the Hall.

"I don't want to say anything to Betsy without speaking with you first," Hope began. "So what would you think if I asked her if she would like to visit Switzerland with me?"

"I think she would enjoy that very much. It is a wonderful idea."

"And you would have no objection?"

"None at all."

Twenty minutes later Betsy and Hope were outside together. Betsy had hold of Hope's hand pulling her along, again toward the woods.

"I have a question to ask you, Betsy," said Hope. "How would you like to come with me when I leave next time—to Switzerland?"

"Oh yes . . . yes! When can we leave!" exclaimed Betsy. All thought of the bird's nest instantly disappeared from her mind.

"It is not quite so simple as just getting on a train," laughed Hope. "There will be much to do. But we will begin making preparations to-morrow."

♦ ♦ ♦

Later that evening, after Betsy was in bed and Hope and Jocelyn were alone, the two women were discussing a number of practical matters concerning this waif whom the Lord had so unexpectedly dropped into their lives.

"We will have to get her a passport, of course," Hope was saying, "which may be somewhat difficult without birth records and knowing as little about her as we do."

"It might be that we will need to file for some sort of temporary legal guardianship," suggested Jocelyn. "I had already been thinking along those lines. I haven't been able to get a word out of her about other relatives, but it is something we have to consider."

"Yes, that would certainly be advisable."

"I will telephone Lieutenant Langham in the morning," said Jocelyn, "and Timothy as well.—Oh no . . . what am I thinking? Lieutenant Langham is away from London with Lieutenant Forbes."

She thought a moment. "Well, the naval office can tell me when he will be back," she said. "In the meantime, Timothy will do whatever he can. I have needed to look into Betsy's affairs and report what happened to someone, but I wasn't quite sure what to do."

"If we could arrange for something temporary, that would be good," said Hope. "Then, if and when we learn anything further, more permanent arrangements can be made for the girl."

"I will talk to Timothy, and perhaps Lieutenant Langham about it," said Jocelyn. "How long were you thinking of Betsy visiting?"

There was a brief silence.

"What I would ultimately like to do," began Hope slowly, "—that is, if we are able to confirm that Betsy has no one else—is adopt her."

"Oh, Hope, that is wonderful!" said Jocelyn. "Would it be possible?"

"With my dual citizenship, I would think it could be done."

"Have you said anything to Betsy?"

"No, only about going to Switzerland. I want to investigate the matter thoroughly first. But mostly I wanted to know what you think. After all, the Lord did lead her here first."

"And led you to come too," added Jocelyn, "I think for just this purpose. I didn't know what we were eventually going to do about her, though we certainly would have been happy to keep her indefinitely. I think this is wonderful. I could not be more pleased."

Hope nodded and thought a moment.

"Yes," she said at length, "I do feel that the Lord led me here for Betsy. But I think there is a larger purpose, even than that."

"A larger purpose, what do you mean?"

"A larger purpose for you and Catharine and Amanda."

"I still do not see exactly what you mean."

"I believe Betsy's coming here," said Hope, "is the Lord's sign that he is going to use you all, and this wonderful home he has provided for you, in perhaps something of the same way he has the Chalet of Hope."

Jocelyn smiled and was quiet a moment. Then she briefly told Sister

Hope what Amanda had discovered about their home, and the direction
they were praying about following.

Sister Hope shook her head and laughed lightly. "Remarkable," she
said when Jocelyn was through.

"Why do you say that?"

"It is so like the Lord to give a vision, only then to take away the
very means, in *our* eyes, for it to be fulfilled. I think of his promise to
Joseph, only to be followed by Joseph's being sold into slavery."

"I see what you mean," replied Jocelyn.

"He filled my heart with a vision for missions," Hope went on,
"which he is now fulfilling at a chalet in Switzerland. Foreign missions—I could never have foreseen his way of fulfilling that vision. In
the same way, I am certain that even should you leave Heathersleigh,
you will look back on it as fulfilling his purpose."

Jocelyn smiled a sad, nostalgic but bittersweet smile. "I always
dreamed of a happy family," she said, "and then later as we began living
as Christians, I dreamed of serving the Lord together with our children,
all of us the best of friends, into the teen years and that friendship growing richer in adulthood. I will never understand why God put family so
deeply into Charles's heart and mine only to have it turn out as it did."

"It may be another example like Joseph," replied Hope. "Perhaps that
vision he put in your heart *will* be fulfilled . . . is even now being fulfilled.
But perhaps God's higher purpose is for your experiences, even your
grief and heartbreak and Amanda's prodigal years, to help many more
families than just your own."

"How ironic that our experience may help others know what we were
never able fully to experience ourselves. I am not altogether sure I like
it," said Jocelyn sadly, "or would have chosen such a road had I been
able to foresee it."

"But for those who pray to be made like our Lord," rejoined Hope,
"as, now that I know you, I am certain you and Charles did pray together, such decisions are not ours to make."

"Yes, you're right," said Jocelyn. "Charles continually prayed the
prayer of Christlikeness. I am sure that if the Lord had asked Charles,
'Are you willing to lay down your life and your dreams for my sake?' he
would have answered that he was willing."

"Once that prayer is prayed, our lives are no longer our own," said
Hope. "We have embarked upon a road that is difficult, often lonely, a
road that has been called the Calvary Road. But it has been the road of

God's saints of obedience through the centuries. And I know, had you any choice in the matter, you would not have wanted your Charles any other way."

Jocelyn nodded, a tear or two creeping into her eyes. "As long as he was with me, I could bear the heartache of Amanda's being gone," she said. "She was always in my heart, every day, every moment all those long years. I ached constantly with love for her. Yet somehow I could bear it... with Charles. But to have him gone, and George with him, when Amanda returned... oh, Hope, it is *so* hard to bear."

Hope rose, went to Jocelyn's side on the couch, and placed a tender hand on her arm.

"Perhaps by your own prayers, and those of your dear husband," she said, "and the dreams that seem that they will never be fulfilled... perhaps by them you are the sacrifice, laid down that our Father might work healing and reconciliation and homecoming in many other hearts."

Before she was through speaking, Jocelyn was quietly weeping. Hope stretched a loving arm around her.

"He will fulfill the ministry he intends for you and your two lovely daughters," Hope said, "perhaps in ways none of you expect. I believe the day will come, Jocelyn, as it did for me through my own grief that I did not think would ever end, when you will rejoice and thank God... maybe not *for* what has happened, but *through* what he has been able to do by putting it to use in his kingdom."

It was silent a minute or two as Jocelyn wept at the magnitude of what Hope had just said.

"Lord," began Hope, *"I pray for your blessing on this home, this place, and these three women who are your servants and whose hearts desire to serve you. I pray that you will strengthen my dear sister Jocelyn. Though she feels weak at this moment—and how I remember the feeling—remind her every day that your strength is made perfect in weakness. You will use her, as you will use her home, the love that is in her, a love poured out on the altar of sacrifice, to demonstrate your love to others. Even now I pray for the people like Betsy you will send to receive that love, that you would be preparing their hearts for the ministry they will receive from these, your women. Continue to guide Jocelyn and Amanda and Catharine as they seek your will about what to do."*

A long silence followed Hope's prayer.

"Thank you, Hope," whispered Jocelyn at length. "I hear what you have said, and I receive it into my heart. It will always be hard. I will always miss Charles. But God is good."

She paused a moment, then added, "Life may always be hard . . . but God is good."

"Amen," added Hope softly. "God *is* good."

60

Mediterranean Coast

A warm but persistent late summer rain had pounded the Mediterranean coastline all day. And now as evening began to fall, the wind accompanying it by degrees grew chillier, and was finally downright cold.

The docks of Marseilles at such a time were particularly unfriendly if you had no place to seek cover from the downpour, as the visitor to this city did not.

That he was well dressed and could have afforded the best hotel in the city did not stop the bite of the wind against his rain-soaked coat. He was not one who enjoyed being miserable, and was about ready to give up on the clandestine rendezvous to which he had been summoned.

He glanced down at his watch. Another ten minutes; then he would go find someplace to stay and let them make other arrangements.

Amanda had been in subconscious prayer most of the day. This time neither her own future nor that of the estate lay heavily on her mind, but rather the sudden remembrance of something Timothy had said months earlier—*"We must forgive those who injure us whether or not they ever acknowledge their wrongs. There is no other way to move on in life."*

She wanted to move on in life. In many ways she felt she had been moving on. But suddenly with the reminder of Timothy's words came the realization that a huge roadblock lay in the middle of her path. That roadblock's name was Ramsay Halifax.

If she was going to allow God's forgiveness to enter her heart to enable her to forgive herself, she also had to forgive those who had wronged her. Ramsay most of all.

It was all she could do not to *hate* him. But forgive him! The idea was almost more than she could take in.

He had trapped her . . . used her. He didn't deserve forgiveness, she said to herself. Even if he did . . . she didn't *want* to forgive him.

Amanda walked into the heather garden. Immediately she felt enveloped in an attitude of prayer. The spirit of her father still hovered over this place into which he had invested so much of his time and energy. Little did she know that this had always been to him a special place of communion with both Father and wife on behalf of the wayward daughter whose life was now flowering with the fruit of those years of prayer.

As she went Amanda conversed with God, already resigning herself—willingly yet with the normal struggle of her flesh against the spirit—to what she realized was an inevitable necessity. She *must* forgive. She knew it. Yet she was not quite able to go so far all at once. She knew she would need help, for it was not an act she could carry out in her own strength. For now all she could pray was to be made *willing* to forgive. The prayer of willingness, however, is often taken into the heart of the Father as nearly as good as the act itself, for willingness at the beginning almost always leads to obedience in the end.

"God," she said quietly, *"help me forgive Ramsay, even though I am not sure I want to. Fill my heart with your forgiveness where I feel none of my own. Wherever Ramsay is at this moment, even if right now I cannot bring myself to say I love him or forgive him, I know that you do, and so I ask you to touch his heart with your love."*

As Ramsay stood in the cold, rainy dusk of the French port, his thoughts turned inexplicably toward the past, his years in England before the war, and finally to Amanda.

He remembered the first day he had seen her at the Kensington Lawn Tea, then their happy weeks together afterward.

Had he really cared about her, or only wanted to use her? Had his attraction at first been wholesome, or had deceit been in his heart even then? He would probably never know. Such questions were so far from the realm of his normal mode of thought that he quickly dismissed them. He and Amanda had had some good times, and that was as far as he could go with it.

He glanced around, trying to shake off thoughts of the past. The rain had stopped and the wind died down a little. He walked a few steps along the dock, then back, taking advantage of the lull in the weather to light a cigarette.

But he could not get Amanda out of his mind. Where was she now? he wondered. Had she begun a new life, or had she been swallowed up as one of a million innocent casualties of the war?

What if somehow they met again? Would anything be different? Did she hate him now? Or . . .

What was the use of such reflections, he tried to tell himself. He could never walk away from this life he had made for himself. He was in too deep.

Or was he?

Even if such a thing were possible . . . would he want to?

He kicked petulantly at a stone underfoot. Such reflections probed in unpleasant ways against his drowsy conscience. Might he have gone a different way? Maybe Amanda had been his chance, he thought. What could have been their life together had they remained in England and she been reconciled to her family? He could have become a gentleman, the son-in-law of an important man. Amanda might have given him a bright future.

He laughed morosely. Perhaps brighter than what he had to look forward to at present.

Was it too late for them to make a life together? Could he even find her if he wanted to . . . and what would she say?

A sound interrupted Ramsay's thoughts.

He tossed his cigarette into the water and looked out toward the sea.

The low chugging of a boat's engine had gradually intruded into his hearing. Ramsay peered through the wet dusk. Ahead of him faintly came into view through the mist the outline of a small vessel bearing straight toward him.

He watched as it slowed and closed the distance. Two or three shapes moved about on deck in readiness to tie onto the dock. It was not a large craft—probably thirty feet in length, and old. It had no doubt at one time been the handsome pleasure yacht of some Mediterranean aristocrat. It had seen better days, thought Ramsay as he watched its approach, and was now probably lucky to stay afloat at all. This must be his contact. There didn't appear another human being anywhere near this remote portion of the harbor where he had been told to wait.

Another two or three minutes he stood as the outline of the vessel's shape slowly came into sharper focus.

Suddenly footsteps sounded behind him.

Ramsay turned.

Two dim figures approached through the thickening darkness. He stood waiting as they walked toward him, then stopped five feet away.

The brief illumination of a match being struck to a cigarette revealed a short, balding man with an evil glint in his eye.

"Scarlino—what are *you* doing here!" exclaimed Ramsay as the flicker reflected off the face.

"My employer this time is the Alliance," replied his erstwhile companion. "They needed a delivery. Now that I've made mine, you've got to get this fellow to Vienna."

"Why me?"

"That is your region, not mine. He must get to your safehouse."

"Why?"

"I thought that was explained in the communiqué you were sent."

"Nothing was explained."

"No matter. From Vienna he will be seen to by central command."

"How am I supposed to get him there?" asked Ramsay irritably.

Scarlino nodded to the boat now mooring behind them. "That is your transportation. You will be on the coast of Italy by morning. Reaching Vienna should not be a problem from there."

"Who is he?" said Ramsay, nodding toward the tall shadow.

"That is not for you to know."

Ramsay pulled out another cigarette and took a step toward them as he now struck a match of his own. He held it out slightly where it lit up the face of the man beside Scarlino.

A sharp intake of breath registered his shock.

"Put that out, Halifax," said a voice Ramsay recognized as clearly as he just had the face. "Don't try to get cute."

Ramsay threw the match to the ground.

"—You didn't tell me our contact was a Brit," the man added to Scarlino.

"You two know each other?" said Scarlino in surprise, glancing back and forth.

"Let's just say our paths have crossed," replied Ramsay in a tone of irony.

"All right, so now you know, Halifax," said the Englishman. "It changes nothing."

"But I thought—"

"You and your mum and Barclay aren't the only moles coming out of hiding," interrupted the man in anticipation of his question. "So can you get me to Vienna?"

"I can get you there. But why you, Forsythe? You helped Churchill break up the lighthouse operation."

"I had to keep my cover intact. I had no choice at the time, when Barclay's security broke down. I couldn't save the operation."

"That still does not answer why."

"We all have our reasons, Halifax," replied Colonel Forsythe, "and mine are my own business."

61

Happy Departure

The scene this time at the Milverscombe train station was much different than at Sister Hope's previous departure. Betsy was flitting about hardly able to contain herself. She and Catharine were running down to the end of the platform like two energetic youngsters to see who could be first to spot the approaching train, whose slowing engine and giant white puffs of smoke they could already hear and see in the distance.

"Timothy will meet you at the station," Jocelyn was saying.

"Yes," nodded Hope almost absently, checking their tickets again, uncharacteristically nervous now that the moment of her departure with Betsy had come.

"He should have all the necessary papers when you arrive," Jocelyn went on. "If not, he says it will be another three or four days at the most."

Her statement seemed to bring Hope to herself.

"Imagine, Betsy and me in London for three days!" she laughed. "What have I got myself into? I will have my hands full!"

"You will love it," smiled Amanda. "Betsy won't let you do anything but have a great time."

"Perhaps everything is already in order," added Jocelyn. "Timothy sounded optimistic when I spoke to him last evening."

"The train is coming!" came Betsy's excited shriek into their ears as she pounded down the wooden platform toward them, Catharine on her heels.

It did not take long now. The train slowed and stopped. A few smiling glances followed. The beginning of tears, then suddenly the four grown women rushed forward into a solid bundle of arms and whisperings, kisses and farewells, while Betsy impatiently grabbed one of the bags and ran to the conductor who had just stepped from an open door of the nearest coach.

"I will never forget any of you," said Hope, eyes glistening as she glanced at all three of them one by one.

"Nor we you," rejoined Jocelyn.

"Don't forget your promise to visit."

"I doubt Amanda will let me," laughed Jocelyn.

Hope and Amanda found one another's eyes.

"Amanda . . ." began Hope.

But there were no words.

Of one accord they embraced and held each other tight.

"Thank you, Hope," whispered Amanda. "Thank you for everything . . . I love you."

"'Board!" came the call from the conductor behind them. Hope pulled away, smiled into Amanda's face one final time, then turned.

"May the Lord bless and prosper you," she said. "All the sisters will keep you in their prayers."

She and Betsy boarded the train and found seats. Soon Betsy was eagerly leaning out the window.

"Good-bye, Betsy!" called Catharine.

"Write us a letter, Betsy," added Jocelyn.

The train began to move. Betsy shrieked with glee. Catharine, Amanda, and Jocelyn lifted their arms and slowly began walking along the platform in the direction of the motion, continuing to wave until the train was out of sight.

Gradually the metallic clattering of the train's wheels along the steel tracks receded into the distance. In another minute it had faded altogether from their hearing. The three women turned and walked quietly back through the station and to their car.

"Suddenly everything is so still," said Catharine.

"I hadn't realized how much Betsy had changed Heathersleigh," smiled Jocelyn. "You're right—it is quiet. Perhaps the Lord sent her to remind us that even in death there can still be life."

"As much as we have lost," added Amanda, "think of poor Betsy. At least we have each other. She has no one."

"Except for Hope," her mother reminded her. "Who knows but that this may be the beginning of a wonderful new life for them both."

◆◆◆

Later that evening Amanda went to her father's study on the first floor, sat down at his desk, and telephoned London.

"Hello, Timothy," she said when the minister answered. "It's Amanda. Did Betsy and Hope arrive all right?"

"Yes, and both are in fine spirits. They should be on their way to the Continent within two or three days."

"Well, give them our love again.—I called, Timothy," Amanda now began more seriously, "to say that I have decided to follow your advice and file for an annulment. I would like you to look further into the legalities, if you don't mind, and tell me what I should do."

"Of course, my dear. I will be only too glad to help."

62

Shootout at Sea

♦ ♦ ♦

The HMS *Livingstone*, a frigate of the British Royal Navy, ploughed through the waters of the Mediterranean, growing calmer now after the night's brief squall.

The grey of dawn had just come to the horizon. The officer standing at the prow with binoculars scanning the distance for sign of their quarry only hoped they were not too late.

How much better had they been able to get to them before Marseille. Once out to sea, finding them became nearly impossible. But they had to stop the escape vessel before it reached Italian shores—or before encountering an Alliance warship themselves—otherwise many high-level military secrets could reach enemy hands.

Suddenly the faint outline of a vessel appeared in the distance against the grey light of morning.

The officer squinted and adjusted the focus of the lenses. It was a boat, all right, and bearing almost due east.

He turned and ran to the bridge to alert the captain. Within a minute the *Livingstone*'s course had changed by fifteen degrees, which would exactly intercept the boat as they reached it.

Forty minutes later the frigate pulled alongside the small yacht. The latter had given no response to repeated messages and commands.

"Stop or be fired upon," called a voice over the loudspeaker. "This is the British Royal Navy. This is your final warning."

Still no response was evident.

Captain Logan turned to his second in command. "Mr. Briscoe, send a shot across their bow."

Thirty seconds later a small torpedo fired out from the *Livingstone*. It sped through the water just below the surface, missing the bow of the yacht by a mere thirty or forty feet.

At last the smaller craft cut its engines and began to slow.

The captain gave the stop-order to his engine room. On deck the crew made preparations to board the yacht. Still they had seen no one.

"All right, Lieutenant," said Captain Logan, turning to the officer at his side who had spotted the escape craft. "I suppose it's your operation now. Tell us what you want us to do."

"Thank you, Captain," replied Lieutenant Langham. "Lieutenant Forbes and I will climb down to see if the man is indeed on board."

"You still cannot tell me who it is?"

"We may be wrong, Captain. If he is here, you will know soon enough."

The two naval officers on special assignment from the headquarters of the First Lord of the Admiralty prepared to finish the job they had been sent to do. Several petty officers tossed the rope ladder over and secured it. Langham immediately climbed over the rail and made his way down the side of the frigate. Lieutenant Forbes stood in readiness a moment, then followed.

Suddenly a figure appeared at the stern of the yacht below.

"That looks like . . . Colonel Forsythe . . . of the army!" exclaimed the captain where he stood at the railing.

"I'm afraid you're right, sir," Forbes called behind him as he climbed over the ship's side. "We hoped we were wrong. But intelligence reports said that the colonel might try to make a run for it. It appears we were just in time."

Lieutenant Langham was nearly down by now. He jumped to the yacht's deck, losing his balance briefly, then stood and began walking calmly toward Forsythe.

"It's over, Colonel," he said. "You have no place to go. Give it up, and perhaps—"

"You're not taking me alive, Langham!" shouted Forsythe, suddenly pulling a gun. "I've come this far . . . I'm not going back now!"

Langham froze. On the deck of the frigate a dozen or more officers immediately pulled their weapons and trained them downward. For a second or two, everything stood still.

Behind him, Langham heard Forbes's booted feet now thudding onto the deck.

Forsythe glanced toward the noise. Langham took the momentary diversion as his opportunity and rushed forward to disarm the traitor.

But Forsythe saw the movement and reacted instantly. Any thought that he was bluffing immediately disappeared when two shots rang out, one followed by the ricocheting *ping* of a miss against the steel hull of the frigate. But as the second died out Langham fell with a groan on the wooden plankway. The same instant Forsythe turned and ran for below.

Forbes sprinted after him.

"Get down there!" shouted Captain Logan to his men. "Briscoe... take the colonel alive!"

Half a dozen more forms scurried down the rope ladder. In several seconds the would-be escape yacht swarmed with the white and blue of the Royal Navy.

Langham pulled himself slowly to his feet. His vision was blurred and pain seared his body. He staggered forward, trying to pull his own gun. Three or four uniformed officers ran by.

"Stop, Forsythe!" Forbes cried. "—You others... to the bridge!"

Langham's senses were dulled. He could barely see clearly. Everywhere men were now running and shouting. More shots rang out. Forbes returned the fire as he ran.

Langham grabbed at a rail and tried to steady himself and focus, but with difficulty. In the midst of the commotion, a man stepped from behind a steel pillar. Langham recognized him vaguely, but in his blurry confusion could not place the face. The man had a gun and now aimed to shoot. Langham lifted his pistol. His arm was heavy. He staggered a step or two. Behind him someone returned the fire. He heard a cry of pain and the sound of a fall. Bullets were screaming and ricocheting everywhere, the air filled with gunshots and metallic, pinging echoes.

Langham struggled a step or two, then stumbled over a body.

"There are two dead," he heard one of the officers say.

Gradually the gunfire died down.

"We've got the control room," shouted one of Logan's officers, running out and signaling up to the frigate.

"Drop your weapons!" came the captain's voice over the loudspeaker.

Langham shook his head to clear his vision, then saw Lieutenant Forbes emerge from below, gun poised on Colonel Forsythe. He tried again to walk toward them. A wave of pain surged through his limbs. Suddenly his vision faded and he fell senseless.

Meanwhile, Lieutenant Forbes shoved Colonel Forsythe across the deck until he was in the hands of several others, then turned and ran back to his fallen comrade.

On board the *Livingstone*, Captain Logan continued to shout down orders. "Briscoe, take charge of the yacht," he said. "The rest of you make sure it is secure."

"What about the dead, sir?" Briscoe called up.

"Give me a report on wounded and casualties, then we'll bury the dead at sea.—See to Lieutenant Langham first."

"And the crew?" asked Briscoe.

"Bring everyone aboard and put them in the brig. We'll escort the yacht back to French waters and sort it out later. I don't know what we've uncovered here, but we'll let Lieutenant Forbes tell us what the navy wants us to do."

63

A Caller

◆ ◆ ◆
---

*N*ews of events in the Mediterranean had still not reached Heathersleigh when a stranger arrived at the door of Heathersleigh Hall.

"Lady Jocelyn," said Sarah at the door of the sun-room, "you have a visitor."

Jocelyn glanced up as she began to rise.

"How did he come?" she asked. She had been absorbed in the book in her hand and had heard nothing.

"By car, ma'am—here is his card."

Jocelyn took the card and glanced over it. The name meant nothing to her. She followed Sarah out of the room toward the front door.

She approached to see a man standing in the entry where Sarah had left him.

"Good morning, Lady Rutherford," he said, extending his hand. "My name is Bradbury Crumholtz. I am a solicitor from Exeter. I wonder if I might speak with you about a matter that may be of some importance."

"Of course . . . come in, Mr. Crumholtz," replied Jocelyn. "Would you care for some tea?"

"Yes, thank you, that would be very nice."

"Sarah," said Jocelyn to the housekeeper, "we will have tea in the east sitting room."

"Yes, ma'am."

Jocelyn led the way. The solicitor followed.

"You are no doubt unaware of it," began Crumholtz when they were comfortable, "but my firm has had some previous dealings with the Heathersleigh estate."

"No," replied Jocelyn shaking her head, "—you're right, I know nothing about them. My late husband was accustomed to employing a solicitor in London."

"Yes, I am acquainted with Mr. Hastings," nodded Crumholtz. "The matters I speak of, however, did not concern you or your husband directly."

He went on to explain in general terms that his firm had been called in to represent certain Heathersleigh interests many years before during the time of Crumholtz's father and uncle.

"Most recently," he went on, "I represented Mrs. McFee, whom I understand is a close friend of your family, in the matter of her will."

"Yes, now I remember your name," nodded Jocelyn. "—Excuse me, Mr. Crumholtz, would you mind if I asked my two daughters to sit in on our conversation?"

"Not at all."

"We have been thinking a great deal about our future lately. You see, my husband died at sea last year."

"Yes, I was aware of it. I am very sorry."

"Thank you. That is why I would like my girls to know about whatever you have to say."

Jocelyn left the room briefly. When she returned, Amanda and Catharine walked into the room at her side. As she proceeded to introduce them to the solicitor, Sarah entered with a tray of tea things.

"Maggie—Mrs. McFee—told us about her visit to you," said Jocelyn as they prepared their cups, "and of her request regarding the disposition of the cottage."

"Ah, I was not aware you knew," said Crumholtz. "Perhaps that will simplify things. At that time Mrs. McFee was most concerned about confidentiality. I should perhaps speak with her further. Be that as it may, there is another matter that has arisen, and about which I confess I find myself most concerned. That is why I have come, notwithstanding her request. That confidentiality, it seems to me, is precluded by these new circumstances."

"I am afraid I do not follow you," said Jocelyn.

"Right. Let me explain... you know, I believe, a certain Gifford Rutherford from London?" asked Crumholtz.

"Yes... he is my husband's first cousin," answered Jocelyn.

"So I have been given to understand."

"What does he have to do with it?"

Crumholtz did not answer immediately, but glanced down, apparently marshaling his thoughts.

"Just this," he began again after a few moments, "—Mr. Rutherford came to me some months back to employ me in a most curious manner. The more I delved into it, the more I could not, in good conscience, proceed without speaking to you. Tell me, are you aware of any dispute to the title of your late husband's estate?"

"None," replied Jocelyn, concern registering in her voice. "I am certain my husband knew of nothing either. Why?"

"Mr. Rutherford—Mr. Gifford Rutherford, that is—employed me to initiate proceedings against your claim to the title."

"What!" said Jocelyn.

"I knew I didn't trust him!" exclaimed Catharine fiercely. "Do you mean he is trying to take Heathersleigh from Mother?"

More disbelieving exclamations and discussion followed. As Catharine grew more and more heated by the news, Amanda remained strangely quiet and calm, almost smiling to herself at the irony of it. Jocelyn saw her reaction and knew what she was thinking.

"I still do not see exactly why you have come to us, Mr. Crumholtz," said Jocelyn at length. "If you represent Gifford, are you not bound to do as he has employed you to do?"

"The matters of confidentiality and conflict of interest are rather murky, I admit," he answered. "But I am bound by higher laws."

"What laws, Mr. Crumholtz?"

"The law of right," he answered. "I felt there may have been something untoward in what I was asked to do. The moment he came to me, I knew something to be amiss. Complicating the matter further, my firm represented a certain bishop Arthur Crompton many years ago—"

At the name, all three of the women glanced at one another.

"—which fact additionally obscures my loyalties in the case."

Crumholtz now removed from his coat a sealed envelope, obviously old.

"This envelope," he said, "presumably containing a document of some kind, has not been opened in more than sixty years. It was entrusted to my firm for safekeeping along with Bishop Crompton's will, with instructions that it not be read until such time—"

Here Crumholtz paused, then cleared his throat.

"The matter is a bit awkward," he said, "as you shall see, but as I read the instructions left me by my father and uncle, this envelope is to be opened at the death of the last remaining living relative of a certain Orelia Moylan, to whom, as you know, the bishop deeded the property known as Heathersleigh Cottage . . . which, as I see it, would indicate the death of your friend Mrs. McFee."

The room fell silent. Catharine, Amanda, and Jocelyn all glanced at one another again.

"But . . . Maggie is alive and well," said Jocelyn at length. "Surely . . ." Her voice trailed off.

"Yes, I realize, as I said, the awkwardness of my bringing up such a matter," rejoined Crumholtz. "But after Mr. Rutherford's request, I felt something was afoot I did not care for. Therefore, to get to the bottom of it, I am willing to suspend the bishop's request and open his letter now. But I do not feel I should do so without the permission of Mrs. McFee, since she is the last living heir spoken of in his will and the instructions to the transfer of the deed to the property. Yet you are also deeply involved, as you are the owner of the estate to which the cottage originally belonged. You can see, I think, my predicament, and why, as I say, the case is extremely complex."

"Mother," said Amanda, "Grandma Maggie would do whatever you say."

Jocelyn thought for a moment.

"No," she said, "we must respect Bishop Crompton's wishes."

A long silence followed.

"I think I know what is in the envelope, Mother," said Amanda at length.

Crumholtz glanced toward Amanda, surprise evident on his face.

"It is proof of what happened that night," Amanda added.

"You may be right," agreed Jocelyn. "But we must still act on the truth we know, even without the letter. I think our plans must proceed without reading it."

Jocelyn paused, then looked toward the solicitor.

"We appreciate your coming to us very much, Mr. Crumholtz," she said warmly. "However, it may be that the entire matter may be resolved without further action on your part, and without the need of opening

Bishop Crompton's letter prematurely."

"How, if I may ask?" inquired the solicitor.

"Let me ask you a question," returned Jocelyn.

"Certainly."

"Do your present, uh . . . obligations with respect to Maggie and my husband's cousin . . . do they preclude you from representing us in a matter we would like you to handle for us?"

"In ordinary circumstances, perhaps," Crumholtz replied. "But these are not ordinary circumstances. It would, of course, depend on the exact nature of the matter you have in mind. Is it possible for you to be more specific?"

Jocelyn waited several moments before replying. At length she spoke.

"It is this, Mr. Crumholtz," she began, "—my daughters and I—that is," she added with a smile, glancing toward Catharine, "—*one* of my daughters—we are still working on Catharine, aren't we, my dear—even prior to your visit we had come to the realization ourselves that Gifford's suspicions, of which we had some idea, were indeed accurate."

"You cannot—" began Crumholtz.

Jocelyn nodded. "We believe, Mr. Crumholtz, that the envelope you are holding actually contains proof substantiating his claim."

"I see. This is most unexpected," replied Crumholtz slowly. "I confess . . . this is not at all what I had anticipated."

"I had planned to speak with Mr. Hastings soon," Jocelyn continued. "But as you have already had so much to do in the situation, I think it would be best if you and he worked together."

"I will be happy to talk to him on your behalf. I have to be in London next week. What do you want me to do, then?"

"We would like you to begin drawing up papers for the transfer of Heathersleigh Hall to my husband's nephew."

The solicitor, though he said nothing, was clearly stunned by Jocelyn's words.

"As I said," Jocelyn concluded, "we are convinced the letter that was left in your possession supplies proof that it should have belonged to his family all along."

"And you wish to begin proceedings even without that proof?"

"We have all the proof we need, Mr. Crumholtz."

"And the cottage . . . the McFee cottage?" he asked.

"As I understand it, the cottage was legally sold when Bishop Crompton purchased it," replied Jocelyn. "As it has not been connected to the estate since that time, I see no reason why it should be included in the transaction. It will, therefore, remain in the hands of Mrs. McFee as long as she is alive."

"What will you and your daughters do, Lady Rutherford?" asked Crumholtz, still reeling from this unexpected twist in developments. "Surely you want to make some provision for yourselves."

"The Lord will provide for our needs, Mr. Crumholtz," replied Jocelyn. "Nor do I think Geoffrey will object, as you suggest, to some modest provision being made for my daughters. I am sure you will advise us accordingly as we work out the details."

"But as to accommodation and . . ." the solicitor attempted to continue. But he hardly knew what to say, and his question trailed off.

Jocelyn was silent a moment. She appeared to be turning something over in her mind.

"You said you wanted to talk with Mrs. McFee?"

"Yes," answered Crumholtz.

"We will take you to her.—Amanda, will you ask Hector to hitch the large carriage?"

Amanda nodded and left the room.

♦ ♦ ♦

When Maggie opened the door of the cottage twenty-five minutes later, her astonishment at having visitors was all the greater at seeing her own solicitor standing beside Jocelyn and the girls. Perplexed, she invited them all in, hobbling in front of them toward the sitting room, with the four following slowly.

"Mr. Crumholtz has some matters to discuss with you," said Jocelyn as they sat down, "and so do we. We have told him to begin proceedings to transfer the house and grounds to Geoffrey."

The news did not come altogether as a surprise. Jocelyn had spoken about it several times with her aging friend.

"And the cottage?" said Maggie, not exactly afraid of losing her beloved home—she could be happy anywhere—but a little sad for the news she thought must surely be the purpose of the visit, that she was to be told she needed to vacate this place where she had spent most of her life.

"The cottage will not be included in the transaction to Geoffrey," replied Jocelyn.

Maggie glanced at her in confusion.

"Mr. Crumholtz asked what we were going to do," Jocelyn went on.

"What do you mean, *do?*" asked Maggie.

"What *did* you mean, Mr. Crumholtz?" said Jocelyn, turning toward the solicitor.

"Where will you live, how will you provide for yourselves?" he said. "It still seems to me, I confess, that you have not adequately considered all the implications of the action you are contemplating."

Jocelyn smiled and turned again toward Maggie. "What the girls and I have been thinking," she said, unable to keep from being amused at the solicitor's consternation over their other-worldly method of resolving a dispute most of his clients would have kept quiet about, "is this— since you plan to will the cottage to Amanda and Catharine eventually ... we wondered if you would have us *now?*"

"*Have* you ... what can you—" began Maggie.

"Would you like us to come live here at Heathersleigh Cottage with you as soon as the Hall is Geoffrey's?"

"Oh, I cannot believe my ears!" exclaimed Maggie, already beginning to shed tears of happy disbelief. "I cannot think of anything more wonderful!"

64

Temporary Lodgings

♦ ♦ ♦

Two or three days of chilly, blustery weather signaled that autumn was well on its way to Devon. When Timothy Diggorsfeld arrived in Milverscombe with the one heavy trunk—mostly books—two carpetbags, and three small boxes, which represented the sum total of his earthly possessions, the wind had begun to blow in such a manner as to let most of the locals know that rain was not far away.

Timothy had just lugged his belongings into the station when Jocelyn arrived with the Peugeot.

"I think I will have to come back with Hector and a wagon for my trunk and the boxes," said Timothy. "Hopefully we will be able to beat the rain."

"Would you like to drive, Timothy?" asked Jocelyn as they walked toward the car.

"Me! Not for a minute. I have not been behind the wheel of an automobile in my life."

"I will teach you. Both the girls are learning."

"Another day, perhaps," laughed Timothy.

"Well then, we will have you snug in your new room within the hour," said Jocelyn, climbing in behind the wheel. "You will be able to sit at your writing desk, cozy and warm, a fire blazing in the hearth, and look out on a Devonshire rain."

"You make it sound delightful."

"The girls are so excited about your coming. They have been working all day to get everything all ready for you."

Timothy laughed with delight. "They are dears," he said. "You are all very kind to take in a wayfaring pilgrim changing homes and occupations so late in life."

"Nonsense," laughed Jocelyn. "You make it sound as if you are a stranger. You are family, Timothy."

"Nevertheless, I am very grateful."

"Have you thought any more about what you will do?" asked Jocelyn as they drove.

"Of course, but without much resolution. I will settle in and see how Devon suits me. As much as I complain about the city, I have been a city man most of my life. I may try to write, as the girls suggest. There are a number of my former congregation with whom I must keep in touch.—By the way, I invited Hugh and Edlyn down for the weekend a fortnight from now. I hope you don't mind."

"Of course not. That will be wonderful! Oh, Timothy, I am sorry you will have to leave so soon after coming. I wish you could stay at Heathersleigh forever."

"On the contrary, I am privileged to be able to share with you in the laying down of this grand house," rejoined Timothy. "It is a lovely place, the loveliest I know on the earth. Some of the happiest times of my life have been spent here. But we are all pilgrims after all. And to be able to give up our treasures is the greatest privilege of all. We cannot truly possess what we cannot let go of. Otherwise, they possess us."

"Wasn't it the Scotsman who said that in the giving do we most truly make something our own?"

"I forget his exact words, but something very like that, I believe. As for me, the Lord will provide me new quarters where I know I will be happy. I do not need a mansion. I only need friends, and those I know I have when I am in Devon."

"Well . . . we are here!" said Jocelyn as she drove up in front of the great old grey mansion. "Welcome to Heathersleigh Hall, your new, if temporary, home!"

65

Revelation in Hyde Park

Autumn progressed.

Gifford Rutherford's investigation continued as he schemed and connived how best to win a suit against Jocelyn in court. All the while he was unaware that his efforts had been rendered moot by that which his cousin's wife had already set in motion.

Meanwhile, knowing nothing of the events about to sweep him into the middle of their vortex, his son was changing in ways the father had no idea of.

One day when noon came, rather than lunch with his father or colleagues of the bank, Geoffrey decided to go to the park. Strange things had begun to gnaw at him, beckonings from a world whose language he did not at first recognize.

Why *him?* the reader asks.

Why Geoffrey Rutherford, seemingly the last young man on the face of the earth who would be inclined to heed the silent call of that deeper world?

Yet the question might also be asked, why *not* Geoffrey Rutherford? What makes some men and women gradually attentive to the world's *whys?* What causes some to begin looking upward and inward for answers, while the great majority of the masses remain oblivious to the very currents of life they were put on this earth to discover?

Who can identify that invisible germ of distinction between the askers and ponderers, and the contented unthinking blind? Such will forever remain an eternal question of great mystery.

Whatever the reason, whatever spark prompts the opening of a heart's door in one but not another, as unlikely as it might seem, Geoffrey was now showing signs of being one of those who had begun to cast his gaze inward.

What had triggered this season of introspective melancholy, even he could not have said.

Was it the feel of mortality, the gradually receding hairline even at twenty-five, the lack of energy he had felt for some time? He had consulted a doctor without telling his father. The man had pronounced him fit, but Geoffrey harbored doubts. He still didn't feel quite himself. What was it? Were the changes physical . . . or was something else going on within him?

The previous winter had been difficult. There had been a few nights, after days upon days of ceaseless coughing, that he had lain awake fearing he had somehow contracted something. Yet the condition had eventually left him, and he had been fine all summer. But now, with the cold rainy season approaching, he could not help but be anxious. He was not looking forward to another London winter.

But chiefly his unease originated in his soul. He wasn't happy at the bank, and he knew it.

He left the office, took a cab to Hyde Park, and walked slowly around for three-quarters of an hour carrying the apple and sandwich his mother had packed for him that morning, yet scarcely thinking of them. He wasn't hungry.

As he walked, Geoffrey saw things he had never noticed before, ducks scurrying and quacking and swimming about everywhere, what remained of the autumn flowers, children at play, a gentle breeze on his face, the clouds suspended in the blue above.

It really was a beautiful world, he thought, even in the city. Why had he never paused before to drink it in? But did the beauty all around him *mean* anything? Was there more to life than money and investments and compound interest?

He smiled thinly. Even without his father's money, he was well on his way to becoming a rich man in his own right. But what did it matter? It had certainly not made him happy.

He was almost tempted to quit the bank and move to the country.

His father would hit the roof. But did he want to spend the rest of his life pursuing only profit? What had it accomplished for his father? He was a selfish, lonely, greedy man, Geoffrey thought. He had no friends, no interests besides money. Geoffrey had never seen him read a book for pleasure. Did he want to end up the same way himself?

If nothing changed . . . toward just such a future he was probably heading.

A little boy ran by chasing a tiny flock of walking ducks. Geoffrey glanced up, glad for the interruption to his broodings, and watched the boy's energetic antics for a few moments. He was followed a minute later by his mother.

"Mummy . . . Mummy, may I please have a coin to throw into the fountain!" cried the lad as he reached the bridge over the little pond.

"I'm sorry, Fraser," she replied, "but I have none."

Geoffrey watched the two another moment, then rose and walked toward them, hand fishing into his trousers.

"Excuse me, ma'am," he said to the lady, "I couldn't help overhearing. I have a coin or two to spare in my pocket. I would like to give them to the boy, if you don't mind."

"Oh . . . thank you, that is very generous of you, sir," she replied.

Geoffrey walked toward the lad, holding out his hand.

"Here, son," he said, "throw these into the water and make a wish."

The boy glanced up into Geoffrey's face, then down at the five large copper pennies in his hand. The next instant he scooped them into his chubby fist and began tossing them into the pond toward the spraying fountain in the center.

Geoffrey turned, smiled at the lady as he tipped his hat, and continued on his way.

"Mummy, Mummy," he heard behind him, "the man gave me five coppers!"

Geoffrey smiled to himself. *That was nice*, he thought.

In fact, as he went, he realized that the tiny act of generosity had made him feel better than the thousand-pound profit he had added to his account last month from one of his many investments.

Geoffrey chuckled to himself as he walked, then began laughing outright. Maybe giving *away* money was the secret to happiness rather than *accumulating* it.

The simplicity of the revelation jolted him.

He shook his head as he continued to revolve it in his brain, still chuckling as he walked . . . giving not getting.

Incredible!

Ha, ha, ha! he laughed inwardly. *What would dear old Dad think of that?*

66

New Resident in Milverscombe

When Terrill Langham appeared at the door of Heathersleigh Hall after Timothy had been in residence about a week, Catharine was the first to arrive to open it. He held an umbrella in his left hand and clutched a cane in his right.

"Hello, Miss Catharine," said the lieutenant.

"Terrill!" she exclaimed.

"I hope you do not mind an unannounced visit."

"Of course not.—But what happened to your leg!"

"A bit of an accident," he replied, attempting to shrug it off.

"Come in.—Mother . . . Amanda!"

Lieutenant Langham lowered his umbrella, set it in the stand next to the door, and hobbled in after her. As they entered, Timothy was just coming downstairs with a book under his arm.

"Oh, Timothy," said Catharine as she saw him, "meet Terrill Langham . . . *Lieutenant* Terrill Langham, I mean."

"We know each other, Catharine," said Timothy, approaching with a smile. "—How are you, Lieutenant?" Catharine looked on in surprise as they greeted one another.

"Fine, Rev. Diggorsfeld," replied Langham as the two men shook hands, "except for the leg, that is. I didn't expect to see you here."

"Actually, I am living here at present."

"What about your church?"

"I am afraid I am no longer in the pastorate," replied Timothy. "In fact, I was just on my way out to the village to scout about for more permanent lodgings."

"Will I see you later?" asked Langham.

"I should be back in time for tea."

"I would take your umbrella if I were you," said Langham as Timothy walked toward the door. "It was raining just now as I drove up."

"I appreciate the warning."

Timothy left the house with happy sounds of welcome and greeting behind him as Jocelyn and Amanda now arrived from upstairs and the kitchen.

The brief rain had let up as Timothy walked away from the door and down the drive. The damp smell of autumn was in the air, and he breathed in deeply of its fragrance. He would take the long way to the village.

He reached the main road and turned left along the river. Tucking the crook of his umbrella over his forearm, he now opened the book he had brought along—as so befitting the occasion, one of his favorites, the Scotsman's *Annals*—and began to read the thoughts that so mirrored his own at this moment of life. Though he was not coming to a new parish as a minister as in the story, he was coming to a new home, and could not help wondering what the Lord might have in store for him here.

Timothy entered Milverscombe forty minutes later. His mind was still occupied with the fictional old Rogers and the carpenter shop of the tale. Would this village provide *him* such treasures?

He prayed as he walked that the Lord would direct his steps, and that if his future was indeed in this place, a home would be provided where he would be able to do whatever God had for him to do.

Here and there as he went, he poked his head into several of the homes and shops, greeting many of the friends he had made through the years during his many visits, finally approaching the large stone church, where he turned aside to spend a few minutes visiting his friend Vicar Stuart Coleridge.

67
News and No News

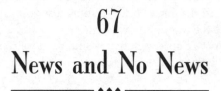

*A*driane Grünsfeld suspected the worst.

Something must have happened to Ramsay. He should have been back weeks ago. She had no way to know for certain except by visiting his mother, and that she was not about to do. She never wanted to see that place in Vienna again. She could probably write the woman, but that was nearly as distasteful a thought as going to her in person.

She would continue to wait. If something had happened, no one would think to contact his mistress.

What else could she do? If Ramsay made an unexpected appearance, her fears would be put to rest. If he didn't . . . well, then she would know that he had either gone back to the English girl . . . or else was dead.

◆ ◆ ◆

The telegram that arrived at Nr. 42 Ebensdorfer Strasse in Vienna was not entirely unexpected. Hildegard Bronislawgh Halifax knew things were getting dangerous and that the war was not going well.

She took the envelope from the messenger and went into the darkened sitting room before opening it. She did not exactly feel a sense of apprehension. In truth, it would have been difficult to tell what the woman felt. She had hurt so many lives for so long, and had ceased caring about the feelings of others so long ago, that now when she needed to feel something for herself, she scarcely was able to do so.

Baroness Bronislawgh, as she now called herself, sat down and opened the yellow envelope.

She read the brief message.

No tears came.

Ramsay's mother had steeled herself against the natural emotions of her womanhood for so many years that she had lost the capacity to feel at all. She had grown cold and hard, and now must pay the price by her inability even to weep for the loss of her son.

68

Impromptu Meeting

*W*inter came early to Devon. Even in this southernmost part of England, by late November two storms had produced several inches of snow. The second had fallen just two days before, leaving Milverscombe, for the present, as picturesque as a Christmas card.

Lieutenant Langham, with his wounded leg, made several more visits to Heathersleigh, each a little longer than the previous. Jocelyn invited him, as his duties allowed, to use one of their many guest rooms and come for two or three days at a time.

Letters from Hope and Betsy began to arrive. Both seemed very happy with the new arrangement. According to Hope, Betsy's presence had injected the chalet with new energy and life. She and Sister Galiana were already the best of friends. Several letters came from Hope, forwarded from New Hope Chapel, addressed to Timothy. His lengthy replies took up a good deal of Timothy's time.

With Timothy's help, Amanda filed papers for her annulment application according to British law. The procedure was somewhat dubious, since the so-called wedding had occurred on foreign soil. The outcome was thus uncertain. The process made Amanda thoughtful and a little sad. She spent much time during these weeks alone.

Timothy occasionally took supply positions throughout Devon as word of his presence and availability spread. He had never been happier, and had already begun, as time between letters to Hope and his former parishioners permitted, to write some memoirs. After five weeks at the Hall, what he declared to be the most perfect accommodation imaginable became available in the village.

Maggie continued to recover from her fall, yet did not seem altogether herself. Jocelyn could not help but be concerned that she now spent more time indoors sitting in her chair without the energy to prepare her garden for the winter. She appeared tired.

———— ◆◆◆ ————

A knock came to the door of the three-room flat above Mrs. Feld-stone's shop after Timothy Diggorsfeld had occupied it a week and a half. The former minister rose to answer it.

"Come in . . . come in, my friend!" he said enthusiastically to the visitor standing before him.

A tall young man in his late twenties, well shaped, lean but with muscular definition to shoulders, arms, and chest, entered carrying a book in his hand, limping slightly. "How do you like your new lodgings?" he asked.

"Wonderfully well," replied Timothy. "I am already feeling very much at home. Now that I have my books reshelved, I am no longer alone. Indeed, I always feel in the midst of a great silent company of wise mentors, as the Scotsman said of the authors of his books, whose friendship I can call upon anytime I choose, but who will make no intrusion upon me when I wish to be alone."

The visitor laughed. "A wonderful way of putting it."

"Sit down. I will put on water for tea," said Timothy. "—Tell me, what did you think of the third volume of the sermons?"

"Invigorating and challenging," replied his visitor, "although in places too deep for my feeble brain."

"Your feeble brain, indeed!" rejoined Timothy. "You are about to graduate, as I hear it, with honors."

"We shall see."

"Well, the sermons always require two or three readings for me as well," laughed Timothy.

"The one entitled 'Justice' was worth its weight in gold."

"My favorite! It is one of the few spots I have discovered in the mines of his writings where the Scotsman seems willing to speak boldly and openly about the controversy."

"How I wish some of my friends at the university could be introduced to his writings. Atheism is so prevalent in the Oxford environment."

"Perhaps a few of your scholar friends will meet the Scotsman. One never knows where a book will find its way into a person's life."

They continued to chat freely, and gradually the discussion moved in many directions.

After an hour Timothy's visitor rose to leave, another two borrowed books in his hands. "I will get these back to you soon," he said. "I will have to read them before next session."

"No hurry," said Timothy. "A book being read is infinitely better than a book sitting closed on a shelf."

The young man descended the stairs and turned absently into the sidewalk from the narrow stairway. Suddenly a young woman coming toward him from around the corner crashed straight into him.

"Oh, excuse me," began Amanda, startled as she recovered herself. "I didn't—"

"Hello, Amanda," said a deep voice.

Amanda glanced up into the face that went with the chest she had just ploughed into. She flushed, then hesitated momentarily.

The young man smiled. The expression was enough to take any girl's breath away.

"You don't know who I am, do you?" he said.

"I, uh . . . it's just that you caught me off guard," she flustered.

"It's Stirling . . . Stirling Blakely."

"Oh . . . Stirling—of course!" exclaimed Amanda, laughing. "I don't know what I was thinking. My mind was occupied and—"

She smiled as her eyes flitted about his face.

"—To be honest," she said, "you're right, I guess I didn't recognize you . . . it must be the moustache."

"An easy mistake!" laughed Stirling. "My mother says it makes me look atrocious."

"No, it's very becoming," rejoined Amanda. "I will just have to get used to it, that's all."

"Well, you may be excused on account of not seeing me for some time."

"That's right—I heard you were away tutoring someplace in the north between terms at the university."

"I only just got back a few days ago. To tell you the truth, though I needed what the job paid me, I am relieved that the assignment is over. I don't think I am cut out for teaching—at least not the sort of youngsters I had," he added laughing.

"But what are you doing here?" asked Amanda.

"Chatting with Rev. Diggorsfeld."

"I was just on my way to visit him myself.—But do you know Timothy?"

"Oh yes, we are good friends. He supplies me with books."

"Are you finished at the university, then?"

"Nearly. I have one more term. I will return to Oxford after the first of the year. I am greatly in your family's debt. I will never forget it."

"What do you mean?"

"For my education," replied Stirling.

"I still do not understand you."

"Your father... he paid for my entire schooling at Oxford. I assumed you knew."

Amanda smiled and shook her head slowly as the revelation dawned on her. "No," she said, "there are a great many things about my father I am only now finding out."

"Well, I must be going," said Stirling. "It was nice to see you again, Amanda."

"And you, Stirling. Come and visit us at the Hall when you can."

"Thank you... I will!"

69

Christmas 1916

*C*hristmas of the year 1916 was a time of happy contentment.

Timothy, Hugh and Edlyn, Lieutenant Langham—who had been down for several weekend stays and was now walking without his cane—Stirling and Agatha and Rune Blakely, as well as Maggie, though looking frail, Sarah Minsterly and her widowed sister from London, Stuart Coleridge, and Hector Farnham all gathered with the Rutherford women on Christmas afternoon at Heathersleigh Hall for a joyous dinner and final celebration of this phase in Heathersleigh's history. Not everyone present, however, knew of the changes about to take place that would stun the entire community.

None of those who did know were sad. This was a *celebration* of sacrifice rather than a time of mourning. "We have enjoyed Heathersleigh as the Lord's provision for a season," Jocelyn had said many times. "Now we will relinquish it with equal thanksgiving in our hearts."

Edlyn and Jocelyn began to reminisce about their memories of Christmas in India. Amanda and Catharine listened with fascination as the sisters talked about another life and another time halfway around the globe. The holiday began a new season between the two Wildecott sisters. Once the door was opened to talk candidly about the past, their respective childhoods, and their parents, a great healing began between them that led to a new and much deeper friendship than they had been able to know as children. Edlyn's husband, Hugh, developed a great respect for his sister-in-law as a result.

An unplanned time of gift giving began after the plum pudding had been served. Though hers was such a giving heart, Jocelyn, as it turned out, came in for the largest share of the receiving, as perhaps befitted the honor in which she was held by all those present. And she was equally able to receive with the graciousness of the true lady she was.

Stirling started it by presenting her with a paper he had written for one of his university classes, for which no small amount of research had been required, representing a compilation of the events, both military and political, of the entire career of Sir Charles Rutherford, his academic benefactor.

Timothy then presented her with an autographed copy of the Scotsman's *Salted With Fire*, the last of his realistic novels, which Timothy had purchased and taken with him to have signed in Italy. As she opened it, he leaned over and whispered to Amanda that she might be interested in it as well, and might find it healing for her own situation.

Jocelyn presented both Sarah and Hector an envelope with a monetary token of her appreciation for their many years of faithful service to the family. And finally she gave each of her daughters brooches left her by her own mother.

◆ ◆ ◆

Two weeks into the new year, Bradbury Crumholtz arrived at Heathersleigh with the final documents for Jocelyn's signature.

As they sat in the formal lounge, Jocelyn glanced over at her two daughters with a smile and sigh. A few final tears were shed. Yet Amanda and Jocelyn were also filled with excitement about what the

Lord was now planning to do in their lives. Catharine had been slow to accept the coming change, yet trusted her mother enough to know it was right. While Amanda *felt* the rightness of it, Catharine had learned to give thanks for the change in the absence of feelings, through *faith*.

"Do you want me to deliver the papers?" asked Crumholtz after they had discussed all remaining matters pertinent to the documents and Jocelyn had finalized the transfer with her signature.

"No," replied Jocelyn, "I think this is something we need to do in person."

An invitation was sent off that same afternoon to London.

70

Telegram

◆◆◆

*W*hen the telegram arrived at the Rutherford house on Curzon Street, Martha Rutherford's heart skipped a beat when she saw whom it was from. As she read, Martha had no idea what Jocelyn was speaking of, but she could hardly wait to show it to Gifford and Geoffrey.

> *Dear Geoffrey, Martha, and Gifford,* the telegram read,
>> *We would like the three of you to visit us at Heathersleigh Hall at your earliest convenience, this weekend if possible. We have a matter to discuss with you of great importance concerning our future and yours. Please telephone if this will be convenient.*
>> *Yours warmly,*
>> *Jocelyn Rutherford*

Gifford could make nothing out of it that evening either. He had hoped that his next visit to Heathersleigh would be under different circumstances, namely, to present thirty-day eviction papers to the wife of his cousin.

But what could they do, he said to himself, other than consent to go make another call, as outsiders, one last time? Within six months he would have his cousin's brood out of the place anyway.

After revolving the thing in his mind a minute or two, he glanced across the room to his wife.

"You may telephone her as she suggests," he said. "This weekend will be acceptable."

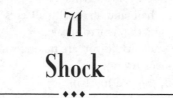

71

Shock

*W*hen Gifford walked through the doors of Heathersleigh Hall, he was taken aback to see Bradbury Crumholtz on hand, and apparently on intimate terms with the current residents of the place. The banker and the solicitor nodded to one another stiffly.

"Hello, Gifford . . . Martha!" said Jocelyn, giving Martha a warm hug. "I am so glad you have come—please come in . . . hello, Geoffrey!"

"Good morning, Cousin Jocelyn," replied Geoffrey, smiling pleasantly.

"Hello, Geoffrey," said Amanda, stepping from beside her mother and embracing her cousin. "It is good to see you again."

The gesture did not seem to surprise Geoffrey as much as it did his father, and he returned the hug with kindly affection.

"You are looking well, Amanda," he said stepping back. "—Hello, Catharine!"

"Hello, Geoffrey," returned Catharine with a cheery smile, shaking Geoffrey's hand.

Gifford stood in gloomy silence as his wife now hugged each of the women in turn, thinking how absurd were all these trivial pleasantries. And that wife of his cousin's—that hideous mark on her face . . . with everyone pretending it wasn't there.

"Come in, all of you!" said Jocelyn. "We have a nice tea all spread out in the east sitting room."

What was this! thought Gifford as he followed the obnoxiously cheerful troop inside. While the rest visited and while his wife fought back the tears, all he could think was, what was this all about? The infernal woman must have set him some trap. It was just like them, always lording it over his side of the family.

The guests sat down. Jocelyn and Sarah served tea and cakes. Out of the corner of his eye, Gifford noted the sheaf of papers Crumholtz was silently holding, and concluded the worst. He was so accustomed to adversarial relationships that he could conceive of nothing but that Jocelyn must be intent on some scheme of her own.

Jocelyn took a chair and gradually all eyes came to rest on her. Amanda, however, was the first to speak.

"Mother," she said, "while you are talking with the others, I think I would like to tell Geoffrey myself."

"Certainly, dear," replied Jocelyn.

Amanda rose, turning toward her second cousin. "Geoffrey," she said, "would you come with me?"

"You're not taking me to the tower again?" he kidded good-naturedly as he rose from his chair.

"No," replied Amanda. "I think you will find what I have to tell you far more interesting than the tower."

They left the house. Amanda led the way across the lawn east of the Hall.

No one ever heard, and Geoffrey never told another soul, exactly what Amanda said to him during the next thirty minutes as they made their way slowly through the paths of the heather garden. But when they returned to the house, he had tears in his eyes. They were the first he had shed since boyhood. They would not be the last.

They paused at the door and turned toward one another.

"I . . . I don't know what to say," said Geoffrey.

"You don't have to say anything, Geoffrey," replied Amanda, placing her hand on his arm. "It is the right thing to do. The Hall should rightfully be yours."

"Perhaps, but . . ."

Geoffrey glanced away, overcome yet again by this sudden alteration in his fortunes. They had both changed more than either had realized. From this moment on, though neither would have anticipated it years earlier, they would no longer be mere cousins, but would also be friends.

Geoffrey turned again to face Amanda after a moment. Slowly they embraced with the affection of true relational love. They fell apart without another word, then turned and entered the house to rejoin the others.

Inside the sitting room, meanwhile, Jocelyn was explaining the situation to Geoffrey's parents, doing her best to remain upbeat in spite of

Gifford's stiff formality. Gifford kept one eye warily on Crumholtz, who sat expressionless and unmoving.

"It is quite simple, really," Jocelyn had just said. "It is our belief that the possession of Heathersleigh Hall many years ago followed the wrong family line—"

At the words Gifford's ears perked up. He glanced toward Jocelyn with a jerk of his head.

"To right this error," Jocelyn continued, "we have undertaken legally—"

She glanced in the direction of the solicitor.

"—with the help of Mr. Crumholtz, to transfer the deed of Heathersleigh Hall and its grounds, as well as the title 'Lord of the Manor,' to Geoffrey, who, as of the first of March, will be rightfully entitled to both."

She stopped. The room was silent as a tomb for several seconds.

Gifford sat as one stunned.

He could make no sense of the words. They were actually *giving* the estate to them . . . *without* fighting it out in the courts!

The next instant Martha burst into an incoherent babble of weeping. She rose from her chair and within seconds was smothering Jocelyn in a large, exuberant embrace. Her joy came not because they were being given Heathersleigh but from such a gesture of familial love. The poor lady was so hungry for companionship with her kind that her soul gushed with tearful thanksgiving. They could keep Heathersleigh for all she cared! To have a friend like Jocelyn was to her worth any ten country estates!

"But surely you will stay," she was saying through her tears. "You cannot leave . . . there will be plenty of room for all of us . . . won't there, Gifford . . . we will be so happy together . . ."

"Thank you, Martha," said Jocelyn, "but we have made other arrangements."

"I . . . could not, of course . . . leave the bank," Gifford was saying, speaking more to himself than the others. "And . . . Geoffrey, well . . . we, er . . . will of course have to consider how best . . ."

He could scarcely find words to speak out of his spinning brain.

" . . . although no denying that . . . we cannot help but acknowledge your . . . er, your generous foresight in this matter . . ."

It was clear he and Martha had absorbed the sudden information differently. Martha immediately thought what a joy it would be to live in the Hall, both families together. Gifford on the other hand wondered what all his prior machinations had not caused him to reflect on, namely what impact the possession of a Devonshire estate would have on his banking career. Neither had he yet absorbed the fine print of Jocelyn's disclosure, that the estate was not being transferred to him at all, but to his son.

But all these details would filter down into his grey cells over the course of the following days. Why they had chosen to ignore his own claim to the title, once the fact dawned on him, caused him to chaff anew. But once they were out and his own son was legally installed as the owner, he would see what steps might be taken to correct Jocelyn's blunder in passing him over.

"What... other arrangements?" asked Martha. "Surely... you will remain at the Hall."

"Not knowing your plans," replied Jocelyn, "and whether Geoffrey would take residence, we have made plans to remove ourselves to Heathersleigh Cottage with Mrs. McFee. Charles's military pension will see to our needs more than adequately."

These words of Jocelyn's registered nearly as much disbelief in Gifford's mind as what she had said a moment ago. Not only were they voluntarily relinquishing a deed and title worth hundreds of thousands of pounds, they actually planned to move off into some silly little cottage in the woods! Charles's whole family was a pack of simpletons and idiots!

Amanda and Geoffrey walked in. Geoffrey saw from the expressions on the faces of both his parents that they had received the news much as he—with stunned disbelief.

"Our plans are to be out in two months," Jocelyn continued. "Many of our possessions and much of the furniture, several horses, as well as a large part of the library, we will not have room to keep at the cottage. We hope you will not object to our leaving the greater part of our possessions here. And actually many of them belong to the Hall." As she spoke, she glanced toward Geoffrey rather than Gifford.

"Uh... oh, no... of course not, Cousin Jocelyn," he replied. "No objection whatever. Leave anything you like for as long as you like. But anything you want... you may... it goes without saying, you may come for at any time."

The visit did not last much longer. Jocelyn invited them to stay the weekend. Two rooms were ready for them. Martha's countenance brightened immediately at the prospect. But Gifford insisted they must start back for the city where he had pressing business. In truth, he was so uncomfortable, though delighted, at this unbelievable turn of events that all he could think was that he had to get out of the place.

The following Monday, without consulting his father, Geoffrey Rutherford walked into the office of the president of the bank to present written request for an indefinite leave of absence, effective March 1, to consider and reflect upon his future.

PART V

1917

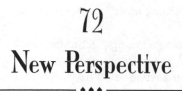

New Perspective

Geoffrey Rutherford was still wondering what he had been wondering for weeks—was this all a dream?

What was he doing in the master bedroom of Heathersleigh Hall, with Sarah Minsterly and Hector Farnham calling *him* "my lord"?

After a month in Devon, he knew he had reached a crossroads of life. Whatever had come before, he could never more be the same person he had been till now. But the transformation was not one of mere outward circumstance. What was taking place was a fundamental change in who he was... or perhaps more importantly, who he wanted to be.

What Amanda and Jocelyn had done had shaken the foundations of everything his father had taught him to believe—namely to get all one could however possible. Never had the thought of putting another ahead of oneself entered the creed of Gifford Rutherford, banker, entrepreneur, and amasser of wealth. And that creed he had zealously transmitted to his son from almost the moment he could crawl out of the cradle.

From his earliest childhood Geoffrey's father had exhorted and pushed him to get ahead, to take advantage, to connive and scheme, even to sneak and lie if it suited his purposes.

Geoffrey had some time ago begun to realize the bankruptcy of such a way of life, however, and knew it made him no happier than it had his father. When and how that divergence with the mammon-philosophy of his upbringing had begun, who could say? It had probably been growing slowly for years. But in all that time, it had not actually occurred to him as a defined and conscious idea in Geoffrey's mind that such an empty value system, such a hollow and meaningless way of life, could be—more than could be, *ought* to be—replaced by anything else.

His response during those slow-growing years of unease had been chiefly negative. He only knew that he did not want to follow in his father's footsteps. When he thought to himself that something more in life might be gained than what his father had achieved in his, the idea was merely a vague sense of what he did *not* want.

What that "something more" might be, he had not stopped to consider.

Suddenly the changes taking place in his cousin Amanda were striking root in the soil of Geoffrey's consciousness. She had been just as self-centered as he. If anyone could have been said to be out for herself, it was Amanda.

Yet . . . look at her now!

She had changed—noticeably, visibly. She was a wholly different person.

Why? What had happened? Had she merely "grown up," or was there more to it?

Geoffrey suspected the latter.

What they had done was such an extraordinary thing! They had turned their backs on, set aside, given away, nearly all they possessed. And they had done so by giving it . . . to *him*.

What a hugely unselfish act! The realization of the enormous consequences involved had set off a series of domino-like topplings to his moral and emotional equilibrium.

As he had pondered the incredible thing in recent days, gradually had come into Geoffrey's brain the familiar verse he had heard recited how many dozen times out of the prayer book while sitting dutifully between his father and mother through the years trying to keep from falling asleep.

If a man will deny himself . . .

Over and over the words hounded him—*deny himself . . . deny himself . . .*

That's what they had done. They had given away *everything!* They had carried out the essence of that principle in a way he had never witnessed before. In light of their sacrifice, this was no stale dogma, but living reality!

Could *this* be the something more, the specific missing ingredient in his life? Did this account for the change in Amanda? Had she tapped into some new source of life whose foundations lay in the realm of this incredible thing called self-denial?

He rose, left his room, and walked upstairs to the library. Was the family Bible still where Amanda had pointed out to him all the familial clues she had discovered? He wanted to check the exact wording of the verse. Now that it was repeating itself over and over in his brain, he had the sense that he wasn't remembering the whole thing correctly.

Geoffrey entered the library and flipped on the light. The place still appeared substantially the same, though Jocelyn and Amanda had removed a few books. He went straight to the old secretary whose secret mechanisms and compartments Amanda had shown him. Right now, however, he was interested in secrets of another kind.

There was the Bible lying flat and open to the Psalms.

Where would the verse be... probably somewhere in the Gospels. He should have paid more attention when he was younger. He was hopelessly illiterate when it came to this book. He began turning over the large pages.

Wasn't there something... some reference in the back that helped locate what you were looking for?

He turned quickly to the back of the Bible... yes, here it was. He began scanning down the lists of words, flipping two or three more pages.

In a minute or two he had located the passage in the sixteenth chapter of Matthew. *If any man will come after me*, he read, *let him deny himself, and take up his cross, and follow me... for what is a man profited, if he shall gain the whole world, and lose his own soul? or what shall a man give in exchange for his soul?*

How perfectly did the words illuminate the difference between his father and Amanda's. The one had spent his life seeking profit, and in so doing, at least for the present, had lost his soul. The other had laid down one of the most prestigious political careers in all of England that he might serve the man he called his Master, Jesus Christ. Charles Rutherford had been mocked as a fool. Geoffrey had heard his own father deride him with scorn. He had even joined in his father's laughter.

And yet... if this verse was true, it was *Charles* who had discovered the secret of life through that very self-denial, while his father would perhaps gain the whole world... but lose everything in the end.

Geoffrey read the words again, then a third time, then turned and left the library, pondering the remarkable principle that the meaning of life was backward from all he had been taught, and that for most of his life he had believed.

It was not merely self-denial, he thought. It was self-denial for the sake of following Jesus Christ. It was not enough to give, to deny, to lay down oneself for others, but to do so *while following Christ.* Exactly as Charles Rutherford had done.

Was this what Amanda's example signified? Did this explain the remarkable change that had come over her, just as it explained Charles's transformation twenty years before?

The next instant—not yet having again even reached his own room, but there in the corridor near the second-floor landing of the staircase of Heathersleigh Hall—Geoffrey Rutherford paused, then sank to his knees.

"God," he prayed softly, *"I am sorry for what I have been. But I want to be more. Help me to make something of what is left of my life, and to follow the example I have been given of what self-denial truly means."*

73

The Hall and the Cottage

◆◆◆

*G*eoffrey Rutherford awoke several mornings later feeling strangely at peace with his new surroundings.

His mother and father, who had come down for the weekend, were still sleeping. Geoffrey dressed slowly and went out. He walked toward the stables. Before he had actually planned it, he had mounted his favorite horse and was on his way across the meadow in the direction of the cottage.

As he went, nature whispered secret sights and smells he had never noticed before. What had begun as mere hints that afternoon in Hyde Park now blossomed fully in his heart. The world was indeed beautiful, and was his to enjoy.

When he drew closer to the cottage he saw evidence of the clearing through the woods for the new roadway that would make the cottage accessible by automobile both to the Hall and the village.

He approached to the pounding of Rune Blakeley's hammer out behind the barn, where he was constructing new stables for horses and one or two carriages. Despite the hour, the place was alive with activity.

And there was Amanda in Maggie's garden picking some of the first new flowers of spring.

She glanced up as Geoffrey rode toward her.

"Geoffrey, you're out early!"

"No earlier than everyone around here by the look of it!" he laughed. "Maybe the country does that to you."

Geoffrey dismounted and tied his horse.

"How do you like it after a month?" she asked.

"I am getting used to the quiet," he replied. "I have to admit that not having to be at the bank every day is a welcome change, though it has been a surprise to find that I do miss being around people."

He paused a moment. Amanda was climbing to her feet and did not see the poignant and reflective smile that passed across his lips.

"And," he added, "I have been making changes *inside* that are probably more significant even than this change in my outward circumstances that you—you and your mother—are responsible for."

"I am intrigued!" smiled Amanda.

"Perhaps one of these days we can go for a long ride and I will tell you about it," said Geoffrey. "Right now I am still trying to understand exactly what it all means."

"I shall look forward to it."

"For now, let me just say that I am learning to pray—for the first time in my life, really."

Amanda smiled and nodded, adding, "It is something I have begun to learn as well."

"And to ask what kind of person God wants me to be," he added. "That is not so easy a thing when you have never done anything in your life other than what you yourself wanted."

"It is a difficult change to make," agreed Amanda. "How well I know! You have described me exactly."

"I have the feeling you are a little ahead of me," laughed Geoffrey. "In my case it has only been a matter of days. So when I have made a little more sense of it, we shall take that ride."

They walked through the flowers a moment or two in silence.

"Do you think you will return to London and the bank eventually?" asked Amanda as slowly they made their way together toward the cottage.

"I honestly don't know, Amanda," Geoffrey replied. "As I find myself thinking about these new perspectives—I am also thinking hard about my future, about goals and priorities. It is so new to me. I am going to need more time than anything. But I do like it here in Devon. And I think too that the climate might agree with me. It is warmer than London. I haven't really felt well for some time."

"And you are better now?"

"I think somewhat. Winters are always difficult—congestion in the lungs, fevers, you know... I am extremely susceptible. Sometimes I cough and hack for weeks on end. But this month here so far has been quite good on that score."

"I am happy to hear it."

"I am thinking in time of perhaps opening a small branch of the bank in Milverscombe," Geoffrey went on, "not primarily for investments and that sort of thing, but in order to help the residents with everyday needs, purchasing motorcars, home building, the seasonal requirements of the farmers and sheepherders, and so on."

"That sounds wonderful. What does your father think?"

"That the idea is ridiculous," laughed Geoffrey. "He says that no money can be made in such an out-of-the-way place as this. But it might be an opportunity to help the community."

"He and your mother will remain in London, then?"

"For the present. Although he is not far from retirement. My mother is anxious to move down to the Hall with me. Perhaps I shall make my father a junior officer in the new bank once I get it established ... just so long as I could keep him away from the customers!"

"Why do you say that?" laughed Amanda.

"He is too surly. He would drive them away!"

"Geoffrey, you are too mean!"

"I know," he chuckled. "But the sad fact is ... it is true. My father is ... well, you know what he is like—you practically lived with us for a good while when you were in London. He never did warm up to you, except briefly when he concocted that scheme that we should marry and pushed me to propose to you.—By the way, I *am* sorry for that. I was a nincompoop back in those days."

Amanda laughed. "Oh, Geoffrey, you weren't a tenth as bad as me. I was positively awful. I apologize to you too for the uppity way I treated you."

"I suppose we have both changed since. But you know what I am saying about Father. Even me he treats like a colleague, not a son."

"I see what you mean. You're right. It is sad."

"I love him in spite of it," said Geoffrey. "But he is a trying man to live with. I hope in time the people of this community, if he spends enough time down here, might help him see that there is more to life than money. But . . . we shall see. They are here for the weekend," Geoffrey added. "That's one of the reasons I came over, to invite you all for tea this afternoon."

"I am certain we will enjoy it very much," said Amanda as they arrived at the door to the cottage. "Come in and have morning tea with us."

Jocelyn and Catharine received Geoffrey warmly as he entered with Amanda.

"You are just in time for tea and bread!" said Jocelyn as she walked toward the door. "Sit down and join us. I won't be but a moment—I want to run out to see if Rune can take a break from his work."

She left the kitchen just as Maggie made her way slowly in from the sitting room.

"Let me help you get to your chair, Grandma Maggie," said Catharine, taking her arm.

"Thank you, dear," said Maggie. "Oh—hello, Geoffrey. What do you think of my little cottage?"

"Bustling, Mrs. McFee," laughed Geoffrey.

The place was so vibrant and full of life, thought Geoffrey as he continued to watch and listen. This family had lost nothing by giving away Heathersleigh Hall. The life of the place had come *with* them, right across the meadow just as he had come a few minutes ago. The life was here *without* the Hall, *without* the possessions, *without* the library, *without* the history, *without* the title.

They were the life, these wonderful, giving, gracious, loving people.

The Hall stood now mostly quiet and empty. His father had so long coveted it. Yet it was just an empty shell. Without people within its walls, it was mere mortar and stone, while here in this simple two-story cottage there was such—

Geoffrey's reflections were cut short as Jocelyn and Rune Blakeley walked in chatting and laughing. They sat down at the remaining two places at the table.

"This is a tight squeeze!" said Jocelyn. "I think this is the largest group we have had since moving to the cottage."

"We shall have to get a larger table, Mother," said Amanda.

"It sounds like a big new table will be next on my list after completion of the stables," laughed Rune.

Gradually it quieted and they all joined hands. How long had it been, thought Geoffrey as his right hand closed about Amanda's soft palm, and his left was swallowed up by the great rough-textured fingers of Rune Blakeley's fist, since he had held hands with another human being? He could not even remember. The feeling of companionship and brotherhood filled him with such a warm feeling that he could think of no place he would rather be at that moment than right here.

"Thank you, our Father," prayed Jocelyn, *"for this day you have given us, for your provision, for your love, for your constant goodness to us, and for dear friends with whom we are able to share life. Thank you for Geoffrey and Rune and their presence with us today. Thank you for this wonderful cottage with Maggie where we are all so happy. And we pray that you will bless and prosper Geoffrey's tenure in the Hall, and make this a wonderful season in his life. Amen."*

The humble simplicity and genuine warmth of the prayer went straight to Geoffrey's heart, and he found a lump rising in his throat. It was with difficulty at first that he was able to enter into the friendly conversation that began immediately as Jocelyn poured tea and the girls began passing around plates laden with bread, cakes, cheeses, and meats.

"Geoffrey, would you care for a scone?" asked Catharine.

"Why, yes . . . thank you, I would," replied Geoffrey, trying his best to focus his mind on the plate in front of him.

"Geoffrey has just been telling me of his plans," said Amanda to the others. "He is thinking of opening a small bank in Milverscombe."

"Progress comes to the country, eh!" said Rune.

"I suppose something like that," rejoined Geoffrey. "I am not at all anxious to return to London. You see, Mr. Blakeley, I am on indefinite leave at present. But I cannot just lounge about forever. I shall have to do something. And banking is all I know."

"Milverscombe *is* growing," put in Jocelyn. "A bank would no doubt be a boon to the community."

"I would hope so," said Geoffrey. "But what about all of you?" he added, turning toward Jocelyn. "What will *you* do here?"

"We intend to pray for God to keep us busy and involved with people. We may even take in a few young people now and then if he leads them to us."

"But is there room?"

"Oh yes. We will take you on a tour of the cottage after breakfast. The first floor has a small sitting room and four bedrooms. Granted, they are small, but adequate. We each have a room of our own at present. And this floor has another two bedrooms, the large sitting room, this kitchen ... we shall have plenty of space."

Geoffrey listened with a nod and gentle smile. "I think it sounds lovely," he said, then paused. "In a way," he added, "I almost envy you."

"You will have the chance to minister to people too, Geoffrey," said Amanda.

"I must admit I had never thought of banking in quite *that* way before!"

"Any occupation is full of opportunities to help, wherever people are involved."

"One always thinks of money and banking as the opposite of what you call *ministry*."

"It is the worship of money that is the root of all evil, Geoffrey," said Jocelyn, "not money itself. Properly used, money is a tremendous tool for good in the world. My husband was always very grateful for what he had. It allowed him to do a great deal for others."

"Amen to that!" chimed in Blakeley enthusiastically. "Me and my family are living proof of the man's generosity, God bless him!"

"Charles was always fond of a certain passage of the Scotsman's.— Amanda," she said, turning to her eldest daughter, "—would you mind fetching the Scotsman's *Curate*?"

"I think the passage you want is in *Faber*, Mother," replied Amanda, rising. "I'll go see."

She left the room and returned a minute later with two old books bound in red boards. She handed one to her mother and immediately began scanning the other herself. The others waited.

"Ah, here it is, Mother," said Amanda after a couple of minutes. "It's in chapter seven, where Wingfold is preaching."

She handed the book across the table to Jocelyn, who found the familiar spot.

"Yes, this is it ... I always get the two books a little mixed up.— 'Friends,' " Jocelyn began to read, " 'cast your idol into the furnace. Melt your mammon down, coin him up, make God's money of him, and send him out to do God's work. Make of him cups to carry the gift of God, the water of life, through the world—in lovingkindness to the oppressed, in rest to the weary who have borne the burden and heat of the day, in joy to the heavy-hearted, in laughter to the dull-spirited.

" 'Ah, what true gifts might not the mammon of unrighteousness, changed back into the money of God, give to men and women! How would you not spend your money for the Lord if he needed it from your hand! He *does* need it, for he that spends it upon the least of his fellows spends it upon the Lord.

" 'To hold fast to God with one hand while you open wide the other to your neighbor—that is true religion, that is the law and the prophets.—Lord, defend us from mammon. Hold your temple against his foul invasion. Purify our money with your air and your sun that it may be our slave, and you our master. Amen.' "

Jocelyn closed the book. The kitchen fell silent.

Geoffrey pondered deeply the words he had just heard. "A wonderful passage," he said at length. His voice was unusually quiet.

"You see, Geoffrey," said Jocelyn, "it is all about turning money into *God's* money, and using *whatever* he gives us—possessions, talent, money, the work of our hands, our energies, the love in our hearts, even such a thing as simple friendliness . . . using *all* he gives us to carry the water of life to a thirsty world."

"What a creed that would make for the banking industry," added Geoffrey with a reflective smile.

Perhaps, he thought, he had just found the direction he had been seeking for his own future.

74

More News

Lieutenant Langham's call to Devon on the present occasion was twofold. He must speak in private with both the Rutherford girls. He had arrived the evening before and—as was now his custom since the family had left Heathersleigh Hall—spent the night in Timothy Diggorsfeld's guest room.

The seriousness of the first of his two objectives could be seen by the expression on his face when he asked to talk to Amanda alone after calling at the cottage the morning after his arrival. They walked out the front door and slowly made their way through the paths of Maggie's flower garden.

"I have some news to report to you, Miss Rutherford," the lieutenant began slowly. "Apparently it occurred several months ago during the incident Lieutenant Forbes and I were involved in. But at the time we were not aware of the identity of some of those involved."

"Lieutenant, what are you talking about?" said Amanda. "I have never heard you sound so serious."

"Just this, Miss Rutherford—we have just learned that Ramsay Halifax is dead."

Amanda took in the words with strange detachment, then slowly began to cry, for sadness, but also relief.

She took out a handkerchief. They walked on in silence, except for an occasional sniffle.

"What happened?" asked Amanda at length.

"He was killed in the aborted escape attempt of Colonel Forsythe I told you about before," replied Langham. "He was one of those buried at sea. Unfortunately, at the time I was unconscious from my own wounds and did not actually see the body. No one else on board knew him. I wish I could have notified you sooner. News only just reached us through an intercepted communiqué listing the names of those on the escape yacht."

"Was it Ramsey who shot you?"

"It may well have been," answered the lieutenant. "The last thing I remember was catching a momentary glimpse of him. At the time I didn't put the face together with the incident at the lighthouse. But in retrospect I now realize it was Halifax. I saw him raise his hand. He was holding a pistol. I heard a volley of shots, then everything went black."

"Did . . . did *you* kill Ramsay, Lieutenant?"

"No. I never got a shot off," he said. "There is no way to know, really, who actually fired the shot that hit him. The ship exploded with gunfire for several seconds, or so they tell me, much of it from the frigate, before the colonel and the crew of the yacht gave up."

Amanda pondered this sudden development seriously, continuing to wipe at her eyes and blink away the tears.

"Well . . . thank you, Lieutenant," she said at length. "This certainly changes things. I don't suppose there is much point in pursuing my annulment papers now."

"You had filed for an annulment?"

Amanda nodded. "Rev. Diggorsfeld has been helping me. I suppose I should go into town and talk to him and let him know."

They had circled back in the direction of the house. Amanda took in a deep breath and glanced about. "I need to find my mother," she said. "I think she is out with Rune."

"Is your sister at home?" asked Lieutenant Langham

"Catherine . . . yes—she is upstairs in her room."

"Would you mind telling her that I am here?"

"Of course not, although I am certain she is already aware of it."

Amanda walked inside the cottage and returned in a couple of minutes. "She will be right down, Lieutenant," she said.

"Thank you," replied Langham. "Well, again, I am so sorry to have to be the bearer of such tidings. But I wanted you to hear it from a friend."

"Thank you, Lieutenant."

"Good day, Miss Amanda."

Langham turned for the house. Amanda walked toward the barn to find Jocelyn, who was conferring with Rune Blakeley about the timbers he had just had delivered for the roof-beams for the enclosed portion of the new stable area.

Half an hour later Amanda was still outside by the stables when Catharine and the lieutenant left the house, walked toward the barn, saddled and mounted two horses, and cantered off through the woods for a ride together. She did not see Catharine for the rest of the day.

◆ ◆ ◆

Catharine returned late. Lieutenant Langham went straight to the village without coming back into the cottage. Catharine was quiet as she entered, but one look on her face as she went toward the stairs and up to her room after greeting her mother and sister said clearly enough what she had been trying to hide for months, that she was in love and didn't care who knew it.

Amanda was the first one down for breakfast the next morning. A few minutes later Catharine bounded in with a big grin that a night's sleep had not removed from her face.

"Guess what, Amanda?" she said, walking up close and speaking in a whisper. "Terrill asked me to marry him yesterday."

"Oh, Catharine!" exclaimed Amanda. "I am so happy for you! Why didn't you tell us last evening?"

"He asked me to wait until today. He's going to talk to Mum again this morning."

"Again?"

"He said he had already spoken with her about me months ago."

"I didn't know that!"

"Nor I."

"Well, she certainly kept his secret," laughed Amanda. "I want to know what he said to her."

"Me too!" said Catharine. She went to the window and looked out but saw nothing. "Oh, I wish he would hurry and get here!"

75
Summer 1917
••••

Four months went by. Spring matured and at last the summer of 1917 came to Devon.

Again the war began to intrude. A rash of ship sinkings in the English Channel once more had the people of England in panic. In April the United States entered the war against Germany and Austria-Hungary. Little did the rest of the world realize, as news of it spread throughout the year, to what an extent the successful Bolshevik Revolution, then under way in Russia, would alter world affairs and change the course of history itself. At the time it was hailed as a step toward democracy in the East. Though the fighting seemed far removed from Devon, Catharine continued to worry that her new fiancé would be called for service at sea, the one thing she feared above all else.

The war did not affect the fortunes of Stirling Blakeley, however, whose bad leg had prevented his involvement. He graduated from Oxford, as predicted by Timothy, with honors in physiology and literature, and a third in history. Jocelyn, Amanda, Catharine, and Timothy accompanied Rune and Agatha Blakeley to Oxford by train for the commencement ceremony. After his return, throughout the summer, Stirling was to be seen around the cottage on most days helping his father with the felling of timber to make way for the new road, and with the completion of the stables.

Gradually the move to the cottage changed the feel of life for the three Heathersleigh women. For the first time since Charles's and George's deaths, life began to feel right again. There was just so much to do. If anything they were busier than ever, moving in, unpacking, and with all the work they undertook about the place. They all went to sleep each night fatigued but at peace. And of course Maggie couldn't have been happier.

Life for Jocelyn seemed to have turned a corner. Amanda, however, still found herself wrestling with inner doubts whether she would ever truly be able to put her father's death behind her. Tears often still came when she was alone.

The flowers of Maggie's garden bloomed profusely throughout the spring and summer, but Maggie herself did not seem to care for them with the same passion as before. The long, cold winter had taxed her reserves, and she was noticeably weary. She always brightened when one of the others brought in a bouquet, or when they took her out for a walk outside the cottage. But no longer could she tend the garden herself and surprisingly, she did not seem to mind.

In her quieter moments, Jocelyn was anxious that her dear aging friend was no longer her sharp-witted self. She knew the girls noticed the change as well, though they did not talk about it. More and more all three found themselves tenderly waiting on Maggie as they might a child, though with this difference, that reverence and honor filled their every thought and tiniest act of ministration on her behalf.

Jocelyn moved herself down to the ground floor into a small room next to Maggie's, which had been used prior to that time primarily for storage. She wanted to be nearby, especially at night. The narrow staircase rising from the corridor between the large sitting room, Maggie's bedroom, and the back door of the cottage rose to the first floor to open onto a large rectangular landing around which sat the four bedrooms and sitting rooms of the upper story. Two extra bedrooms—one on the ground floor and the fourth second-story bedroom—they made up as guest rooms.

The smallest of the bedrooms on the ground floor they were slowly converting to a tiny library. The intent was to fill it with the entire collection of the Scotsman's volumes, Charles's Bible collection, and assorted other of their favorite books from the Hall. Stirling's first project upon returning from Oxford was to construct bookshelves along each wall, from floor to ceiling, all around the room.

Timothy continued to write, though in time he was so involved with people dropping by either to borrow books or talk about one thing and another, in addition to mounting requests for his occasional services in the pulpit throughout Devon, Cornwall, and Dorset, that he declared himself busier than he had ever been in London.

Upon learning of Ramsay's death, Amanda knew her future was obviously greatly altered. After much thought, she decided to continue with annulment proceedings in spite of the news. Though it would make little practical difference, she wanted legally and ethically to put forever behind her the Halifax season of her life. Finalizing an annulment, she judged, was the best way to do so.

Knowing the town name Looe they had heard from Betsy, and having as yet had no response with regard to the girl from their inquiries, Timothy traveled down to Cornwall himself to speak personally with the police chief of the coastal town. The name Scully Conlin was well known to the man the instant Timothy mentioned it.

"Not such a bad bloke, as they go," the chief said, "but mixed up with some rum ones, he was—smugglers, they were, and Conlin got the worst of it."

"Worst of it . . . how do you mean?" asked Timothy.

"Shot him dead, they did. Some kind of a brawl at his place. That's where we found him."

"What happened to the men who did it?"

"Gone . . . gone without a trace and never been seen again."

"What about his daughter?"

"Didn't know he had none, Reverend."

"Yes, he had a daughter by the name of Elsbet."

"No one seen nothing of a girl after that . . . though now that you put my mind to it, I do recollect some of the neighbor folk asking the same thing. A mystery what had happened to her, they said. Most of them figured she must have got killed herself, or else run away."

"She was born in Looe?"

"Don't know, Reverend."

"Did the man have any other relatives?"

"None, leastways not around Looe. You know something, Reverend?"

"I may," replied Timothy, rising and shaking the man's hand. "I will talk to you again before I leave town."

From the station Timothy went immediately to the rectory to speak with the local vicar. The man was familiar with the case but knew no more than the policeman about any family. Timothy told him about Betsy, and that she was now safe and happy in Switzerland.

"I am more happy than I can tell you to hear of it," replied the vicar. "I had been worried about the girl and had assumed she must have been kidnapped or killed. She is decidedly better off where she is. It was a bad life she lived here. Everyone wondered what would happen to the poor child when she came of age. I am sorry about what happened, but it sounds to me as if it may be for the best."

"Still, if other relatives appear, someone should know her whereabouts," said Timothy.

"Of course," said the vicar. "And now that I know, I will make inquiries among those few who knew her. But what is to become of the girl in Switzerland?"

"The woman I told you about—Mrs. Hope Guinarde—intends to adopt her," replied Timothy. "She has only been waiting for me to learn what I could of her past."

"I have told you all I know, and I am reasonably confident that is all there is to be known. Conlin was a loner. I doubt anyone will step forward to claim the child."

Timothy thanked him, paid a last visit to the chief of police to tell him what he and the vicar had discussed and to inform him of Hope's plans, then started on his journey back to Devon.

The moment Timothy returned to Milverscombe, he began a letter to Hope telling her what he had learned. He also put her in touch with Bradbury Crumholtz, saying he had informed the solicitor that she would be contacting him, and suggested, as he was well known throughout Cornwall and Devon, that she pursue the adoption filing through him.

Chelsea Winters was a regular visitor to the cottage through the summer months. By and by a few other girls of the village began dropping by with her. The fact that there were interesting things going on, and always a biscuit and cold milk to be had in Jocelyn's kitchen, was incentive enough to make Heathersleigh Cottage a place of regular visits by the youngsters of the town. Whereas in Amanda's childhood the clearing in the woods had been feared, now a generation later it was a popular hub of constant activity. Catharine organized regular rides on horseback through the countryside with whatever boys and girls came to the cottage to join her.

Geoffrey settled into life in the community with remarkable ease. He never missed a Sunday at church and gradually came to occupy a role similar to that Charles once had during the visiting time afterward. He and Timothy were nearly always the last to leave, and most times left together. When Timothy was not elsewhere, it became their custom to spend Sunday afternoons with one another and have tea together in the evening, each at the other's home on alternate Sundays.

Geoffrey and Stirling Blakeley also became good friends.

Gifford and Martha came down from London at least once a month. Martha looked forward to Sundays in Devon more than any of the dreary pastimes that occupied her time in London. While Gifford left church to return alone to the Hall, his wife and Jocelyn spent many an afternoon together calling on one or another of the villagers, especially among the elderly of the community.

Catharine and Terrill Langham talked about their plans as often as the lieutenant could get down to Devon. They had decided to wait until the war was over to marry. Jocelyn could not bear the thought of Catharine moving to London. Lieutenant Langham requested a transfer to Plymouth, which appeared likely to be granted after the cessation of hostilities.

In early November a packet arrived at the cottage bearing the stamp of the firm Crumholtz, Sutclyff, Stonehaugh, & Crumholtz. It was addressed to Amanda.

Half suspecting what it contained, she went into the sitting room to be alone.

She sat down, slowly opened the envelope, then pulled out and looked over the enclosed documents. They represented the final annulment papers, signed and witnessed by the necessary authorities both in Vienna and London. Though nothing could erase the memories of that time, and the foolishness she would always feel for the immaturity that had landed her in such a fix, in the eyes of the law at least, her marriage to Ramsay Halifax was now as if it had never happened.

She was once again *Amanda Rutherford*.

Amanda heard the sound of soft footsteps approaching. She glanced up to see her mother.

Jocelyn walked forward, sat down beside her on the settee, and placed a loving hand around Amanda's shoulder. Amanda's eyes filled with tears of sad relief. She set the papers aside, then slowly leaned against her mother and melted into her comforting embrace.

For several minutes neither spoke. At last Amanda let out a long sigh.

"Finally, Mother," she said, "I think it is finally over."

76

Stroke

*O*ne morning late in the year, Maggie did not appear for breakfast.

"Have either of you seen Maggie yet?" Jocelyn asked her two daughters when they had all gathered in the kitchen.

Catharine shook her head.

"No . . . I haven't either," said Amanda.

Jocelyn left the kitchen and went straight into Maggie's room. Immediately she sensed that a change had come over her old friend. Maggie was lying in her bed awake, eyes open but motionless.

"Good morning, Maggie," said Jocelyn cheerily. "Would you like to get up?"

Maggie did not reply, only smiled. She followed Jocelyn with her eyes, yet to all Jocelyn's entreaties, her only response was a smile.

"I shall bring you some tea," said Jocelyn and left the room.

She returned to the kitchen. It was obvious from her expression that she was shaken.

Immediately she sent Sarah—who was sharing duties both here and at the Hall until Geoffrey had decided on his permanent plans—for Dr. Armbruster.

Within ninety minutes he was at Maggie's bedside. He sat speaking kindly while he took her pulse. Jocelyn stood quietly to one side.

Maggie's smiling but speechless face moved slowly from one of them to the other, her eyes seemingly the same, still aware of the activity around her. But not a sound came from her lips.

At last Dr. Armbruster rose, nodded to Jocelyn, gave Maggie a kindly pat on the shoulder, and left the room. Jocelyn followed.

They returned to the kitchen, where Amanda and Catharine were waiting. Dr. Armbruster took a chair.

"I am afraid Maggie has suffered an apoplectic seizure," he said, "otherwise known as a cerebral hemorrhage, or what we now commonly call a stroke."

"What does all that mean, Cecil?" asked Jocelyn.

"A blood clot of some kind, probably in the vessels of the brain."

"Goodness!" exclaimed Jocelyn, her face growing pale. Slowly she eased into a chair. "What can be done?"

"Unfortunately, nothing. Either the clot passes, or it continues to block the vessel or artery, causing paralysis and often, as in Maggie's case, loss of speech."

"How long . . . does the paralysis last?"

"There is no way to know," answered Armbruster. "There could be improvement with some motor function and speech. But sometimes such skills are permanently lost. It depends on the size and severity of the clot and its exact location. Most often hemiplegia, or paralysis, affects one lateral half of the body, usually the right side. But apoplexy remains a great mystery to medical science. That is why, as I say, there is nothing that can be done but wait . . . and see what course the stroke takes. She could still live for many years."

"But . . . could it be—"

Jocelyn glanced away.

"Just a year ago she was so vibrant and active," said Catharine. "I do not understand how she could become so . . . so frail . . . so quickly."

"She is seventy-nine, my dear," replied the doctor. "Sometimes when the end comes, those we love fade quickly. It is never easy to see, but it is part of life. And especially in the case of a stroke, there are often no warning signs whatsoever. One day a tiny invisible clot comes from somewhere in the body's blood supply and . . . as you have seen, the change is instantaneous."

PART VI

❖❖❖

1918-1919

77

Farewell

As 1918 opened, and with the United States now fully mobilized and involved on the side of the Allies, there were signs throughout Europe that the war was at last winding down. Though its allies were nearly exhausted from the fight, Germany launched a final all-out offensive on the western front that represented the dying gasp of a losing cause. The smaller countries allied with Germany and the Central Powers, however, had had enough and began throughout the year to sue for peace.

Geoffrey prepared to move ahead with the Milverscombe branch of the Bank of London. He made several trips back into the capital and returned one day in February with the news that his proposal had been approved. He opened the following month in a small store space while plans were being made to construct a new building. Sufficient capital was provided for him to begin making a few loans and teaching the country folk of the region how to do business with a bank. He hoped to open the doors of the new building by August of that year.

The managers of the Bank of London hired a construction firm from Exeter to build the new bank in Milverscombe. Within weeks construction was under way on the building to be situated across from the train station. Because many young men in the area were overseas with the war, Geoffrey made certain that those who were available and needed work were hired as laborers, including Rune and Stirling Blakeley. Through the spring months they were at the cottage early, usually by seven in the morning, where they worked for three or four hours before returning to the village for the afternoon.

Letters continued to arrive from Hope and Betsy.

Though Jocelyn, Amanda, and Catharine had all been mentally making themselves ready for the worst, nothing could actually prepare them for the loss of their beloved Maggie. Their ministrations for eight months had been almost continuous, as she had been bedridden since the day of the stroke. Even though she had not spoken a word again since that day, it was still sudden when the time actually arrived.

When Jocelyn entered the room for the first time that August morning, she knew immediately from the pale, vacant look on Maggie's lifeless form that her dear friend had departed for another world during her sleep. Jocelyn could not have wished for a more peaceful passing, yet she burst into tears at the sight.

Slowly she approached and reached out to touch the beloved face. Maggie's skin was cold. She had been gone several hours. It had been such a quiet departure, thought Jocelyn, without even the chance for a final farewell.

"Good-bye, Maggie," she whispered in a choked voice. "We all love you so much!"

Jocelyn turned and left the room and immediately went to find Catharine and Amanda, then sent for the undertaker.

The next day, even before funeral arrangements could be made, Jocelyn boarded the train for Exeter. She must see Bradbury Crumholtz. She knew Maggie's passing had implications he must be made aware of.

Upon learning the news, Crumholtz made immediate plans to attend the funeral. He would bring the appropriate documents, he said, and open them with Jocelyn and her daughters after the service.

People for miles around attended the funeral. That Maggie had been loved late in her life, almost to the point of being considered a saint, was clear from the outpouring of affection expressed by everyone throughout the day.

That same afternoon, in the cottage whose mysteries were at last to be brought fully to light, with Timothy and Geoffrey also present—an hour or so after the gathering in the village had at last broken up—Bradbury Crumholtz explained the provision of the deed to the cottage that had resulted in its being transferred to Maggie's grandmother at the death of Bishop Arthur Crompton. He then opened and read Maggie's will, which passed on the cottage and whatever of her worldly possessions might go along with it to George, Amanda, and Catharine Rutherford.

"As you know," he went on after completing the will, "several documents were left for safekeeping with our firm, the deed and the will I have just read being of a legal nature. There was also a personal letter by Bishop Crompton, to be opened at the death of the final living heir of Orelia Moylan. As that time has come, I will now open the bishop's letter."

He opened the envelope and pulled out two sheets of paper. He glanced over it a moment and then began to read.

"To whomever it may concern," he began, "I write the following to testify to certain events concerning the births of twins, a son and a daughter, to Henry Rutherford, lord of the manor, Heathersleigh Hall, by his wife, Eliza, births attended by me to which I gave false witness at the time."

He went on to read of the events of that night.

"As through the years," the letter concluded, "my conscience made me more and more ill at ease with what I had agreed to, I went back to the parish registry during a visit to my former church. I felt that to alter the entry I had made earlier would be to compound my sin. Therefore, I added a marginal reference to Genesis 25 and Psalm 27, adding my initials beside them, in hopes that someone would one day unearth the deception and perhaps do more than lay in my power at that time to right the wrong. I further sought to make it right with this letter, explaining what had happened, so that the truth, should this ever be read, would be clearly known."

Crumholtz set the papers aside and glanced around the room.

"It appears Amanda was right," said Jocelyn. "This confirms her conclusions exactly. It seems that we did the right thing... as we were already certain of."

Geoffrey sat listening in silence, amazed anew at what they had done. The fact of this proof now coming to light in no way changed the enormity of the fact that they had given him the estate voluntarily.

78

In the Chicken Shed

♦ ♦ ♦

As Geoffrey had little interest at present in any of the animals at the Hall other than horses, Jocelyn and Catharine and Amanda, with Hector's help, had transferred their chickens, a few goats, as well as four of Heathersleigh's seven horses to Maggie's cottage. They planned also to raise a few sheep and add several cows. Thus Rune and Stirling would be kept busy for some months as their time permitted, not only with the road and stables, but clearing space for grazing as well as enlarging the barn and adding several new pens and enclosures.

As Amanda stepped out of the cottage a week and a half after Maggie's funeral, the morning sun seemed especially warm and cheery. She stood on the doorstep and basked for a moment or two in its pleasant warmth, vaguely aware of shouts and pounding coming from the direction of Rune and Stirling's work in the distance. With basket in hand, she set out for the chicken shed, thinking of Geoffrey and the changes that were so apparent about him. How could she have once felt so differently about him, and now consider him—strange as it was even to think it!—as a friend?

It was truly remarkable, Amanda thought, how real and tangible and down-to-earth God's grace actually was. It really could get inside people and *change* them . . . transform them . . . make new people of them.

Geoffrey, her cousin, had actually become a kind, gracious, and likeable young man.

And what about her? She knew *she* had changed under the influence of God's grace too.

Yet she knew that there was still something missing. Something was still wrong deep inside her. She could see Geoffrey through different eyes . . . but could she ever see *herself* through different eyes?

She opened the door to the old and dilapidated chicken shed and went inside. Cackling and squawking greeted her entry as several of the hens scurried about in front of her. She stooped down to gather the eggs one by one and began setting them into her basket. When she rose and turned toward the next row of nests, she saw a figure standing in the doorway.

"Stirling!" exclaimed Amanda, laughing as she gave an involuntary jump. "You gave me a fright. I didn't hear you!"

"I am sorry," he smiled. "I saw you coming this way and followed you in. I was on my way to ask you something. I must say, you handle those eggs with great care."

A strange smile came over Amanda's face.

"Someone at the chalet said that to me too," she said. "I had nearly forgotten, it had been so long since I had gathered eggs. It made me realize how much of my childhood and homelife I had blotted from my memory."

"They had chickens there too?" asked Stirling, looking about and probing in the straw to see if he could find any eggs.

"And cows and goats and donkeys," said Amanda, continuing to work her way around the small enclosure.

"Here's one," said Stirling, handing Amanda his find. "Is that why you want so many animals around here?" he asked. "It seems like it will be a lot of work."

"You're right," agreed Amanda. "But it is such good and wholesome work. There is nothing quite like animals to help get in touch with one's feelings and with the world. That's how the sisters at the chalet keep busy, and I know it certainly helped me begin to think a little more clearly."

"What was it like at the chalet?"

"It was wonderful," replied Amanda. "Making butter and cheese and tending goats and cows and donkeys—it gives the people who come to the chalet, like me, a sense of responsibility that forces them to think about something other than their own problems. And of course the most important thing of all was the love that was present from all the sisters. Yes . . . it was a wonderful experience. Yet I hardly realized just how wonderful during the time I was there."

"What do you mean?"

"It was like my years at home when I was young," Amanda answered. "I was too full of my own self to appreciate all I had until I was gone."

Stirling smiled. "I am sorry, Amanda. I didn't mean to bring out painful memories."

"They are becoming less painful every day," she said, returning his smile. "God used the chalet, just like he is using my memories of my past to teach me what I need to learn."

Amanda finished gathering the eggs. Stirling handed her another two or three, and they left the shed and began walking back to the cottage together.

"What were you going to ask me?" said Amanda.

"Oh, right . . . my father and I were thinking that you probably need a new chicken house too."

"I suppose that old one is falling apart," laughed Amanda, looking back over her shoulder. "I never really thought about it. It's been there and looked just the same all my life. I suppose you should talk to my mother."

"I will. My father has an idea for a new spot next to the barn that he thinks will be better than this."

"What will you do now, Stirling?" asked Amanda as they neared the cottage.

"Well . . . we'll finish the stable first, then—"

"No!" laughed Amanda. "I mean, what are your plans now that you are through at university? I can't imagine you gaining all that knowledge just to fix barns and build stables."

"Maybe in a way that's not so far off," Stirling replied.

Amanda glanced over at him with a curious expression.

"I want to do something for people," Stirling added. "I want my life to count for something permanent, something that makes a difference in people's lives—like how you hope God uses this cottage."

"Tutoring again, perhaps?"

Stirling smiled. "I doubt it," he said. "But though I don't know exactly what it is I will do, I am sure it will have something to do with helping people."

79

Dreams

♦♦♦

*T*hey walked into the kitchen. As Amanda put away the eggs, Stirling sat down at the table and continued to talk.

"In a way, I envy you, Amanda," he said.

"Me! Why would you envy me?"

"You've seen so much of the world."

"And *you've* studied. That's an even greater thing."

"Perhaps, but I would like to travel and see more of the earth than just England."

"I have seen enough of it," laughed Amanda. "I truly am content here."

"Don't get me wrong—I love Devon," rejoined Stirling. "But I would like to see India, Japan, the United States, maybe even California and Australia. You've traveled to France and Greece and Austria—what are they like?"

"Greece was nice," replied Amanda. "And Paris, but the rest of

France and Austria were so involved in the war. All I did was travel quickly through them. I was hardly aware at the time what I was looking at through the train windows. And Austria . . . I suppose in a way Vienna was beautiful and historic. But I can hardly separate my images of it from horrible memories I would rather forget. But you should see the Mediterranean—the blue is so deep and clear. And it is so still—not like our seas, so cold and rough. When you are on deck looking out over the Mediterranean, it is somehow like a dream. Time seems to stand still. Yet when I think about it, all of that time in my life is so tinged with sadness that it makes it impossible for me to enjoy the memories. It was a dark time for me."

They were silent a moment or two.

"I don't know, maybe I'm just a dreamer," said Stirling at length. "I dream not only of traveling, but of doing things too. Do you ever dream, Amanda, really dream of doing something great?"

"I used to," laughed Amanda. "That's what got me into so much trouble. I am trying to learn to be content with life as it is."

"I understand that. But I can't help but dream about . . . I don't know, traveling, writing a book, maybe inventing something . . . like a cure for polio."

"Did you have polio? Is that what—"

Amanda hesitated, suddenly feeling awkward at bringing up Stirling's handicap.

"No," answered Stirling. "I was just born with a weak and deformed leg. No one knows why. But the similarity between my leg and polio made me feel a special empathy with people who were afflicted by it. I was intrigued. That's why what I would really like to do more than anything is become a doctor."

"Did you study medicine at university?"

"No—I never thought there was a chance of continuing to medical school. And," added Stirling as he lowered his voice, "don't you dare say a word of this to your mother."

"Why not?" said Amanda.

"Because she might get it into her head to try to help send me back for more schooling, and she and your father have already done enough."

"What about Dr. Armbruster . . . have you spoken with him?"

Stirling nodded. "He lets me come to his office and borrow books," he said, "and lets me help him and go on calls for small things occasionally."

"Really . . . that's wonderful. Perhaps you could apprentice with him."

"Perhaps, but you still have to go to school to be a real doctor."

"Somehow, Stirling, I have the feeling you will see all those places you speak of one day," said Amanda, "and probably become a doctor too."

"That would take a great deal of money."

"Why don't you talk to Geoffrey? Maybe it wouldn't be as difficult as you think."

"I don't know—maybe I should. But I imagine I will have to content myself to do my traveling and doctoring through books."

"I doubt that. You will probably be an important man one day. Rich and famous and important. I can see it, the famous author doctor and world traveler and inventor, Stirling Blakeley."

Stirling laughed.

"My father was the same way," Amanda went on. "Although now that I think about it, that was early in his life. Later on, his priorities and ambitions changed."

"I admired your father, though more for what he did late in his life than before."

A pained look came over Amanda's face. Stirling did not say anything further for several long seconds.

"I've been wanting to tell you something," he said after a moment, "but didn't want to bring it up. However, since you already mentioned the pain of the past . . . I've been reading in my New Testament, and everywhere you look we are reminded to turn the painful hurts of life into occasions for thanksgiving."

Amanda nodded.

"I have had to do the same thing," Stirling went on. "I remember how my father used to be. It is not as though I have forgotten. But long ago I knew I could let what had happened ruin me, or I could use it to make me a stronger person and a forgiving person. I think you have that same opportunity."

Amanda took in the words thoughtfully. "I know . . . thank you, Stirling," she said. "You're right. But it is hard."

"Of course it is hard. It is not easy to be a Christlike person. But isn't that the highest form of faith there is, to be strong even though it is hard, to suffer with grace, knowing that Jesus suffered too?"

Jocelyn walked into the kitchen just as Stirling finished speaking.

"Good morning, Stirling," she said.

"Good morning, Lady Jocelyn," he replied.

"Rune and Stirling think we need a new chicken shed, Mother," said Amanda.

"I am sure they're right," replied her mother. "There is a great deal around here that is older than I am, much of it probably even older than Maggie was."

"Would you like me to get started on it this week?" asked Stirling.

"I think the hens will be content for a while longer," replied Jocelyn. "To tell you the truth I would like to get our books out of their boxes. And there are still a few more from the Hall we would like to bring over. Whenever your father can spare you from the stables, I think I would rather you start on the bookshelves for our little library in the spare room."

Stirling laughed. "It sounds as though you have enough to keep me busy for a year or two before everything is completed!"

80

The Prayer Wood

─────── ♦♦♦ ───────

The door of Maggie's cottage had originally been placed in just the right spot to receive the morning sun when it shone above the treetops from the southeast. Maggie, her mother, and her grandmother before her had all been in the habit of opening the door early in the day to invite the sunshine indoors, and throughout the summer it stood open most of the day.

Amanda woke early, dressed, and came downstairs. There was her mother standing in the doorway soaking in the morning light, though there wasn't much warmth yet so early in the day.

Jocelyn turned when she heard Amanda's step. Amanda came forward and gave her a hug. She saw that there were tears on her mother's cheeks.

"What is it, Mother?" she asked as she stepped back.

"I have just been standing here realizing how happy I am," replied Jocelyn.

"Happy?" said Amanda. "That isn't what I would have expected so soon after Grandma Maggie's death, and with . . . you know, all that has happened these three years."

"I know," nodded her mother. "I think it caught me off guard too. That's what I was thinking about just as you came down. Earlier I might have said contentment or acceptance or even that I was at peace. But this morning I just felt . . . *happy*. I saw my face in the mirror a few minutes ago and suddenly realized how thoroughly gone are my feelings of self-consciousness about my scar. That alone is a miracle. But then I realized too that, even with the pain I will always feel for missing your father and brother and now Maggie, I am still . . . well, I am happy, and I can say life is good in spite of the pain."

"I don't know if I will ever know that peace, Mother," said Amanda. "I can't imagine being able to put it behind me."

"You mean your father and George being gone?"

"No, although that makes it a hundred times worse. I mean the guilt I feel for having made such a mess of my life, for hurting so many people, especially you and Father."

Jocelyn thought for a moment. "Let's go for a walk, dear," she said.

She led Amanda from the house. After five or ten minutes Amanda realized her mother was leading her to her father's prayer wood.

"I didn't know you knew about this place, Mother," said Amanda in some surprise. "I've never seen you come here."

"Your father showed me this wood years ago," replied Jocelyn as they worked their way through the narrow opening in the branches. "He told me how special it was to him and how many of his deepest times of prayer happened right here. He also told me about the day you followed him here."

"He knew!"

"Of course. He was aware of most of what was going on inside you. He knew you better back in those days than you knew yourself."

"I should have known," said Amanda, shaking her head.

"He always prayed that you would come on your own one day and someday be able to make this your own place of communion and retreat."

Amanda smiled. How many of her father's prayers for her had been answered! She would probably never know.

"Did you and he ever come here together?" she asked.

"Once or twice," replied Jocelyn. "But not often. He always said that a person's prayer closet ought to be reserved mostly for that person and the Lord. Usually when we prayed together it was in the heather garden."

A silence fell between mother and daughter. They emerged into the damp green clearing, walked about for a minute or two, then sat down on two large stones. For several minutes neither said a word as they drank in the peaceful silence of the morning.

"You probably don't realize it, because you were so young," began Jocelyn at length, "what a struggle this birthmark on my face was for me. It dominated my whole life as a girl and a young woman. After your father and I gave our hearts to the Lord, it was a tremendous struggle for me to reorient my thinking. Becoming a Christian doesn't make you suddenly think and respond differently. My heart had changed, but I had to *learn* how to think anew. I knew that God was good, but for the life of me I could not see that my red face was good. That prevented me from being able to fully accept his love . . . for *me*. I knew that he loved the world, that he loved everyone *else*. But that he loved *me* . . . that was very difficult to accept. In my heart I knew he was supposed to work all things for good. But I could not find a way to apply that goodness to my face."

"That's exactly it, Mother," agreed Amanda. "I know in my heart that God forgives all things. I can accept that he forgives murderers—the men who killed Betsy's father, for instance. But bringing that principle into my *own* life is far more difficult. I cannot help still feeling such a weight of guilt and condemnation. It is far easier to accept that God forgives other people than to accept that he forgives me."

"I think I understand."

"How *do* you accept it, then—God's love, I mean . . . his goodness . . . his forgiveness? How did you finally realize that God truly loved you as you were?"

"The breakthrough came when I decided to give him thanks for my birthmark."

"You actually . . . *thanked* him for it?"

Jocelyn smiled to think how absurd the idea had seemed to her when Charles first confronted her with it.

Jocelyn nodded. "I finally simply had to decide to put the past behind me. I had to determine that from that point on I would think differently—about God, about my scar . . . about the person I was. That all began when I decided to give him thanks for it. I had to say, 'God, you gave me this birthmark because you love me, not because you don't. Therefore, I thank you for it, as a sign of your love.' "

"Knowing what I am going through, that must have been very difficult."

"It was the hardest thing I have ever had to do as a Christian—just say to him *Thank you . . .* and really mean it."

"And you say you *decided* to give him thanks?"

"Yes," nodded Jocelyn. "That's when I realized that accepting his full love was my choice. I could go all my life never accepting it completely. Or I could decide that I, Jocelyn Rutherford, was included in his love and goodness—red face and all. I could no longer think that God's goodness applied to everything else in the world *except* me and my face. If I was serious about being a Christian, then at some point I had to believe what the Bible said—that God works good in *all* things. If I was going to continue not believing that my disfigured face could be turned to good, then what did my faith really mean? I think it might be the same for you."

"But it's so hard, Mother."

"I know, Amanda. Believe me, I know. At least strangers don't stare at you and know about your past. *Every* stranger stares at me. But there comes a point where you have to decide to accept God's forgiveness. His grace is there, but you have to reach out and take it. God's mercy doesn't change. It isn't conditional. That's what I had to learn. It even applied to my birthmark, just as it applies to you and everything that has happened—yes, and even all the things you did that you wish you hadn't. God's forgiveness is available for everyone no matter what they have been, or done. Some people live forever unable to accept that forgiveness and never forgiving themselves. They live in guilt and self-condemnation every day. But they don't have to. That burden can be lifted. But each person has to reach out and decide to take what God has offered."

"But . . . how . . . *how* do you take it?"

"It is something you have to do in your heart and mind. It's a spiritual decision to say to yourself and to God, 'I know you are a good and loving Father. I know you have forgiven me. Therefore I will accept that forgiveness, and I will walk in that forgiveness every day.' "

Amanda did not reply. They sat awhile longer, then slowly rose and gradually made their way back to the cottage.

81

New Bank and the Stable Roof

♦♦♦

*B*y the middle of September the new bank was completed. A great celebration was planned for the sixteenth of September when the doors would open for the first time.

Several executives from London, as well as Gifford and Martha, were on hand for the opening. A few brief speeches were made, the ribbon was cut, and clapping went around the gathering.

Then Geoffrey stood and announced, "The Bank of Milverscombe is officially open for business!"

Most of the crowd came in for tea and biscuits, then gradually dispersed and made their way back to homes and a few of the shops. The London contingent would be on hand for about another hour, then would return on the midday train.

Even before the day of the opening it was obvious that Geoffrey was a hit in the community. Everyone loved him. His father hardly recognized the son he had raised and trained to follow in his footsteps. He had trimmed down, and was so openly friendly with everyone as to make Gifford cringe. A banker couldn't be friendly with his clientele; he must maintain an edge of aloof superiority. But Geoffrey's months in Milverscombe had made a new man of him, driving into the village early on most days, walking about in the morning before opening and at the lunch hour greeting new acquaintances. Already many had had him in their homes for tea. As Gifford watched the proceedings on this day, therefore, and observed the laughing and informal exchanges between Geoffrey and every farmer and sheepherder for miles crowding through to shake his hand, he could not help but consider his son a sap, mixing and on such terms with this backward lot. What kind of nonsense was this all about? And that idiotic plaque on the wall about melting mammon down to do God's work. Gifford could make no sense of it whatever.

Was his son becoming a country bumpkin like all the rest of these louts! He was strangely like his cousin Charles. Was there something about the air at Heathersleigh that took away a man's ambition? How could this bank possibly make any money with such a creed behind the manager's desk? The sooner he got back to London, thought Gifford, the better. It was mortifying for the rest of the executive committee to see this! He would have to keep a close eye on Geoffrey's dealings in the future.

Maybe Heathersleigh Hall *was* haunted with the ghost of old Henry's wife, he thought to himself as he stepped aboard the train with several of his colleagues an hour later—making lunatics of all its residents. Perhaps the children's rhymes of his childhood around here hadn't been so far off after all. This was as bad as what had happened to his cousin with all his religious fanaticism.

Martha wanted to remain for a week. Let her stay on in Devon as long as she wanted. He had had enough of this place!

◆◆◆

On their way walking back to the cottage, Amanda, Catharine, and Jocelyn were talking about the bank opening and their plans for the remainder of the day.

"Poor Gifford looked uncomfortable, didn't he, Mother?" said Amanda as they went.

"I did seem to notice him squirming behind the collar when Mr. Mudgley pressed by him. He isn't much of a countryman."

"And when Geoffrey was talking to Mr. Roper about building a new barn," added Catharine.

"Somehow I don't think that is quite what Gifford had in mind for this bank. What Stoddard needs is a new crib," Jocelyn added, laughing. "Have you seen Cordelia lately? She is so huge, if I had to guess, I would say she is carrying twins."

"But everyone does love Geoffrey," rejoined Amanda. "If I wasn't seeing it with my own eyes, I wouldn't believe it. He really seems to like the people."

"I know, and I think it is wonderful," said Jocelyn.

A brief silence fell.

"I picked up a few yards of ribbon this morning from Mrs. Feldstone's," she added. "Would you girls like to help me tie up some bunches of lavender from the garden?"

"Just so long as I save time for a letter to Terrill," said Catharine.

"When do you see him again?" asked Amanda.

"Next week, I hope. But he is so involved right now with the war nearly over, he is having a difficult time getting away."

"I'd like to, Mother," said Amanda. "It sounds like fun."

"We also want to save time to prepare a late tea, because Geoffrey is bringing Martha for a visit after the bank closes for the day."

"Are they staying on awhile?"

"Only Martha. Gifford is returning to the city today."

"Why don't we wait to tie up the lavender when she is here?" suggested Amanda. "She would enjoy working on it with us."

"Do you think so?" asked Jocelyn.

"I am sure of it, Mother. She is very clever with things like that. She helped me make some lovely dresses. Did you know that she made yards and yards of bandages for the war effort?"

"Then I think that is an excellent idea. We will invite her over tomorrow."

The sounds of shouts interrupted their conversation as they entered the clearing approaching the cottage.

"That sounds like Rune," said Jocelyn. "Wasn't he in town this morning?"

"Apparently not, Mother," replied Catharine, pointing ahead, "because there he is up on the stable roof—look."

They hurried ahead.

"Amanda!" shouted Stirling the moment he saw them, "—come quickly! The board is slipping . . . grab the end of it, would you, and help me steady it."

Amanda handed Jocelyn her handbag and ran toward him, Catharine right behind her. Amanda and Catharine took hold of the end of the huge beam a few feet from where Stirling held on while doing his best to keep from falling off the ladder. The board was slanted steeply up to the upper section of one of the vertical walls where Rune was struggling with the other end while trying to keep from falling down.

"I thought we could hoist these joist beams up ourselves," said Stirling, moving up a little higher on the board now that he had more hands to work with. "But with the ladder and weight, it was too awkward for us. All right . . . let me see, Catharine, I think I have it now—if you could hold on to the ladder and steady it . . . I'll try to climb a little higher."

Catharine let loose of her portion of the board, hurried over, and placed her two hands firmly on the ladder, while Stirling took a step or two up.

"Amanda," he said, "if you can just hang on where you are long enough for me to step up and take the weight off your end . . . good . . . I think we're getting it. Steady, Catharine, I'm going to take another step, but I've got to keep both my hands on the board, so don't let me fall."

"Stirling, don't say that!"

"I'll be fine.—How are you doing up there, Father?"

"It's coming," Rune shouted down. "Another two or three feet and I'll be able to balance it on the end joist and swing it up and over."

"Oops—my end of the board is too high!" exclaimed Amanda as the beam began to pivot, her hands now outstretched above her head. "I can't hold it anymore."

"It's all right," said Stirling. "It's high enough . . . Father, I'll give it one more shove . . . good . . . got it?"

"Push it my way another foot. . . ."

Suddenly the beam swung the rest of the way up as Rune balanced it in its center.

"That's it!" cried Stirling. "Hold it there, Father, I'll be right up."

Stirling let go and scrambled up the ladder, then crawled out on the frame opposite his father.

"Stirling, be careful!" Amanda called up to him. "You're moving around up there too fast."

Stirling laughed, but continued along like a spider on the wall edge.

"All right, Father," he said in a moment, "I'm ready . . . swing it around in my direction."

Father and son struggled a minute to coerce the board into position, then all at once with a great thud, the heavy beam settled into place.

"Whew!" sighed Stirling as he worked his way back to the top of the ladder and climbed down. "Those extra hands made a big difference. I wasn't sure what we were going to do. You came along at just the right time."

"I doubt we did that much good," laughed Amanda as Jocelyn now walked up to join them.

"It was all a matter of balance," said Stirling. "I don't think we'd have managed alone. I thought we'd be able to, but these boards were too much for us.—And ... we have another eight beams to get up there. What do the two of you say to lending us a hand?"

"Do you mind if we run in and change into our work dresses?" asked Catharine.

"Not at all. We'll take a breather."

"I doubt that my sister will be content to hold up a ladder the whole time," said Amanda. "She will want to be up on the roof with you."

"That might be arranged!—You might bring your gloves too!" Stirling called out after the two girls as they ran for the cottage.

82

How Can I Forgive Myself?

———— ◆◆◆ ————

The afternoon several days later was sultry and still. Little work was being done inside the cottage, and the heat seemed to take everyone's energy.

After lunch Amanda wandered outside. She walked toward the new road through the woods. She saw Stirling, shirt off, chest dripping from the heat, chopping at a foot-thick pine that had to come down. He paused and wiped the sweat off his forehead as she approached.

"Working alone today?" asked Amanda. "Where is your father?"

"He left a little while ago," replied Stirling. "He had some things to do at home. Now that we've got the stable roof finished and the sheathing over the rafters—thanks to you and your sister—we plan to start thatching the barn and stable tomorrow."

"You look hot—would you like some lemonade?"

"That sounds as wonderful as anything I can imagine!"

"I'll be right back," said Amanda. She turned and went back to the cottage, returning five minutes later with a pitcher. "I brought you the whole thing," she said, pouring out a tall glass. "I have the feeling you'll need it by day's end."

She handed the glass to Stirling, who drained it to half in one swallow.

"Positively delicious—thank you!"

"I'll put the pitcher over here," said Amanda.

She turned and left him to his work. Stirling watched her go for a minute or two as he slowly finished the glass of lemonade. It was obvious something was on her mind. She seemed quieter and more distant than usual.

Amanda found herself walking unconsciously toward her father's prayer wood. As she went she continued to think about Stirling. How could he be so at peace with himself and who he was? How could he enjoy such closeness with his father when he had had it far worse than she? Never a word of complaint had she heard from his mouth. Why had *she* been so angry with her father, when *he* had all along been able to accept his father, flaws and all? Was a young person's attitude toward such things not so dependent on his or her parents at all but upon one's own attitude toward life? Why had she been so angry, so irritable, so argumentative, so challenging, so full of hostility toward authority? Maybe it had had nothing to do with her father at all. Would she perhaps have been just the same had he never placed a single restriction upon her independent nature? And yet . . . there was Stirling—whose life had been hell compared with hers—who had grown up with a sweet disposition, content with his lot in life and without an ounce of resentment toward anyone.

How could it be? What was the difference between them? Where had the anger and irritability come from that had so characterized her nature for twenty years? And where had Stirling's gentleness originated?

Had they each perhaps *chosen* their opposite paths of personality, *chosen* them in a thousand tiny invisible ways every day, *chosen* to react differently? Had she chosen her anger without even knowing it? Had he chosen his gentleness, perhaps equally without knowing it?

The face of Rune Blakeley came into Amanda's mind. When and how had the change, so evident now, come upon him? He had been around nearly every day since they had moved to the cottage. She had become so accustomed to his presence as to mostly forget what he used to be like. She had come to take his presence for granted. Yet how different he had once been. She had considered him a cruel tyrant.

How did Rune Blakeley cope with *his* memories of the past? Amanda wondered. If *she* struggled with her guilt . . . how much worse must be his!

She was still thinking of the father and son as she entered the wooded sanctuary and sat down on her favorite large stone. It was quiet and still. Amanda felt like the only person in the world. She tried to pray but could not. Her prayers were silent. God was silent. If she was going to move on in life, she had to put this obstacle she was struggling with behind her . . . but how?

At last she rose and began the return walk the way she had come. Where could she go for help? Who could understand the mental torment of the words that had once come out of her own mouth—horrible words, biting and cruel words—constantly stinging at her memory? Words that would never go away no matter how many times she asked for God's forgiveness. Even if God had forgiven her, the words were still there, words of anger, hatred, bitterness toward her father.

As she went, it began to come on her that there might be only one person who could really understand what she was facing, and perhaps who had even felt what she was feeling. Memories of her past association with him flooded back into her mind. The very thought of going to see him filled her with dread. But once the thought came, she knew she had to face him no matter how hard it might be.

Rather than return to the cottage, therefore, she continued along the ridge of a low hill just north of the cottage, winding her way at length back down into Milverscombe. Minutes later she was at the Blakeley's door.

Agatha Blakeley answered her knock.

"Hello, Amanda . . . come in."

"Hello, Agatha—is your husband at home?"

"Yes, dear," answered Mrs. Blakeley slowly, looking at Amanda with a questioning expression, "—he is working out back in the barn."

"Do you think he would mind if I went to see him?"

"Of course not," replied Stirling's mother, still uncertain why Amanda would want to see her husband. "Come this way, I'll let you out through the kitchen."

Amanda followed. Moments later she was walking across the grass behind the house toward the small barn. The door stood open. Agatha left her and returned to the house.

It was cool and dark as Amanda entered. She heard Rune pounding away on a piece of machinery at the far end. She walked across the hard-packed floor toward him. He sensed the approach, put down his hammer, and turned. Amanda stopped as he faced her.

The two looked at one another for a moment, the one surprised to see this unexpected visitor, the other intimidated now that the moment had finally come when she was standing before the man she had once both hated and feared. This was not an encounter either would have anticipated.

"Uh . . . Miss Amanda," said Rune, nodding hesitantly.

"Hello, Mr. Blakeley," said Amanda. "I wonder if you would mind if I talked to you for a minute."

"Not at all, miss." Blakeley set down the hammer and unconsciously wiped his hands on shirt and trousers, though they were covered with as much dirt as his palms and the action accomplished little by way of cleaning them. He was a tall man and sturdily built from having labored hard all his life. His round face was perspiring freely in the heat and bore a splotch or two from the back of his wrist rubbing against it earlier. His forehead had receded to the crown of his head, and thus about half his hair was gone. What remained was thin and graying. The lines and cracks about his eyes and mouth gave them what might be called a hard expression. In it, however, were mingled hints of both remorse and weariness, for he had been a difficult man for most of his life. But largely thanks to Amanda's father, he had won the battle against drink, though it had done its best to age him before his time. Behind the rough exterior that remained, his eyes now shone with life and his lips were eager to smile.

"I saw Stirling a little while ago," began Amanda. "He was cutting down a tree."

"The lad's a good worker, all right," nodded his father. "I can't keep up with him no more."

Amanda forced a smile. A brief silence fell. Rune shifted his weight on his feet a little nervously. It was uncomfortable having the daughter of the most important man and woman in the region standing in his poor little barn, and he hadn't a notion what she was doing here.

"I . . . I don't know how to say this, Mr. Blakeley," began Amanda again. "But I am . . . I am having a hard time since my father's death . . . I feel very badly about how I treated him when I was younger, things I said, and then leaving like I did—"

She hesitated and glanced down at the floor.

"I understand, miss. He was a good man, your father."

"Yes . . . yes, I know that now," said Amanda. "But, you see . . . I didn't know how good he was when I was young. You probably don't know it, but I was terribly cruel to him. I said very horrible things to him and treated him very badly. I once told him I hated him, and then stood and watched with fire in my eyes, wanting to hurt him—God forgive me!—while he just sat, saying nothing, and slowly began to cry. The memory of it haunts me almost every day."

"I can hardly imagine it of you, miss." In truth, everyone in town knew how difficult Amanda had been, and most had seen firsthand how she treated father and mother.

"It is true, Mr. Blakeley. I was a very angry and self-centered girl. And now my father is gone . . . and sometimes I am miserable with guilt over how I was to him. I've told God that I am sorry and I try to tell myself that both God and my father forgive me. But I can't help it, I still feel so bad that sometimes all I can do is find a place to be alone and just cry."

"I'm sorry to hear it, miss. Your father—he forgives you . . . I can tell you that for sure."

Again Amanda hesitated.

"I don't mean . . . I don't want to be rude . . . this is very awkward, Mr. Blakeley—I don't want to pry or get personal, but—I know that you . . . I mean you know that I wasn't very nice to you either, before, you know . . . I saw how you—"

"Don't trouble yourself to say it, miss," said Rune. "I was a bad father and a bad husband, and anybody with eyes to see for miles around knew it. You won't hurt my feelings none by saying it to my face."

Amanda smiled awkwardly. "I don't mean to bring up the past," she said. "But . . . do you ever think of . . . you know, do you remember how you used to be?"

"Of course, miss," replied Blakeley. "You don't forget how you were."

"How well I know that."

"I remember how bad I was every day."

"Then how do you stand it?" said Amanda. "That's what I came to ask you, because . . . I thought you might understand what it is like for me. It must be very painful for you."

"Sometimes I *can't* stand it," answered Blakeley. "Sometimes I got to do just what you said, and come in here, to the barn I mean, where I can be alone and I just have to cry for a spell, to get it out."

"I'm sorry . . . I didn't mean to—"

"It's all right, miss," rejoined Stirling's father. "How can a man like me not sometimes get overcome with memories of what he did to the poor boy? Sometimes there's nothing else to do but let a few tears out."

The man sniffed and glanced away, sending the back of his giant wrist against cheek and eyes again, though this time not from heat and sweat.

Amanda was touched. She had never expected a man like Rune Blakeley to be so free with what was in his heart.

"I think," she said after a moment, "that perhaps to some extent I have accepted God's forgiveness. It is hard, but I think I know that God forgives me. Do you know what I mean?"

"I think so, miss."

"But forgiving myself is even harder," Amanda went on. "And—"

She hesitated and looked away.

"Say anything you want, Miss Amanda," said Blakeley. His voice was almost tender. He had never had a daughter, but if he had had one, he was now showing the side of his nature that would have loved one with the special love of a father.

"What I was going to ask," Amanda continued slowly, "after the way you... you know, how you treated Stirling when he was young... how—"

She paused again, glancing away. She could not look directly into his face.

"—how did you ever... how did you come to forgive yourself? That's what torments me, Mr. Blakeley—how can I ever forgive myself? I *wanted* to hurt my poor father, and I *did* hurt him, and it torments me—"

Amanda now glanced up helplessly and again took courage to find Rune's eyes.

"I have to know," she said, eyes glistening as she blinked at them hard, "how do *you* forgive yourself?"

Tears now came into the man's eyes in earnest. But he did not look away or resist her imploring gaze.

"I know what you're talking about, Miss Amanda," he replied. "You're right about that—I do understand. A lot of folks couldn't probably know what it's like, even for a pretty young lady like yourself. But I know what guilt can do to a person. I've lived with it all these years. That's why I would drink sometimes. Even now I sometimes look at Stirling's bad leg, and my heart gets so sick... God help me, that—"

His voice caught in a sob.

"I find myself thinking," he struggled to continue, "that maybe I caused it myself one time, when I was mad with whiskey, by hitting him when he was young... Oh, God—"

He glanced away, voice choked in convulsive breaths.

"I know it can't be," he struggled to continue, "on account of Dr. Armbruster said he was born with it. But that's how the guilt eats at me. It's a terrible thing, miss. Can you imagine the grief I feel to remember—"

Rune broke down and wept and could not continue for several seconds. Amanda's heart stung her to watch the man lose control of himself. She reached out her hand and placed it on his arm.

"It is more than I can bear sometimes to remember what I did," he tried to go on in a halting voice, "the cruel things I said both to him and his mother... the pain I caused them both. No, Miss Amanda, I won't never forget... I won't never be able to completely forgive myself. It's a burden I have to bear every day. Every day I wake up, it's still there. I can't help it. Those memories are like a knife in my heart that'll never go away. I think they hurt me more to remember than they hurt Stirling."

"But you seem... happy enough. To watch you and Stirling now, you appear the best of friends."

"I'm learning to find happiness in life even with that knife still in my heart."

"So how do you do it?"

"I have the boy to thank for that," replied Rune, wiping at his eyes again, his voice gradually calming and becoming steadier. "I can't... I can't completely forgive myself, to answer your question. But it's Stirling's love for me, and his forgiveness of me that enables me to hold my head up at all and forgive myself a little. It's by watching him love me that I see a little bit of what God's forgiveness must be like. I don't deserve for Stirling to love me, but he does anyway. He even treats me like he respects me and honors me. Think of that! Think of that—he graduated with honors, but he honors me. My Stirling is about the best young man in the world. I don't deserve such a son. He is God's gift to his mother and me. So I try to hold my head up, because of him."

"That is an amazing thing to say, Mr. Blakeley," said Amanda. "It must make you love him very much."

"I do love him, miss. I always loved him, but I was just too mixed up with drink and my own selfishness, and my own sin that made me say and do things I hated myself for later."

"And so . . . now . . . do you feel that God's forgiveness and Stirling's forgiveness helps you forgive yourself?"

"I believe in God's forgiveness all right," replied Blakeley. "Your father helped me, sat with me, prayed with me, even held me in his arms when I wept in anguish for what I had done. And Stirling, my son, bless him, he shows me every day that he cares about me. Yes, that helps me— I can't say I completely forgive myself. I'll never be able to do that, but it helps me be able to look up to God and give thanks more than I ever thought I'd be able to in my life with the mess I made of things. My heart still hurts for the memory of what I did. But I try to live by faith— that's how your father explained it to me, when you try to live one way, even though you might feel a different way. So I do my best to believe in forgiveness, even though I still feel the pain at the memories. And I try to tell myself every day that no one holds my past against me no more."

"Do you think God forgives us *completely*?" said Amanda after a brief silence. "Or do you think he still must be just a little upset with us for how we behaved both to my father and to Stirling?"

"I can hardly imagine God being angry with you, miss," replied Blakeley. "If all your father always told me about him was true."

"So will we ever be able to forgive ourselves completely, then?"

"I don't know, miss. But I think I have an idea what your father might tell me if I asked him that, which I did a time or two."

"I would like to hear it."

"I told him once that I didn't feel worthy of being forgiven. And he asked me if I thought God's forgiveness was based on my worthiness. I said I hadn't thought about it. And he said that if it were, there would be no forgiveness at all, because if there's something to forgive it means someone's sinned. Then he said something I'll never forget. He said, 'We're all unworthy, Rune. We're all sinners. I'm just as unworthy as you, and you're just as unworthy as me. Nobody's worthy of God's forgiveness. We're all sinners together. But he forgives us anyway.' That really helped me, miss. Then he said that once you accept God's forgiveness, there ain't nothing standing in the way to forgive yourself. You just have to decide to do it, he said. You just have to say, 'God, thank you for forgiving me. I accept your forgiveness. So I'm going to forgive myself.'"

Amanda nodded thoughtfully. Once again her own father's words were coming back to her own point of need, just as they had that day on Bloomsbury Way when she was listening to Timothy preach her father's sermon.

"But you haven't been able to do that?" she said after a moment.

"Not completely, miss. But I keep trying every day. And every day it gets a little easier. Sometimes I have to do it over and over. It's like the drink. Sometimes after all these years, if I catch a smell of it, it pulls on me. I have to say no real hard, and remember your father and imagine him there beside me helping me to say no like he done so many times. The guilt pulls on me the same way sometimes, and I have to remember your father telling me that God's forgiven me."

Amanda smiled. "Thank you, Mr. Blakeley... I feel much better already just talking to you."

"I hope some of what I said helps, miss."

"I know it will," Amanda nodded. "Thank you for telling me," she said softly. "Somehow just knowing that you understand what it is like gives me hope."

Amanda paused, then looked up into the dirty, rugged, tearstained face.

"Will you... pray with me, Mr. Blakeley?" she asked.

"You mean... here—right now?"

Amanda nodded.

"I never been much at praying out loud. I never prayed with nobody in my life except your father, when he was helping me get over the drink. But I'd be honored to pray with you, if you really want me to."

"I need to pray with someone," said Amanda, "who really understands how hard it is to live with the kind of memories that you and I have to live with."

Rune nodded. Neither spoke for a moment.

"*Dear, Lord,*" prayed Amanda. "*Thank you so much for Mr. Blakeley, and that he wasn't afraid to tell me what it's been like for him. I pray that you would help us both get over our guilt, and help us know that you love and forgive us, and that both Stirling and my father love and forgive us too. Help us, Lord, because—*"

Her voice cracked momentarily.

"*—because... it is so hard sometimes.*"

The barn was quiet for a minute. Amanda sniffed a few times and drew in two or three deep breaths.

"*Lord,*" said Rune at length, "*I ask you to help Miss Amanda feel better about herself. I know I was with her father a lot when she was gone, and there*" *wasn't nothing in his heart for her all that time but love—"*

At the words Amanda began to cry. They stung all the more with such bitter regret in her heart because she knew they were true. Her father had been forgiving her the instant the words "I hate you" had shocked him into tears of anguish as they had exploded out of her mouth.

"—and I know he forgave her a long time ago," Rune went on, *"so I ask you to help her forgive herself."*

"Yes, Lord," Amanda added softly in a faltering voice, still weeping, *"help me . . . show me how to forgive myself."*

The barn fell silent.

Amanda opened her eyes, wiped away her tears, smiled, then stepped forward to embrace Stirling's father. He took her in his dirty arms and held her close for a second or two. When they stepped back, tears glistened on both their cheeks.

"Thank you . . . Rune," said Amanda. "I will never forget this day, and how honest you have been with me."

Silently the two began walking slowly out of the barn. As they emerged into the sunlight, they saw Stirling coming from the house toward them.

"Amanda!" he exclaimed. "What are you doing here?" As he glanced back and forth between the two, he saw the unmistakable signs of an emotional exchange. What it was about, he couldn't guess, but thought it best not to ask.

"Your father and I were having a talk," replied Amanda with a smile and wiping her eyes again. "And you? The last time I saw you, you were chopping down a tree."

"I broke the ax and had to come for a new one," said Stirling. "Are you going home now?"

Amanda nodded.

"I won't be a minute . . . if you want to wait, I'll walk back with you."

Stirling ran past them into the barn and came out a minute later holding the new ax.

"See you this evening, Father!" he said as he and Amanda walked away.

Rune stood watching as they went. Amanda glanced back again. Stirling's father gave one last nod and smile. Amanda knew they were meant for her.

83

Impromptu Delivery

$\mathcal{S}$toddard Roper ran frantically into Dr. Armbruster's office in mid-morning on the sixth of October.

He glanced hurriedly around. He saw no one in sight but Stirling Blakeley behind the counter perusing a book lying open on the doctor's desk.

"Where's Cecil?" cried Roper.

"He had to ride out to the McDermit place this morning," answered Stirling, rising and walking toward the counter.

"That's eight miles! When's he coming back!"

"Probably not for another hour or two, Mr. Roper. Is there anything I can do for you?"

"Not unless you can deliver a baby! My Cordelia's in a bad way—it came all of a sudden."

"Has her water broken?" asked Stirling.

"I don't know about that, but she made a mess in the kitchen and yelled at me to fetch Dr. Cecil."

"That's her water . . . all right . . . relax, Mr. Roper," said Stirling, "everything's going to be fine."

He paused a second or two, thinking.

"You ever been out to the McFee place?"

"Not since Bobby was alive."

"That's fine, just so long as you know where it is. Ride over there as fast as you can and get Lady Jocelyn and Amanda. Lady Jocelyn knows what to do."

Roper turned for the door. "What about my wife?" he said. "Will she—"

"She'll be fine, Mr. Roper," said Stirling, grabbing his coat. "I'll run over to your place right now and stay with her till you and Lady Jocelyn get back."

Already Roper was out the door and climbing onto the back of his horse. Stirling hurried across the floor after him, then stopped abruptly. He turned and ran back to the desk. Hastily he scribbled a note, just in case Dr. Armbruster returned and set it in plain view. Then he picked up one of the books he had been glancing through earlier as well as the emergency bag Dr. Armbruster had left behind, and ran from the office, turned up the street, and hurried as fast as he could toward the east side of the village.

Eight minutes later Stirling ran into the Roper house without benefit of a knock.

"Mrs. Roper . . . Mrs. Roper," he called, glancing quickly around, "— it's Stirling Blakeley, where are you?"

He heard a faint moan from one of the rooms. He threw down the book in his hand and dashed toward the sound. The woman lay on her bed in obvious pain. Stirling knew instantly that the labor was well advanced.

"Where . . . where is—" she tried to say.

"Dr. Armbruster is away," interrupted Stirling, trying to sound calm. "I was at the office. I sent your husband for Lady Jocelyn. They will be back soon. But for now, you and I will manage together just fine, Mrs. Roper. I know what to do, and everything will be fine. How do you feel?"

"It hurts . . . the baby's coming . . . I can feel it!"

"All right, Mrs. Roper, that's fine . . . do you mind if I have a look to see whether the baby is showing?"

She looked at him with wide eyes but nodded her head.

Gently Stirling took one of her hands as he drew back the blanket. A cry of pain suddenly filled the room.

"Relax, Mrs. Roper," he said. "I know it is difficult, but try to exhale in little puffs as long as the pain lasts . . . that's good. I am going out for a minute to wash my hands, and then we shall see what we need to do."

Stirling left the room. As soon as he was out of sight he grabbed the book he had laid down a minute earlier and bolted outside for the water pump, frantically fumbling through the pages of the book as he went. *Let's see*, he said to himself, *where is it, ah, here . . . contractions . . . two minutes . . . one minute . . . when contractions begin to come less than one minute apart . . .*

He had to hurry!

This baby was on its way, and one look told him that there wasn't a chance in the world it intended to wait either for Dr. Armbruster, Jocelyn, or its own father!

Two minutes later Stirling reentered the bedroom drying his hands, trying to calm himself again, and setting the book on the edge of the bed, open to "Birthing Procedures" just in case he should need it again. There was no time for boiling hot water and sterile cloths . . . or even sterilizing his own hands in hot water.

There wasn't time for anything!

"How are you doing, Mrs. Roper?" he asked gently, again taking her hand and taking his watch out of his pocket. "I'm just going to time your contractions—tell me when you begin to feel pain again."

She nodded. They did not have to wait long. Suddenly she cried out again, her face grimacing in pain.

"Blow, Mrs. Roper . . . gentle puffs . . . blow, blow, blow. That's good."

After thirty or forty seconds, the pain subsided and she lay back down in exhaustion, face perspiring freely.

"Was that the first since I left to wash my hands?"

She shook her head.

"You had a contraction while I was out?"

She shook her head, trying to hold up two fingers.

"Two!" he exclaimed.

She nodded again.

There was no time to lose. Stirling drew in a breath and tried to collect his wits, when suddenly the mother-to-be lurched up again and cried out. Stirling felt his hand nearly crushed by her grip.

He drew back the blankets again. "All right, you're just doing fine," he said. "Your baby is starting to come . . . I see a foot and there is its little bottom trying to squeeze—"

"No . . . no . . . can't," interrupted the woman frantically, struggling to make herself heard in the middle of the pain, "head . . . *head* has to come first."

"Right . . . of course—what am I thinking!" said Stirling. *Don't be an idiot!* he added to himself. *You need to calm down . . . get hold of yourself. What are you thinking!* "Yes, it's breech, Mrs. Roper," he said aloud, "but we will take care of that."

Gradually the contraction subsided.

Stirling stood and hurried around the bed to where the book lay, scanning through the pages quickly. He bent down and hastily read the instructions for breech births, then walked back to Mrs. Roper's side.

"We shall just turn your little one around," he said. "I will have to put my hand inside you, Mrs. Roper, and turn him around. . . . It may be a little uncomfortable, but I will be as gentle as I can. . . ."

She nodded up and down vigorously. She knew it was necessary.

Eleven minutes later Stirling heard footsteps and voices outside. The next instant the outside door of the house crashed open.

"I'll get water boiling, Mother!" he heard Amanda's voice say. Almost immediately Jocelyn ran through the bedroom door. She stopped in the middle of the room and stood looking at the scene before her with eyes wide in astonishment.

"I am afraid you are too late, Jocelyn," said Stirling with a smile. "Mrs. Roper and her daughter are already asleep."

Jocelyn came slowly forward, her bewilderment now changing to a smile. Gently she lifted back the blanket to take a quick peek at the infant at its mother's breast, then turned back to Stirling and began to laugh with delight.

"Stirling . . . but how—"

Amanda, who had heard Stirling's voice, now entered the room.

"It would seem that you are already a doctor, Stirling," she said as she quickly surmised the state of affairs.

They were interrupted by the sounds of more footsteps coming through the door outside.

"I think you should be the one to tell him, Stirling," said Jocelyn. "Amanda and I will begin cleaning up and see to your two patients."

Stirling nodded and walked out of the bedroom.

"Congratulations, Mr. Roper!" he said, reaching out his hand as he met the anxious father. "You have a new baby daughter!"

84

The Banker and the Client

Stirling Blakeley awoke earlier than usual. He had spent a fitful night thinking about Amanda and what she had said to him several weeks earlier. And now the incident with the Roper baby confirmed it all the more—medicine was indeed something he wanted to pursue. He knew he was too old to think realistically about going back to school for another three or four years. As it was, he had been several years older than most of his fellow students at Oxford. But if it was a dream worth pursuing, why should he not do as Amanda suggested?

Stirling got out of bed, dressed quietly, and stole from the house. A few minutes later he was out walking through the village. It was dark out, with the first hints of light only just now creeping up the horizon in the east. Slowly he made his way toward the center of town, thinking of the people who lived in the homes along these streets and throughout the community, thinking what it would be like to be entrusted with their lives, to deliver their babies, to help them in sickness, to ease their elderly gently into the life to come.

What a high and sacred calling. Was it really what he wanted . . . more importantly, was it what *God* wanted for him?

As he continued to walk, images of Amanda filled his mind again. What a lady she had turned out to be, gracious, warm, giving, soft-spoken. He would never guess, to look at her now, that she had ever been otherwise. There was no one—except perhaps Timothy Diggorsfeld—he enjoyed talking to quite like Amanda. She was . . . an interesting person. In the two years since their impromptu meeting outside Timothy's flat, she had become a true friend.

Fifteen minutes later Stirling found himself standing in front of Dr. Armbruster's small surgery. He stood for several minutes quietly contemplating the possibility that someday *he* might occupy just such an office, in some small town like this, with *his* name on the sign above the door.

"*Lord,*" Stirling prayed softly, "*if this is your will, you must open the door and make a way. It seems too distant and out of reach. If you truly are speaking to me through Amanda's encouragement, make a way for it to happen.*"

Even as he prayed, the conviction came over him all the more that he should follow Amanda's suggestion and see what came of it.

Six hours after his early morning walk, it felt to Stirling Blakeley as if every eye in the village was upon him as he walked into the new Bank of Milverscombe dressed up in his best shirt and trousers, tie and coat, and with his hair combed down flat and wet on his head. He could not help being nervous.

Geoffrey saw Stirling enter, smiled and waved him over to his desk, then greeted him with a shake of the hand, and offered him a chair. Stirling sat down. The two chatted informally for a few minutes.

"I, uh . . . I don't know how to say this," began Stirling, "but I want to talk to you about money . . . about maybe a loan . . ."

"Of course, Stirling," replied Geoffrey. "For what purpose?"

"Actually, I . . . I would like to return to university, medical school actually . . . I would like to study to be a doctor."

"Right . . . I see—yes, the whole town is abuzz about your delivery of the Roper girl. Congratulations."

"Thank you," smiled Stirling. "It was an unexpected adventure."

"Medical school would be an expensive proposition," said Geoffrey. "There could be collateral difficulties as well. I doubt such a loan would be approved by London without sufficient collateral."

"Collateral?"

"Tangible assets," replied Geoffrey, "to set against the note in case of default."

"You don't think I wouldn't pay it back?"

"No, of course not, Stirling. I know you, and know you to be a man of your word. But banks must be very cautious and skeptical when loaning money. The way London would look at it would be to ask what would happen if you died, for example, or if you got halfway through the medical program and then for some reason were unable to continue. Their money would be gone, and you would not be in a position to repay. That's why they always look for something, as I say, to set against the loan to insure that they will not lose out in the end. The loan committee would be very doubtful of loaning that much money, as they would see it, on speculation of future earnings."

"Oh ... right, I see," nodded Stirling, beginning to feel uncomfortable.

"And too ... have you considered," Geoffrey went on, trying to sound warm and sympathetic, though he realized he was probably dashing Stirling's hopes with every word he spoke, "the future burden such an indebtedness would place on you after your education was completed?"

"But the opportunity to be a doctor would make it worth it," said Stirling.

"Perhaps," rejoined Geoffrey. "But country physicians don't earn a great deal. It would take years to repay."

Stirling nodded, then shuffled in the chair and began to rise.

"I am sorry not to be more encouraging," said Geoffrey, rising with him.

"Don't mention it, Geoffrey, you're just doing your job—I know that. I didn't think it would hurt to ask."

"No ... it never hurts to ask. I will look into the matter further, and shall certainly see what I can do."

They shook hands. Stirling left the bank, feeling far more awkward than when he had walked in. He turned along the street, praying that Amanda didn't happen to be in town. He didn't think he could face her right now.

As he limped quickly along, he thought to himself that the only thing he wanted to do was get home and get out of these fancy clothes!

85
The Banker and His Thoughts

❖❖❖

*D*arkness had fallen over Milverscombe. Its residents were long since in their homes and all its shop doors closed.

A lone desk lamp, however, still burned in the newest of Milverscombe's buildings. The doors were locked, and the only two employees of the bank other than its manager had gone home for the night.

Geoffrey Rutherford sat at his desk looking over the papers in front of him. There wasn't a chance Stirling Blakeley's hope to further his education would be approved. There wasn't even any use sending it in. Every loan application in the last three months had been turned down. His father sat on the loan committee, and for the life of him, Geoffrey could not understand it.

The requested funds for Stoddard Roper's new barn . . . for Mary and Sutton Thurmond's house . . . for the new store building that had Hiram Spenser's hopes so high . . . these and three or four other small applications had all come back denied.

London wasn't interested in small high-risk loans like these. They made their profits off business loans in the city. Their objective in opening a country bank like this was in securing deposits, not making loans. He had been naive to think he could do the people here any good. The rejected applications were piling up, and eventually he was going to have to summon the courage to tell these poor people that the money they were planning on was not going to come through.

Just today he had had two new requests, including Stirling's. How could he face these people if all he ever had for them was bad news? Where would the bank be a year from now if not a single loan were approved for the people of the village? Most would eventually go back to keeping their money in their beds or in the floors of their cottages.

He had wanted so badly to help this community. But all his high hopes were gradually giving way to the reality that the loan committee did not intend to back up his optimism with actual cash.

Geoffrey rocked back in his chair and let out a long sigh as he glanced over the papers again. Slowly he rose, put on his coat, then gathered up a few of the files to take home with him for further review. As he turned from his desk, his eyes fell on the plaque hanging behind his desk that Catharine had lettered and nicely framed for him. He read over the words again: *Melt your mammon down, coin him up, make God's money of him, and send him out to do God's work. Make of him cups to carry the gift of God, the water of life, through the world.*

Geoffrey smiled thinly. A fine sentiment, he thought. But how could he implement it without the backing of London?

He moved to the door, turned off the light, and walked outside. He glanced about. The evening was already chilly. He was glad he'd brought the car. The cold sent a shiver through his frame. He coughed a time or two as he walked to the side of the building. It was starting already, he thought rubbing at neck and chest, the winter hacking in his lungs . . .

and it was still only November. He'd go see Dr. Armbruster tomorrow and get a new supply of lozenges.

Slowly he drove through the deserted streets of Milverscombe, out of town, and finally up the long, winding drive to Heathersleigh Hall, cheered to find that his new housekeeper Wenda Polkinghorne, Sarah Minsterley's sister-in-law, recently widowed from Exeter, had a bright fire, hot pot of water, and inviting tea all waiting for him.

* * *

In the middle of the night, Geoffrey awoke suddenly out of a deep sleep.

It had begun to rain outside, and somewhere he thought he heard a faint *drip, drip, drip.* Coughing lightly, he glanced toward the window, wondering where the sound was coming from, then sat up and turned on a light. It wasn't the rain against the windowpane that had roused him, however, nor the congestion in his chest, but rather a startling idea.

So startling it had jolted his brain awake as if an electric current had surged through it.

Geoffrey threw on a robe and walked to his desk, where still lay the loan files he had brought home that had troubled him the day before.

He glanced through them again. A smile spread over his face.

Then slowly the smile turned to laughter.

Why not? he laughed to himself. *Why not! I will cast him into the furnace, melt him down, and coin the mammon up to make God's money of him . . . then send him out to do God's work!*

86

Excitement in Milverscombe

*T*hree weeks after his visit to the bank, a brief letter was waiting for him when Stirling came home midway through the afternoon.

"Mr. Rutherford brought this by for you this morning," said his mother, handing him the envelope.

Stirling,
I haven't seen you around town for several days. Would you be able to come by the bank at your earliest convenience? I would like to talk to you again about your proposal.

G. Rutherford

Stirling was out the door the next instant and on his way toward the center of the village. Some distance from the bank he saw Stoddard Roper walking toward him on his way home.

"Stoddard," said Stirling, "—from that smile on your face, I would say you have had some good news."

"I just found out the loan for my new barn and several new cows went through," replied Roper as he and Stirling shook hands. "I will have three hundred pounds in my hands by next week."

"I am delighted to hear it. How is that little girl of yours doing?"

"Well... very well, thanks to you. My wife and I will never forget what you did."

"It may be that I shall be indebted to you, Stoddard," rejoined Stirling. "I hope to return to university one day to study toward my physician's license."

"Good for you, Stirling. When will this happen?"

"I don't know. I'm on my way to the bank now. I am hoping the bank will be able to help me finance it."

"And why not? Besides me, did you hear that Hiram Spenser is going to build a new store to sell farm equipment?"

"No, I hadn't heard," replied Stirling. "Is he being financed by the bank too?"

Roper nodded. "That Rutherford's about the best thing to happen to this town in a long time."

"Maybe this will be my lucky day too!"

"I hope so. Good luck to you, Stirling, and thanks again."

Stirling continued on to the bank, not pausing to realize until he was walking through the door that on this occasion he had not so much as combed his hair and was still wearing his work clothes. Geoffrey, however, did not seem to notice.

"Stirling," he said as they shook hands, "I have some good news for you—your loan application has been approved."

"To go back to university!"

"That's right," said Geoffrey with a smile. "Come and sit down so that we can talk about it."

"But what about the collateral?" said Stirling. "This is wonderful news . . . but I thought you said—"

"They waived the requirement," said Geoffrey. "I told them that the risk would be minimal and that I would personally vouch for you. It will be called an unsecured loan."

"Thank you, Geoffrey. I don't know what to say."

"I suggest you begin looking into the various medical colleges and making your application," Geoffrey went on. "Perhaps you will be able to enroll next year. Meanwhile, I will have the paper work ready at whatever time you feel you need to begin receiving the funds."

"I can't believe it," said Stirling enthusiastically. "Just wait until I tell Amanda—thanks, Geoffrey!"

"I do have one favor to ask of you," said Geoffrey, his voice taking on an almost apologetic tone.

"Anything—just name it."

"I wondered if you wouldn't mind coming by the Hall one of these days. I think a leak has developed from this recent rain, but I can't find it anywhere."

"That often happens with the first rains of the season," nodded Stirling. "Wood and roofs and plaster and joints shrink from the summer heat and tiny cracks develop. And if there's one thing about rain, it will find the cracks as soon as autumn comes and it cools down again. I'd be glad to have a look."

"Good, thank you—perhaps at the next rain."

Stirling rose and, in a stupor at this sudden change in his fortunes, stumbled out of the bank. He turned immediately for Heathersleigh Cottage. He had to tell Amanda!

He half ran, half walked, half limped all the way, such that he was perspiring and breathing heavily by the time he stuck his head into the open door of the cottage.

"Amanda . . . Lady Jocelyn . . . Miss Catharine—is anyone home around here!"

"In here, Stirling . . . come in!" Jocelyn's voice called out from inside. Stirling hurried inside.

"I've got great news!" he said. "Where's Amanda?"

"She's at the Hall looking for a few more books she wanted to bring over. What's got you so excited?"

"Just this—my application has been approved for a loan to return to university to study medicine!"

"Stirling, that's wonderful news. I just heard yesterday that Andrew and Sally Osborne are getting a loan to enlarge their cottage as well. Those twins of theirs are growing into strapping boys."

But Stirling hardly heard her. He had already turned and was heading out the door on his way through the woods to Heathersleigh Hall.

------------------- ◆ ◆ ◆ -------------------

Within weeks everyone who had needed money for any project or family need, large or small, had received similar good news. It was almost as if manna were being sprinkled down from heaven in the form of one-, five-, and ten-pound notes!

Farmers were anticipating more extensive crops for the following spring. Gresham Mudgley himself was too old to tend his sheep, but his son had added several new Wensleydales and Oxfords to their flock. Other farmers from the community were purchasing cattle, bulls, and equipment, and planning improvements to barns and houses. Vicar Stuart Coleridge had even spoken to Geoffrey about some badly needed repairs to the church building that lay outside the budget of the diocese.

But not all the changes in and around Milverscombe were as a result of loans at the new bank. Improvements of various other kinds began to come to the neighborhood. One of the first such resulted when word began to go through the community—no one knew how it started, but within weeks no one was talking about anything else—that funds were being made available for certain home improvements. These were not loans which must be repaid, but grants of some kind, money simply being provided for the betterment and modernization of the community. Because finances were involved, the whole thing was being handled by the bank, though it was not directly involved. Clearly, everyone said, no institution like the Bank of London would just *give* money away.

Whoever was responsible had indicated, through solicitors, so as to keep their identity secret—so Geoffrey told those who came to inquire—that funds were to be distributed by application to local residents for the purpose of wiring their homes for either electricity or telephones, for the installation of plumbing to provide indoor water, or toward the purchase of an automobile. The money was available now, he said, up to £125 per household. It was more money than half of them made in three months.

It was all very mysterious, though no one was inclined to complain. Within two weeks, Rune and Stirling Blakeley, well trained by Charles Rutherford, were busier with more wiring orders than they could finish in a year.

Because of the likely increase in demand, Geoffrey spoke with Hiram Spenser about adding an automobile or two to his inventory when his new building was completed. If Hiram was interested, said Geoffrey, he would see to it that his loan was increased by a sufficient amount to cover it.

It was obvious that some wealthy benefactor had taken an interest in Milverscombe. The reason would apparently remain a mystery. Rumors were rampant, though no one was successful at getting to the bottom of them.

Most suspected Amanda and Jocelyn of having a hand in the affair. Had not Sir Charles and Lady Jocelyn been the leading citizens and well known to be just the kind of man and woman who would carry out such a plan? Some maintained that no doubt Sir Charles's will had just been finalized and must have carried such a provision for the benefit of the community he loved. It was just what he would have done.

Jocelyn, however, steadfastly denied it. And as certain as they were that Sir Charles might well give away half his estate, those who knew them were equally certain that Lady Jocelyn would never utter so much as a word that wasn't true. In the end they had no alternative but to believe her innocent of any knowledge of the source of the strange goings-on.

Other rumors, therefore, began to circulate in time that Geoffrey and the bank *had* to be involved. The new bank's manager, however, displayed no more knowledge of the peculiar affair than anyone, and confessed himself merely a go-between acting on behalf of the ultimate source of provision and the good people of Devon.

Stirling Blakeley's application to medical school at Oxford was accepted. He made plans to leave the following fall.

87

Changes

◆◆◆

At long last the countries of Europe breathed a collective, though weary and painful, sigh of relief when the war known as the Great War, and the War to End All Wars, concluded in November of 1918. The cost in human life had been terrible, and scarcely a family in Europe had not been affected. But it was now time for the world to put the conflict in the past and move forward into the modern era.

For several weeks after Geoffrey's request to Stirling, no rain fell in Devon. But in early December a drenching storm swept over southwest England, turning rivers and streams to swollen floods of brown. The downpour began late one Friday evening. By Sunday half the roofs in Milverscombe were leaking, including that of Heathersleigh Hall.

As soon as church was over, Geoffrey sought Stirling Blakeley where he was talking with Amanda, Catharine, and Terrill Langham, on leave for a weekend visit.

"Would it be convenient for you to come out to the Hall this afternoon?" asked Geoffrey. "—As a matter of fact, now that I think about it, why don't you and your father and mother come for tea?"

"It sounds good to me," replied Stirling.

"Good," said Geoffrey, glancing about through the dispersing congregation, crowded into the church building on account of the storm. "—I'll go talk to them and invite them myself. About three?"

Stirling nodded.

"Better yet," added Geoffrey, "it's so wet, I'll come for you all in the car. Perhaps I'll ask your father if he would like to drive us back to the Hall!"

Stirling laughed. "Then maybe I shall get out my umbrella and walk!"

The four enjoyed a delightful tea together later that day. But despite all the efforts of the three men searching high and low, they were not able to find the source of Geoffrey's leak. They could hear the faint dripping that had plagued him—loudest near the guest room next to the east gallery on the second floor of the north wing—but nowhere could they find evidence of wetness. Rune's conclusion was that the sound must be echoing from somewhere outside on the roof, a common occurrence, and that no actual leak into the house existed. In the absence of a damp ceiling anywhere, it seemed the most logical explanation.

♦ ♦ ♦

The storm passed, and winter finally settled in earnest over the land, slowing down the various projects about the community, though Rune and Stirling continued to wire homes as weather permitted.

The winter proved to be a relatively mild one, though rainy. Geoffrey suffered again through the cold, wet months. When not employed elsewhere, Geoffrey kept Stirling busy at the Hall with one thing and another, always paying him at least double what Stirling considered appropriate.

"You've got your medical school to think of, Stirling," said Geoffrey. "Your time is valuable to me, and I insist on your receiving a fair wage for your efforts."

Whenever Stirling was at work at the Hall, Geoffrey was right beside him. Though his experience in practical skills had been minimal, he was an eager learner, and through the companionship of such shared labors, their friendship steadily deepened.

Amanda often joined them, adding to the friendship a threefold cord of pleasure and spontaneity that only a woman could bring. Sometimes the three laughed and talked together more like three children than three adults in their late twenties. Never had Amanda imagined that Geoffrey could be so much fun. Never had Geoffrey imagined that he could enjoy his cousin so dearly. Never had Stirling imagined that his two closest friends would one day be the aristocratic daughter of an M.P., and a wealthy London financier.

They all had suffered severe handicaps early in life, which perhaps contributed all the more to their closeness during this happy season of second childhood they were enjoying together. But Stirling's leg and upbringing, though visible and physical, had in truth not been handicaps at all but had worked to the strengthening of his character. Geoffrey's training in seeking financial gain, and Amanda's hatred of authority, on the other hand, had been significant detriments to their development. They were both on the road toward selflessness and virtue now, and glad of it. Yet because he had been seeking such qualities longer, they recognized Stirling, though his roots were humbler, as the acknowledged spiritual leader of the trio.

In time, Amanda showed her two friends every secret passageway of the Hall, retracing the discoveries George and Betsy had both made, and laughing with Geoffrey as together they told Stirling of their childhood dispute in the tower. Together they took out the tower key ring, made their way through the panel in the wall to the library. There Amanda again told them of the mysterious cabinet where the family Bible had been hidden for so many years, demonstrated the mechanism and key by which it had been discovered, and showed Stirling the passages that had led her to the knowledge that the Hall should rightfully have belonged to Geoffrey all along. For the first time, even Geoffrey finally understood everything, and at last were the mystery of all the keys and doors and passageways laid to rest. But Amanda still confessed herself puzzled, she said, by the odd construction in the garret. Why did old Lord Henry enlist Webley Kyrkwode to build the secret garret room George had discovered years earlier, a room only accessible through a maze of hidden passages?

They gathered one stormy evening in the mysterious chamber, wind blowing a gale outside, laughing and excited like three children, then sat down together, turned out the light, and told one another ghost stories to see who could most successfully frighten the others.

"What's that noise?" asked Geoffrey as a silence fell at the conclusion of Stirling's tale.

"I think it's a loose tile," answered Amanda, glad for the diversion. She was still trembling a little from the creepy images of the story she had just heard. "Betsy discovered it, but we could never figure out exactly where it was."

"That could be the source of the leak," said Stirling, standing up and trying to listen. "I'll have to take a look at it. If a tile comes off, then you will really have a problem. Can you turn on the light?"

Amanda was only too glad to do so.

They all listened for a few seconds.

Stirling placed his ear against the wall. "Yes," he said, "I can hear something."

"We'll investigate it later," said Geoffrey as he coughed a time or two. "And you're right," now pressing his ear to the wall, "there's that dripping sound again—it's even louder here than next to the gallery."

"Geoffrey," said Stirling, "you ought to do something about that cough. I don't like the sound of it."

"It's nothing. I have to put up with it every winter. I think I'm allergic to rain and cold."

"But this little room is completely dry," said Amanda, still thinking of the dripping sound. "If the room were leaking, we would see some evidence of it."

"It must be coming from the other side," said Stirling. "Let's go have a look."

They returned through the labyrinth to the main part of the house, walked to the northeast corner, up the tower stairs, and finally into the eastern portion of the garret that had been walled off from the rest by Kyrkwode's mysterious construction. But upon reaching the opposite side of the wall they had left a few minutes earlier, they found wall, floor, and the underside of the roof above them all perfectly dry.

The next day the sun returned and their explorations continued. Now that he finally had straight all the ins and outs of the place that had become his, Geoffrey said he was anxious to see the twin cabinet fashioned by Maggie's great-grandfather. A romp across the field and through the woods to the cottage followed.

From her kitchen window, Jocelyn saw the three running toward her, happy and talking freely. Her heart warmed to see the two cousins and their friend acting like children again. Neither Geoffrey nor Amanda had had the chance to be exuberant and spontaneous when they were young. Now they were enjoying all the more the opportunity they had let pass the first time.

———————— ♦ ♦ ♦ ————————

With the coming of the new year of 1919, life at Heathersleigh Cottage centered for several months around plans for Catharine's upcoming wedding, which was sure to be the most celebrated event in Milverscombe since the memorial service for Charles and George. There were dresses to make, food to plan, and invitations to send out. Catharine's wedding dress was being made in London, but Jocelyn was making her own and Amanda's. Catharine had chosen the pale greet fabric from a catalog at Harrods.

Jocelyn, Amanda, and Catharine all traveled to Lincoln to meet Terrill's family. The retired admiral—who had served with Charles in his early naval days—and his wife could not have been more pleased with developments. They returned the gesture several weeks later by traveling down to Devon, where Geoffrey put them up at the Hall. Catharine's cousin insisted on helping as much with the wedding plans as they would allow, and would house all the guests from Lincoln and London at the bride's former home. Sarah and Wenda were already at work getting rooms ready that had not seen inhabitants since Charles had entertained his parliamentary colleagues.

Catharine and Terrill Langham were married in the first week of April 1919 in the Milverscombe church, with Timothy Diggorsfeld officiating.

When the bride and groom departed for their honeymoon in Scotland, all Devon seemed to grow quiet without Catharine's boisterous, cheery laughter and smiling optimism. Heathersleigh Cottage felt especially dreary and deserted.

Amanda was sober for several days. Jocelyn could see that a melancholy was stealing over her. How difficult it must be, she thought, to watch her sister happily married with the support and blessings of an entire community, and then to remember what she had done.

Jocelyn came upon Amanda three mornings after the wedding, alone in the family lounge quietly crying.

"Oh, Mother," she said in a forlorn voice as she glanced up through red eyes, "it was so beautiful and happy—I threw so much away!"

"God will restore the years the locusts have eaten, Amanda dear," said Jocelyn as she sat down beside her. "I do not know how, but with the Lord nothing is lost forever."

Amanda did not reply but quietly continued to weep.

She did not know how either. The promise seemed impossible to grasp. *So* much had been lost. She had thrown away not only precious years, but even her memories of childhood, which should have been happy ones. How could any of it be restored?

But gradually the tears dried as they had in the past, and life settled once more into a routine.

Now there were only two of them left. Bobby was gone. Charles was gone. George was gone. Maggie was gone. And now Catharine was gone.

In October Stirling Blakeley left on the train for Oxford. Now Milverscombe seemed all the more deserted. Half the village was at the station to see him off. Amanda stood between her mother and Geoffrey, waving as the train gradually rumbled and clattered out of sight. As she turned away a few moments later, she was surprised to feel tears in her eyes.

PART VII

---◆◆◆---

1920-1923

88
End of a Tumultuous Decade

Stirling's departure left a void in Geoffrey's life, just as it did in Amanda's. Frequent letters passed between them, of course, and though Amanda and Geoffrey still saw one another frequently and were by now the best of friends, it was not the same without their mutual friend. The two could not alone capture the joy the three together had shared.

Terrill and Catharine Langham spent the first six months of their married life in London, then, much to the delight of the mother of the bride, settled in Plymouth following the lieutenant's transfer.

Timothy Diggorsfeld had nearly completed a book of devotional memoirs. He was being encouraged by all his friends to take the train into London to talk to a publisher.

They heard from Sister Hope that Betsy's adoption had been finalized. Adoptive mother and adoptive daughter could not have been happier. There continued to be talk of visits in both directions between Switzerland and Devon.

Stirling Blakeley's homecoming after his first year at medical school was, if possible, a happier time for Amanda and Geoffrey even than for Stirling. They found that the threefold friendship had not been injured but had deepened from Stirling's absence. Not a day went by that the three were not together. They took turns reading aloud to one another the Scotsman's simple tale of the love between Dawtie, Sandy, and Andrew—the childlike trio—and prayed for themselves some of their prayers after setting the book aside for the day. More and more of Stirling's time, too, was taken up at Dr. Armbruster's side.

At the end of the summer Stirling left again for Oxford. His second and third years passed more quickly than he would have imagined. Milverscombe and the surrounding area continued to grow and thrive. More and more of its residents took out loans and availed themselves of the resources for improvements. With the war over, prosperity and progress were coming to the world, and Devon came in for its share.

Accustomed now to having a local bank, and growing comfortable with liens, mortgages, monthly payments, and interest rates, the people of the community were adjusting to and enjoying the march of progress.

The appearance of prosperity and growth were evident wherever one looked. New homes and a few new buildings were in progress in the village. Everyone said that Geoffrey Rutherford must surely have been endowed with the same giving nature as his cousin Charles.

When Stirling Blakeley returned to Milverscombe in the spring of 1922 at the end of his program, his medical studies complete, all that stood in the way of a practice of his own was a period of apprenticeship with Dr. Armbruster.

If anything, thought Amanda when she saw him step off the train, he was more handsome than ever with his bright, lively countenance, flowing light brown hair, and golden moustache. His limp seemed to have lessened, too, though she wondered if she were imagining the improvement.

Amanda glanced away briefly as he approached with a great smile. Her heart was beating a little too fast, and she had to try to calm herself.

She stared down at the boards under her feet.

A moment later a large shadow on the platform engulfed her. Amanda could feel him standing less than two feet away.

Slowly she glanced up. "Hello, Stirling," she said softly.

"Amanda, you look radiant!" exclaimed Stirling exuberantly. "I could hardly wait to get home. It is so good to see you again!"

Amanda smiled and their eyes met. In that moment both realized that something had changed between them.

89

Private Talk

❖❖❖

As handsome as Stirling appeared to Amanda, he could not say the same about Geoffrey as the two young men, both now over thirty, greeted one another. He had noticeably lost weight and his face seemed pale.

"Geoffrey!" said Stirling, giving his friend a warm embrace. "How are you!"

"Now that you are home for good," replied Geoffrey, "I am certain I will be better than ever."

The affection between the three friends resumed as if no time had passed at all.

"Geoffrey and I have discovered a new book this spring," said Amanda excitedly, recovering her trembling emotions once Geoffrey and Stirling were talking together. "We've been dying to show it to you, haven't we, Geoffrey?"

"Absolutely."

"I can't wait!" said Stirling. "How about tomorrow... I should spend the rest of today with my father and mother."

"Today's Friday—why don't you both come over to the Hall tomorrow for lunch?" suggested Geoffrey.

"Agreed?" asked Stirling, glancing toward Amanda.

"Agreed!" she consented eagerly.

Inwardly Stirling was more concerned about Geoffrey's lean and pallid appearance than he let on. After a pleasurable reunion with his parents, he walked to Dr. Armbruster's surgery for a brief visit. After they had chatted for a few minutes, he brought up the subject of Geoffrey's condition.

"I know," sighed Armbruster. "It has been progressively worsening for a couple of years."

"Do you see him regularly?" asked Stirling.

Armbruster nodded. "I do what I can, but it's mostly limited to lozenges to try to reduce the coughing, and reminding him to bundle up and keep warm."

"I don't like the sound of it."

"Nor do I. But I don't know what to do."

"Do you think..." Stirling's voice trailed off.

"I don't know, Stirling," sighed Armbruster. "All I know is that these winters are not good for him, and every year his capacity to fight off infection seems to decline."

♦♦♦

On Saturday the three enjoyed much talk and laughter together, with Amanda and Geoffrey taking turns sharing passages out of their new favorite of the Scotsman's books.

Sunday's church service was a special time of rejoicing for Stirling, made all the fonder in that his heart had missed these people and the rich fellowship for so long. He sat next to Amanda and Jocelyn, with Geoffrey to her left, and his own parents to his right. Even as the service was concluding he decided that today was the day to do what had been growing in his mind for more than a year now.

After the service Stirling waited for a moment when she was not with Amanda, then approached Jocelyn.

"Is it good to be back, Stirling?" she asked.

"Better than you can imagine," he answered. "As they say, absence makes the heart grow fonder. This will always be my home."

Stirling hesitated briefly.

"I wondered," he went on, "if I might come over and talk with you this afternoon?"

"Certainly, Stirling—would you like to come for tea about four?"

"No . . . I mean, thank you . . . but I meant in private."

"Oh . . . right, I see—of course. Well, come anytime, then, and if you would like to stay for tea, that would be fine too."

"Will . . . uh, will Amanda be home?"

"I believe so," answered Jocelyn, "although I think she is going over to see Esther Spenser immediately after church."

"Could I come right away then . . . I would rather talk to you when she wasn't nearby."

"Of course, Stirling," said Jocelyn, growing more curious by the minute why Stirling, usually so confident and self-assured, had all of a sudden become so fidgety.

An hour later, Stirling sat down in the large lounge of Heathersleigh Cottage, nervousness written over every inch of his face. Jocelyn could see his discomfort but waited patiently for him to begin.

"This is hard, Lady Jocelyn," he began at last, "but I don't think there is any easy way to say it, so I will just start."

He paused, took a deep breath, then continued.

"I wish I could talk to Sir Charles about this," he said, "but I know you and Sir Charles were of one mind, and you are head of the family now, so it's you I have to ask. The last thing I want to do is bring Amanda any more pain. I care too much for her to do that. But at the same time, I want to tell you what I am thinking, which is just this—"

He stopped and drew in a long breath, then let it out slowly.

"I know it seems presumptuous," he continued, "even to think there could be anything between us. And she's been my friend first of all . . . but I've been praying and talking to the Lord about it for almost a year now, wondering if he may have in mind for us to live our lives together. So that's what I want to ask you about, if you think there could be any chance, and if you'd have any objections."

Jocelyn smiled. She should have seen it coming.

"I can't think of anything that would delight me more, Stirling," she said.

"It is kind of you to say it."

"And don't be too sure about there being no chance. Amanda is very fond of you. Have you mentioned anything to her?" asked Jocelyn.

"Oh no . . . not yet," he said, shaking his head. "I don't know if she is healed enough from all that happened, you know . . . her past and the marriage to Mr. Halifax, and everything. But I wanted to ask you if you thought there might be hope."

"I do, indeed, Stirling. And you certainly have my permission to speak with her, if that's what you are asking. You and Amanda are both over thirty years of age and well able to make up your own minds what God wants for you, but decisions like this need lots of support. I appreciate your coming to me."

Relieved to have the ordeal over with, Stirling let out another long sigh.

"Thank you, Lady Jocelyn," he said. "I was really nervous."

"I could tell!" smiled Jocelyn.

Outside, they heard Amanda's voice singing the closing hymn from church as she approached the cottage after her visit with Mrs. Spenser.

Quickly Stirling stood. Jocelyn rose also, went to him and embraced him warmly, then stepped away.

Stirling turned and made for the door.

"Hello, Amanda," he said as he hurried past her outside and toward his horse.

"Stirling . . . I didn't know you were here," she said. "Did you—"

But already Stirling was climbing into the saddle and galloping away.

Bewildered, Amanda continued on. She met Jocelyn at the door.

"What did Stirling want, Mother?" she asked.

"He had private business with me," answered Jocelyn.

"Private business with you!" laughed Amanda. "What is that sup-posed to mean . . . what kind of business?"

"I told you—private business."

"And he didn't even want to see me?"

"I am sure he will talk to you when he feels the time is right."

"Talk to me about what?"

"Never mind. Just be patient."

Amanda continued into the cottage to change her clothes, more per-plexed than ever.

90
Another Private Talk

*A*manda did not have long to wait for an answer to Stirling's curious behavior.

Four hours later, as the warmth of late afternoon gradually began to cool, he appeared again, this time in a two-seater buggy.

Hearing the clattering sounds of the approach, Amanda came to the door just as he pulled up in front of the cottage.

"Stirling!" she laughed. "What are you doing? Where did that fancy buggy come from?"

"I borrowed it from Geoffrey," Stirling replied.

"I knew I recognized it, but what—"

"Would you come for a ride with me, Amanda?" As he spoke, he seemed distracted and nervous.

"But . . . what—now? Like this? You're all dressed up, like you're going to church or a party or something."

"Never mind about that. Just come with me for a ride—yes, as you are."

Amanda leaned the broom in her hand against the wall, then called inside the open door, "Mother, I'm leaving for a while with Stirling."

She walked to the buggy, climbed up, and sat down on the other side of the padded bench seat. Stirling flicked the reins, pulled the horse around, and cantered off back the way he had come. But instead of

continuing on toward the Hall, about halfway Stirling turned onto another dirt carriage track leading toward the hills northwest of the village.

He did not utter a peep. He was obviously growing more and more
restless by the minute. Amanda began to think something was seriously
wrong. There must be some dreadful news he had been waiting to break
to her after returning to Milverscombe.

"Stirling," she finally said, "please . . . what is going on? If something
is wrong, you can—"

"Nothing is wrong," he said abruptly.

"But you are so quiet and serious. I've never seen you like this."

Stirling did not reply.

Suddenly Amanda realized what it must be.

"Oh no . . . Stirling—you're going to move! You're leaving Milverscombe. Have you told Geoffrey yet?"

"No . . . I'm not leaving," he said. "Actually . . . Dr. Armbruster has
offered me a post as his assistant for as long as I want it."

"That's wonderful. But—"

Amanda paused.

"Is it . . . it's Geoffrey, then, isn't it," she said, "—something's wrong
with Geoffrey?"

Again Stirling shook his head.

It fell quiet for another minute as they bounced slowly along.

"Then what is it?" implored Amanda at last. "You're making me
worry!"

Finally Stirling slowed the buggy, then eased it to a stop. While the
horse stood calmly snorting and shuffling its hooves, Stirling tried to
collect himself. He made several attempts to speak, drawing in long
breaths and exhaling slowly. Amanda continued to sit, not exactly patiently but quietly waiting. At last Stirling turned toward Amanda.

"You know, Amanda," he began, "I'm not what you'd call a romantic.
I've read the romantics of literature, and I always considered all that a
bit soupy for my tastes. But you're my friend, actually probably the best
friend I've ever had along with Geoffrey. I like being with you, as a
friend . . . but also as a woman."

Amanda felt her face suddenly getting very hot and knew it was
turning red.

"These years away," Stirling continued, "made me think about a lot
of things. I know you've had a lot of difficulties to face . . . and I know

you said you'd never marry again . . ."

At the word "marry," Amanda's heart began to pound.

" . . . and I can respect that if it's the way God is leading you. I would be the last person on earth to try to talk you into doing anything other than what you think God wants for you, even for my own sake."

Stirling exhaled deeply and squirmed a little where he sat. He then stared straight out over the peaceful Devonshire countryside.

"But at the same time," he went on, unable to look at her now, "I've been finding myself realizing that I want to spend the rest of my life with you, because . . . it's just that . . . well, that I love you as more than just as a friend."

Amanda's brain was spinning. Was Stirling saying what he seemed to be saying . . . that he *loved* her!

"And so what I'm saying," said Stirling, taking a deep breath and then letting it out, "if you don't think it's too presumptuous for a commoner like me to approach a lady like you, if you should ever change your mind about your future . . . you know, what you think you're supposed to do—about marrying, I mean . . . if such a time should ever come, I would . . . what I'm trying to say is that I would like to ask you to be my wife."

Amanda's eyes flooded with tears.

A commoner! Stirling Blakeley was no commoner! He was the finest young man she had ever known!

Who cared about station nowadays? Was she not her father's daughter after all, and had he not liberated her from thinking about class and station long ago?

But though her brain was exploding, Amanda could find no words to reply. Her heart was too full. It had been slowly dawning on her for some time that the bond she felt with Stirling was growing into something more than friendship alone. When she was with him she felt things she had never felt with anyone. They could talk about anything. She was relaxed and comfortable, yet somehow more aware of life than at other times. She felt more whole, more complete . . . more herself. And when she had seen him at the station, she'd realized her feelings about him were changing.

But despite the vague growth of such sensations in her own heart, it had not occurred to her to imagine—she would not even have dared dream!—that similar feelings had taken root within Stirling. He was good, wholesome, kind, intelligent, gentle, virtuous . . . how could *he* ever love one like *her*, knowing what she had been and done?

Amanda's head swam at the very thought! How could she find words to tell him all that was in her heart and mind to say?

Slowly she moved closer to Stirling on the seat of the buggy, slipped her hand through his arm, and gently laid her head against his shoulder.

For now it was enough that they loved one another . . . and that at last both knew it. When her swirling head calmed down a little, she would try to find words to tell him what she felt.

91

Storm Clouds

The summer passed like a dream for Amanda. She had not imagined that she would ever be completely happy again. Now suddenly from out of nowhere, great joy had exploded into her life. Every day she awoke having to remind herself again that it was not a dream, but that a wonderful man of God loved her . . . loved *her*—and that they were planning a life together such as she had given up imagining she would ever know.

"Mother," she said almost every day, "I cannot believe it . . . I simply cannot believe it!"

"God is good," returned Jocelyn with a quiet smile. "He loves you and wants nothing but the best for you. When that best is something that makes you happy, he delights to see you so."

Amanda and Stirling and Geoffrey were together nearly every day as before, but now, as things stood between her and Stirling, it could not but be changed. Geoffrey understood and was delighted for them. He had never been in love with Amanda, and knew it. Nothing could have made him happier than for his two best friends to fall slowly and quietly in love with each other, as it was now obvious they had been doing for some time. In his quieter moments, with a knowing smile on his lips, Geoffrey, like Jocelyn, said to himself that he should have seen it all along. Once it had happened, it almost seemed as if there could be no other way for Stirling and Amanda's friendship to flower than this.

The winter of 1922 to 1923 came early and was especially severe in Devon. Geoffrey seemed tired, and his cough grew incessant.

Many outbreaks of cold, fever, flu, and various minor infections kept Dr. Cecil Armbruster and his new young assistant busy. Dr. Armbruster was now in his midsixties, and with the community growing as it was, he could hardly keep up with all its needs. Until Stirling made other plans or had a better offer, the older doctor was more than glad to share both his caseload and income with his young protégé.

As the cold grew more severe, Geoffrey was seen walking about town less and less. Stirling went into the bank to say hello on most days. To his eyes, Geoffrey seemed to be wasting away. Yet there was no fever or other troublesome outward signs, only the cough and loss of weight.

In the second week of February 1923, a thaw came, then a sudden warm, dry spell. All Devon, indeed all of England, breathed a sigh of relief to see and feel the sun again. Coats and hats and umbrellas were discarded, and some of the more intrepid gardeners wondered if an early spring had come.

On Tuesday of the following week, the sun rose again in spectacular glory for the eighth successive day.

Geoffrey Rutherford came down to the breakfast room in fine spirits.

"Good morning, Wenda," he said to Mrs. Polkinghorne. "A splendid day, what?"

"Indeed, it is, sir."

"If this warmth keeps up, my lungs will clear and I will finally get rid of this cough."

"I am glad you are feeling better, sir. What would you like for breakfast—eggs and bacon?"

"My appetite is still a bit off . . . just tea and toast, thank you."

Geoffrey wandered to the window.

"Yes . . . a fine day," he repeated. "And I have not been getting enough exercise lately. That's what these tired lungs of mine need— fresh air and exercise. I think I shall walk to town today."

"But, sir, don't you think—"

"It is a beautiful warm day, Wenda. I am convinced the walk will do me good."

As the day progressed Geoffrey's spirits remained buoyant. The oasis in midwinter had turned everyone's thoughts toward postponed projects and activities, and the bank was unusually busy. He did not get out all day; nor was he aware that as the afternoon advanced, an ominous blackness had appeared on the horizon. The storm approached rapidly, sending gusts of wind and a chill ahead of it to announce the end of the warm, dry week.

When Geoffrey closed the bank door at 6:10 and walked out into the evening darkness, a fierce rain had already begun to pour down. He now realized his foolishness in not bringing the car that morning.

He went back into the bank to fetch an umbrella, then returned again to the street.

There was nothing for it, he said to himself as he gathered his coat tightly about him and raised his umbrella, but to launch out into it and get home as quickly as possible.

By the time he reached the Hall he was chilled and nearly soaked to the bone, for the wind had blown about him on the road with such intensity, with the rain pelting him from all directions, that the umbrella did little but keep the rain from getting into his face.

Mrs. Polkinghorne had a fire and hot pot of tea waiting for him.

Shivering uncontrollably, Geoffrey fumbled into dry clothes and tried to warm himself. Despite his efforts, soon he had no choice but to go straight to bed.

By the next morning it was obvious that he had caught a severe infection. He tried to get up but could not. He rang for his housekeeper to get a message to Mr. Miles at the bank that he would not be in. He lay almost motionless for three days. Mrs. Polkinghorne kept the fire in his room burning, and soup and tea warm and ready in the kitchen. But it was all she could do to get him to sip at it. She did not like the sound of the coughing she heard day and night coming from his room.

On the fourth morning she came to his room. No sounds came from within.

"Mr. Rutherford," she said. "Mr. Rutherford . . ."

At last she heard a croak from behind the door.

She opened the door and timidly crept in. The fire had gone out. The room was freezing. Geoffrey lay in his bed staring out with red gaunt eyes, his face a ghastly pale.

"Wenda," he whispered hoarsely, "please go for Jocelyn at the cottage."

Terrified, the poor woman hurried from the room and sped across the field and through the woods in the rain without so much as remembering to put on her boots.

In less than an hour Jocelyn and Amanda, Stirling and Dr. Armbruster all stood at Geoffrey's bedside. Dr. Armbruster had just finished listening to his lungs with his stethoscope. Now Stirling was bent down listening as well while Amanda and Jocelyn stood waiting anxiously.

At last Stirling stood. Dr. Armbruster nodded to him, and they both began moving toward the door.

"Wait, Doctor," Geoffrey called after them weakly from the bed. "You don't need to go outside to confer. I want to hear what you're thinking."

Both men paused and turned back.

"It is just that we can never be one hundred percent certain," Dr. Armbruster began.

"You will have to tell me eventually," insisted Geoffrey.

"But sometimes these things—"

"Doctor," interrupted Geoffrey, "what do you think it is? I can see from your expression that you consider it serious. If you do not tell me, I will insist Stirling does. He is my dear friend and will not be able to refuse."

Dr. Armbruster nodded, glanced at Stirling, and sighed. "Right . . . well," he began, "—but as I said, I cannot be completely certain . . . I didn't want to let myself admit it at first . . . but from the look and sound of it, I would say there is a chance . . . that you may have tuberculosis."

At the dreaded word, a cry escaped Amanda's lips.

Geoffrey took in the news calmly. "I thought as much," he said. "I did not want to let myself admit it either."

"But you've got to keep hope, Geoffrey," now said Stirling. "There are new advances being made all the time. There is a good chance you can beat it."

Geoffrey nodded. In front of Amanda and Jocelyn he would maintain an optimistic front. But he knew the odds as well as Stirling did.

"What . . . what can be done?" said Jocelyn.

"Keep him warm, well fed, plenty of fluids, keep a good fire in his room," replied Dr. Armbruster, "and pray for warm weather to clear out his lungs. We will pray that rest will enable his body to turn the corner. Otherwise, of course . . . as you know, ultimately when one is unable to take care of oneself—"

"We will not talk of sanitariums now, Doctor," said Jocelyn. "We will all help Geoffrey to rest and make a full recovery.—I will call your mother right away, Geoffrey."

"No ... no, please, Jocelyn. She would be on the first train down. Her fussing would be worse than this cough. I do not want to worry her. I love my mother, but ..."

"I understand. But don't you want her to know?"

"She would fret herself into a dither," replied Geoffrey. "Perhaps if there is a change."

92

Decline

♦ ♦ ♦

For the rest of the month never had a sick man two such devoted friends to nurse him as Amanda and Stirling. Everyone warned them to be careful, for the disease was well known to be highly contagious.

"I have spent my whole life thinking of nothing but myself," was Amanda's reply. "It is time I thought about someone else."

And for Stirling's part, if medicine was the profession he loved and had chosen to follow, how could he run from the first difficult case to present itself?

For the first week after the diagnosis, Jocelyn and Amanda took turns spending the night at the Hall to be near in case Geoffrey's condition worsened noticeably.

As the bank's business had grown, Geoffrey had hired two new employees, including an assistant, Welford Miles, who had almost as many years experience as he himself. Therefore, Geoffrey's absence caused no disruption to business and was not even reported to London. Stirling met with Miles to apprise him of Geoffrey's condition, passing along the message that when he was up to it, he would send for him and they would confer about whatever needed to be discussed.

Within a week Geoffrey was back on his feet, though did not plan to resume his duties at the bank until cleared by Dr. Armbruster. Either Amanda, Jocelyn, or Stirling continued to call on him and sit with him every day. But though he could move slowly about inside with relative ease, Geoffrey's strength did not improve as they had all hoped, and his cough remained extremely troublesome.

It continued to rain, lightly but incessantly. The wind that had heralded the storm soon dropped to a light breeze, but the thick grey mass of cloud water settled over England like an unmoving heavy blanket and continued to pour down, not buckets, but cupfuls of water, day after day, night after night, without a letup. Again rivers and streams filled, and the ground became soggy and waterlogged like an overfull sponge.

All at once for no visible reason, Geoffrey took a sudden turn for the worse. The day had begun well. He ate a tolerably adequate breakfast, dressed and read most of the morning, enjoyed the *Times* crossword puzzle with a laugh or two, even conferred with Miles, who had been coming to the hall with a report every several days about noon.

In midafternoon, however, a wave of light-headedness and nausea came over him.

"I am feeling tired, Wenda," he said as she brought him afternoon tea. "I think I shall go to my room for a rest."

"Shall I send for Dr. Armbruster?" she asked.

"No . . . I am fine. I just need a little nap."

Jocelyn called later in the afternoon. But when Mrs. Polkinghorne informed her that Geoffrey was sleeping, she left without disturbing him.

No one saw him again that afternoon.

The rain continued to pour down. In the middle of the night, suddenly Geoffrey awoke from the sound of a great breaking crash somewhere above him.

Trying to gather his wits, he coughed and hacked painfully, groped for the light beside his bed, then rose, tried to clear his head, and pulled on his robe.

He went to the window. Apparently the rain had finally stopped. He turned back into the room and, between violent coughing fits, tried to listen.

Upstairs, he was sure of it, there was water dripping somewhere inside the house.

On uneasy legs, he made his way out of the room into the corridor, turned on a light, and followed the sound up to the second floor. He was far too weak for such activity, but curiosity over the persistent mystery of the strange dripping sounds gradually gave him energy to continue the search.

Struggling to the top of the stairs, he made his way along the north wing. Ahead in the dimly lit corridor he saw what seemed to be the glittering of falling water droplets. Was his mind playing a trick on him? It looked like it was raining inside the house!

He shuffled forward weakly until he came to the source of the sound that had awakened him. Wherever the rain had been leaking into the house from above, it had apparently worsened suddenly, then accumulated throughout this storm to the point where the ceiling above, roughly between the library and the armory, could no longer contain the weight. On the floor in the middle of the corridor was splattered a water-soaked pile of lathe and plaster that had crashed down from above.

Geoffrey looked up to see a hole in the ceiling a foot or more wide. From it water continued to trickle onto the floor in front of him.

The loose tile on the roof must have finally given way. But, he thought, if the roof had been slowly leaking all this time, why had they seen no water in the garret directly above where he now stood? How could the water get from the roof through to this corridor... without first making a mess in the garret?

He couldn't worry about that now. If something wasn't done within another hour, the water in this pile of plaster would leak down onto the first floor and create a dreadful mess on carpet and furniture and ceiling. He had to try to find a way to clean it up. He could go rouse Wenda. But she was working hard enough already and would only scold him for being out of bed. He would do it himself.

Geoffrey glanced around. He would try the guest room across the hall. Soon he had gathered every available towel and sheet and brought them to the scene of the minor disaster. Within thirty minutes he had the mess tolerably cleaned up, though the carpet would need to be cleaned or replaced. Thankfully by now the dripping from above had stopped. If it began to rain again, he would have to put containers down to catch it.

He carried the wet towels and sheets and cleaning bowl in which he had placed the broken bits of wood and plaster to the empty guest room. He put the bowl on the floor and dumped the wet things on the bed to be seen to in the morning. It wasn't the best solution, he thought as he walked out of the room, breathing heavily and surveying the scene again, but it should keep the damage from spreading.

Feeling energized from the work, and hardly realizing his danger,

Geoffrey continued to puzzle over the dry garret. He looked up into the wet hole in the ceiling. *Why* had they seen no evidence of this leak all this time?

Perhaps it had not developed to that extent when they were last in the garret. He would check it again.

He turned, walked to the library, through the panel in the wall, struggling finally as he climbed up into the secret garret room Amanda had shown them.

Glancing about, he saw that it was *still* dry. How could it be? They had heard dripping behind the wall. The leak must be directly below him.

He left the garret room, retracing their steps from that previous occasion, to the tower and finally, as Geoffrey thought, to the opposite side of the wall he had just left.

But here too everything appeared completely dry.

He stood looking about in mounting bewilderment. Had he not just cleaned up a great mess directly underneath this very spot? The leak *had* to be coming through the garret from the roof down to the corridor below... but where!

Still puzzling over the strange incongruity, Geoffrey returned to the corridor below and stared up yet again into the black vault where the ceiling had broken through. There was only one way to find the source of the leak. He had to get up into that hole. He would get a ladder and have a look for himself.

The next moment he was on his way back to the library, returning two minutes later dragging the five-foot stepladder used to reach the highest of the library's bookshelves. Struggling with it as quietly as possible, and at last beginning to realize that he had taxed his body far too greatly, he managed to stand it up under the hole. All that remained now was something to see with once he got up there.

He hurried back down to his bedroom, stopping several times to lean against the wall for a brief rest, returning a few minutes later with a kerosene lantern. Grasping it carefully with one hand, he made his way cautiously up the ladder, then held the lantern aloft over his head, stuck it up into the round black void and chipped away a few wet, loose pieces of plaster so he could get his head up through the hole as well.

He was dangerously high on the ladder. He knew he was weak, that his legs were wobbly, and that what he was doing was risky. But he had to find out what was up there!

Grasping the wet edge of the ceiling hole with his free hand for balance, although the plaster and lathe would never support him if he fell, he cautiously now extended his right foot to the top of the ladder, then slowly followed with his left. Carefully he stood and tried to extend shoulders and chest through the small opening, which he had now managed to enlarge to some fourteen inches in diameter. When his head was through the ceiling, he glanced about in the eerie flickering light of his lantern.

He had not broken through to the garret at all, or at least not to any part of it he had ever seen. He was looking up into a narrow chamber no more than three feet in width, stretching above him to the uppermost outside roof of the Hall, from which an occasional drip continued to fall on his head. This was the garret all right, but somehow a portion of it walled off from all the rest.

And as he glanced about, what he saw next took his breath away.

He had finally begun to hallucinate from his weakened condition, or else he had discovered a mystery connected to this place that no one else in all the world could possibly know about.

A hidden storage vault!

Eyes still wide and brain reeling from the discovery, he climbed down a few minutes later and hurried again to the secret room of the garret. There he knocked and pounded against the only wall that could possibly connect with the tiny chamber he had found. Yes, he could hear behind it now what sounded like hollowness.

It was a false wall!

No wonder they had never seen the leak from the garret room. This wall and that of the tower corridor were not the same at all as they had always assumed! The two walls had been separated by a three-foot wide space, creating the vault he had just left. Had this been the intent of the mysterious construction Amanda had told them about which had been carried out by Mrs. McFee's great-grandfather, a construction designed to *hide* this small three-foot storage chamber so that its cache would never be discovered?

And it might never have been, thought Geoffrey, had not a rainstorm brought a leak to this *exact* spot and had not a loose tile of the roof finally given way, sending the storm tumbling straight down into the second-floor corridor.

But how to get into the hidden vault from here? This garret room must have been intended as the entry. There had to be access to it of some kind.

Excitedly Geoffrey probed the floor at the base of the false wall with his fingers, knocking, pushing, and feeling about. His excitement seemed to give him a new injection of energy.

There ... he felt a tiny bit of wet along the base of floor and wall. Frantically he now pounded and pushed and scraped. All at once he felt one of the floorboards give way a little at the corner. He pressed down. Three feet away the other end popped up an inch. As it did, the corner end sunk below the level of the floor.

Geoffrey tried to lift the board, but it was still connected somewhere.

He continued to push and pull at the curious floorboard. Now he felt it slide a quarter of an inch as the corner end slipped beneath the wallplate.

Pushing now with more force against the raised end, the board slid farther along some hidden track. But it had grown difficult from lack of use and did not slide smoothly. Geoffrey pushed with all the limited strength he possessed until he had slid it some twelve inches. The effort taxed him. He paused to grab his handkerchief, coughed terribly three or four times, then bent down to examine the opening under the board.

Hidden in the floor beneath it had been constructed a small, concealed brass lock.

This was obviously the means of entering the invisible vault behind the wall. How, he couldn't immediately see—probably by some unseen panel in the wall that the lock released.

And why not? The fellow Kyrkwode had been a master of such ingenious devices. The place was full of them!

Staring at the lock, Geoffrey coughed again. But where was the key?

The only keys he knew were on the key ring in the tower. He closed his eyes and sighed. He was too fatigued to investigate further.

He would try them later. He had to get back to bed. He had made a remarkable discovery; that was enough for now. He would investigate the lock in the morning.

Exhausted and hacking, he slid the floorboard back in place, then made his way down the corkscrew staircase out of the garret room, back through the labyrinth to the library. As he went he was thinking of the consequences of what he had just found. No one must know of it yet, especially his father. He must cover up the evidence of the discovery while determining what to do about it.

With great effort he managed to clean up the additional mess he had made, then dragged a piece of rug from the guest room over the stain in the hall carpet.

But what about the hole in the ceiling?

He had to cover it up with something. A blanket, he thought.

But how to tack it to the ceiling?

A hammer and some small nails would do it. The next moment he was on his way creeping down to the storeroom next to the kitchen to fetch them.

Within five minutes he was again on the ladder carrying out the final part of his clean-up operation.

But tacking the blanket to the ceiling robbed him of his last ounces of strength. He nearly collapsed as he feebly climbed down, replaced the ladder, and staggered back to his room. He was exhausted and growing faint. But he knew well enough that if something happened to him, his father would be here the next day to take possession of the Hall. And he mustn't let his father come here and find this.

But *someone* had to know what he had found, thought Geoffrey. And that could only be one person.

That person was not his father... but his cousin. He must tell Amanda!

He struggled into his room, coughing constantly by now, but trying his best to mute the sound with his handkerchief for fear of waking Mrs. Polkinghorne. He sat down at his writing desk and took out a piece of paper. With quivering hand he made a crude drawing, then followed it with a brief letter.

A terrible paroxysm of coughing finally shook Geoffrey's entire body and forced him to stop. His lungs felt like they were exploding. He groaned in exhaustion, rose, wobbled a few steps, and fell onto his bed. As he removed the handkerchief down from his mouth, the red-stained mucus all over it told him what he knew Dr. Armbruster had long feared.

Gradually he fell into a fitful sleep.

93
Farewell

The next morning Geoffrey did not appear for breakfast.

Mrs. Polkinghorne waited as long as her patience could endure, then began to climb the stairs with trembling foot and a premonition of dread clutching her chest. Just as she reached the first-floor landing, she heard the bell ring for her. In a delirium of relief, she quickened her step toward her master's bedroom.

"Yes, Mr. Rutherford," she said cheerfully as she entered. "How are you this morning?"

Her voice caught as the "morning" left her lips. One look at his wasted form, deathly white skin, and gaunt red eyes told her everything. A terrible smell of sickness pervaded the room.

"Wenda," he said nearly inaudibly, then paused as another fit seized his lungs. "Please," he struggled to go on, "please... send for Stirling Blakeley... only Stirling... no one else."

◆ ◆ ◆

When Stirling entered the sick room fifty minutes later, his heart nearly failed him. Mrs. Polkinghorne's warnings had not been sufficient to convey to his imagination the drastic change that had come over his friend in the thirty-six hours since he had last seen him.

Geoffrey smiled thinly and extended a weak hand.

Fighting tears, Stirling rushed to the bedside.

"Stirling, my dear friend," he said wearily, "I can see in your face that you already know what I brought you here to say—"

"You have merely had a temporary relapse," said Stirling. "The winter is nearly over and—"

Geoffrey's thin white hand waved weakly up from the bed to interrupt him.

"I am dying, Stirling," he said. "Let us not lie to ourselves. I have been coughing up blood. . . ."

Stirling glanced away momentarily, blinking hard, then turned his face back to the bed.

"I want to talk to you about Amanda," Geoffrey went on. "I know you and she love one another. I am so glad of it. But I have no sister, and now Amanda has no brother. I am the closest she has to one. I was a fool for many years . . . I hope I am now learning some of life's lessons. I love her . . . with the love of a brother."

Stirling nodded.

"Take care of her, Stirling," said Geoffrey.

"I will."

"Be good to her."

"I promise . . . I will."

"And when I am gone, give her this," said Geoffrey. "But not a word of it before then. Keep it safe . . . guard with your life. I found something . . . last night . . . too much to try to tell you . . . this will explain."

Geoffrey gave him two folded pieces of paper.

"Do you understand, Stirling?" persisted Geoffrey, "—important . . . see that Amanda gets this. She has to get it!"

Stirling nodded and took the papers, folded them again, and shoved them into his pocket. Then he stooped down and embraced his friend.

"I love you, dear friend."

"And I you, Stirling," said Geoffrey in barely more than a whisper. "You have been the best friend I could imagine. It has been an honor to know you. And . . . and we shall see one another again . . . very soon."

Stirling was weeping freely and could hardly hold Geoffrey's gaze.

"Do you want me to bring Amanda?" he asked through his tears.

Geoffrey shook his head.

"Time is short . . . first I must see Rev. Diggorsfeld . . . something I must do. Please . . . go for him . . . go for him now."

Stirling nodded again, tried to smile as he gazed lovingly one last time into Geoffrey's sunken eyes, then turned and left the room.

He thought no more of the incident with the papers for the rest of the day.

94
Geoffrey and Timothy

◆◆◆

Stirling left Heathersleigh Hall in tears, ran across the entry to his horse, and galloped into Milverscombe. He hardly needed to say a word when Timothy answered his knock. The moment the minister saw his face, he was grabbing up coat and hat and the next instant was out the door.

"Hello, Geoffrey," said Timothy as he came forward toward the bed less than ten minutes later. "I hope you are comfortable."

Geoffrey smiled up from the pillow. "All that matters to me now is that my mind is comfortable. That is why I sent for you. Everyone wants to play silly games . . . pretending I am going to be better soon. I don't think you will do that . . . will you, Timothy? You are not afraid of death . . . are you?"

Timothy shook his head. "And you, Geoffrey?" he said, sitting down in the chair beside the bed.

"No," replied Geoffrey. "Now that it is staring me in the face . . . I find the thought of it almost comforting."

"As it should be. I believe God intended it so."

"Of course, I wish I had been better all my life."

"We all do," smiled Timothy.

"Perhaps, but it took me far too long to begin seeing things, as I hope I have begun to do, in something like their proper light."

"Such is the case with us all."

"But I was so self-absorbed—"

"We will all say the same thing when our time comes. I will say it too. We are *all* self-absorbed. It is one of the misfortunes of our earthly condition that death is meant to cure. But God will make all things that were wrong down here right in the end. And you can take comfort from the fact that you accomplished a great deal of good in this community."

"What do you mean?"

"Come, come, Geoffrey," smiled Timothy, "do you think I do not know the source of the mysterious grants to improve people's homes? I have been watching you, the personal interest you have taken in the work, walking about checking on everything, supervising the work, suggesting various improvements... no mere administrator of someone else's money would conduct himself in such a manner. I have also taken note of the plaque on the wall behind your desk at the bank. You have done God's work in this community, and I know great blessing awaits you."

Geoffrey smiled at Timothy's assessment. "You haven't... no one else—"

"Rest easy," rejoined Timothy. "I could see what was in your heart to do. I have spoken to no one. I doubt anyone else suspects."

"I am relieved to hear it."

"You can take great satisfaction in what you have done, Geoffrey. You may, as you say, have begun a little late. But once begun, you gave God's water to drink to those around you, and did so faithfully and diligently. I am confident you are well prepared to meet your heavenly Father."

"I hope I am. Remnants of fear cannot help occasionally cross my mind... as if he could not wait to punish me... for every little thing I did wrong. But listening to Vicar Coleridge... knowing you these three years... have nearly purged my brain of such notions. I know... he is a good Father who will... welcome me home in spite of all that."

"I am so glad to hear it, Geoffrey," smiled Timothy. "If only more men and women reached the end of their earthly sojourns with that same peace."

Geoffrey tried to draw in a breath. It caused a series of coughs. Timothy waited for the fit to subside.

"Timothy," said Geoffrey at length, "I do not have a will... not time to send for a solicitor. I would like you to take this down... if you would. When I am through... you and Stirling witness it... will be legal."

"Of course, Geoffrey."

"You will find paper... pen and ink there on the writing table."

Timothy rose, went to the desk, and sat down. Slowly, interrupted by many coughing spells, Geoffrey dictated his final wishes, which Timothy took down verbatim.

95
End of the Fight

*W*ord of Stirling's madcap dash into town, followed by Timothy Diggorsfeld's buggy tearing off toward Heathersleigh Hall but a few minutes later, was enough to set the town abuzz with speculation.

Amanda, who had come to the bakery for fresh bread and rolls, caught wind of it and rushed home. She and her mother hurried toward the Hall only moments later, and were running through the door of their former home as Timothy slowly and almost reverently descended the stairs with papers in hand, eyes wet with tears, after his poignant interview with the invalid. They saw the expression on his face, sadness mingled with a strange light, and surmised the truth in an instant.

"Timothy!" exclaimed Jocelyn, running to him. "Is he—"

Timothy shook his head.

"He is still hanging on," he said. "But he is failing."

Stirling, who had been waiting for Timothy in the drawing room and now hearing their voices, rose quickly and came out. Amanda went to him weeping. He took her in his arms.

"Is there ... any hope?" said Jocelyn, glancing back and forth between Stirling and Timothy.

Timothy glanced toward Stirling.

Slowly Stirling shook his head. "I am afraid not," he said. "Even if we could get him to a sanitarium now, I fear it is too late."

A cry burst from Jocelyn's mouth. "I must call Martha, then," she said, "no matter what Geoffrey says."

She turned and ran up the stairs toward her husband's former office.

"I need to go to Dr. Armbruster," said Stirling. "I will be back as soon as I can." He turned to go.

"Geoffrey would like to see you for a moment," interposed Timothy, handing Stirling the papers in his hand.

Stirling nodded.

"Is it all right for me to see him?" asked Amanda as she and Stirling began to climb the stairs together.

"Of course," replied Stirling, who, now that the full truth was apparent, was beginning to be concerned for the health of his wife-to-be. "Only please, for my sake," he added, "do not sit too close . . . and wash well after you leave the room.—Just give me a minute alone with him," he said, "then you can talk to him while I go to Dr. Armbruster."

In tears Amanda nodded, hating the thought of having to protect herself from one she had come to care for so dearly.

Timothy, meanwhile, went to find Mrs. Polkinghorne, to tell her, as gently as he could, that her master was dying.

⸻ ♦♦♦ ⸻

Knowing that their son had been having a bad winter, but without any idea how serious the condition was, Gifford and Martha Rutherford arrived in Milverscombe on the late-afternoon train that same day. Jocelyn was standing on the platform waiting to greet them. At sight of her, Martha burst into tears and ran into her arms. Gifford approached stoic and expressionless.

They had arrived in time but only by a few hours. Jocelyn rushed them to the Hall, where by now a small crowd had gathered. After contacting Martha, Jocelyn had also telephoned Catharine in Plymouth. She and Terrill were expected within the hour.

With Stirling leading her up the stairs, Martha rushed up to the room. Stirling closed the door behind her and waited outside. Mother and son exchanged a few last poignant expressions of love. The father, however, trudging up the stairs slowly after them, then opening the door and walking in without so much as a nod to Stirling, had little to say. Geoffrey tried to speak but could barely croak out the words.

"Father . . . Father," he tried to begin.

"Don't try to speak, boy," said Gifford. "You just get your rest. We will talk later."

"I . . . I want you to know—" struggled Geoffrey.

But he could not continue. The words of love with which his heart was full at this final hour of earthly meeting would have to wait until the next life to be spoken.

Downstairs, as millings and sighs and tearful whisperings continued, a bleary-eyed Wenda Polkinghorne and Sarah Minsterly kept tea and food coming, the only way they knew to be of service to Geoffrey's family and friends. But few appetites were working to capacity.

Geoffrey drifted in and out of sleep throughout the evening. Visitors came and went, but he said little. Toward the end he seemed hardly aware of them.

A little before midnight, a change came. Dr. Armbruster gently aroused Amanda and Catharine, who had both dozed off in two of the chairs in Geoffrey's room, then went to find Stirling and Jocelyn. Jocelyn immediately went to the guest room where Gifford and Martha had retired a short while ago. After knocking lightly, she opened the door a crack.

"Cousin Gifford... Martha," she said, "Dr. Armbruster thinks you should come."

An hour later, Geoffrey slipped away.

96
Stratagems

$\mathscr{F}$or three days a pall descended over Milverscombe. What curse existed here, asked some of the more superstitious residents, that took its Rutherford men, the best of the community, in the prime of their lives?

The bank closed in honor of its founder and manager. Its doors would remain locked until after the funeral, scheduled three days later.

Jocelyn remained almost constantly at Martha's side doing her best to comfort the disconsolate mother.

Gifford Rutherford slipped out of the Hall unnoticed shortly after noon on the day after his son's death. He did not like the thought of walking all the way into town, but did not want to call attention to himself by taking Geoffrey's automobile. When he arrived in the village, he went straight to the bank, let himself in with one of the keys on the ring he had found in Geoffrey's room, relocked the doors behind him, and proceeded to spend an enlightening hour or two going over his son's loan files in some detail.

Revolving many things in his mind, he returned to the Hall. Entering, he did not pause to greet wife or cousins or any of the others whose voices were coming from the formal lounge. Instead, he walked straight upstairs to Charles's study, where he began searching the files and folders in the desk for additional documentation concerning Geoffrey's financial activities since leaving London.

Satisfied at length, and carrying a small leather satchel full of papers, he descended the stairs again and entered the sitting room.

"Martha," he said, "urgent business compels me to return to the city immediately. I will take the three-o'clock train."

"But, Gifford," she began, "the funeral—"

"I will return by tomorrow evening."

Gifford returned on schedule, carrying yet more papers that would prove of extreme interest to all concerned.

Geoffrey Rutherford was buried the next day in the churchyard of the Milverscombe church, as had been, much to his father's annoyance, his expressed wish. His funeral was attended by everyone for miles.

With his wife in tears beside him, as he stood listening to Timothy Diggorsfeld speak on the victorious hope of the life to come, Gifford could not help inwardly blaming all these bumpkins for the changes that had come over Geoffrey in recent years, leading him to move to this godforsaken place and thus causing his contraction of tuberculosis.

But he would get his revenge, Gifford thought, now that Heathersleigh Hall would at last be his. If only he could have found Geoffrey's will among the boy's effects, it would have made matters simpler.

But that's what solicitors were for. He and Martha would obviously inherit the boy's estate.

97
Thirty-Day Call

The day after the funeral, when Welford Miles went to the Milverscombe bank to reopen for business, he was surprised to find the lights already on and someone inside at the manager's desk.

"Good morning, Mr. Miles," said Gifford. "I will tentatively be assuming management of the bank until other arrangements can be made."

"Yes, sir," said Miles, wondering if those arrangements would include him.

"Our first order of business," Gifford began in a businesslike manner as if nothing out of the ordinary had transpired, "is to draft thirty-day due notices for the loans made since the bank's opening. I want to have them all delivered within two days. Then we shall begin preparing foreclosure papers for those cases in which it becomes necessary."

Stunned by what he had heard, Geoffrey's assistant manager did his best to respond.

"But, sir, if I might," said Miles, "none of the people in the community will be able to pay off their loans within thirty days."

"That will be unfortunate," rejoined Gifford. "However, the terms of the loans are quite clear that such is the prerogative of the bank. And since I am a vice-president of the bank and chairman of the London committee overseeing the activities of this particular branch, and since I deem it a necessity, they will have to do what they can."

"But surely, sir . . . there must be some other—"

"Don't argue with me, Welford," snapped Gifford, "or you will find yourself out of a job. Now I have all the files here, and I want you to get to work immediately on the call notices.—Oh, and, Welford," Gifford added, "please see that this is destroyed."

He rose, took down Geoffrey's plaque from the wall, and handed it to the assistant manager.

"Such notions," he said, "no longer represent the policies of this bank and will not be tolerated."

In stunned disbelief, Miles took the plaque, then sat down at his desk and began the odious assignment of filling out thirty-day call notices for the notes of the friends and neighbors he had grown to care about since coming here. As he filled in the specific information, he knew that not one of these people whose names he was writing down possessed so much as an extra ten pounds in ready cash. What he was doing would cost them all their homes and businesses unless some miracle intervened.

♦♦♦

When word of the first round of call notices reached Jocelyn the following day at the cottage, at first she thought there must be some mistake. Within minutes she was on her way to town. Even as she and Amanda were hurriedly hitching the buggy, the uproar of angry speculation was mounting to a frenzy in Milverscombe.

A gathering crowd, hearing that Jocelyn was on her way, milled about anxiously at the edge of town. If anybody could straighten this all out, everyone said, Sir Charles's wife could.

The moment Jocelyn's horse appeared galloping toward them as fast as her shouts had been capable of urging the animal, a few cheers sounded that quickly grew to a low roar. The crowd parted. Jocelyn flew through it and made straight for the bank, with the gathered throng running and hurrying behind her.

She reined in almost recklessly, jumped down without even tying the buggy reins to the nearby rail, and half ran toward the door.

Gifford saw his wife's cousin walk through the door. He had been expecting her. A few townspeople followed her inside while most of the throng remained milling about outside looking through the windows. Jocelyn slowed, trying to calm herself with a few deep breaths, and walked across the floor to Gifford's desk.

"Hello, Gifford," she said in a friendly tone. "I have been hearing various reports from anxious people that their notes are all being called due. As you can imagine, some of them are quite upset. I assume that there must be a misunderstanding."

"No, Jocelyn," replied Gifford without expression. "It is not a mistake."

"But why would the bank suddenly call all the notes due?"

"Geoffrey's death changes things," said Gifford calmly. "Surely you understand that."

"No ... I am not sure I do."

"He is no longer in charge here."

"I do not see what difference that should make. Geoffrey would never have done such a thing. He wanted to help the people of this community."

"Yes, that is all too clear," rejoined his father with a hint of sarcasm creeping into his tone. "But I am the manager now, and it is not at all certain whether the bank will be able to continue. I am afraid circumstances thus compel me to call in all the notes made by the bank thus far. Then everything will be reassessed."

"But why, Gifford ... *why?* If the notes represent viable, profit-making loans for the bank—"

"Ah, that's just it, Jocelyn," Gifford interrupted. "They do not."

"What do you mean?"

"It is very simple. Nearly all the loans in question were either turned down by the loan committee in London, or would have had they been submitted on their own merits."

"Turned down ... I do not understand."

"The Roper loan ... the Spenser building project ... and most certainly the Blakeley loan for medical school—these and a dozen more ... yes, Jocelyn, I am afraid they were all turned down."

"Turned down? I don't understand what you are saying. The loans were made."

"Yes, because Geoffrey, apparently overcome by a wave of sentiment, more likely idiocy, took it upon himself to guarantee these loans himself."

Jocelyn stared at her husband's cousin, bewildered.

"In cases where there was no tangible collateral," Gifford went on, "such as the Blakeley matter, he advanced the money straight from his own account."

"Do you mean that *Geoffrey* paid for Stirling's schooling, not the bank?"

"I am afraid so. In the cases of home and building construction, he co-signed the loans, guaranteeing every one with the backing of his own assets. And this unbelievable crusade to install electricity, telephones, and indoor water," he added, unable to keep himself from chuckling sardonically, "—I cannot imagine where such a foolhardy notion originated, but in carrying out his Good Samaritan scheme, Geoffrey only succeeded in squandering nearly his entire asset base."

As she listened Jocelyn sat as one stunned. Geoffrey had brought all this enthusiasm and prosperity and growth to the region in secret... *himself!*

"But the loans are being repaid," she insisted. "There is no risk to the bank. Why can you not let things continue?"

"It is simply out of the question," replied Gifford. "With Geoffrey gone, all the loans must be renegotiated according to bank policy. As I said, most were made under, shall we say, unusual circumstances. With Geoffrey's assets gone, none have adequate collateral. The notes must be called due. If you will check the fine print, every one contains a thirty-day call clause, which option can be exercised at the sole discretion of the bank. I could not prevent my son from doing what he did, but I *could* protect the bank's interests. Once paid in full, of course, anyone who wishes may apply for financing under the bank's normal terms."

"But you know they cannot repay," insisted Jocelyn. "This will bankrupt the community and make the bank the owner of half the property in Milverscombe."

"The bank... *or* whoever buys off the notes," he added.

In truth, Jocelyn was exactly right—most of the loans in question were very secure, and their payments being made on schedule. If he could get his hands on them and raise the interest a couple of percentage points—Gifford was reminded again of another of his son's foolish gestures, that of writing all these loans at considerably lower rates than current London levels—they should turn him a handsome profit for years to come.

But Gifford's chief objective was Heathersleigh Hall. It would come to him because of Geoffrey's death, of course. But then there would still be the outstanding lien against it. The simplest way was for him to purchase the mortgage from the bank. In the unlikely event that the disposition of Geoffrey's assets proved troublesome or were contested, his ownership of the Hall would thus be insured.

That done, he would also buy up the rest of the foreclosures for the outstanding amount of the notes. Two months from now, he would end up owning most of Milverscombe as well as the entire Heathersleigh estate.

"I regret that all this has turned out to be the unfortunate result of my son's philanthropic policy," Gifford went on in an attempted sympathetic tone. "But as you can see, as the bank's representative I have no other choice. Now really, Jocelyn, I am very busy with my audit of the bank's loans and the execution of the call notices. There is a great deal of paper work to attend to. I am sorry to say, this bank is in a sorry state. I must do what I can to right things. So you really must excuse me. Good day."

Too stunned to be angry, Jocelyn turned for the door. The few people who had come in followed her through the door into the midst of the clamoring and questioning throng outside. One look on Jocelyn's face, however, told them that she was not bearing good news.

98
The Will

♦ ♦ ♦

*W*ithin an hour of Jocelyn's interview with Gifford, everyone in town knew that her efforts had been unsuccessful.

That afternoon Timothy rode out to the cottage.

"Jocelyn," he said, "I have something to tell you that may affect all of this—on the day of his death, Geoffrey dictated a will to me."

Jocelyn's eyes widened.

"I had intended to speak with you, and perhaps consult a solicitor about what I ought to do. But then with the funeral, and now suddenly all this . . . somehow the time never seemed right. Now it seems I need to act quickly before this situation escalates further."

"Does his father know?" asked Jocelyn.

"I haven't any idea," replied Timothy, "although I doubt it. I imagine he would have been to see me by now had Geoffrey told him."

"What happens next?" Jocelyn asked. "Aren't wills usually read aloud to the family and those involved?"

"Right, but by a solicitor," rejoined Timothy. "I must admit, this is a first for me. I don't really know what to do."

"Why are you telling me, Timothy?" asked Jocelyn.

"Perhaps in light of what is happening, the will could change things. Without divulging its contents, I will only say that we need to get a solicitor here, and quickly, to make certain that legalities are complied with."

"Mr. Crumholtz," said Jocelyn. "—I will telephone him immediately."

Meanwhile, throughout the village, anger mounted to such an extent that Jocelyn herself began to fear for Gifford's safety. As the day progressed, more due notices were delivered by Welford Miles, who, sympathetic as he was with the plight of the recipients, nonetheless had to put up with a good deal of verbal abuse as a result of the notices.

The next morning it was Timothy who walked calmly into the bank.

"Mr. Rutherford," he said, "I have a matter that requires your immediate attention."

"What kind of matter?" asked Gifford, looking up from his desk, annoyed at the interruption, especially from this fellow.

"That will all be explained," replied Timothy.

"Then explain it or go about your business."

"Please, sir, come with me," insisted Timothy.

"What the deuce for?"

"As I said, that will be explained. Now I really must insist that you accompany me."

"Go to the devil. I am busy."

Timothy did not budge.

"I am sorry to be so importune, Mr. Rutherford," he said. "Your wife, Lady Jocelyn and her family, Stirling Blakeley, Vicar Stuart Coleridge, and Mr. Bradbury Crumholtz, are all waiting for us at the church."

"I know Crumholtz. What does he have to do with anything?"

"Lady Jocelyn and I contacted him to be present and to see to the legalities in the reading of your son's will."

Gifford sat bolt upright in his chair. Suddenly Timothy had succeeded in getting his attention.

"I see," he said after a moment. "I was unaware my son had spoken with a solicitor."

"He did not, sir. He dictated his final wishes to me the day of his death."

"Ha—then it won't be legal anyway," humped Gifford as he rose.

"Mr. Crumholtz has read it and has advised me to the contrary," rejoined Timothy. "Your son was keenly aware of the law and observed every necessity to insure that the document would stand."

Unnerved by this unexpected development, Gifford at last consented and followed Timothy out of the bank. They walked to the church together in silence.

As they entered, a forced round of greetings and a few stiff handshakes followed. Jocelyn and Timothy did their best to remain cheerful, but one cloudy countenance is usually enough to dampen the spirit of any gathering, and grey skies were written all over the lines on Gifford's forehead.

"Right, then... shall we begin?" said Crumholtz, moving to the front while the others sat down in the first two pews. "I have here," he went on, "the last will and testament of Mr. Geoffrey Rutherford, turned over to me this morning by Rev. Diggorsfeld, to whom it was dictated. If there are no objections, I will proceed with the reading."

Crumholtz cleared his throat, adjusted the pince-nez on his nose, then began to read the will. It was simple and brief, leaving all his interest in Heathersleigh Hall and the property associated with it to his second cousin Amanda Rutherford, naming her mother, Jocelyn Rutherford, as executrix of his estate—"

"What is this!" exploded Gifford. "This cannot be possible! My son would never—"

"Please, Mr. Rutherford," said Crumholtz firmly, for he had been expecting something like this, "reserve your remarks until the reading is concluded."

"But this whole thing is preposterous!"

"As you see it, perhaps. But as I say, the instrument is legal. Now, with your permission, I shall continue."

He looked down at the papers.

"Where was I—ah yes, '...Jocelyn Rutherford as executrix, and whatever small sums might be left in my various investments and bank accounts should be applied against the outstanding loans bearing my cosignature at the discretion of my estate and the bank. Finally, I leave whatever of my possessions remain at Curzon Street in London to my parents, Mr. and Mrs. Gifford and Martha Rutherford.'"

Crumholtz paused and glanced up.

"The instrument is properly signed," he concluded, "is witnessed by the signatures of Rev. Timothy Diggorsfeld and Mr. Stirling Blakeley, and appears to be in order in every way."

As quiet descended within the ancient church, Geoffrey's father sat in angry and gloomy silence.

"Well," he said at length, "it would appear, Jocelyn, that you have succeeded in thoroughly poisoning my son against me."

He stood to leave. "But this changes nothing," he said. "Whether this so-called will is legal or not hardly matters. There are extenuating circumstances which make it a moot point. I *will* have Heathersleigh Hall, and nothing you can do will stop me."

"What sort of circumstances?" asked Jocelyn slowly.

"My son's foolishness," replied Gifford, "was not limited merely to making unwise loans to the community—he also jeopardized his own financial standing. And when his own account went dry and he no longer had cash reserves to cover the loans he was guaranteeing, Geoffrey took out a sizeable mortgage against Heathersleigh Hall in order to continue his folly."

"He mortgaged ... *Heathersleigh Hall?*" said Jocelyn in disbelief.

"A foolhardy decision, I grant you, but unfortunately true."

Jocelyn's head was swimming.

"But ... I have a few assets left," she said. "Perhaps if I guaranteed—"

"Tut, tut, Jocelyn, my dear ... believe me, the amounts in question are far beyond the scope of your limited means. The amount due against the Hall alone is £14,500, not to mention all the other loans. The total indebtedness created by Geoffrey's benevolence amounts to more than £30,000. So you see, his sham of a will does nothing but tie around your daughter's neck the noose of Geoffrey's indebtedness."

He turned to go.

"But ... but what will you do?" Jocelyn asked after him as the others continued to listen in silence.

Gifford paused and turned. "It is really quite simple, my dear. I shall return to the bank immediately, where I will set in motion the steps necessary to fulfill Geoffrey's obligation against Heathersleigh Hall."

"What kind of steps?"

"Those prescribed by law under the terms of the note. It is called foreclosure. The Hall and all its assets will be sold by public auction, and the other notes called due. There is simply no other way."

"But surely, Gifford . . . selling off the Hall by auction—how can you do such a thing!"

"Why do you not see what you and others in the community can raise?" suggested Gifford, raising one eyebrow and glancing about at the others. "Perhaps, that is if the people of the community were behind you and you all banded together . . . you might buy back your old home."

Even as he spoke, Gifford knew that what the community could probably raise, pooling every penny together including what was in Jocelyn's account—the balance of which he had checked on himself before setting his plan in motion—would not amount to more than two thousand pounds.

"If not, however," he added, "the mortgage on the Hall remains . . . and remains *due*."

He turned to Amanda.

"So unless you can come up with fourteen thousand pounds within the month, my dear," he said, "you will have but thirty days to enjoy it."

He turned again and now left the church and returned to the bank.

Even as he walked along the street, Gifford knew he had no intention of letting the thing be decided by an auction where he would run the risk of some wealthy Devonshire land baron coming in to outbid him. The Heathersleigh property was easily worth over £100,000. He would, before then, quietly pay off the debt in a private transaction with the bank, and then foreclose on Amanda himself.

Back in the church, the others sat stunned for perhaps a minute.

"Mr. Crumholtz," said Jocelyn at length, "may I ask a question . . . even though what Gifford says is correct about the outstanding mortgage against the Hall, who actually owns it now . . . right now?"

"Technically," replied the solicitor, "no one. It is included in Geoffrey's estate; therefore, the formalities of an actual transfer of title will take time to sort out. However, as benefactress, your daughter's claim is legally undisputable, there is little doubt that she could be viewed as the owner, and you as executrix of the will may deem it best to expedite her taking possession pending the actual transfer of title. In fact, to avoid awkwardness and any contestation of the will, I would recommend it.

But I am afraid Mr. Rutherford is right concerning the lien. Once title is transferred, you will be liable for the amount. If it is called due by the bank, as appears certain, you will have to pay the amount in full or forfeit the property to its creditors."

"In other words . . . the bank," said Jocelyn.

"So it would appear, Lady Jocelyn. I am sorry. I wish there were something I could do."

"Well, if it is Amanda's until then," said Catharine in a huff, "I suggest we go there right now and take possession. Otherwise, Gifford will take it over as his. I am sorry, Cousin Martha."

"Think nothing of it, dear," replied Martha, dabbing at eyes which wept as much for her husband as her son. "You are no doubt right. Gifford tends to do what is best for the bank without thinking of anyone else."

They all rose and began moving toward the church door.

"Mr. Crumholtz," said Jocelyn, "would you like to join us for tea before your drive back to Exeter?"

"Yes, thank you," replied the solicitor. "There are a few signatures I will need as well."

"Jocelyn," said Martha, "I think I shall go back to the inn. I am very tired."

"It must be very difficult for you," said Jocelyn, giving her a warm hug. "I am so sorry again about Geoffrey."

Martha nodded, shook hands with Vicar Coleridge, then left the church. The others followed.

"Timothy, will you join us?" asked Jocelyn as they emerged again into the sunlight.

"I don't want to intrude if there are legal matters—"

"Nonsense," interrupted Jocelyn. "You are our advisor. Please come. We will have tea together, and perhaps talk further about what we should do."

Word had spread that some sort of meeting in the church was in progress with Lady Jocelyn, a solicitor from Exeter, and Mr. Rutherford. Fifteen or twenty people were, therefore, milling about hopefully outside. They had seen Gifford Rutherford storm out a few minutes earlier and walk briskly through their midst.

And one look at Lady Jocelyn's face now told them that the situation with the bank remained unchanged.

Within thirty minutes a public announcement was posted outside the bank, per regulations, which would, as much as the circulation of the call notices, set the community all the more aflame against Geoffrey's father.

NOTICE OF PUBLIC AUCTION OF ASSETS
IN SATISFACTION OF DEBT

Three weeks from today, on the 26th of March, 1923, at 2:00 in the afternoon at the estate known as Heathersleigh Hall, Milverscombe, Devon, a public auction will be held of all assets on the premises, including approximately 120 acres of land, the building of Heathersleigh Hall, and all its furnishings—to be sold as single lot. Auction will be by sealed bid. No bid less than £14,500 will be accepted.

99

Deliverance

◆◆◆

Two automobiles drove slowly up the long entry to Heathersleigh Hall. It felt different now that, for a short time at least, Amanda was the owner again. Yet it seemed so empty and lifeless. Not even Sarah or Wenda were present, for Jocelyn had brought both women to the cottage to be with them after Geoffrey's death. Not a voice, not a sound, came from within the old, cold grey stone walls.

The seven walked inside. It was chilly and quiet.

Slowly Amanda walked toward the stairs while Jocelyn went to the kitchen to start a fire and begin preparing tea.

"Where are you going?" asked Stirling.

"I want to see Geoffrey's room again," Amanda replied.

They climbed the stairs and walked into the room that had belonged to her parents for so many years and in which Geoffrey had died only five days before. Amanda glanced about with a sad smile. The sight was familiar yet distant. It was so silent and sterile. It almost smelled like a hospital ward after the cleaning Sarah and Wenda had busied themselves with after Geoffrey was gone.

They stood several moments in silence.

"Wait... what am I thinking!" Stirling suddenly exclaimed in the midst of the solemn atmosphere.

"What?" said Amanda as she turned toward him, jarred by his sudden statement.

"Geoffrey gave me some papers to give to you," he said. "In the grief over his death and the funeral, I forgot all about them."

"What were they?" asked Amanda.

"I don't know. He said they were important, that I should guard them with my life, and—what else... he said he had found something."

"Where are they?"

"That's what I am trying to remember," said Stirling, frantically searching his pockets. "But they're not here—I must have been wearing a different shirt and pair of trousers."

He paused, thinking hard.

"No—I was wearing my heavy coat. It was chilly that day. I'll run home and see if I can find them."

"I'm going with you!" said Amanda, following him from the room and toward the stairs. As they went, somehow a sense of urgency came over her. By the time they reached the door, she was as anxious to find the papers as Stirling. "We'll take the Peugeot," she said. "I'll drive!"

Four and a half minutes later Charles Rutherford's Peugeot, once the talk of the community but now becoming an automotive relic, nearly skidded to a stop on the dirt street in front of the Blakeley home. Now the villagers had something to talk about other than the call notices on their loans—the fact that a dozen of them had nearly been run down by Amanda Rutherford speeding through town.

Stirling ran inside with Amanda on his heels.

"Hello, Agatha... Rune," said Amanda, hastily greeting Stirling's parents.

"What are the two of you—?" began Agatha.

But the brief conversation was interrupted a moment later when Stirling ran out of his room carrying his coat in one hand and fumbling in the pockets with the other.

"Here it is," he cried. "—Amanda, I've got it!"

He rushed to her and handed her the papers. Amanda sat down in the nearest chair, unfolded them, scanned both the letter and drawing, then calmed herself and began to read.

Two minutes later she glanced up, tears in her eyes from what Geoffrey had written. She had just heard his voice speaking to her from beyond the grave.

"I think we had better get back to the Hall," she said. "This time you should drive. I don't think I could keep my hands from trembling."

"Why . . . what did he say?" asked Stirling.

"I will tell you on the way," replied Amanda, hurrying from the house, while Stirling's mother and father stared after the two, knowing no more what was going on than when they had rushed in.

For the second time in less than an hour, Stirling and Amanda entered the doors of Heathersleigh Hall. But this time they burst through at a run.

"Catharine . . . Catharine!" cried Amanda. "Catharine, where are you—you have to see this!"

Already she was flying up the staircase, Stirling on her heels. Catharine arrived from somewhere on the ground floor, called for Terrill, then chased after her sister.

Catharine caught the other two just as Amanda had reached the second-floor landing and had turned toward the library. Lieutenant Langham's footsteps could be heard behind them taking the stairs two at a time.

"What is it!" asked Catharine as she overtook Amanda.

Amanda paused as she saw the makeshift piece of rug on the floor in front of her. She glanced above her to see Geoffrey's patchwork repair on the ceiling.

"Right there," she said, pointing to rug and blanket, "—*that's* what it's all about."

"What are you talking about?" repeated Catharine.

"Do you remember," replied Amanda, "how George always thought there was another mystery to be discovered about the garret? Even after he discovered the secret room?"

"Of course. He was always sure there was more."

"It turns out he was right," said Amanda excitedly. "Geoffrey apparently found out what it was just a few days ago, during that big storm we had.—Look!"

She handed her sister the papers as she opened the library door.

"Where are we going now?" said Catharine, trying to scan them quickly as they went.

"To the garret room."

"But it's just an empty room."

"Not if you know where to look."

"What in the world are you two talking about?" laughed Catharine's husband as he tried to make sense of the conversation.

"Come with us, Terrill," said Catharine. "You'll see!"

Three minutes later, the four young people, still being led by Amanda, scampered up the narrow circular staircase into the garret room and closed the floor-door behind them.

"And there's no access to this," said Langham, "other than through that hidden passage?"

"That's right," answered Catharine. "That's why no one knew about it for years until our brother discovered it."

"According to Geoffrey's drawing and explanation," said Amanda, "the board in this corner . . ."

She scooted to the corner on hands and knees and began probing about with her fingers.

"—There, look . . . this end just slipped down!"

"Let me slide it back," said Stirling, who had just read Geoffrey's directions again.

It slid easier to Stirling's touch than it had to Geoffrey's. A moment later, all four faces were bent down close to each other in amazement over the concealed lock in the floor.

"It's just like the mechanisms in the two cabinets!" said Catharine. "Maggie's great-grandfather must have been a mechanical genius."

"How does it open?" asked Terrill. "I don't see a key."

"There isn't one," said Amanda. "Geoffrey suggested the key ring in the tower."

"Let's go!" cried Catharine.

They pulled open the trapdoor again, squirmed through the small opening, descended the stairs, then rushed off through the labyrinth, this time to the northeast tower of the Hall. A few minutes later they were on their way back, the key ring jingling in Stirling's hand.

"But all of these keys are accounted for," said Catharine. "There is the large tower door key, the medium-sized one that unlocks the door in the opposite wall into the hidden passageway, and the small key that opens the hidden panel of the cabinet in the library. There aren't any extras."

"We'll have to try them," said Amanda. "Perhaps the same key opens two locks."

Scrambling up into the garret room, again they knelt down.

"It's obviously not the big one," said Stirling, looking at the keys and lock. He held the next one down toward the floor.

"No, that couldn't be it either—too big. How about the secretary key?—Here, Amanda, it looks about the right size . . . you do the honors."

Amanda took the key from Stirling's hand and slowly pointed it down into the lock, then attempted to insert it. It slid smoothly into the mechanism. Slowly she began to turn the key.

From somewhere in the wall facing them, they could hear a metallic click of retracting bolts. In front of them a hidden panel that had been built into the wall measuring some two feet wide by four feet high swung back, revealing a darkened chamber behind it. It had no floorboards, only the back side of lath and plaster from the ceiling below between the joists, and had obviously never been intended to support any weight.

"It's exactly as Geoffrey described it!" exclaimed Amanda. "A tiny vault between the two opposite garret walls."

Three wood shelves had been built on the wall of the vault and contained various objects, trinkets, a book or two, a tattered blanket, a knife, a spyglass, a pocket watch, and a compass. Evidence was apparent of the leak in the roof above and the hole where the lath work had fallen into the corridor below.

"What's that!" said Catharine. "Look!"

On the lower of the shelves sat what had first drawn Geoffrey's attention as well—an ancient chest approximately a foot long, six inches wide, and nine inches deep, with top rounded from front to back, silverish in color with hammered designs and patterns engraved in the metal.

Stirling reached across with one hand to pick it up.

"It's heavy—I can't lift it!"

Crouching forward, he now lifted the box with both hands and withdrew it into the larger room, where he set it on the floor with a heavy thud.

"You're not going to believe this," said Terrill, "but that is a Turkish money box. I would recognize it anywhere. I saw one in a museum once. I recognize the engravings."

"It looks like something out of *The Arabian Nights!*"

"Actually, you're not so far wrong," said Langham.

"Open it, Amanda!" said Stirling. "What are you waiting for? The Hall is yours now. I presume that means so is that box."

It fell silent a moment. A sense of awe descended upon them in anticipation of what their eyes were about to see.

Slowly Amanda raised the unlocked latch, then lifted the lid.

Gasps of incredulity and astonishment broke from all four mouths at once.

"Can that possibly be . . . what it *looks* like!" exclaimed Catharine, the first to find her voice.

Terrill reached toward the gleaming sight and picked up one of the coins with which the box was filled, examined it a moment between thumb and forefinger, then tried to judge its weight by tossing it up and down in his hand.

"It's gold all right," he said. "It looks like a Turkish coin, probably a seventeenth- or eighteenth-century *ducat*. There are legends of Turkish pirate vessels all along the coast down in this part of the country at that time. I would say the history of this chest must be connected with some such activity."

"But what is it doing *here?*" said Amanda, still incredulous at what sat on the floor before her eyes.

"If this place has been boarded and locked up as long as it appears," said Langham, "we may never know. It could have been here for more than a century."

"And it's not *only* gold," added Catharine, who, after her initial shock at the sight, had plunged her hand straight into the pile of coins. "Look at this."

She pulled out a small leather pouch which had been buried in the midst of it.

Opening it, she glanced inside.

"Diamonds!" she exclaimed. Carefully she poured out a few of the radiant jewels onto her palm. "I can't believe it!"

More exclamations went around the small group.

Gently Catharine replaced the gems into the pouch and set it back in the chest with the coins.

"What were pirates doing here, Terrill?" she asked.

"They had business with smugglers who brought their merchandise ashore into England all along the coast of Devon and Cornwall."

As they were talking Stirling had been looking over some of the other items on the shelves on the wall of the vault, and was now examining the pocket watch.

"Look at this," he said. "It's engraved on the back with the initials *B.R.*"

A few glances went around.

"*Broughton Rutherford?*" suggested Amanda, looking at Catharine. "What do you think?"

"Who was he?" asked Stirling.

"Our great-grandfather's uncle," replied Catharine. "He lived at the end of the eighteenth century."

"That would fit," said Langham. "If he is the one who brought this box here, then he must have been trying to hide it. If he somehow managed to steal this treasure from Turkish pirates or smugglers, he had good reason to be afraid."

"And look at this knife," said Stirling, who had continued to examine the items on the shelves as the others were musing on the origin of the treasure. "Here's a name . . . *Rufus Powell* . . . on the handle."

"Powell!" exclaimed both Catharine and Amanda nearly at once.

"I take it you know the name," said Langham.

"Yes—they are a powerful Devonshire family," said Amanda. "Their estate once bordered Heathersleigh."

"Isn't there a rumor about some old Powell being murdered?" asked Catharine.

"It does sound familiar, now that you mention it," remarked Amanda. "I wonder how he and Broughton Rutherford were connected."

"And didn't Lord Henry's uncle die suddenly, Amanda?" asked Catharine.

"I think so. Then Lord Henry inherited. But that's strange, now that I think about it. Remember Daddy telling us that Lord Henry had been forced to sell off part of the estate?"

"Right—that's how the cottage got into Bishop Crompton's hands."

"Obviously, then, Lord Henry never knew about this treasure."

"Why do you say that?" asked Stirling.

"If he had known, he would have used this instead of selling land to raise cash."

"Which means—wait . . . Amanda, remember that chest George found," said Catharine, "the one that had the ship's logs and other old records in it? I wonder if it contains any clues."

"Where is it?" asked Stirling.

"In an old storeroom in the west wing—that is, unless Geoffrey did something with it."

"I doubt that," said Amanda. "Let's go have a look."

"What should we do with this chest?" asked Stirling.

"Bring it!" replied Amanda.

Ten minutes later they were poring over the chest that had first led George to the discovery of the hidden passages, half its contents on the floor, including journals, papers, a few books, and an old diary Amanda was already engrossed in, with the name Jeremiah Rutherford stamped in gold on the front of its leather cover.

"By the way, Amanda," said Stirling at length, "what did Geoffrey say in his letter?"

Amanda smiled. "It's mostly instructions about what his drawing meant and where to find the concealed lock," she replied. "He said he didn't want to make it known until I was again in possession of the Hall, because of his father. He said he wanted me to have it."

Amanda paused and dabbed once or twice at her eyes.

"The rest of it is personal," she added. "He . . . well, he just told me that he loved me and hoped I would be happy."

She paused, then added, "I am really going to miss him."

It was silent another moment. Stirling nodded. So would he.

"How much do you think is here?" asked Catharine, ever the pragmatist. "What do you think it is worth, Terrill?"

"There would be the historical value to consider," he replied, "as well as the pure value of the gold itself."

"What about the diamonds?"

"I'm not sure they would have any antique worth—but they are no doubt valuable enough in their own right."

"What do you think, then—how much is it all worth?"

"I don't know . . . a good sum."

"How do we . . . but . . . is it *ours*?" asked Amanda.

"Who else would it belong to after a hundred and fifty years?" said Catharine.

"Wherever the pirates got it from," added Terrill, "there is no way to know. This is one of those legitimate cases where possession truly is nine-tenths of the law. This sort of thing is not all that uncommon, actually, and absent clear right of ownership, those making the discovery are always entitled to keep what they have found. But you might consult a solicitor just to set your mind at ease."

"Supposing it is ours... *mine*," said Amanda, "what should we do with it?"

"If you like," said Terrill, "I will take some samples back to Plymouth and talk to some people—antique dealers, collectors, historians, one or two museums."

"Yes... I would appreciate that," nodded Amanda. "But right now I think we should go downstairs and tell the others. We can ask Mr. Crumholtz about it immediately."

As they walked into the lounge a few minutes later, where Jocelyn, Timothy, and Mr. Crumholtz had already finished their first cup of tea, Jocelyn glanced up with surprise.

"What have you four been up to?" she asked. "I heard tromping, running footsteps, a few shrieks, then nothing for the last half an hour. I began to wonder if you had disappeared into one of George's secret passages."

"Mother," said Amanda with a smile as she came forward, "we have something to show you."

100

More Stratagems

*C*atharine and Terrill returned to Plymouth the following day, taking with them several of the Turkish gold ducats.

That same morning Jocelyn, Amanda, Stirling, and Timothy spent quietly passing through the community, individually visiting all those they knew had been affected by the bank's call notices, telling them to have hope, be patient, and not do anything rash. They were continuing to do what they could, they assured them, to resolve the situation. But they could not do so without everyone's peaceful cooperation. Most of the people consented. They had always been able to depend on Sir Charles and Lady Jocelyn and would not stop now, even though matters looked dark and hopeless.

In early afternoon two days later, Amanda and Jocelyn left for Exeter.

After visiting with Mr. Crumholtz again, and obtaining from him names of several reputable jewelers in the city, the following morning they first visited a bank of Mr. Crumholtz's recommendation, then boarded the train for London.

Their first order of business in the great metropolis was to consult with the diamond dealers.

Their second was a visit to the headquarters of the Bank of London. There they asked to be allowed to see the President.

After they explained their relationship to a certain one of the bank's vice-presidents and late manager of its Milverscombe branch, as well as to the late Sir Charles Rutherford, they were at last shown into the expansive fifth-floor office of Mr. Giles Fotheringay. Amanda was amazed to see her mother walk into the private room with such confidence.

"Hello, Mr. Fotheringay, I am Jocelyn Rutherford," began Jocelyn. "This is my daughter Amanda. I am the wife of the late Charles Rutherford, who was your own Gifford Rutherford's first cousin."

"So I have been given to understand," replied Fotheringay. "It is a pleasure to make your acquaintance."

He shook both their hands, then sat down behind his desk.

"What may I do for you, Lady Rutherford?" he asked.

"Simply answer a few questions, if you do not mind."

"I will do so to the extent I am able."

"I mean no disrespect," Jocelyn went on, "and if you answer yes, you need have no fear of my reaction—we will leave peaceably—"

As she spoke Fotheringay stared at her with a puzzled, though concerned, expression.

"—but what I have to ask you is this," Jocelyn continued, "—are you aware, or is it by your, that is the bank's directive, that the town of Milverscombe in Devonshire, where your bank opened a branch three years ago under the management of Mr. Rutherford's son Geoffrey . . . that this town is about to be financially ruined?"

"I am sorry, Lady Rutherford," said the bewildered Fotheringay, "but it would appear I am at a disadvantage, as the situation you refer to is not one with which I am familiar."

"I am trying to learn," Jocelyn went on, "whether Gifford Rutherford is operating under your orders to call due every loan made by the Milverscombe bank since its opening. The loans *have* been called due, and not one of the local residents will be able to pay off the notes within thirty days. Most will be ruined as a result. If this directive comes from

London . . . from you, sir," she added, "I do not think it the kind of policy that will enhance your reputation should the public learn of it. The banking business, as I think you understand, is based on trust. I doubt the public will desire to place its trust in an institution that cares so little for the welfare and financial security of all its customers in an entire community."

Fotheringay shook his head in continued perplexity.

"Of course, of course, Lady Rutherford," he said, "but I assure you that I haven't an idea what you are talking about. I would appreciate it if you would be so good as to explain."

Jocelyn went on to give him the details of what had taken place in Milverscombe during the course of the week.

"Well," said Fotheringay when she was through, "these are grave charges. Now I begin to understand why you are so upset. It may well be, however, that Mr. Rutherford is exercising a legitimate option under the terms of the notes as drawn, in a manner he deems in the best interests of the bank."

"I am certain he has done nothing illegal or unethical according to the letter of the law," said Jocelyn. "I only question whether his judgment in the matter is in the best long-term interest of the bank's public reputation."

"Yes . . . yes, I see."

Fotheringay knew well enough what effect a letter to the *Times* by one such as Charles Rutherford's widow would have on depositor confidence. The bank could certainly not run the risk of letting this complaint escalate publicly.

"I assure you," he said, "that we at the London branch did not authorize such a course of action on Mr. Rutherford's part. That is not to say that we do not find call notices occasionally necessary, but such a wholesale call inflicted upon an entire community . . . yes, I see the difficulty. Believe me, we will look into the matter. I will telephone Mr. Rutherford immediately and—"

"Please, Mr. Fotheringay," said Jocelyn, "if you could allow us to handle matters for a short time in our own way, we would be most appreciative."

"Under the circumstances, it is the least I can do. Little will change in that time."

"Thank you," nodded Jocelyn. She and Amanda rose to leave.

As they descended the stairs a minute later, a smile crept over

Amanda's face. "Mother," she said, "I have never seen you like that in my life. For one who says you used to be afraid to be around people, you had that poor man trembling in fear."

"I can fight if I have to," smiled Jocelyn, "especially if it's for someone else."

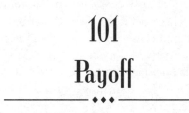

101

Payoff

*T*wo days before the thirty-day deadline and scheduled public auction of the assets of Heathersleigh Hall, Amanda Rutherford walked through the doors of the Milverscombe bank.

She made her way straight to Gifford's desk and set down in front of him a cashier's check, drawn on an Exeter bank, for £14,500.

"I believe this should clear off the outstanding balance on Heathersleigh Hall," she said. "When you have calculated the accrued interest due, I will write you a personal check on my account to cover it."

"What . . . what *is* this?" huffed Gifford, picking up the check and giving it a cursory glance. "Is this your idea of a joke? I know well enough that you haven't anything close to such an amount in your account."

"Do you make it a practice to pry into the finances of your customers?"

"It's just that—"

"It is no matter," said Amanda. "As you can see, this check is drawn on my account in Exeter. I am sure you will find that there are ample funds to cover it. Good day, Cousin Gifford."

Chagrinned, Gifford watched as she turned and walked toward the door. Slowly it was dawning on him that he was apparently going to be denied yet again being able to get his hands on the place.

"There are still the call notices on the other loans," he called after her angrily, as if to remind her that whatever she did, he still held the fate of the rest of the town in his hands.

Amanda paused and glanced back.

"We shall see, Cousin Gifford," she said. "We shall see."

Amanda and Jocelyn's most recent visit, with Stirling accompanying them, to the bank in Exeter a few days earlier had had another purpose than only arranging for the cashier's check. Amanda had also withdrawn a large sum of cash, mostly in twenty-, fifty-, and hundred-pound notes. They left immediately for Milverscombe, not wanting to be away from home with such a sum of cash any longer than absolutely necessary.

The evening after her brief interview with Gifford, Amanda and her mother spent visiting all those with pending call notices due on their loans. Every visit was met with the same tearful disbelief and gratitude when Jocelyn extended her hand with a sheaf of cash notes in it.

"But, Lady Jocelyn . . . Lady Amanda," most of them began, "we cannot accept such generosity."

"You must not see this as a gift from us," was Jocelyn's reply. "The money is in fact not ours at all. It is what we think to be a portion of an ill-gotten pirate's or smuggler's treasure hidden for years at the Hall. It does not belong to us more than to anyone else, and the best way to cleanse such wealth and turn it to good is to give it away and turn it to a use that benefits the entire community."

The following morning, almost from the instant he unlocked the bank's doors, Gifford was greeted with a steady stream, mounting about an hour later to a deluge, of men and women, all asking to see him, then telling him that they had come to pay off their loans according to the terms of the thirty-day call notices they had been sent. Well able to guess the source of this sudden flood of wealth, and furious at being so thoroughly foiled by his cousin's daughter, he had no alternative but to mark every note "Paid in Full."

What else could he do? The people were carrying in fistfuls of bank notes in cash!

That night the bank of Milverscombe closed its doors with more cash in its safe than at any time since its opening. The next day Jocelyn telephoned Mr. Fotheringay in London, informing him that all the notes had been cleared.

Three days later, still reeling from the week's events and the cash payoff of every single outstanding loan as well as the Heathersleigh mortgage, Gifford Rutherford was yet more stunned to look up from his desk to see Mr. Fotheringay himself, the President of the bank, striding across the floor toward his desk. The look on his face was stormy and unpleasant. Slowly Gifford rose, wondering what this could possibly be about.

"Mr. Rutherford," said Fotheringay without benefit of any pleasantries, "if I might have a word with you."

"Of course, Mr. Fotheringay... what an unexpected pleasure to welcome you to—"

"Spare me your pleasantries, Mr. Rutherford," interrupted Fotheringay. "I am afraid it will not be such a pleasure when I inform you that you are relieved of your duties here, effective immediately. Mr. Miles will take over temporarily. As for your future, I will speak with you next week in London. Good day."

Fotheringay turned and departed as abruptly as he had come, leaving the bank's employees, who had heard every word, standing in stunned silence.

Mortified, Gifford wasted no time in hurrying from the building, turning in the opposite direction the moment he was through the door.

♦ ♦ ♦

If the truth were known, Giles Fotheringay had been awaiting an opportunity to slap Gifford Rutherford's hands for some time. He was furious at what had been done in the matter of the call notices. Even though serious repercussions had been preempted by the payoff, he still considered it a stain on the bank's reputation.

Even as the papers throughout England were full of news and speculation about the enormous discovery made in the garret of Heathersleigh Hall, Gifford was called on the carpet immediately upon his return to London. Fotheringay told him bluntly that he was seriously considering not only demoting him from his vice-presidency but firing him altogether. Pending a final decision, however, he informed Gifford that effective immediately, he was on two-week suspension, without pay.

Gifford slunk from the building in disgrace.

Hearing of what had transpired through Martha, Jocelyn returned to London to plead with Fotheringay to reconsider, making a recommendation to the bank's president which, she said, she was certain would do Gifford more good in the long run than any disciplinary action.

Fotheringay thanked her warmly and promised to consider it.

102
An Offer

$\mathscr{A}$nother summer came to Devon.

That of 1923 brought with its warmth a time of peace and also a new dawn of change to the community of Milverscombe in Devonshire.

Until a manager was chosen, Welford Miles acted as assistant manager and continued the policies begun by bank founder Geoffrey Rutherford. Geoffrey's plaque, which he had not destroyed, hung again behind the manager's desk. The electrical and plumbing improvement projects instituted as Geoffrey's personal vision were resumed in joint cooperation between Amanda and the bank. Amanda also donated half of what remained of her newfound wealth to the establishment of the Charles, George, and Geoffrey Rutherford Foundation, whose purpose was to benefit community progress and development. She named Rune Blakeley, the man who would soon be her own father-in-law, chairman of the foundation, arranging for him to receive an annual stipend of £200 to oversee its activities.

Catharine announced in midsummer that she and Terrill were expecting their first child.

Jocelyn and Amanda had been so happy and content in Maggie's cottage that neither were anxious to leave it. Throughout the spring and early summer, therefore, they continued to reside at the cottage, though they kept Sarah, Wenda, and Hector on at the Hall to keep the place up. They visited on most days, gradually coming to feel as if they had two homes, and making preparations for whatever changes might be in store for the grand old Devonshire mansion.

After the humiliating disciplinary measures against him by the bank, Gifford was offered one of two options concerning his future—early retirement, *or* the position of manager of the Milverscombe branch of the bank, where, he was told, if he chose to continue his affiliation with the Bank of London, he must learn to place customers' interests first. Martha was in ecstasy at his acceptance, after a week of healthy and humbling deliberation, of the latter of the two options.

Soon after the announcement was made, the London Rutherfords received the following letter in the post:

> *Dear Cousin Gifford and Martha,*
>
> *Having heard of your acceptance of the position at the Milverscombe branch of the bank, and looking forward to your future as residents of Devon, it is our pleasure, if you have no other plans, to make you welcome at Heathersleigh Hall for as long as you may wish. The place is huge, as you well know. There is no reason why it cannot house two Rutherford families. Our own plans remain uncertain at this time, although we may be reoccupying our former quarters in the east wing. But we are prepared to offer you a portion of the west wing of the first floor to use as your own rooms and apartments. There are many rooms, some very spacious. You would be most welcome to put them to use any way you like. At present, Wenda, Sarah, and Hector make use of only three. Gifford, perhaps you would like to convert one of the unused guest rooms into an office. The corner room with windows looking out both north and west offers a lovely setting, and Charles often thought it one of the nicest rooms in the entire Hall.*
>
> *We look forward to sharing the ancient estate of our mutual family with you.*
>
> *Jocelyn and Amanda Rutherford*

As she was now viewed as even more a local hero than ever, when Jocelyn urged everyone in the neighborhood to give Gifford the benefit of the doubt when he came, most were only too happy to comply. Almost from the moment they arrived in Devon to begin their new life, the community smothered Gifford and Martha with kindness. Martha thrived and blossomed, gave back tenfold, and in time was almost as great a favorite among the women as Jocelyn herself. The friendliness of the country, as he considered Devon, annoyed Gifford considerably. He took every possible opportunity to return to London, where he kept up the house on Curzon Street, to see to his many investments and conduct what bank business was necessary. Yet the change in environment would accomplish its work in time. The human flower withers only when turned in upon itself. But when the sunlight of kindness shines bright in its face out of the eyes and smiles of its brothers and sisters, what can even the most surly, droopy, grumpy man do but revive and draw strength and begin to stand tall in the invigorating air of love. As such influences began to operate on Gifford, he did his best to combat them. Martha rarely accompanied him into the city. She was home at last and couldn't have been happier. And she could see her husband gradually softening, and in her heart thanked God for the change.

◆ ◆ ◆

"What will you do, Mother?" asked Amanda as they walked away from the post after delivering a letter to Sister Hope and Betsy about final plans for Amanda's upcoming marriage.

"I had assumed that you and Stirling would move back to the Hall after the wedding," answered Jocelyn. "It *is* yours now."

"I will always think of it as yours and Daddy's," smiled Amanda. "But if we did, you know that I would love nothing more than for you to remain with us. Besides," she added with a light laugh. "I am not at all sure I could handle Cousin Gifford and Martha without you!"

Jocelyn laughed. "To tell you the truth, dear," she said, "I have been thinking about remaining at the cottage."

"Actually, Mother," said Amanda after a moment, "Stirling and I have been talking about it . . . and, well, if you don't think you would mind . . . *we* would like to live with you in the cottage."

"That's wonderful, dear!"

"We cannot think of any better place to raise a family."

"And when it gets crowded with children, or even before, I may move to the Hall. Then I shall have Gifford and Martha all to myself!"

They walked for several minutes, quietly thinking about the changes that were coming.

"What do you think the Lord has in store for our future?" said Amanda at length.

"What do you mean?" asked her mother. "You will raise a family, and—"

"I know . . . I mean beyond that. What *else* will he give us to do?"

"I'm sure he will show us. Perhaps, as we've spoken about before, he will send us other Betsys as he sends people to the chalet."

"I cannot think of anything more wonderful than doing what the sisters do there."

"Whether or not something like that happens, there will always be plenty to do with the people of the community," added Jocelyn. "You will be very involved as the wife of a doctor. I'm sure that will keep you busy, especially with the area growing. Thinking about it reminds me of my nursing days. There is always so much to be done. You and Stirling will be a great team. I am certain the Lord will use you together in ways you cannot imagine."

Amanda smiled thoughtfully.

"Do you remember when we talked about the Lord restoring the locust years... at first I didn't think it could be possible. I was so discouraged. Yet now... I cannot imagine a greater blessing than what the Lord has given to me."

"Hope for answers to prayer according to our own timetable is a common false expectation," smiled Jocelyn. "I had to learn that in praying for you. I wanted you home *immediately*. Yet now that you are here, I realize that there were maturing influences God had to deepen within you to make you ready to come home. My prayers were right, but my expectation of timing was self-motivated."

Amanda nodded. Remembering the pain she had caused would always be hard. She was silent a moment or two.

"I know, Mother," she said. "I realize that sometimes things happen slowly. Yet for so long I wondered if my prayers had been heard at all."

"As did I when you did not return home right away," rejoined her mother. "—But what about Stirling? What is his vision for the future?"

"To help people through medicine, to meet physical needs as a doorway into helping the Lord bring healing to their spirits."

"What a wonderful ambition," exclaimed Jocelyn. "He is quite a young man."

"I know, Mother. And here he was so close to me all the time. It took so long for the Lord to open my eyes to many things—Stirling included."

"But you do know, don't you, Amanda," said Jocelyn, "that it was you who caused us to pray for Stirling in the first place, and then get involved with his family?"

"What do you mean?"

Jocelyn went on to explain how she and Charles had begun praying more actively for the Blakeleys after the day when she and Amanda saw Rune and Stirling in the village.

"Whatever the Lord has for us," Jocelyn concluded, "we must all continue to pray for those he sends us, whether now or in the future—people in the community, those Stirling will tend to through his medicine, Gifford and Martha perhaps, even those in whom we do not immediately see what the Lord is doing. What if, for example, we pray for another ten years, and without knowing it our prayers are all directed toward a single individual God is preparing to come into our lives at some time in the future, some wayfaring Robinson Crusoe who will need our help to turn his or her steps toward home. Our prayers may be tilling the soil in that heart even now."

"You are quite a woman, Mother," smiled Amanda.

"I don't know about that," laughed Jocelyn. "But speaking for myself, I am going to continue to pray for what is ahead. There is a great deal God still may want to do with me. I am only sixty-three years old, and I feel as young as ever. My husband is gone, both my daughters will soon be married. It has even occurred to me to go back to India and work in a hospital. There is such a great need there. I have been reading some of Amy Carmichael's writings, and I want to give whatever years I have remaining to the service of others. Whether at the cottage or the Hall—and I have the feeling he will use both places together—I plan to continue to pray that he will send people to whom we can be of service."

"Amen! That will be my prayer too."

103
Loving Admonition
♦♦♦

Jocelyn and Amanda took up residence at the Hall in September so that Stirling and Amanda could have time to fix up the cottage and make it ready to be their new home.

Hope and Betsy arrived two weeks before the wedding. Betsy had grown into a lovely young lady of twenty-one. Amanda scarcely recognized her. She spoke fluent German, radiated a deep peace, and was more beautiful than any of them could have imagined.

Amanda waited for Catharine's arrival before showing Betsy the secret vault they had found and to tell her the story of its discovery in which she had played a part herself. Soon after the Langhams arrived, the three girls were off like excited children, running through the passages laughing and talking. Catharine, however, was now the last of the three rather than leading the charge.

"I remember the day I crept up into the attic all alone and got lost," said Betsy as they hurried along. "And then the day you took me to the secret room, Amanda, and led me to the Lord. I will never forget that day."

"Nor will I."

"It changed my life almost as much as the day I wandered frightened and hungry into your barn."

"Just wait until you see the secret room now."

Betsy led them scrambling up the circular staircase and through the trapdoor into the garret room.

"Whew," puffed Catharine as she slowly reached the top. "I don't remember these stairs tiring me like that!"

"I don't see anything," said Betsy, glancing around. "It looks just the same as I envisioned it."

"Remember the storm and the noise you heard?" said Amanda. "It turned out to be a loose tile on the roof, and the leak from it led to the discovery of what we are about to show you."

———— ◆ ◆ ◆ ————

Betsy took Hope back to Looe, the town of her early childhood. At last, with Hope's help, she was ready to remember her past and seek full healing in her heart for those tumultuous early years and the shock of her father's death.

By the end of the week, Timothy was seen accompanying Betsy and Hope almost constantly. Word had begun to spread through the community of a beautiful young woman from the Continent visiting at the Hall, and a few young men from the area began calling, hoping to catch a glimpse of her.

Several days after her arrival, Hope and Amanda found themselves alone in the sun-room an hour or so after breakfast.

"You seem very happy, Amanda," said Hope. "I am so glad for you."

"I am happy," smiled Amanda. "God has been good to me. I have you to thank for much of it."

"You have God to thank."

"Of course. But God works through people, and in my life he used you."

"We can both thank God together."

"And *you* look well too," said Amanda, "—as does Betsy!"

"Yes, isn't she lovely?" Hope agreed.

"How did she turn out to be so beautiful! She is positively radiant."

"And with such a sweet spirit," returned Hope. "She has been a greater blessing than I could have ever hoped for."

It fell silent a moment.

"How are you doing... inside, Amanda?" Hope asked after a moment. "Is it resolved... with your father?"

"Resolved, hmm..." replied Amanda slowly. "Perhaps... but it is hard whenever I think of it. It will always be hard."

"What we talked about when I was here before—the guilt you felt at first. *Have* you forgiven yourself?"

"I don't suppose it is resolved on that front," said Amanda. "It is a struggle... no, perhaps I haven't," she added quietly.

"You may always hurt from the memory of what happened," said Hope. "But there comes a time when you have to put it behind you, completely. You accepted accountability for your wrongs. But in the midst of accountability, forgiveness must also flow. If you do not forgive yourself, you are rejecting the very gift God has given you, namely *his* love and forgiveness toward you."

"You never mince words, do you?" smiled Amanda.

Hope laughed lightly. "You do not want me to, do you?"

"No—that is how I know you love me... you are not afraid to speak the truth, to make me face my own wrong attitudes."

"Then let me add this," said Hope. "Who knows when we will have the opportunity to speak together like this again? So I will put this before you in hopes that you will take it to the Lord in your own heart and ask him what to do about it."

"I am ready for whatever you have to say to me," returned Amanda humbly.

"Amanda dear," began Hope, "lack of forgiveness is a cancerous growth inside many a heart that hinders full relationship with the heavenly Father. Unforgiveness prevents more people from intimacy with God than anything. It is one of *the* most lethal human diseases. For most it is an unresolved bitterness toward another person, often a parent. But unforgiveness toward oneself can be just as blocking to the Father's love. You have come a long way, Amanda. You know that I love you and would not say this otherwise. But there remains one obstacle standing in the way of your relationship with God until you remove it."

"But that is what I struggle with," said Amanda. "*How* to remove it... how to forgive myself?"

"I think you know," answered Hope. "By *taking* what God has been offering all along. His love and forgiveness must be *received*. That is something no one can do for you... not even him. Jesus died on the cross that forgiveness might flow. Not only forgiveness for our sins that we might know God's salvation, but also that we might experience wholeness as his sons and daughters. There is a tiny door in your heart blocking the full entry of God's forgiveness. That door is unforgiveness toward yourself. God's forgiveness is what enables you to forgive yourself. But at the same time, forgiving yourself is what enables you to experience the fullness of God's forgiveness. Eventually you will have to complete that circle within your heart, or else your growth in the Father's love will slow."

Amanda took the words in thoughtfully, but said no more.

104

Closing of the Circle

◆◆◆

Stirling and Amanda left the house the evening before the wedding and strolled hand in hand across the grass toward the heather garden. Behind them in the Hall, the Langhams, Timothy, Stirling's parents, Hope and Betsy, and Gifford and Martha were all enjoying tea together after a sumptuous supper following a discussion of the wedding particulars.

"Tomorrow is the big day," said Amanda softly. "I can hardly believe the time has finally come."

"Are you afraid?" asked Stirling.

"A little... and you?"

"Of course. It is a big step."

"Any last-minute doubts?"

"None... you?"

"No."

"I love you, Amanda Rutherford."

425

"Thank you," smiled Amanda. "Sometimes I can hardly believe it. And I love you, Stirling."

They sat down on the same bench on which Charles and Jocelyn had prayed so many times.

"Do you ever worry," said Amanda after a moment, "like you said on the day you asked me to marry you, that we are not romantic enough?"

"We are not as young as most couples who marry," replied Stirling. "Perhaps that is the reason."

"I have wondered if it is because I was married before. I am sorry to bring that up at a time like this, but it does concern me sometimes."

"I am not all tingly like a schoolboy either. But we are both thirty-three years old. What I feel is so much deeper than a schoolboy falling in love. I may not be starry eyed every moment, but that changes nothing about my wanting to be with you . . . always. It's more than just a feeling. Do you know what I mean?"

"Of course. That's exactly how I feel. God has brought us together. It's not a storybook romance. It's better. It gives me even more confidence as we move ahead. But I do love you very much."

They sat a long while in silence, each simply enjoying the other's presence.

At length Stirling rose.

"Do you want to come back inside. It's a little chilly . . . and I think my parents may be about ready to be getting back home. We've got a big day ahead of us!"

"I think I will sit here a bit longer, if you don't mind," said Amanda.

"Then I'll be going."

He reached down and gave her hand a squeeze.

"Until tomorrow, then."

"Until tomorrow."

Amanda watched Stirling go. Hope's words of the previous week had been with her constantly and now came back to her more urgently than ever. If an obstacle still remained in her heart toward being able to fully accept God's love, she didn't want to enter marriage with it still unresolved. Yet there was very little time left.

Amanda knew in her heart that the moment had finally come. In obedience she would take the final step, by faith, of accepting God's forgiveness . . . and forgiving herself.

Perhaps Hope was right and there was no great mystery to it. All she had to do was accept and receive it . . . and take what God had been offering her all along.

Amanda rose and walked deeper into the heather garden. It was getting dark. She heard the hooves and wheels of the Blakeleys' horse and buggy gently clomping and crunching down the drive toward the road. It was the last time Stirling would go home with his parents as a single man. By tomorrow at this time . . . she would be his wife.

Amanda drew in a deep breath.

"Lord," she whispered, "*it seems I am always coming to you saying I am sorry for being such a slow learner. Now here I am again. But I am at last ready, I think. Help me . . . because this is even more difficult than knowing you forgive me. I don't know if I can really forgive myself. So all I can do is do so by faith. . . .*"

Her prayers fell silent.

Slowly Amanda sank to her knees on the soft, moist earth.

"*God, help me,*" she said softly. "*I . . . accept your forgiveness. I will take your love all the way into my heart, far enough and deep enough inside me to allow me to say . . . yes, Lord, I will say it—I forgive myself. I will say it again . . .* I forgive myself! *Because you love her, and because Jesus died for her, Amanda Rutherford is clean, whole, forgiven.*"

At the words, Amanda burst into sobs of release and relief. She could utter nothing further.

She wept for another minute, hard, deep, aching, convulsive tears of cleansing.

At last the storm began to subside, and she knew the battle was over. A change had come. She was ready to go on . . . to a new dawn in her walk with God . . . to a new life as the wife of Stirling Blakeley.

She drew in a deep breath, then another.

"*Thank you, heavenly Father,*" she whispered as she rose to her feet. "*Thank you!*"

105
Joining of the Two

♦♦♦

$\mathcal{S}$tirling Blakeley and Amanda Rutherford were married on October 24, 1923.

Catharine was Amanda's maid of honor, Betsy her bridesmaid. Catharine's plumpness had just begun to show, but her large frame and the loose cut of the dresses they made for the occasion hid her condition from all but those who knew. The radiance on her face, however, was indication enough that she was very happy, following in her mother's footsteps, in her new life as the wife of a naval officer.

Rune Blakeley stood proudly next to his son as Stirling's best man, with Terrill Langham beside him.

Martha sat in a place of honor next to Jocelyn. Betsy and Sister Hope, along with Hugh and Edlyn Wildecott-Browne, filled out one side of the front row in the Milverscombe church. Agatha Blakeley, her brother and sister from Exeter, and Rune's sister and her family from Bristol occupied the front row on the other side of the aisle. Almost from the first strains of music from the organ, Jocelyn, Martha, and Hope began to cry. All eyes turned to see Amanda in a lovely cream-colored satin dress beginning to come toward them.

Amanda had asked Gifford, as her closest male relative, to walk her down the aisle and formally give her away. As Amanda slowly came forward on his arm, the expression on her countenance was neither so expansive nor exuberant as shone on her sister's beaming face. Rather her smile spoke of quiet peace, gratitude, and contentment. If a hint of sadness could yet be detected as a reminder of the pain she had endured growing into readiness for this day, she would have said it was a *good* sadness from which she would not shrink in order to become all that God would have her be. And in its own way, its presence somehow made her yet more beautiful.

As they went, happy faces turned toward them, all eyes upon Amanda, the girl many of them had known as a tempestuous child, watched leave home as an independent youth, and then seen return as a young lady who was quickly growing into a woman of dignity and virtue just like her mother. Among the guests, to Amanda's surprise and pleasure, she saw Gwendolen Powell and her husband, and Hubert Powell with his second wife. She gave a slight nod and extra smile as she passed them.

Stiffly Gifford did his best to retain his inexpressive poise as they walked. But even he could not help the edges of his mouth twitching upward occasionally in that most foreign of movements with which his facial muscles were unfamiliar—reflecting back the bright faces of Amanda's and Stirling's many friends with the hint of a smile.

"Dearly beloved," began Timothy a few moments later with a great smile on his face, "we are gathered together this day to unite this man and this woman in holy matrimony...."

◆ ◆ ◆

A huge reception was held that afternoon at Heathersleigh Hall. Nearly everyone in town was present. There was more food and drink than any three communities of such size could have consumed in a day, accompanied by much laughter and talk and well-wishing, which even occasionally brought from the cousin once removed of the bride a moment or two of unguarded chuckle and reply.

In late afternoon the bride and groom departed in the Rutherford Peugeot for Torquay. From there they traveled through Oxford, where Stirling showed Amanda the sights of his university years and introduced her to a few friends and professors who remained.

They spent several days in the Midlands, then returned to London, and thence followed Betsy and Hope back to Switzerland for the remainder of their honeymoon.

They spent two weeks at the chalet. Many of the villagers remembered Amanda, and by the end of their stay, Stirling was a favorite throughout the entire village of Wengen. He and Herr Buchmann hit it off in particular, with the latter almost promising to visit the newlyweds in England the following summer.

After three weeks away, they returned to Devon and took up residence in Heathersleigh Cottage.

Sarah remained at the Hall to wait on Jocelyn when she came;

Wenda remained in the employ of Gifford and Martha. In his early seventies and though slowing considerably, Hector continued to occupy his room and do what he could to keep up the grounds. He was especially happy now that several of Jocelyn's favorite horses had been returned to his care.

Gifford managed under the circumstances to do his best to preserve that long-standing British tradition of the stiff upper lip. The entire household treated him as if he were master of the place. He occasionally muttered and fussed, but was generally civil and accepted the ministrations of the houseful of women with grudging acknowledgment. Hector addressed him as "my lord." He did nothing to discourage the appellation, and occasionally could be seen briefly afterward drawing himself up a little straighter in the back and carrying himself with heightened dignity.

On most mornings, Jocelyn, Martha, Sarah, Wenda, and Hector, along with Gifford when he was not in London, ate breakfast together, after which Gifford departed for the village and the bank.

"Good morning, Mr. Rutherford!" and other such greetings could be heard addressing him as he made his way through the streets of Milverscombe almost as frequently as they had followed his son. Gifford always nodded, rarely smiled, even more rarely returned the greetings. But the hard shell surrounding the seed of life in his heart was being slowly chipped away by the generous and forgiving natures of the simple folk with whom he now must conduct his business.

106

A Christmas Trip

♦♦♦

In early December, Timothy, Amanda, and Stirling came to the Hall for tea, as was their custom most Sunday afternoons. As they chatted and ate together, Timothy announced that he would be going abroad for Christmas.

"That's wonderful, Timothy," said Jocelyn. "Where are you going?"

"Hope and Betsy have invited me to join them at the chalet for the holidays," he replied.

"Oh, Timothy!" exclaimed Amanda. "You will positively love it. I can't think of anything more wonderful than Christmas in Wengen. And the chalet . . . the crèche . . . oh, I wish we could go too!"

"Why don't you?"

"We just returned from the Continent two weeks ago ourselves!" laughed Stirling. "Please, don't put ideas in her head! I am just a struggling country doctor—we're not made of money, you know."

"Perhaps you shall take up skiing, Timothy," suggested Jocelyn.

"At my age, I hardly think it advisable!"

"Oh, Timothy," added Stirling, just remembering, "I will give you a book I borrowed to take back to one of the villagers with whom I have the feeling you will have a delightful time, a fellow by the name of Buchmann."

"Buchmann," said Timothy. "An intriguing name."

"Not half so interesting as the man himself."

"What can you tell me about him?"

"Only this—that he loves books, and loves to think about things from unusual angles."

"It gets better and better!" laughed Timothy. "He does sound like my sort of man. But what kinds of things does he think about, as you say, from unusual angles?"

"I shall leave you to discover that for yourself!" said Stirling, joining him in laughter. "I assure you . . . he will not disappoint you. Take several of your own favorite volumes with you to share. I will tell you this much, he is also an avid friend of the Scotsman."

"I can hardly wait to make his acquaintance!"

◆◆◆

Two weeks later, a small steam locomotive pulling a single coach behind it pulled slowly into the tiny station of Wengen high in the Swiss Alps and puffed to a steamy stop.

The entire countryside was white, snow piled in drifts alongside the tracks up to four feet. As Timothy stepped out of the train and glanced around, it seemed to him that he had stepped into a fairy wonderland. The sky was clear, his breath was visible in front of him, for the temperature of the air was well below freezing, and above the rooftops loomed the gigantic presence of the great mountain of which he had heard so much. From somewhere could be heard the tinkling of bells.

There stood Hope on the platform waiting for him, a smile on her lips, tears in her eyes.

Timothy smiled and walked slowly forward. Their eyes met. Timothy's were also glistening.

Neither spoke a word. Gently they embraced, and held one another several long moments.

Ten minutes later, with Timothy's bag's safely in the station to be retrieved later, they began the walk out of the village to the chalet, Hope's hand through Timothy's arm. Still few words were spoken, but it felt to both that at last their hearts had come home.

107

A Young Crusoe

*O*ne day in May, as flowers were bursting alive all around the quaint but roomy dwelling formerly known as Maggie's cottage, a knock came to the door, which stood open to the spring sunlight.

Amanda had been working in the garden most of the morning and had just gone inside to begin preparing tea and lunch. Stirling had been out on calls all morning, and she expected him back any moment.

Thinking it was he, she came to the door, wiping her hands on her apron.

"Why did you knock—" she began, then paused in midsentence.

There in front of her stood a girl of fifteen or sixteen, a bewildered expression on her face.

"Good morning," said Amanda. "I'm sorry, but I thought you were my husband. How can I help you?"

"Someone told me in the village that you might be able to help me. They told me how to get here."

"Why don't you come in and tell me about it?" said Amanda. "What kind of help do you need?"

"I'm afraid I've made a mess of many things," the girl replied, following Amanda into the kitchen. "Now I want to go home. But I have no money and don't know how to get there."

"Where do you live?" asked Amanda, offering her a chair.

"It is a very long way. I came to England . . . to get away, and . . . then my bag was stolen. I am miserable and don't know what to do."

"Would you like some tea?"

"Yes . . . yes, I would, thank you."

"And something to eat?"

She nodded and smiled. "Thank you—to be honest, I *am* quite hungry."

"Then we will take care of that right away," smiled Amanda. "You're from America, aren't you?"

The girl nodded.

As Amanda filled the kettle with water, she quietly studied her visitor. The poor girl looked so forlorn, she was reminded of her own wayward years. *"Thank you, Lord,"* Amanda prayed silently, *"for sending this one of your children to me. I pray that she will not only get home, but I also pray for her healing, just as you healed me when I was so far away. Show me how I can help her."*

"There," she said aloud, "while we are waiting for the water to boil, let's see about washing up.—Do you have a suitcase?"

"Yes, I left it at the station."

"That's fine. My husband will bring it for you later. And why don't you begin by telling me who you are," added Amanda as she led her guest into the cottage toward the washroom.

"My name is Sally," smiled the girl.

Epilogue
Knotted Strands

— ❖❖❖ —

The girl named Sally remained at Heathersleigh for a month, spending half her time with Jocelyn in the Hall when she was not with Amanda. After contacting her parents and making arrangements, they took her to Southampton and put her on a ship bound for home.

Timothy had returned to England after the Christmas holidays, but only briefly, to pack his few belongings and make arrangement for their transport to Switzerland. He and Hope Guinarde were married in Wengen in March 1924. Amanda, Stirling, and Jocelyn all attended the simple ceremony held in the great fireplace room of the chalet.

Betsy married a young Swiss man from Wengen three years later. When she moved into her new home as a young bride, she could still see the chalet from her kitchen window.

Amanda and Stirling Blakeley had five children—two sons and three daughters—all of whom grew up calling Heathersleigh Cottage their home. Two years after their marriage, Dr. Armbruster retired, turning over his entire practice to Stirling. They came to be known throughout the community as Lady Amanda and Dr. Stirling.

Jocelyn was revered by everyone for miles, and Amanda and Stirling, if possible, came in later years to be yet more loved than had been Amanda's parents a generation earlier. Jocelyn and Hope visited India together, though Jocelyn did not stay there to work.

Rune Blakeley so skillfully managed the affairs of the Rutherford Foundation that it began to receive donations from other sources. By the latter years of his life, he was frequently sought after—traveling throughout England in suit and tie and briefcase in hand—as a consultant to other foundations and communities desirous of following the Milverscombe model for development and modernization.

Catharine, meanwhile, had two sons and a daughter. The family followed Terrill through the country wherever his career led him. Catharine never had the opportunity to attend university as she had once dreamed, but continued to read avidly. Like his father, Terrill rose to the rank of admiral, commanded a battleship during the Second World War, then returned again to Plymouth. After his retirement, they moved to a small estate in the Devonshire countryside about six miles from Milverscombe. Catharine and Amanda, still the closest of friends, saw one another at least weekly, and spoke on the telephone with each other every day.

Martha and Jocelyn were together on most days as they grew older. Gifford kept mostly to himself, even after he retired from the bank. Gradually, however, he began to strike up a few acquaintances in the community. Curiously, this included a friendship with Gresham Mudgley's twenty-five-year-old son after the death of his sheepherder father. The simple young man often came to the Hall, smelling of sheep, to consult with Gifford about one thing or another. His simple trust in and inexplicable affection for the aging banker did Gifford far more good than either realized. Though it was late in his life, Gifford at last began to grow inside, which is the best thing that can ever be said of any man or woman.

Timothy wrote several books, which were published in London. They sold modestly and never generated much income, but came to be highly regarded in certain circles where spiritual inquiry was valued above dogma. He died in 1941. Hope outlived him by fifteen years. At her passing, Betsy and her family moved back to the chalet in order to continue its ministry. Betsy died in 1984. Today the Chalet of Hope is in the hands of two of her daughters, who carry on the vision of its founder in giving hope to all those who come.

After hiring a young assistant in his medical practice, Stirling spent many subsequent summers traveling to various hospitals, wards, sanitariums, universities, and research facilities, furthering his own interest in and participation in the quest for a cure for polio. He frequently contributed to various prestigious medical journals, and in time became recognized as one of the most highly respected names in British polio research. He was offered any number of lucrative positions with some of England's major hospitals and research facilities. He accepted none of these, however. He was a country doctor, after all, he said, and he was happy and would remain content with his wife and family in Devon.

As she grew older, more and more Amanda came to resemble her father. His creative restlessness, his spiritual priorities, his interest in so many things, and his desire to help people, all found themselves lived out in the daughter. Amanda was especially thankful for the ways in which her father had taught her to think. Though she had misused the precious gift early in life, she put it to good use throughout the remainder of her years in helping whomever the Lord placed in her path.

As if God were adding a blessing of years in exchange for the ones lost by Charles's and George's early passing, the rest of Jocelyn's family lived long, healthy, and productive lives, and not a single son or grandson was lost to the next war when it engulfed Europe in the 1940s.

Gifford lived to be sixty-eight, Martha seventy-seven. Jocelyn herself lived to be ninety-three. Her passing in 1953 was greatly mourned by all of Devon.

At the marriage of their eldest daughter to one of the Osborne twins, Amanda and Stirling, themselves now over fifty, moved back again to occupy Heathersleigh Hall in order that a new generation might be able to raise its family in Heathersleigh Cottage. They yet had four children who remained with them, ages ranging from nineteen down to eleven, who now delighted in romping through the halls and rooms and hidden passageways that their mother and Aunt Catharine and Uncle George had explored before them.

Terrill Langham died in 1968, five months shy of his eightieth birthday. He was given a full naval funeral with honors, though by his own request was laid to rest with Catharine and her family in the small Devonshire town of Milverscombe. Catharine Rutherford Langham lived to be eighty-one and died in 1975, leaving behind eight grandchildren who loved her dearly.

Dr. Stirling Blakeley died in 1973. He was eighty-three.

Lady Amanda Rutherford Blakeley passed away, again to join father and mother in that great reunion which awaits us all, in 1976 at the age of eighty-six.

Amanda and Stirling were mourned by all who knew them, especially by sixteen grandchildren, four great-grandchildren, and the citizens of Devon, many of whom had come under their influence and learned from them of the mysteries of the kingdom.

Heathersleigh Hall is today in the hands of two of the Blakeley daughters and their husbands, in addition to the eldest son and his wife and the family of their son.

Heathersleigh Cottage is occupied by Amanda and Stirling's youngest daughter and her husband, along with their two unmarried daughters, both in their twenties.

The Rutherford plot in the Milverscombe churchyard, first begun with the burial of Geoffrey Rutherford, is now one of the most visited and revered sites in the small cemetery.

Gifford and Martha Rutherford were laid to rest beside their son.

Simple granite headstones commemorate the loss at sea in 1915 of Sir Charles Rutherford and George Rutherford.

Jocelyn Rutherford's grave, by her request placed as near that of Margaret and Robert McFee as possible, is flanked by Amanda and Stirling Blakeley on her right, and Catharine and Terrill Langham on the left.

The tombstones of the three Heathersleigh women are never without fresh flowers.

Ideas in Fiction
A Personal Postscript From the Author
❖❖❖

𝒯here are many kinds of fiction.

I enjoy writing contemporary fiction, fantasy fiction, and am considering one day attempting a series of futuristic novels. Most of my work, however, including this series you have just completed, would fall into that broad classification known as "historical fiction."

There is a huge variety of historical fiction types as well. Set within a historical framework, authors write to distinct audiences, attempt to accomplish different purposes, and emphasize a multitude of varied themes. One of the most familiar and prevalent subgenres is "romance" historical fiction, where relationships and romance predominate. There are also "family sagas," histories of nations and races, church histories, and political histories. Most good historical fiction interweaves many elements together—romance, politics, family struggles, geography, religion, geology, racial and cultural factors, etc.—even though one or two particular themes will usually be elevated above the others.

I love history, I love geology and archaeology and politics, and there are parts of the globe and certain periods within its history that particularly draw my interest. I am like Adam Livingstone in this regard (*A Rift in Time* and *Hidden in Time*)—few things fascinate me more than beginnings. So in my books, many of these disciplines and themes find their way into the narrative.

But there are two things that fascinate me more than all the rest, which I love to explore as much as history itself. One does not usually find these two components, however, as dominant influences in historical fiction because many readers do not care to pause long enough in their pursuit of the story to think about them. But because they interest *me*, and because I cut my literary teeth on the works of George MacDonald, who also emphasized them, these two features usually tend to pervade the landscape within the stories I tell.

The first is *ideas*.

The second is *personal growth*.

Interwoven within the context of history, ideas and personal growth tell the story of the human drama on the earth far more than romance, geography, politics, or archaeology will ever be capable of doing.

If my fiction had to be categorized into a subgenre of its own, therefore, perhaps I would call it "idea fiction" in which, by confronting *ideas*, by confronting themselves, and by confronting God, the characters in my books *grow*.

That's why I get mail from readers calling my books tedious and boring, and at the same time from others who say they are stimulating and challenging. Some people like to think about ideas, others don't. Just as some people like to read detective stories, others don't. Every genre and subgenre is not for everyone.

But ideas are dangerous things.

In a detective story or romance novel, there's not much to *disagree* with. You may like the story and characters, or not like them. But you're unlikely to get mad at the author as a result. Ideas, on the other hand, are a little hotter to handle. Ideas can, and do, make people mad.

Books such as this, which present certain concepts that lie outside the boundaries of traditional evangelicalism, often rouse controversy and irritated response from readers. Those who respond in such manner to ideas outside their comfort zones invariably frame their objections under the broad charge of "unscriptural." But as we have seen, the Scriptures can support either side of nearly any debate. Evangelicals take biblical truth no more literally than anyone else. All Christians choose different places where they will read the Bible literally and where they will give interpretation more latitude. Taking the Scriptures "literally," as is clear from John 12:32 and Philippians 2:10–11, is in the eye of the beholder.

In this series, as noted in the introduction to *Wild Grows the Heather in Devon*, I have been attempting to shed light on a historical period with an emphasis on the *ideas* of that period, namely the late nineteenth and early twentieth centuries. In the case of the theological dispute between Timothy Diggorsfeld and his denominational leaders, I had hoped—not to argue for or against a particular point of view, for in fact *both* points of view are presented, but—to illuminate a debate which was raging at that time but which western Christendom has largely lost sight of today. It was not and is not my objective to attempt to argue for or against any point of view, but to accurately set the historical climate of the church of that day.

It is the *ideas* that fascinate me, on both sides of many such theological discussions. It was a heated time in the life of the church, and God's people were engaged in debate on a number of issues. I don't mind whether you agree or disagree with Timothy Diggorsfeld. I have tried to articulate his view fairly, as well as the more traditional position, because I am well familiar with the arguments on both sides. But as to a conclusion, I would say, with Diggorsfeld, "I do not know the answer to this scriptural conundrum." Meanwhile, I continue to pray that the Holy Spirit will give me the mind of Christ.

I am always astonished when I discover how many find ideas such as these threatening, and respond in anger. I never see such a response in the life of our Lord. Jesus was a man of ideas. Hypocrisy angered him, but never ideas. Read through the Gospels with an eye to the controversial statements he made that ran counter to the accepted theology of the first century, and you will find yourself highlighting every page. When you understand the historical climate of the time, Jesus was a figure of *controversial*, even *radical* theology. A man of ideas. Sometimes very unusual ideas.

In THE SECRETS OF HEATHERSLEIGH HALL, the frequently mentioned Scotsman is, of course, George MacDonald, who lived out his later life in Italy almost until his death in 1905. Timothy Diggorsfeld's fictional visit to the renowned Scottish author in the 1890s coincides with the final slowing years of MacDonald's writing productivity.

As always, so many of my own ideas and much of my outlook originate in the writings of MacDonald. I am particularly indebted to him for the idea of the dormant garden coming back to life, as Timothy explained to Amanda. This concept and some of the descriptions of the process came from MacDonald's book, *Paul Faber, Surgeon*—published by Bethany House as *The Lady's Confession*—and represents one of my favorite MacDonald passages. From that same book comes the powerful idea, as read aloud by Jocelyn, of coining up mammon to do God's work. There are several other such "borrowings" from MacDonald—the surrounding friendship of books and authors, not following a witness with a plan of salvation, the "daystar of understanding," and the "condition of heart" (obedience), which alone makes comprehension of the Bible possible. Jocelyn's care of Betsy and some of the explanations of it are taken from that of Janet Grant in *Sir Gibbie*—published by Bethany House as *The Baronet's Song*. And the overall theme of relinquishment of an ancient family home is the central theme in MacDonald's book *Castle Warlock*—published by Bethany House as *The Laird's Inheritance*. I hope those who noticed such embedded references to MacDonald, and others I have perhaps forgotten to mention, will take this as my grateful acknowledgment, though I did not interrupt the story by footnoting each one. As C.S. Lewis said, "I never wrote a book in which I did not quote MacDonald." I recently received a letter from a young man who said, "I do believe MacDonald was close to the heart and passion of Jesus more than any other man I have read or listened to so far." That statement, it seems to me, sums up with perfect clarity just why Lewis and myself and others find it virtually impossible to write without "quoting" MacDonald every time we turn around.

In *New Dawn Over Devon*, Timothy's experience was modeled after that of George MacDonald himself. After two years in the pulpit of the Congregational Church at Arundel, on the coast of England south of London in the 1850s, MacDonald was urged to resign on the basis of four points: the possibility of animals in heaven, his views on the Sabbath, an expressed hope that provision was made for the heathen after death, and liberalism in his theology. What I have tried to give in this account, therefore, is a historical document of the times.

Despite the attacks which will surely come as a result, I decided to leave these controversial points in this book. I want to challenge you who read my words to exercise maturity of thought and judgment, rather than dismissing them out of hand. But if you are one who has been upset by some of the ideas raised, I am sorry to have been a stumbling block. If this has been difficult for you, then please put my words aside and return to the Gospels of our Lord. We can never go wrong when we steep ourselves in his life and teachings. And I would urge you to inquire of the Lord whether *he* is himself the author of the annoyance you feel toward what you have read, or whether he might have depths of his divine plan he wants you to explore more deeply. But have no fear—you will not find such controversy in most of my other books. They are written about different historical eras when such ideas as these were *not* at the forefront of people's thinking.

And to those of you who are challenged and stimulated in growth-producing ways by the "idea fiction" I try to provide, and which we have discovered so uplifting in the works of George MacDonald, let me say that we appreciate the words of encouragement many of you send us, sharing your own spiritual inquiries, struggles, journeys, thinkings, doubtings, questionings, and awakenings. I pray for you as I write, and always enjoy hearing about life on the other side of those prayers.

Pray for us too, Judy and me and our family. We, like you, live in the midst of daily weakness, seeking the practical reality of the truth that in our weakness does God give strength. As the church at the turn of the last century was inundated with ideas—evolution, temperance, women's suffrage, universalism, and a host of social issues—the church of today is facing an unprecedented attack on the family. Very few families are unaffected. Perhaps historians will look back on this period and write about the fractured family unit and the impact its fragmentation has had on the church. The most serious result has been to diminish the capacity of today's men and women to understand the concept of God's family, especially his Fatherhood. It was largely in response to this attack that we decided to write the SECRETS OF HEATHERSLEIGH HALL series with the emphasis it has. Other themes might have been more exciting to fashion into a story. But none are more important. We *must* arise and seek our Father.

To the extent it is possible across the miles, through the mysterious yet very real bonds of unity that exist within the body of Christ, we love you and are so grateful for your life-sustaining encouragement in our lives. We truly do draw strength in the knowledge that many of you are praying for us, as we do for you.

How wonderful and remarkable a thing is the unity of our Father's family!

We should all pray, too, for the rest of that family, for the entire body of God's people, that it will be infused with that hunger I spoke of . . . a hunger for all God's truth, God's *whole* truth . . . a hunger, as Paul prayed when writing to the Ephesians, "to grasp how wide and long and high and deep is the love of Christ."

One final point: Heathersleigh Hall, Milverscombe, and the Chalet of Hope are entirely fictional, as are all the characters of the series.

If you are interested in Great Britain, especially Scotland, may I suggest my series CALEDONIA: *Legend of the Celtic Stone* and *An Ancient Strife.*

If you have difficulty locating other of my books, small brochures containing a list of available titles, both of mine and MacDonald's, are available on request. Responses can be directed either to the publisher, or to P.O. Box 7003, Eureka, CA 95502.

Michael Phillips